New York Times and *USA Today* bestse

..., annoying man and beast alike. Darynda lives in the Land of Enchantment, also known as New Mexico, with her husband and two beautiful sons, the Mighty, Mighty Jones Boys.

Visit Darynda Jones online:

www.daryndajones.com
www.facebook.com/darynda.jones.official
@Darynda

Praise for *A Bad Day for Sunshine*:

'*A Bad Day for Sunshine* is a great day for the rest
of us – captivating characters, great writing, pace,
humour and suspense'
Lee Child, *New York Times* bestselling author

'*A Bad Day for Sunshine* is everything you want from Darynda
Jones . . . and more! Laugh-out-loud funny, intensely suspenseful,
page-turning fun with a sassy new heroine you will love.
Prepare to be hooked by this witty, sexy, and thrilling
new series from one of my favourite authors!'
Allison Brennan, *New York Times* bestselling author

'Swoon-worthy heroes, quirky characters, and a page turning
mystery. Move over Stephanie Plum, Sunshine Vicram
has arrived. Prepare yourself. This book is a keeper!'
Christie Craig, *New York Times* bestselling author

'Darynda Jones has done it again. With trademark humour,
eccentric yet relatable characters, and masterful storytelling,
she takes us on a journey we don't want to end. *A
Bad Day for Sunshine* is a great day for readers!'
Tracy Brogan, bestselling author

BY DARYNDA JONES

*ebook only

A
BAD DAY
FOR
SUNSHINE

Darynda Jones

piatkus

PIATKUS

First published in the US in 2020 by St Martin's Press, New York,
an imprint of St. Martin's Publishing Group
First published in Great Britain in 2020 by Piatkus

13 5 7 9 10 8 6 4 2

A CIP catalogue record for this book
is available from the British Library.

ISBN 978-0-349-42717-1

Printed and bound in Great Britain by
Clays Ltd, Elcograf S.p.A.

Papers used by Piatkus are from well-managed forests
and other responsible sources.

Piatkus
An imprint of
Little, Brown Book Group
Carmelite House
50 Victoria Embankment
London EC4Y 0DZ

An Hachette UK Company
www.hachette.co.uk

www.littlebrown.co.uk

For my agent, Alexandra Machinist,
because she is jet-fueled awesome
and she loved this book from the moment
I uttered my bizarre, seven-word pitch.
She gets me.
She really gets me.

ACKNOWLEDGMENTS

Thank you, dear reader, for picking up this book! I'm so excited to share Sunshine's story with you. And Auri's. And the lovely, lovely Levi's. Le sigh . . .

This book owes a lot of thanks to a lot of people, first and foremost those who believed in this book even before I did: my wonderful agent, Alexandra Machinist, and my incredible editors, Jennifer Enderlin and Alexandra Sehulster. Alex, let's be honest, this book would have sucked without your incredible insight and genius-level storytelling abilities. I thank you. My family thanks you. My readers thank you. Because sucky books suck. Nobody needs sucky books in their lives.

Thank you to everyone at St. Martin's Press, Macmillan Audio, and ICM Partners for all the work you do, even when a manuscript shows up a few days (ahem) late. A special shout-out to Marissa, Mara, Brandt, and Anne-Marie, who are like my gang if gangs drank wine and talked books.

But I also had a *ton* of help from professionals in law enforcement who made it look like I knew what I was doing (insert maniacal laughter), and I am forever grateful for their willingness to answer all my stupid questions because, yes, for the record, there are such things as stupid questions. But thanks guys, for not caring and answering them anyway. Ursula and Malin Parker, Donna Mowrer, Keith Thomas, and Wendy Johnson, I hope I done you proud. Thank you especially, to Uschi and Wendy for reading the book and giving me invaluable feedback.

And, as always, thank you to my ace-in-the-hole, the crazy-talented Trayce Layne, who puts the lime in the coconut and laughs inappropriately with me, because inappropriate laughter is the very best kind.

And thank you to the lurves of my life, Netters and Dana and Quentin, whose identities I stole for a little while to make this book that much more fun.

Last but not least, thank you to my family. You make every breath worthwhile.

A
BAD DAY
FOR
SUNSHINE

1

Welcome to Del Sol,
a town full of sunshine,
fresh air, and friendly faces.

(Barring three or four old grouches.)

Sunshine Vicram pushed down the dread and sticky knot of angst in her chest and wondered, yet again, if she were ready to be sheriff of a town even the locals called the Psych Ward. Del Sol, New Mexico. The town she grew up in. The town she'd abandoned. The town that held more secrets than a politician's wife.

Was she having second thoughts? Now? After all the hubbub and hoopla of winning an election she hadn't even entered?

Hell yes, she was.

But after her night of debauchery—a.k.a. her last hurrah before the town became her responsibility—she thought she'd conquered her fears. Eviscerated them. Beaten and buried them in the dirt of the Sangre de Cristo Mountains.

Either Jose Cuervo had lied to her last night and given her a false sense of security, or her morning cup of joe was affecting her more than she thought possible.

She eyed the cup suspiciously and took another sip before looking out the kitchen window toward the trees in the distance. The snow had stopped last night, but it had restarted with the first rays of dawn. Snowstorms weren't uncommon in New Mexico, especially in the more mountainous regions, but Sun had been hoping for, well, sun her first day on the job. Still, snow or no snow, nothing could stop the brilliance that awaited her along the horizon.

Thick clouds soaked up the vibrant colors of daybreak and splashed them across the heavens like a manic artist who'd scored a new bottle of Adderall. Orange Crush and cotton candy collided and dovetailed, making the sky look like a watercolor that had been left out in the rain. The vibrant hues reflected off the fat flakes drifting down and powdering the landscape.

Sun was home. After almost fifteen years, she was home.

But for how long?

No. That wasn't the right question. Somewhere between her karaoke rendition of "Who Let the Dogs Out?"—which bordered on genius—and her fifth shot of tequila, she and Jose had figured that out the night before as well.

This was the opportunity she'd been both anticipating and dreading. Since she had a job handed to her on a silver platter, she would stay until she found the man who'd abducted her when she was seventeen. She would stay until he was prosecuted to the fullest extent of the law. She would stay until she could shed light on the darkest event of her life, and then she would put the town in her rearview for good.

The right question was not how long she would stay but how long it would take her to bring her worst nightmare—literally—to justice.

She tucked a strand of blond hair behind her ear and appraised the *guesthouse* her parents had built, studying it for the umpteenth time that morning. The Tuscan two-bedroom felt bigger than it was thanks to the vaulted ceilings and large windows.

All things considered, it wasn't bad. Not bad at all. It was shiny and new and warm. And the fact that it sat on her parents' property, barely fifty feet from their back door, was surprisingly reassuring.

She'd worked some long hours as a detective. Surely, as a sheriff, that wouldn't change. It might even get worse. It would be good to know that Auri, the effervescent fruit of her loins, would be safe.

The kid felt as much at home in the small tourist town as Sun did, having spent every summer in Del Sol with her grandparents since she was two. The fact that she'd twirled through the apartment when they first saw it like a drunken ballerina? Also a strong indicator she would be okay.

Auri loved it, just like Cyrus and Elaine Freyr knew she would. Sun's parents were nothing if not determined.

And that brought her back to the malfeasance at hand. They were living in an apartment her parents had built. An apartment her parents had built specifically for Sun and Auri despite their insistence it was *simply a guesthouse*. They didn't have guests. At least, not guests that stayed overnight. The apartment was just one more clue they'd been planning this ambush for a very long time.

They'd wanted her back in Del Sol. Sun had known that since the day she'd left with baby in hand and resentment in heart. Not toward her parents. What happened had not been their fault. The resentment that had been eating away at her for years stemmed from a tiff with life in general. Sometimes the hand you're dealt sucks.

But if she were honest with herself—and she liked to think she was—the agonizing torment of unrequited love may have played a teensy-tiny part.

So, she ran, much like an addled schoolgirl, though she didn't go far. Also, much like an addled schoolgirl.

She'd originally fled to Albuquerque, only an hour and a half from Del Sol. But she'd moved to Santa Fe a few years ago, first as an officer, then as a detective for SFPD. She'd only been thirty minutes from her parents, and she'd hoped the proximity would make her abandonment of all things Del Sol easier on them.

It hadn't. And now Sun would pay the price for their audacity, their desperate attempt to pull her back into the fold. As would

Auri. The fact that they didn't take Auri's future into consideration when coming up with their scheme irked. Just enough to cause tiny bouts of hyperventilation every time Sun thought about it.

Auri's voice drifted toward her, lyrical and airy like the bubbles in champagne. "It looks good on you."

Sun turned. Her daughter, short and yet somehow taller than she had a right to be at fourteen, stood in the doorway to her room, tucking a T-shirt into a pair of jeans and gesturing to Sun's uniform.

Instead of acknowledging the compliment, Sun took a moment to admire the girl who'd stolen her heart about three seconds after she was born. Which happened to be about two seconds before Sun had declared the newborn the most beautiful thing this world had ever seen.

Then again, Sunshine had just given birth to a six-pound velociraptor. Her judgment could've been skewed.

Though not likely. The girl had inherited the ability to stop a train in its tracks by the time she was two. Her looks were unusual enough to be considered surreal. Sadly, she owed none of her features to Sunshine. Or her grandparents, for that matter.

Auri's hair hung in thick, coppery waves down her back. Sunshine's hair hung in a tangled mess of blond with mousy brown undertones when it wasn't French braided, as it was now.

Auri's hazel eyes glistened like a penny, a freshly minted one around the depths of her pupils and an aged one that had green patina around the edges. Sun's were a murky cobalt blue, much like her grandmother's collection of vintage Milk of Magnesia bottles.

Auri's skin had been infused with the natural glow of someone who spent a lot of time outdoors. Sunshine was about as tan as notebook paper.

The girl seemed to have inherited everything from her father. A fact that chafed.

"Mom," Auri said, pursing her pouty lips, "you're doing it again."

Sun snapped out of her musings and gave her daughter a sheepish grin from behind the cup. "Sorry."

She dropped her gaze to the spiffy new uniform she'd donned that morning. As the newest sheriff of Del Sol County, Sun got to choose the colors she and her deputies would wear. For both their tactical and dress uniforms, she chose black. Sharp. Mysterious. Slightly menacing.

And because she wanted to look her best first day on the job, she'd opted for the Class A. Her dress uniform. She ran her fingertips over the badge pinned above the front pocket of her button-down. Inspected the embroidered sheriff's patch on her shoulder. Marveled at how slimming black trousers really were.

"I do look rather badass, don't I?"

Auri adjusted the waist of her jeans and offered a patient smile. "All that matters is that *you* think you look badass."

"Yeah, well, it's still crazy. And if I'm not mistaken, illegal on several levels." How her parents got her elected as sheriff when she'd had no idea she was even running was only one of many mysteries the peculiar town of Del Sol had to offer. "Your grandparents are definitely going to prison for this. And so am I, most likely, so enjoy my badassery while it lasts."

"Mom!" Auri threw her hands over her ears. "I can't hear that."

"Badassery?" she asked, confused. "You've heard so much worse. Remember when that guy pulled out in front of me on Cerrillos? Heavy flow day." She pointed to herself. "Not to be messed with."

"Grandma and Grandpa won't go to prison. They're too old."

Unfortunately, they were not too old. Not by a long shot. "Election tampering is a serious offense."

"They didn't tamper. They just, you know, wriggled."

Sun's expression flatlined. "I'll be sure to tell the judge that. Hopefully before I'm sentenced."

Auri had been about to grab her sweater when she threw her

hands over her ears again. "Mom!" she said, her chastising glare the stuff of legend. The stuff that could melt the faces off a death squad at fifty yards. Because there were so many of those nowadays. "You can't go to prison, either. You'll never survive. They'll smell cop all over you and force you to be Big Betty's bitch before they shank you in the showers."

She'd put a lot of thought into this.

Sun set down the cup, walked to her daughter, and placed her hands on the teen's shoulders, her expression set to one of sympathy and understanding. "You need to hear this, hon. You're going to have to fend for yourself soon. Just remember, you gave at the office, never wear a thong on a first date, and when in doubt, throw it out."

Auri paused before asking, "What does that even mean?"

"I don't know. It's just always worked for me." She walked back to her coffee, took a sip, grimaced, and stuck the cup into the microwave.

"Grandma and Grandpa can't go to jail."

Sun turned back to her fiery offspring and crossed her arms over her chest, refusing to acknowledge the apprehension gnawing at her gut. "It would serve them right."

"No, Mom," she said as she pulled a sweater over her head. "It wouldn't."

Sun dropped her gaze. "Well, then, it would serve me right, I suppose." The microwave beeped. She took out her cup and blew softly, having left it in long enough to scald several layers off her tongue, as usual. "But first I have to check out my new office."

While she'd been sworn in and taken office on January 1, she had yet to step foot inside the station that would be her home away from home until the next election in four years. Barring coerced resignation.

She and Auri had taken an extra week to get moved in after the holidays. To prepare for their new lives. To gird their loins, so to speak.

"I need to decorate it," she continued, losing herself in thought. "You know, make the new digs my own. Do you think I should put up my Hello Kitty clock? Would it send the wrong message?"

"Yes. Well?" Auri stood up straight to give her mother an unimpeded view. She wore a rust-colored sweater, stretchy denim jeans, and a pair of brown boots that buckled up the sides. The colors looked stunning against her coppery hair and sun-kissed skin.

She did a 360 so Sun could get a better look.

Sun lowered her cup. "You look amazing."

Auri gave a half-hearted grin, walked to her, and took the coffee out of her mother's hands. That kid drank more coffee than she did. Warning her it would stunt her growth had done nothing to assuage the girl's enthusiasm over the years. Sun was so proud.

"Are you nervous?" she asked.

Auri lifted a shoulder and downed half the cup before answering, "No. I don't know. Maybe."

"You are definitely my daughter. Indecisiveness runs in the family."

"It's weird, though. Real clothes."

Auri had been in private school her entire life. She'd loved the academy in Santa Fe, but she'd been excited about the move regardless. At least, she had up until a few days ago. Sun had sensed a change. A withdrawal. Auri swore it was all in her mother's overprotective gray matter, but Sun knew her daughter too well to dismiss her misgivings.

She'd sensed that same kind of withdrawal when Auri was seven, but she'd ignored her maternal instincts. That decision almost cost Auri her life. She would not make that mistake again.

"You know, you can still go back to the academy. It's only—"

"Thirty minutes away. I know." Auri handed back the cup and grabbed her coat, and Sun couldn't help but notice a hint of apprehension in her daughter's demeanor. "This'll be great. We'll get to see Grandma and Grandpa every day."

Just as they'd planned. "Are you sure?" Sun asked, unconvinced.

She turned back and gestured to herself. "Mom, real clothes."

"Okay."

"I swear, I'm never wearing blue sweaters again."

Sun laughed softly and shrugged into her own jacket.

"Or plaid."

"Plaid?" Sun gasped. "You love plaid."

"Correction." After Auri scooped up her backpack, she held up an index finger to iterate her point. "I *loved* plaid. I found it adorable. Like squirrels. Or miniature cupcakes."

"Oh yeah. Those are great."

"But the minute plaid's forced upon you every day? Way less adorable."

"Gotcha."

"Okay," Auri said, facing her mother to give her a once-over. "Do you have everything?"

Sun frowned. "I think so."

"Keys?"

Sun patted her pants pocket. "Check."

"Badge?"

She tapped the shiny trinket over her heart. "Check."

"Gun?"

She scraped a palm over her duty weapon. "Check."

"Sanity?"

Sun's lids rounded. She whirled around, searching the area for her soundness of mind. She only had the one thread left. She couldn't afford to lose it. "Damn. Where did I have it last?"

"Did you look under the sofa?"

Keeping up the game, Sun dropped to her knees and searched under the sofa.

Auri shook her head, tsking as she headed for the side door. "I swear, Mom. You'd lose your head if that nice Dr. Frankenstein hadn't bolted it onto your body."

Sun straightened. "Did you just call me a monster?"

When her daughter only giggled, she hopped up and followed her out. They stepped onto the porch, and Sun breathed in the smell of pine and fresh snow and burning wood from fireplaces all over town.

Auri took a moment to do the same. She drew in a deep breath and turned back. "I think I love it here, Mom."

The affirmation in Auri's voice eased some of the tension twisting Sun's stomach into knots. Not all of it, but she'd take what she could get. "I do, too, sweetheart."

Maybe it was all in her imagination, but Auri hadn't seemed the same since she'd let her go to the supersecret New Year's Eve gathering at the lake. The annual party parents and cops weren't supposed to know about. The same parents and cops who began the tradition decades ago.

She'd only let Auri stay for a couple of hours. Could something have happened there? Auri hadn't been the same since that night, and Sun knew what could happen when teens gathered. The atmosphere could change from crazy-fun to multiple-stab-wounds in a heartbeat.

"You know, you can stay home a few more days. Your asthma has been kicking up, hon. And your voice is a little raspy. And—"

"It's okay. I don't want to get behind," she said.

"Do you have your inhaler?"

Auri reached into her coat pocket and pulled out the L-shaped contraption. "Yep."

A woman called out to them then. A feisty woman with graying blond hair and an inhuman capacity for resilience. "Tallyho!"

They turned as Elaine Freyr lumbered through the snow toward them, followed by her very own partner in crime, a.k.a. her roughish husband of thirty-five years, Cyrus Freyr.

Sun leaned closer to Auri. "Did your grandmother just call me a ho?"

"Hey, Grandma. Hey, Grandpa," Auri said, ignoring her.

It happened.

The girl angling for the Granddaughter of the Year award hurried toward the couple for a hug. "Mom's worried you guys are going to prison."

Elaine laughed and pulled the stool pigeon into her arms.

"Snitches get stitches!" Sun called out to her.

"Your mother's been saying that for years," Elaine said over Auri's shoulder, "and we haven't been to the big house yet." She let her go so Auri could give her grandfather the same treatment.

"Hi, Grandpa."

Cyrus took his turn and folded his granddaughter into his arms. "Hey, peanut. What are we going to prison for this time?"

Auri pulled back. "Election tampering."

"Ah. Should've known." Cyrus indicated the apartment with a nod. "What do you think of her?"

"She's beautiful, Grandpa."

His face glowed with appreciation as he looked at Sun. "And it's better than paying fifteen hundred a month for a renovated garage, eh?"

He had a point. Santa Fe was nothing if not pricey. "You got me there, Dad." She gave them both a quick hug, then headed toward her cruiser, the black one with the word SHERIFF written in gold letters across the side.

"Sunny, wait," her mother said, fumbling in her coat pocket. "We have to take a picture. It's Auri's first day of school."

Sun groaned out loud for her mother's benefit, hiding the fact that she found the woman all kinds of adorable. She was still angry with them. Or trying to be. They'd entered her into the election for sheriff without her consent. And she'd won. It boggled the mind.

"We're going to be late, Mom."

"Nonsense." She took out her phone and looked for the camera app. For, like, twenty minutes.

"Here." Sun snatched the phone away, fighting a grin. It would only encourage her. She swiped to the home screen, clicked on the app, and held the phone up for a selfie. "Come in, everyone."

"Oh!" Elaine said, ecstatic. She wrapped an arm into her husband's. "Get closer, hon."

The cold air had brightened all their faces. Sun snapped several shots of the pink-cheeked foursome, then herded her daughter toward the cruiser, her father quick on her heels.

When Auri went around to the passenger's side, Sun turned to face him.

He offered her a knowing smile and asked, "You okay? With all of this?"

She put a hand on his arm. "I'm okay, Dad. It's all good." *She hoped.* "But don't think for a second you're off the hook."

"I rarely am. It's just, I know how much you enjoyed putting this place in your rearview."

"I was seventeen. And one shade of nail polish away from becoming goth." She thought back. "Nobody needed to see that." After sliding him a cheeky grin, she stomped through the snow to the driver's side.

He cleared his throat and followed again, apparently not finished with the conversation. "Well, good. Good," he hedged before asking, "And how are you sleeping? Any, you know, nightmares?"

Ah. That's what this was about. Sun turned back and offered him her most reassuring smile. "No nightmares, Dad."

He nodded and opened the door as Elaine called out, "You and Auri have a good day. And don't forget about the meeting!"

Sun looked over the hood of her SUV. "What meeting?"

Elaine sucked in a sharp breath. "Sunshine Blaze Vicram."

She hopped inside the cruiser before her mother could get any further with that sentiment. Nothing good ever came after the words *Sunshine Blaze Vicram.*

She gave her eagle-eyed father one last smile of reassurance as he closed the door, then backed out of the snow-covered drive, confident she'd done the right thing. Telling him the truth would only exacerbate the guilt she could see gnawing at him every time he looked at her. There was no need for both of them to lose sleep over something that happened in Del Sol so very long ago.

2

*There is simply no way **everybody** was kung fu fighting.*

—SIGN AT DEL SOL MIXED MARTIAL ARTS AND DANCE STUDIO

Five minutes later—small-town perks—Sun pulled into the Del Sol High School parking lot. She put the cruiser in park and turned to her auburn-haired offspring. "It's time."

Auri gaped at her. "Oh, god. Mom, not again."

"This is just a refresher."

"It's not really the first day of school. We already had this conversation in August."

"Yes, but that was for the academy. This one is for Del Sol High School. Your new stomping ground."

Auri propped an elbow onto the armrest and dropped her face into a hand.

"Okay, as we've previously discussed, boys are usually born with this little thing I like to call a penis."

Auri groaned.

"And girls are often born with this little thing I like to call a vagina."

"I'm moving in with Grandma and Grandpa."

"But these two components, the penis and the vagina, need never meet." Sun waved an index finger back and forth. "Not ever.

In fact, being a lesbian is very avant-garde. So, you know, you could always go that direction."

"Mom, being gay is not a choice."

"Not if you don't give it a chance."

"Fine." Auri looked around at the growing number of gawkers. "I'll give it a try. Can you just turn off the emergency lights?"

Sun looked around at the faces reflecting the red lights from her cruiser. "They're just jealous. How many kids your age get a police escort on her first day of school?"

"I'm going to have to change my name."

"Now, normally, tab A fits rather nicely into slot B—"

"Mom!"

"—but not in your case." Sun paused for dramatic effect, then looked at her daughter from behind sad eyes. "Honey, I didn't want to tell you this until you were older." She placed a gentle hand on Auri's arm, infusing her expression with concern and something akin to heartbreak. "But I have no choice. Auri, you were born with a horrible, ghastly disfigurement."

"Okay, this is new."

"You know. Down there. In your nether parts."

Auri gazed out the window. "Does our insurance cover therapy?"

"Trust me when I say it's something you never, ever want a boy to see."

"Too late. Scarred for life."

"Especially a boy with a penis."

"People say that, the whole scarred-for-life thing, but I don't think they really mean it."

"You just don't want to open yourself up to that kind of ridicule."

"I, on the other hand—"

"That kind of ostracism."

She turned to her mother in a huff. "This conversation is making me very uncomfortable."

"Okay, I'll stop, but if anything happens, just ask yourself, WWLSD?"

"Mom—"

"No, I mean it. Anytime you get into a hairy situation, ask yourself: What would Lisbeth Salander do?" She gave her daughter a minute, then prompted her. "Well?"

After a heavy sigh, Auri replied. "She'd cut a bitch."

"Exactly. And if that doesn't work?"

Another sigh. "She'd set a bitch on fire."

"Precisely. And if that doesn't work?"

"Mom," Auri whined, shifting in her seat.

"If that doesn't work?"

"Fine. She'd eviscerate a bitch's online presence and get him or her sent to prison for kiddie porn."

Sun placed her hands over her heart. "I'm just . . . I'm so proud of you."

"Can I go now?"

"Absolutely." When Auri opened the door, Sun added, "Just as soon as you tell me what's really bothering you."

Normally, the mere mention of Auri's hero, Lisbeth Salander, cheered her up. Sun had closed with her best material and . . . nothing. Absolutely nothing.

No way would she let the kid go now. If she had to take off yet another day from work, so be it. The last time her daughter had such a drastic about-face, the last time Auri hid what was really going on beneath her dangerously intelligent surface, she was seven years old, and the outcome almost ended in the worst kind of tragedy imaginable.

"Nothing's wrong, Mom."

Sun leaned forward and put her fingers on a switch on the dashboard. "Have you heard the siren on this baby?"

Auri's hands shot up in surrender. "Oh, my god, okay."

Having won, Sun leaned back and gave Auri a minute to compose herself.

After closing the door so no one would hear, she said softly, "It's just, I know how you worry."

Sun's chest inched tighter around her heart, but she forced her expression to stay neutral.

"And my asthma has been bad, and I know that really bothers you."

That did it. "Sweetheart, your asthma doesn't bother me. I mean, I feel horrible for you, but . . ." She thought back to the morning she'd found Auri passed out in the bathroom not two weeks earlier. "When I found you on the floor—"

"I know. I'm sorry, Mom."

"Auri," Sun said, exasperated. "Why do you do that?"

"Do what?" she asked, leaning away as though suddenly self-conscious.

"Every time you have an attack, every time you get sick, you apologize. Like it's somehow your fault."

Auri crossed her arms, her shoulders concaving. "I know. I just . . . I don't want you to be put out."

"Oh, honey." Sun leaned over and draped an arm over her daughter's wilting shoulders. "Why would you even think such a thing?"

"I just don't want to be a problem."

Sun closed her eyes and blocked out the vise crushing her chest. Auri had always been this way. She'd always apologized for getting sick. Or spilling milk. Or, hell, even tripping. What kind of kid apologized for tripping?

And it all started that pivotal period Sun referred to as the Dark Age. Before that summer, she'd had no idea a child, especially one so young, could become clinically depressed. She'd had no idea a child, *most especially* one so young, could become self-destructive.

How bad did things have to be to convince a seven-year-old, *a seven-year-old*, to contemplate taking her own life?

The reality suffocated Sunshine every time she let her thoughts drift back to that summer. It still haunted her to the very depths of her soul. And while she and Auri were about as close as a mother and daughter could be, there was a part of her child that Sunshine had never seen. A shadow. A darkness behind the light that had become her reason for breathing.

She swore she'd never let things get that bad again. She had no choice but to get to the bottom of this. And she was hardly above blackmail. Obvs. "What's bothering you, hon?"

Auri fidgeted with her nails. "It's stupid."

"Hey, if you can't be stupid in front of your mother, who can you be stupid in front of?"

"I guess."

"Spill."

Auri looked out the window again, ignoring the kids gawking, and said softly, "Ever since the New Year's Eve party at the lake—"

She knew it. She should never have let her go.

"—everyone at school thinks I'm a narc."

Her asthma had been getting steadily worse for the last . . . wait.

Sun stilled when her daughter's words sank in. She blinked in surprise, then asked, "I'm sorry, a narc?"

"Two of your deputies showed up and confiscated the keg."

"They had a keg?" Sun asked, her pitch rising an octave.

"And someone said it had to be me because my mom was going to be the new sheriff and the deputies had never shown up before and—"

"Where'd they get a keg?"

"—and so I probably told my *mommy* on them." She'd added air quotes to Sun's title.

"I swear, if—" Then it all made sense. Her BFF's New Year's Eve party. She'd wondered where he'd scored a keg that late at night. "That's where he got all that beer."

"Who?"

"Quincy."

Quincy Cooper had been Sun's best friend since kindergarten. He'd grown a bit since then, however. He was now a cross between a refrigerator and a bank vault door. And he was one of her deputies. What were the odds?

She winked at Auri. "You get enough beer in that boy and he'll strip."

"Mom!" She pulled out her inhaler and took a hit.

"Sorry, hon." Sun switched back into mama-bear mode. "Who? Who would say such a thing about you?" She leaned toward her. "Just give me a name."

"I don't have one. It doesn't matter, anyway. Everyone's saying it now. You can't arrest everyone."

"Arrest them?" Sun snorted. "I'm going to send them a thank-you card. Or a fruit basket. Or a lifetime supply of anti-itch cream. That stuff comes in so handy."

Auri's jaw dropped.

"This solves all my problems." She rubbed her hands together, not unlike a villain in a comic book. "Think about it. The rich kids won't invite you to parties because they think you're a narc. The druggies won't invite you to parties because, again, they think you're a narc. All my worries gone in one fell swoop."

"Mother."

"This is the best news I've had all day. High five?" She raised her palm and gave her daughter a once-over, only to realize the kid wasn't falling for it.

Auri crossed her arms over her chest. "I know you."

"Good thing, since you call me Mom. It would be awkward if—"

"I can handle this. It's *my* problem."

"I know." Sun feigned offense. "But you know, if you happen to find out who started such a vicious rumor—"

"I wouldn't tell you."

"I'm appalled," Sun said, appalled.

"Unlike my new rep, I am not, nor have I ever been, a narc."

Sun knew that for a fact. Boy, did she know. "Fine. Just remember, if you do have to cut a bitch—"

"I know, I know." Auri slid the strap of her backpack over her shoulder. "Don't leave any DNA evidence at the crime scene."

"Oh. Right. I was going to say don't leave any witnesses alive, but that works, too." She leaned over and gave the fruit-of-her-loom a hug despite their ever-growing audience. Cool thing was, Auri let her.

God, she loved that kid.

Having taken the scenic route through town, Sun pulled into her parking space at the station with a nostalgic smile on her face. She'd forgotten how beautiful Del Sol was, especially when blanketed with fresh snow. It was enchanting and mystical and serene.

Passersby would find the town tranquil. Spiritual, even. And it was. She'd give it that. But it was also quirky and charismatic and unpredictable. Just like the people who inhabited it. For the most part.

A large black font graced the side of the stucco building that read *Del Sol County Sheriff's Posse.*

Her posse.

God, she'd always wanted a posse. Of course, she'd envisioned them all on horseback, racing over the rugged countryside in search of a man with a black hat and a handlebar mustache, but this would do.

For now.

Sadly, a sharp rap on her window startled her out of her prepubescent fantasy. She hadn't even gotten to the good part where a Native American named Tarak saved her after the bad guy shot her in the shoulder, and they made sweet, sensuous love by a campfire—apparently, she healed really fast—before resuming the search the next day, capturing said bad guy, and taking him to be sentenced by the Hanging Judge, thus making the Great Plains great again. And bad-guy free.

C'est la vie.

She peered through the window, first at a police-issue flashlight angled against the glass, second at a blond-haired, blue-eyed, half-Latino in a starched black uniform and a gun at his hip. The refrigerator-sized intruder wore a grin that could weaken the knees of a sisterhood of nuns.

Quincy. Of course he'd be there to greet her.

She opened the door and jumped into the arms of her very best friend on planet Earth. Apart from Auri. And her hamster, Gentleman Jack, but he'd died decades ago. So, Quincy had moved up a notch.

She'd warned him at the promotion ceremony he had some mighty big shoes to fill. Or he would have if hamsters wore shoes. But Quincy took it all in stride, confident in his ability to run on a spinning wheel and crawl through plastic tunnels.

They were five. Their aspirations hadn't been particularly lofty.

He lifted her off the ground with a chuckle, and she squealed, the sound very unsherifflike.

"Sunburn Freyr," he said when he put her down and held her at arm's length, "as I live and breathe." He acted like he hadn't seen her in decades when, in truth, they'd met for one meal or another every chance they'd gotten over the years, which wasn't nearly as often as Sunshine would have liked. And they'd even brought in the New Year together. With a confiscated keg, apparently. But the enthusiasm was welcome.

Still, she settled a warning glare on him.

He cleared his throat and made a correction. "Vicram. Sorry, love. Still can't get used to that."

"I've been a Vicram for over fifteen years."

"I'm set in my ways."

"Well, I can't get used to the He-Man you've become." She squeezed his biceps. "How much do you eat?"

"Don't you worry, gorgeous. It's all muscle." He flexed the guns for her appraisal.

Sun snorted. Flirting was a part of their shtick. They'd done it since they were kids, before they'd realized what it meant. But now they were in a professional relationship. Their playful banter would have to stop . . . eventually.

He gestured toward the building. "You ready for this?"

She studied the letters again, her stomach doing somersaults. "I don't know, Quince. How'd they do it?"

"I can't be sure, but I'd bet my last nickel they used a stencil."

"You're funny."

"I like to think I am."

"Spill," she said, infusing her voice with a warning edge.

Quincy laughed and decided to study the snow. "Let's just say your parents are very talented."

Talented they may be, but Sun was genuinely worried about her mom and dad. "They got me elected, Quince. Without my knowledge."

He winced and patted the air, urging her to keep it down.

She lowered her voice to a harsh whisper, which probably carried farther than her voice would have. "How is that even possible? There was a debate, for God's sake!"

"You did great, by the way. I especially liked your ideas on how to eliminate drunk driving."

Sun pinched the bridge of her nose, wondering how she managed to debate the previous sheriff when she'd had no clue she was even in the running. "Someday you're going to have to tell me how they did it."

The grin he wielded like a rapier served two purposes: to disarm and to charm.

And here Sun thought herself immune to the charisma of

Quincy Cooper. Well, okay, she was immune, but she could see the appeal. The allure of the chick magnet—his words—he'd become.

In high school, Quincy had been popular enough. Very well liked. But he'd never been what one would call a ladies' man. Now, the chunky—his description—former sugar addict looked less like a huggable marshmallow and more like a boulder. His waist had narrowed and his shoulders had widened and his smile had grown into something girls of all ages longed to gaze upon every chance they got.

What did the women at her mother's book club call him? Ah yes. *Stupid hot.*

She'd certainly give him that. But deep down, she still saw that sweet kid who fought back tears after skinning his knees on the playground.

And now, after almost fifteen years, the Dynamic Duo—a.k.a. Quincy and Sunshine—was finally back together. Sun could hardly believe the roller coaster of events that had led her here.

"Are you sure you're going to be okay with my being your boss?"

Her chief deputy snorted. "Like anything has changed. When haven't you bossed me around?"

"Good point." She hadn't planned on bringing it up so soon, but she needed to know what awaited her. "All right, Q. Cards on the table. Is the mayor going to let this rest?"

Mayor Donna Lomas seemed to be the only one questioning the legitimacy of Sunshine's win over Del Sol's former sheriff. Well, besides said former sheriff. And Sunshine herself.

Quincy turned away from her, but she saw the muscles in his jaw flex as he worked it, a sure sign that not everything was popping up daisies in the Land of Enchantment.

"I don't know, Sunny. She's pretty worked up about the whole thing."

"And she should be." Sun collapsed against her cruiser. "I

mean, isn't there someone more qualified? You know, someone sheriffier?"

"Okay," he said, joining her at the cruiser with arms folded across his chest, "let's think about this. You have a master's degree in law enforcement. You single-handedly solved one of the highest-profile cases the state has ever seen. And you were the youngest officer to make detective in New Mexico history." He tilted his head. "I'm thinking no."

Sun straightened, faced him, and adjusted his tie before replying, "First off, I have a master's degree in criminal justice, not law enforcement."

"Same dif."

"Second, I was the third-youngest officer to make detective in New Mexico history. I was only the youngest in Santa Fe history."

"Well, then, I take back everything I said."

"And third, no case is ever solved single-handedly." She patted his cheek. "You should know that by now, Chief Deputy Cooper."

He let a calculating smile widen across his face. "Keep telling yourself that, peaches. I read the file."

"Hmmm." Refusing to argue the point, she returned her attention to the building.

"I'll give you a minute," he said, starting for the door. "Let you gather yourself. Make a grand entrance."

"Great, thanks," she said, neither grateful nor thankful.

After he disappeared, she drew in a deep breath and watched it fog in the air when she exhaled before grabbing a box of her personal effects and copies of all the open cases out of her back seat. Then she locked up the cruiser and went inside the pueblo building via a side door.

A hallway separated the station from a small jail that sat in back. From that point, her entrance involved two electronically coded doors in which her master key came in very handy. Once inside, she stopped to take in her surroundings.

The station was nice. More up to date than she'd imagined it would be. Drywall with a light beige paint made up the bulk of the surroundings, but the renovators had kept much of the older wood accents. Remnants of an earlier version of the establishment.

Desks took up most of the main room, and a glass wall separated the public entrance and the administration area up front.

Quincy, who was pretending to be hard at work, spotted her first. He turned in his chair, and the sound of typing and papers shuffling ceased immediately from the other deputies present.

"Hey, boss," Quincy said, leaning back into a giant stretch. "Oh, I meant to ask, how's the bean sprout?"

She nodded to the two other deputies present and the office manager, who doubled as dispatch. Anita Escobar—no relation—was a pretty woman in her early thirties with a wide smile and thick, blond-streaked hair she always wore in a ponytail. According to Sun's ever-studious mother, Anita'd had her eyebrows tattooed on. So, there was that.

Turning back to Quince, Sun balanced her box on two stacks of files that took up half his desk and picked up a pen with a gold deputy's badge on it. After clicking it open and shut several times, trying to decide if she should steal it or if blatant theft would set a bad example for the other law enforcement officers in the room, she said, "Everyone at school thinks she's a narc."

"Sweet. Less trouble she can get into."

She returned the pen and narrowed her gaze on him. "It's bizarre how much we think alike. The accusations stem from a certain raid on a certain New Year's Eve party at the lake."

"Oh, snap. They think she called us?"

"They do."

He snorted. "Like anybody needed to call. Don't they know the secret annual New Year's Eve party at the lake is the least secret event in this town?"

"Kind of like Mrs. Sorenson's breast augmentation."

He laughed out loud, then sobered, his expression wilting a little. "Those aren't real?"

Sun consoled him with a pat on his head. She knew he'd take it hard.

"Poor kid," he said, switching back to Auri. "She's so great. Are you sure she's really yours?"

"I hope so. She borrows my clothes."

She thought back longingly to an amazing burgundy sweater that had never been the same after Auri wore it on a field trip to the zoo in Albuquerque. Something about a boy named Fred and a monkey named Tidbit.

She snapped out of it when she realized all work had come to a complete standstill and her staff was gathering around the coffeepot. She leaned closer to Quince. "Should I address the troops?"

"Price is still out on a call. And besides, you have a visitor." He gestured toward what she assumed was her office.

"Already? I just got here."

"Yeah, well." He cringed, his face lined with sympathy. "Proceed with caution. She's been waiting for twenty minutes."

"And you kept me standing outside chatting for ten of them?" When he offered her a noncommittal shrug, she dropped her head, dread leaching into her pores. "Christ on a cracker."

"Good luck," he said like a manic cheerleader after one too many energy drinks. Then he abandoned her in her time of need to join the other cowards hovering around the coffeepot.

With a withering moan, she lifted her box and headed toward her office to meet her fate.

3

"Aurora?"

Auri had just taken a hit off her inhaler. She put it away and smiled at the administrative assistant behind the counter. "That's me." She didn't bother giving the woman her nickname. She doubted they'd talk often.

"Ah yes." Corrine Amaia, if her nameplate was to be believed, gathered a few papers and handed them to her one at a time. "Okay, the top one is your locker number and combination. Put that somewhere safe."

"Gotcha." Auri took the paper and stuffed it into her binder.

"This is the handbook with the school song and dress codes and such."

"Thanks."

"And this one is your schedule."

Auri brightened, excited to see what her classes were. The usual suspects, of course, but she'd been hoping for a couple of electives her private school hadn't offered.

Trying not to look overly enthusiastic, she took the paper and perused it. She had the state requirements, as expected—English, history, geometry, physical science, and social studies—along with visual arts and American Sign Language.

"Nice," she said, more than pleased. She'd requested three electives, but had only really wanted ASL.

Her old school, a private school in Santa Fe, which also happened to be the home of the New Mexico School for the Deaf, didn't have ASL as an elective, a fact that astounded her. It was only one of several reasons Auri had agreed to transfer here.

Corrine finally stopped long enough to get a good look at the new recruit. "Aren't you lovely," she said, her tone part surprise and part matter-of-fact.

"Oh," Auri said, embarrassed. "Thank you."

"My daughter, Lynelle, is a freshman, too, if you need someone to show you around. Help you find your classes."

"I had an offer over break, but thanks so much."

"Of course. Let me know if you have any questions."

Auri nodded and headed out for her first day at Del Sol High. She glanced around for the girl she'd met at the party, then walked to the vending machines by the front office. They'd made plans to meet there, but the deputies came and everyone scattered. She hoped the girl, who was a freshman as well, a redhead as well, and new as well—though not quite as new as Auri—didn't forget. But that scenario was looking likelier and likelier.

She waited until first bell, but the girl was a no-show. She could hardly blame her. Auri was now officially an outcast. A pariah. A persona non grata, if the glares of hostility were any indication. Squelching her disappointment, she decided to get on with her day.

As she searched for her first-period class, she got the occasional curious glance, and even the outright gawk—she blamed her coloring, which was odd even for a redhead—but if she had to put a number to it, she'd guesstimate that more than half the looks directed her way were full of a venomous kind of resentment.

Who knew denying high school kids the ability to get wasted

was such a big deal? If she didn't know better, she'd have thought she'd set fire to the football uniforms. While the players were still wearing them.

Just as she started down the hall, she happened to glance back through the open doorway and into the principal's man cave. She saw a girl lift a wooden carving of some kind off his desk and stuff it into her jacket pocket.

The principal was in the hall, joking around with a group of kids, so Auri didn't understand why the girl was in there. But she recognized her from the party. Dark hair. Huge gray eyes. Supermodel attitude.

So, while the looting was strange enough, the girl turned, looked right at Auri, and winked at her before walking out.

"See you later, Mom," she said to Corrine.

"Bye, sweetheart. Don't forget about lunch."

"I won't." The girl, who must have been Lynelle, smirked at Auri as she walked out, and Auri couldn't help but feel there was a joke hanging in the air and she'd missed the punch line.

Drawing in a deep breath, she turned to the swarm of kids in the hall half a second before the tardy bell rang.

She could do this. She'd done it before when they'd moved from Albuquerque, where her mom had been working and going to college, to Santa Fe, where she'd gotten her first job in law enforcement as a patrol officer for SFPD. That had seemed like so long ago, but she owed it to her mom to do her best. To go with the flow. To never—*ever*—be a burden.

That was her biggest fear. To be a burden to her mom. Well, any more than she already was.

God, if only her new friend hadn't deserted her. She'd felt an instant connection to Sybil. Maybe Sybil hadn't felt the same about her.

After wandering the halls longer than she should have, growing more anxious by the moment, Auri finally found her first-period classroom tucked into a corner of the main building.

Unfortunately, the tardy bell had rung about two minutes earlier, so plan A, the plan where she would walk in and take a seat before anyone noticed her, fell by the wayside.

Plan B consisted of two steps. One, pull the fire alarm. Two, reenter the building with everyone else once the firefighters gave the green light. But just as she was about to pull the little red lever, she noticed a security camera pointed in that general direction. Thus, plan B had to be nixed as well. Not that she would have done it, but she would've liked the option.

Left with no other choice, she had to opt for plan C, the worst of the three she'd come up with. It basically involved her walking into the classroom and interrupting a lesson already in progress so that the students would turn en masse and give her their full and undivided attention.

Great.

She braced herself and opened the door to Mrs. Ontiveros's English I. If nothing else went her way that day, at least Auri could tell her grandchildren that plan C had worked brilliantly. Every student turned toward her, and she froze.

After an eon passed in which she prayed for the earth to open up and swallow her, she tore her gaze off the sea of faces and scanned the room for Mrs. Ontiveros. She'd assumed the instructor would be the only adult in the room. Instead, she found three, all of them standing at the back, staring at her as expectantly as she was staring at them.

Auri's cheeks went up in flames. She ducked her head just enough to let her hair cover most of her face as embarrassment infused her entire body with a blistering heat.

The movement brought her head around, and she realized what they were all looking at before she so rudely interrupted. A boy stood at the front of the room, holding a piece of paper as though giving a report. A boy she recognized.

She'd seen him a few times at the lake when she'd spent her summers with her grandparents, but she'd never talked to him. In fact, nobody seemed to talk to him for very long. Even though everyone would wave at him or try to convince him to join the festivities, he just sort of hung back and watched everyone else have fun.

But something about him had fascinated her. Now even more so. He was taller than she'd expected. And more . . . built.

She thought she'd seen him at the New Year's Eve party as well, but when she'd looked again, he was gone and there were two patrol cars racing toward the scene in his stead.

"Can I help you?" one of the adults asked, a tall older woman with dark curly hair and black-framed glasses.

Auri cleared her throat and started the long walk to the back of the room to hand the teacher her schedule, gazes still locked on her like laser-guided missiles.

The woman took the paper, welcomed her to the class, and gestured toward a seat, explaining something about a poetry reading, but Auri was already inside herself. Everything outside registered only as a droning hum over the blood rushing in her ears.

At least the teacher didn't introduce her to the entire class. Small blessings.

After she sat down, she ignored the gawkers and fought to claw back out of her self-imposed exile, to reenter the world she shied away from all too often.

And then she heard a voice, soft and deep and lyrical.

She looked up. The boy read from the paper he held, and the words rushed over her like cool water. The poem was about a trapped bird, yet even imprisoned, the bird's powerful wings caused the air underneath them to stir and curl as it fought for its freedom like a hurricane demanding to be set free. One simply had to look close enough to see the power building beneath it before it broke free.

"One simply has to notice," he said before folding the paper and stuffing it into his front pocket.

The class clapped, many with genuine appreciation, and the teacher beamed at him.

"See?" she said as she walked to the front of the room. She looked back at the other two adults. "What'd I tell you?"

Auri hazarded a glance over her shoulder and saw that both adults wore pleased grins on their faces.

"That was beautiful," one of them said. "Mrs. Ontiveros was right, Cruz. You're very talented."

The other woman agreed with a nod, but when Auri turned back to him, his expression was anything but grateful. Either he didn't believe them or he didn't care. He gave his head a quick shake to let his bangs fall over his eyes before he strode to his desk and slid into it.

But in the middle of the slide, when his body was still facing the classroom, he stopped for the span of a heartbeat to look at her. To lock gazes with her. He held it a hairbreadth longer than he should have, the startling intensity of his attention giving her a mild cardiac arrest.

Then he turned in his seat and faced the front as a couple of boys wearing red-and-gold letter jackets patted his shoulder, and a couple of girls wearing sweaters of the same colors graced him with adoring smiles. Again, he didn't seem to want or need their praise, but he took it well.

Auri sat stunned while her heart restarted with heavy thumps against her rib cage, then spent the next five minutes trying to decipher the look he'd given her as another student read a poem about a girl who died after saddling a rocket and riding it to the moon.

She pondered his name. Cruz. She liked it. More to the point, it fit him, though she couldn't reason why.

Forcing herself to look away, she took the next few minutes to scan the other students around her. Some she recognized from her summers in town, but she'd never really gotten to know any of the locals. Faces, yes, but that was as far as it went.

One girl who looked familiar, a pretty blonde, waved when she looked at her and wiggled in her seat with excitement, the smile she wore genuine, and Auri began to breathe a little easier. At least she had one friendly face to turn to.

Sadly, there were a couple of unfriendly faces sprinkled throughout the curious onlookers as well. Both of them seemed to be friends with Lynelle, the girl who'd taken the carving from the principal's office. While Lynelle kept glancing Auri's way, her smile not friendly so much as calculating, her friends glowered outright and kept on glowering through three more poetry readings.

All of this because they thought she'd narced? There had to be more to it than that. They could cool the Sahara with the kind of shade they were throwing her way.

Lynelle leaned over and whispered something to Cruz. One corner of his mouth lifted in response, and another kid, a jock named Liam Eaton, shoved him from behind playfully.

She knew Liam's name because everyone knew Liam's name. He was rich. And cute. And rich.

"Anyone else?" Mrs. Ontiveros asked. "You guys had two weeks to come up with your masterpieces. Surely, someone else—"

A knock at the door interrupted the teacher mid-lecture, and before she could get to the door, the principal walked in with a security guard in tow.

He spoke softly with Mrs. Ontiveros, whose worried gaze flitted across the room and landed on Auri. She froze for the second time that day.

"Aurora Vicram?" the principal said.

Auri hesitated, then offered the barest of nods. Neither man looked happy to be there.

Then, in a tone that could slice concrete, he said, "You need to come with us."

Auri couldn't move at first. Flames engulfed her, and it took her a moment to gather her backpack and start out of her seat. She wouldn't have dared a look around her if not for the giggling squeak that came from one of the two girls.

She glanced over. Lynelle's smile had gone from calculating to lethal, and Auri knew she was in trouble. Payback was a bitch, and they felt they needed retribution for the raid.

Just as she got to the door, she couldn't help herself. She glanced over her shoulder at the boy. Cruz. The poet. The one with dark hair and a full mouth that made hers water in response. But if anger had the ability to shape-shift into human form, she imagined it would look just like him at that moment.

Apparently, the entire school wanted to see her hang.

"Mayor," Sun said as she put the box on a massive oak desk. The room had bookshelves, a computer, and a fortysomething, sandy-haired woman who sat in the only chair in the room. Sun's office chair.

Mayor Donna Lomas stuffed her phone into her purse and stood, giving Sun her full attention. "Sheriff."

Donna was curvy with a button nose, a bouncy bob, and square wire-framed glasses. She was that girl in town all the other girls wanted to be when they grew up. Pretty. Perky. Popular.

The two shook hands for the briefest of moments before the mayor got right to the point. "So, how'd you do it?"

Sun cleared her throat and walked to the window to look out on Main Street. "Well, I wanted to be bold, you know? So, I went for the red first, but then I thought, 'Wait a minute. Is that too bold? Should I tone it down a bit?' That's why I threw in the yellows and the blues. A few peaches to highlight the piece."

She turned back. When Donna only pursed her lips and waited, Sun continued, "Weren't you talking about that time I beat your little sister in the finger-painting competition?"

There had been a lot of pressure that year. Who knew kindergarten could be so competitive? Her classmate Sabrina, a.k.a. Donna's little sister, had never liked her after that, and Sun had felt that same chill every time she'd crossed paths with Donna as well.

"It's okay." Donna clipped on a pair of magnetic sunglasses over her wire frames. "I'll find out on my own."

Sun suppressed a shudder of dread. Honestly, what had her parents done? Making an enemy of the mayor could not have been their best idea. No, their best had been starting that garden and *accidentally* growing marijuana. This one was third, maybe fourth on the list.

"In the meantime, you might want to do a search for a concept called the glass cliff."

Sun tried not to snort. She failed miserably, but at least she'd given her all. "Is that what you think this is?"

The glass cliff was a play on the metaphor of a glass ceiling. Only in this scenario, a woman or minority was put in a position of authority during a time of crisis. In other words, he or she was set up to take the fall when everything went belly-up.

"Is Del Sol on the verge of collapse?"

"You haven't heard?" She tsked as she turned to walk out. "You might want to do your homework."

What did that mean? No one told her there'd be homework. Would there be a test? A research project? Any opportunities to earn extra credit?

"I'll tell you what." Donna stopped and turned back like a runway model at Fashion Week. Either that or Sun's girl crush had been harder than she'd remembered. "I don't really care how you came into office. I appreciate a good law enforcement officer as much as the next person. Especially one with your record."

"My record?" Now she was just embarrassed. "Look, we recorded that in one take. In Quincy's garage. We didn't even have a decent sound system."

"Funny. I particularly liked the part where you beat up that college student who'd murdered that girl, handcuffed him to you, and physically dragged him to the nearest police station."

Sun laughed softly. Good times.

"I'll make you a deal."

That perked her up. "Okay, but I'm keeping my clothes on this time."

"You get me the names of the Dangerous Daughters, and I'll let the whole thing slide."

That time, Sun didn't even try to suppress her snort. She let it rip and then gaped at the woman in front of her. "The Dangerous Daughters? Would you like Santa's address while I'm at it?"

Donna stood unfazed. Her temerity was sobering.

"You can't honestly believe they exist."

"I do," she said. "How else do you explain your win?"

Sun's brows inched together. "I've heard they prefer being called the Diabolical Daughters."

"I've heard that, too. I've also heard them called the Devil's Daughters. The Damnable Daughters. Even the Despicable Daughters. Take your pick. I just want their names."

The Dangerous Daughters were supposedly the members of a group of women who'd, according to rumor, secretly run the town since it went from being a bankrupt mining town to a hippie commune in the 1930s. The Dangerous Daughters were the wizards behind the curtain, so to speak. If it were true, they'd be really old right now. How hard could they be to find?

"And how do you propose I get the names of the members of a group that doesn't exist?"

"You'll think of something."

"Or?"

Her shapely lips formed the smallest, most confident of smiles. "Or I'll go through your past with a razor-sharp machete and rip it apart, thread by fragile thread." She leaned in as though sharing a secret. "No one wants that, now do we?"

When she turned and exited the office, Sun realized she'd been holding her breath with that last threat. She most definitely did not want anyone sifting through her past. She had something to hide. Something she'd give her life to keep hidden. Something Auri could never, under any circumstances, find out.

Thus, she had a choice to make. Did she cut a bitch, set a bitch on fire, or eviscerate a bitch's online presence and get her sent to prison for kiddie porn?

If only her mother had named her Lisbeth Salander. That woman never thinks ahead.

4

Skinny people are easier to kidnap.
Stay safe.
Eat cake.

—SIGN AT THE SUGAR SHACK

After a ten-minute pep talk in which Sun convinced herself Mayor Lomas would find nothing, no matter how razor-sharp the machete she wielded, the shiny new sheriff stepped out of her office to find the whole gang standing stock-still around Anita's desk.

Sun cleared her throat, expecting the deputies to give her their full attention.

They did not.

She cleared her throat again, louder this time.

Still nothing.

She cleared her throat a third time, loud enough to pull a larynx.

No reaction whatsoever.

Giving in, she wove through the obstacle course that was the heart of the sheriff's station and walked up behind her team of deputies, rising onto her toes to see what they were looking at.

She'd taken the previous week to meet one-on-one at a local coffee shop with each of her deputies and her office manager, and had almost succeeded save one. The four deputies she had met with and the one administrative staff member were all present and accounted for, ready to celebrate Sun's first day on the job.

At the moment, however, they were all gathered around a basket of muffins, gazing at it as though it were a basket of tarantulas. Or rattlesnakes. Or claymores. She wondered if they feared all pastries or just muffins in general.

"What's up, guys?"

Two of the deputies started and turned around to her.

"Nothing, Sheriff," Deputy Salazar said, worry lining her face.

The other two ignored the intrusion and continued to stare. Sun looked closer at the muffins, growing wary herself.

She pinned Quincy with her best authoritative glare. "What's going on?"

He offered her one word. "Muffins."

"Yes. I can see that. They look delish."

At that moment, she wedged between Anita and Deputy Price and went in. They were homemade. The muffins, not Anita and Price, who may or may not have been homemade. They could have been conceived in a hot air balloon for all she knew. And the deputies smelled nowhere near as nice as the muffins that, even wrapped in plastic, filled the area with a blueberry kind of heaven.

A microsecond before her fingertips made contact, however, a loud unified gasp echoed around her. Every single person drew back in horror.

She paused and glanced around at each panic-stricken face. The deputies were all taller than she was, so it took a bit of effort.

"What?" she asked, growing annoyed.

Anita glared at Quincy. "She doesn't know?"

Quincy's gaze dropped, along with his chin, the act demonstrative of the guilt he clearly felt.

"You didn't tell her?" Deputy Salazar asked. Apparently, Quincy had been appointed to tell Sun about the muffins and had shirked his duties.

"Tell her what?" another female deputy asked.

Sun turned to the only other person in the room as confused as she was, a new recruit named Azaria Bell. Much like Sun herself, Zee had no idea why every law enforcement officer at the Del Sol County Sheriff's Office was scared of a basket of muffins.

It did boggle the mind.

"Okay," Sun said, growing exasperated, "why are you guys scared of muffins, and who needs therapy because of it? Show of hands."

"These aren't just muffins," Quincy said, his tone hushed as though they were listening. The muffins. The inanimate baked goods just sitting there, begging to be eaten.

"They look like muffins to me," she whispered back.

"Me, too," Zee agreed, not bothering to whisper.

Now Sun just felt silly.

"And they smell like muffins," Zee continued.

"Right?" Sun reached for one again, and Quincy almost dislocated her shoulder when he grabbed her arm and jerked her back.

Sun slapped his hands off her as though they were in a girl fight. Petty but effective. Then she turned to face her posse, her gaze landing on Anita, her office manager and the one person Sun least expected to be afraid of muffins. But her eyes were just as wide as her deputies'.

"That's it." She wielded an index finger like a weapon. "Someone explain what is going on. Are they poisoned? Because if someone is trying to kill us, shouldn't we be investigating?"

"They aren't poisoned," Deputy Salazar said. She was a curvy girl with big brown eyes and a smile that could light up a mental ward. "They were made by Ruby Moore."

"Oh, my gosh." Sun brightened and thought back. "I remember Mrs. Moore. She's so cute, and she was always so nice. Why is she trying to kill us?"

Quincy finally broke the tension with a surrendering sigh. "She's not trying to kill us, boss. It's just every time she sends muffins, strange things happen."

Deputy Price concurred with a nod. "And the bigger the basket, the stranger the events."

Sun squinted in doubt. "What kind of strange things?"

Quincy shrugged. "You know. Traffic accidents. Break-ins. Attempted murders with a cheese grater."

"So, the things we get paid to police?"

"Well, yeah, but—"

"All hell breaks loose," Anita said. "The world goes crazy. No one is safe."

Sun studied the young woman as she spoke, fighting a grin. She didn't want to give away the fact that she found her adorable. And she was the only person in the room shorter than the sheriff.

"The last time Ruby sent muffins," she continued, "Mrs. Papadeaux tried to cut Doug's penis off when he flashed her in the park."

Sun leaned into Quincy. "It amazes me how that man is still the town flasher."

"In an attempt to get away from her, Doug darted out into traffic." Anita was very into the story by that point, acting out Doug, the town flasher, darting into traffic.

"Isn't he, like, a hundred and twelve?" Sun asked him.

"And we had a bona fide pileup."

Deputy Salazar whispered beside her, "He only looks a hundred and twelve."

"He's led a rough life," Quincy said in explanation. "He's only in his early sixties."

"Sixties?" Sun asked, horrified. "Remind me to use sunscreen."

"A pileup!" Anita said, waving her arms in the air.

Sun thought back. "I read about that. It was two cars and a tractor."

Anita nodded. "Which, in Del Sol, is a bona fide pileup. And then, she sent muffins in December, and that very day, Mrs. Cisneros stabbed her husband in the knee."

"Ouch."

"Oh, there's more. So much more. And today, she sent an entire basket of them." Anita pointed to the basket in case someone got confused. "Muffins."

"Okay," Sun said, grasping the problem at last, "so as long as we don't eat the muffins, nothing will happen?"

The deputies shifted their weight and cast sideways glances at one another.

She rolled her eyes as realization dawned. "Are you kidding me? It doesn't matter if we eat them or not? All hell is breaking loose either way?"

A couple of Del Sol's finest shrugged and nodded.

"Well, then." Sun dove in for a muffin and unwrapped it as she walked to the front of the building. She'd seen a suspected thief walk by and decided to do a little recon while enjoying her cursed breakfast.

The others gave in and grabbed one as well. Including Quincy, who walked up behind her, munching on his own blueberry-filled disaster waiting to happen.

They watched Mr. Madrid walk past. The former railroad worker, who was in his early sixties, had a bandage wrapped around his neck and scratches covering both hands.

"You know, Mrs. Sorenson came in again yesterday," Quincy said between bites.

"About?"

He scoffed. "You know what about."

And she did. She'd read all the case files over the break, even cold cases decades old, but she'd known Mr. Madrid, the suspected thief, since she was two.

"That prize chicken of hers," Quince said, filling her in, anyway.

"Rooster."

"She's wondering when you're going to arrest Mr. Madrid for chicken-napping."

"Rooster-napping."

Everyone in town knew about the never-ending feud

between Mrs. Sorenson and Mr. Madrid. Every few months, the two neighbors came up with some new argument. Some new reason to bicker and squabble and caterwaul until the sheriff's office had no choice but to threaten them both with jail time.

The Hatfields and McCoys had nothing on the Sorenson and Madrid.

This go-around, Mrs. Sorenson's prize rooster had gone missing. Since Mr. Madrid had been complaining about the bird's early-morning cacophony for months, he was pretty much their prime—and only—suspect.

But Sun wanted the man to get comfortable. To let down his guard. To come to regret his decision to abduct the most decorated show rooster the town had ever seen.

Who knew a rooster could even be decorated? Where does one even pin a medal onto a rooster?

"You planning on looking into that?" Quincy asked.

Sun lifted a shoulder half-heartedly. "I suppose."

"Before he kills him?"

"I'm pretty sure Puff Daddy can hold his own against the likes of Mr. Madrid."

"That's what I mean." He pointed a finger from behind his muffin. "That chicken is going to kill that poor guy."

"Rooster."

"And then we'll never hear the end of it. It'll go national. All because we let a chicken kill one of our citizens."

"Rooster."

"We'll be the laughingstock of the nation."

"You're that certain we're not already?"

Quincy took a breath to voice his next argument, but he had nothing. He shook his head and took another bite.

"Sometimes these things need to unfold organically." She swallowed and peeled the wrapping lower. "And we can't say those wounds are all from Puff Daddy. Mr. Madrid could've cut himself shaving."

Quince snorted. "Shaving what? A honey badger?"

Sun looked back at her deputies and smiled.

"You glad to be back?" he asked.

"I am. But I thought the gang was all here. Where is my other deputy?"

"Price just got back."

"Yeah, but we're missing Bo."

"Who?" Quincy asked, still studying Mr. Madrid as he limped across Main through a soft layer of snow that was already melting. Freaking New Mexico sun.

"Bo." When he only shrugged, she continued, "Bo Britton? Your lieutenant? The only one to skip out on my one-on-ones last week?"

"Oh, Bo!" He nodded in recognition, then glanced around the station. "Yeah, he must be out on patrol."

"Okay. Can you call him in?"

"Who?"

Seriously? "Lieutenant Bobby Britton? Also goes by Bo?"

"Right. He does."

"He does what?"

"Goes by Bo."

"Okay, great. Now that we've established his identity, I'd like to address the troops. Can you call him in?"

"Who?"

Sun slammed her lids shut and drew in a deep breath. "Lieutenant Britton."

"Oh, right. We usually just call him Bo. Or L-T."

She welded her teeth together and spoke through them. "Can you get him on the radio? I have yet to meet him."

"Who?"

She went completely still. Del Sol was a peculiar place. Sun knew that. She'd known it when she'd accepted the position. She'd known she would have to deal with its own special kind of crazy, but not from Quincy. Not from one of her own.

Realizing there was more to this particular picture than met the eye, she unclamped her jaw and turned to walk away, but Zee came to stand by Quincy, enjoying the last remnants of her own muffin.

Zee was a tall, willowy black woman and the only deputy Sun had wined and dined herself. For good reason.

She had been a sniper for the Bernalillo County Sheriff's Office, and it took a lot of schmoozing, much of it not strictly ethical, to get her to agree to come to the small town of Del Sol.

One could argue that a small town like Del Sol didn't need a sniper.

One would be wrong.

Also, the girl could shoot the wings off a fruit fly at a thousand yards. Metaphorically speaking.

"Have you told her yet?" she asked.

"Crap, I forgot," Quince said. "Zee and I found out we're actually twins separated at birth."

Sun turned back, her interest piqued.

"Weird, right?" Zee asked, nodding in confirmation.

And Zee was the sane one.

"Very," Sun agreed. "Especially since he's half-Latino with blond hair, blue eyes, and a below-average level of common sense and you're a stunning black woman with ebony hair, hazel eyes, and an above-average level of common sense. Way, way above."

"Exactly," Quince said, taking another bite.

"Like, atmospheric."

He nodded. "Weird."

When Sun started back to her office, she heard Zee say proudly, "Did you hear that? She called me *stunning*."

"Yeah, well, since we're twins, it was a compliment to both of us."

"No way. That was my compliment. I get to keep all of it."

"You were always selfish, even when we were kids."

"Insult me again and I'll eat the last cursed muffin."

Sun laughed and continued toward her office with a new vigor. So far, she'd racked up three mysteries that needed solving fairly quickly. First, who were the Dangerous Daughters, and why did the mayor care so much? Second, how was she going to convince Mrs. Sorenson and Mr. Madrid to stop fighting and just date already? And third, what was up with Lieutenant Bo Britton? Because, as subtle as Quincy's evasive tactics were—Note to self: never send that man in undercover—something did not add up.

And it was barely nine o'clock. She could only hope she'd survive the post until noon.

"Hey!" Quincy shouted. "I thought you were going to address the troops."

Sun whirled on her toes and looked at Del Sol's finest.

"Right." She tossed the wrapper in a trash can and stuffed her hands into her pockets.

The deputies gave her their full attention just as Sun's gaze darted to the gas pumps across the street where a truck had pulled in.

A truck she'd know anywhere.

His truck.

Her eyes rounded, and Quincy turned to look over his shoulder.

"Um, thank you guys for being here this morning," Quincy said, coming to Sun's rescue. "You guys are doing great work, and the sheriff looks forward to getting to know all of you better."

A couple of the deputies clapped hesitantly as Sun stood glued to the spot, watching the man she'd been in love with since she was old enough to appreciate boys for what they were: boys.

Across the street, Levi Ravinder climbed down from his black Ford Raptor and slammed his door shut. He was agitated, his movements hurried and aggressive as he loaded supplies into the bed.

A man Sun assumed was one of his plethora of cousins filled up the tank. Levi shouted something to him, and the man showed him a palm in surrender. And then, as though he felt her presence, as though he sensed her focus on him, he turned toward the station and locked gazes with her.

Only he couldn't have. There was no way he could see her, especially where she stood now, in the middle of the deputies' office.

He scanned the front of the building before turning back to his cousin.

"After all this time?" Quincy asked, coming to stand beside her again.

She shook her head, embarrassed. "No. I'm just—" She exhaled, giving up the game. "I haven't seen him in so long."

"Yeah, well, he hasn't changed much."

Holy mother of God, was he wrong. Even from a distance, she could see the changes, and none of them were exactly subtle. His hair had gotten darker. His jaw stronger. His shoulders wider.

She stepped toward the lobby for a better look. She'd seen pictures, of course, a.k.a. she'd stalked his social media, but nothing had prepared her for the real thing. Especially where her bones were concerned, because they'd apparently dissolved.

He turned and went back to work, loading bottles of water and what looked like camping equipment into the truck bed, and Sun realized he wasn't wearing a jacket. His tan T-shirt didn't hide much. She could see the sculpting of sinew and muscle, his forearms cording with every movement, the shadows hugging his biceps ebbing and flowing with every effort. The effect was hypnotic.

Quincy elbowed her softly. "I could bring him in on suspected . . . anything."

Sun laughed softly. "Thanks, but I'm okay. It's better if we don't talk. Or come face-to-face. Or have contact of any kind whatsoever."

"Well," Quincy said, taking a sip of coffee, "good luck with that." He walked away and left Sun alone with her musings.

Sadly, alone with her musings was a dangerous place to be.

Especially when she noticed that even though his coffee-colored hair had darkened, the stubble he'd worn since high school, the stubble that made him look charmingly disheveled, had grown a deeper, richer auburn. And though she couldn't see his eyes, she'd dreamed about them almost daily. The rich, tawny color like whiskey in the sun. The long, dark lashes she would have given her left kidney for. The scythe-shaped brows that always lent him a look of mischief.

She walked closer to the plate-glass windows for a better view. He wasn't a model, but he should have been. The world would have been all the richer for it.

Sun forced herself to snap out of it. She was back and Levi had never left, and the two were bound to see each other now and again. The only question was, how would she survive the stretches in between?

After another glance at the station, one that had Sun retreating back from the window, Levi walked toward the store to pay, and Sun realized just how lucky his jeans were to be able to hug such a perfect ass.

He disappeared inside the building and left her with no other choice but to finally take note of his truck. It had a custom wrap with his company's logo on it, Dark River Shine, and pride swelled inside her.

He'd actually managed to take his family's illegal business— and recipe—and turn it into an insanely successful career as a distiller. Now one of the country's most prestigious makers of corn whiskey, a.k.a. moonshine, his products had been featured in newspapers and magazines all over the world, and he'd won numerous awards for the 100-proof spirits.

Awards. Just like Puff Daddy. Who knew such subcultures existed?

He stepped out of the Quick-Mart and headed back toward the pumps. Sadly, Sun missed most of his reemergence, because a

Mercedes that had been barreling down Main, slipping and sliding on the icy road, jumped the curb and crashed head-on through the plate glass where Sunshine had been standing.

If she hadn't been so preoccupied, she would have seen it in plenty of time and jumped out of the way. Instead, a barrage of splintered glass sliced across her face and hands. And a split second before the car sideswiped her, she realized her deputies might have been right.

Maybe there really was something to the muffin thing, after all.

Auri stood in the hall, staring at a locker that had the word *narc* written on it in red spray paint. She looked from the principal to the security guard and back again.

"I didn't do that," she said, wondering why in the world they would think she did.

"We know," the principal said. A man she thought handsome until about five minutes ago, Mr. Jacobs had smooth dark skin and kind eyes, and she'd noticed earlier everyone still called him *Coach*, a testament to his former position, she supposed.

And his head sat about two feet taller than Auri's. The security guard's a few inches taller than that. There was nothing quite as special as being stared down by two men of authority. And here Auri thought she couldn't feel any more vulnerable than she had earlier.

Mr. Jacobs reached past her and opened the locker with a master key. Inside sat one solitary object: the wooden carving Lynelle had taken off his desk. And Auri suddenly understood.

She took a hit off her inhaler, then asked, "I take it this is my locker?" She had yet to visit it, but it was nice of everyone to make her feel so welcome.

They both nodded.

"Don't tell me," the security guard said. "You have no idea how this got there."

She took a closer look. It was a lion, the Del Sol High mascot.

Appropriate since lions were intertwined with the sun through the zodiac sign of Leo, which was also the name the DSHS mascot.

When she shook her head, the security guard lost it. He huffed out a breath and did an about-face, raking a hand through his hair before turning back to her.

"Do you have any idea how many decades Leo has been passed down from principal to principal? He is a symbol of pride for this school, Miss Vicram. Something you clearly know nothing about."

While Auri backed away slowly, wondering about the guard's mental stability—clearly he took his job way too seriously—she noticed the principal fighting a grin behind a closed fist.

"Okay, Gary," he said, patting the guard on his shoulder, "how about we let her talk?"

Disgusted, the guard turned away from her and jammed his fists onto his hips, the gesture both dramatic and unnecessary. Auri's opinion of him couldn't plummet any lower.

The principal scrubbed his face with his hands, again fighting a grin, then settled an understanding stare on her.

"Do you know who put this in your locker?"

She shook her head.

He raised a warning brow. "I'm willing to bet you do."

"I don't. I'm sorry."

"Even if I were to call your mother? Still nothing?"

Auri stopped breathing and decided to give her shoes a good once-over when she felt a familiar sting in the backs of her eyes. "It's my mom's first day on the job. She doesn't need me messing up her entire day. Again."

"I'm well aware. I used to teach that little firecracker you call *Mom*. And I think you're right. How about we let this slide?" He leaned closer, his expression soft with understanding. "But if you ever want to talk about all of this"—he gestured toward the locker—"you know where my office is. Especially since I'm fairly certain you saw who took this off my desk."

His statement startled her.

"You're just going to let her go?" Gary asked, appalled.

Mr. Jacobs was getting tired of him if his change in attitude were any indication. "Gary, if I weren't married to your sister—"

"I know. I know." The man walked off with a dismissive wave.

But Auri was way more interested in why the principal thought she saw the culprit—a.k.a. Lynelle Amaia—steal the carving. Why he seemed to know she did.

The bell rang before the principal could say anything else, and students flooded the hallway.

"May I go to class now?" she asked him, determined not to be late again.

He gave her a thoughtful gaze, then nodded.

She found her second classroom much easier than the first. Or so she'd thought.

She entered and handed the teacher her schedule as the other kids filed in only to have the teacher point to the paper. "You want the next classroom. Room 47. This is 45."

When a mocking giggle hit her, she turned and saw one of the girls from her first period, one of Lynelle's friends. At least they didn't have this class together.

Auri walked out of that classroom and into the next just as the bell rang. Once again, she handed her schedule to the teacher as the entire class looked on. The instructor, an older man with graying auburn hair and weathered skin, wore a red-and-gold hoodie and matching sweatpants.

"Happy New Year, Coach," a student said as he passed.

"Marks. You're late."

"Sorry." The student hurried to his seat, probably hoping he wouldn't get sent to the office for being tardy.

The coach initialed her schedule and handed her a social studies book. "Welcome to Del Sol, Auri."

Surprised he knew her nickname, Auri glanced up.

"Ah yes, I know your mom. She told me you'd be starting here.

I promised to keep an eye on you. Not too close, though, eh?" He winked, and Auri couldn't help but grin at him.

Friendly faces had been hard to come by of late. At least, she'd thought so until she turned and saw the girl. The blonde who was startlingly happy to see her in first period. She waved again with the same amount of enthusiasm and wiggled in her seat. That was one exuberant girl.

Auri gave a hesitant wave back and went to the only empty seat in the classroom, but not before noticing the poet, Cruz, in the back row. She groaned. Not aloud or anything, but in her mind.

She let her gaze flit past him, because he was staring at her. A nervous energy prickled down her spine. At least he no longer looked angry. Small miracles.

The coach took roll, then proceeded with the lesson. "Okay, we talked before break about the social implications of economy and class, but I want us to shift focus a bit." The coach grabbed a stack of papers off his desk. "Before we left for break, I paired you up. Since you were gone, De los Santos, I'll put you with Auri. How's that sound?"

The coach's gaze landed on Auri, and she nodded. What else could she do? She had no idea who De los Santos was, so she hardly had an opinion.

"That okay with you?" He looked past her toward the back row, where he stopped on the poet, and her heart tried to jump out of her chest when she realized who she'd been partnered with. Cruz De los Santos. This was not happening.

He'd had his head down and didn't bother to lift it when he looked up at the coach from underneath impossibly long lashes and gave a single nod.

"Good deal. Here are your questions." He handed a stack of papers to the first student in each row to pass back. "I'll give you a few minutes at the end of class to partner up and figure out a time when you can meet outside the classroom."

"But, Coach," the tardy kid, a stocky athlete with hazelnut hair, whined. "What about practice?"

"Marks, no amount of practice is going to help your jump shot. I think you can squeeze this in."

The class erupted in laughter. Well, most of the class. Cruz De los Santos was busy eyeing Auri from underneath those killer lashes.

Trying to ignore him, she took the paper and scanned the questions. The basic gist was to get a family history, a fact that caused the teensiest bristle to quake through her.

"This will be due next week, so get on it."

The coach went into his lesson for the day while Auri fought the urge to look over her shoulder. She sank down in her seat and studied the dynamics of the room instead. And the more class went on, the more she saw a strange phenomenon.

The other students seemed to partially ignore Cruz and partially revere him. When they cracked a joke, they'd look at him as though gauging his reaction. When they asked a question, they'd glance back to see if he would . . . what? Back them up?

The girls, Auri could understand. There was no denying the fact that the guy was hot. But the boys? That she found odd.

Then again, she had bigger worries than the student body's fascination with the poet. She'd have to talk to him. Face-to-face. One-on-one. Mano a mano.

Either way, every time she thought her day couldn't get any worse, she'd been proven wrong. She decided to quit thinking altogether. To become a zombie. Zombies didn't sweat the small stuff. She could do that.

5

"He took my daughter!"

A brunette in her midforties stumbled out of the Mercedes that had run Sunshine down just as a trio of deputies swarmed around their new boss.

Looking up from the ground, Sun watched from beside the car as the woman fell to her knees in slow motion. The world had slowed, and she felt like she had that time she'd played quarters as a teen: as though she'd been part of the lunar landing and no one explained to her how to get her balance in the low gravity.

Salazar helped the woman up, but she'd cut her hands on the shattered glass when she'd fallen. Seeing the blood sent Sun into overdrive. Everything hit her at once, much like the car had.

An alarm sounded around them. A deputy was yelling for Anita to get an ambulance there ay-sap. Quincy hovered over her, his face upside down as he spoke, but she couldn't focus on his words just yet. Everything was a blur. Every movement either too fast or too slow. Every sound either too loud or too soft.

When Sun tried to get up, Quincy held her to the ground with a hand on her shoulder. She looked from side to side, trying to orient herself. That was when she saw the tire, which sat about three inches from her face. She could smell the rubber, it was so close. And the engine was still running.

Adrenaline shot through her, and she tried to scramble away from the wheel, worried the car would inch forward.

Quincy caught on and slid her away from the car as though she were a rag doll, heedless of the glass, but he kept her pinned to the ground with a hand on her shoulder.

"Take it easy," he said, his familiar voice finally penetrating her panic bubble. "Let's make sure nothing is broken, okay?"

"I'm okay," she said. The world was only spinning a little. How bad could it be?

She looked for the woman again and found her sitting on a chair the lobby, yelling at sweet Deputy Salazar as Deputy Price jumped in the car and turned off the engine.

"The ambulance is coming," Quincy said, and Sun's annoyance finally took root.

"I'm fine, Quince, really. Can someone turn off that alarm?" She rolled onto her side, and Salazar helped her up despite a warning glare from her BFF.

They steadied her when she swayed, but Quincy took over, wrapping an arm around her for support as she hobbled toward Mrs. Mercedes. The alarm finally stopped screeching.

"Ma'am, do you need an ambulance?" she asked her.

The woman's eyes rounded when she saw her. "I'm so sorry. I didn't mean . . ." She looked at the damage she'd caused and put a hand over her mouth. "Oh, my god."

"Thank you, Deputy," Sun said to the dark-haired tech geek, Lonnie Price, who'd been trying to keep the woman calm. Price had only been with the Del Sol office about six months, and he was the only deputy not originally from the area. But he came with stellar recommendations, and according to all reports, he adjusted quickly.

Price nodded and took a step back to give her room.

With Quincy's help, Sun knelt in front of the woman. "Ma'am, can you tell me what happened?"

The woman seemed to slip into a state of shock. Her expression went blank even as tears slid past her lashes. "He took her. He took my daughter." She blinked and focused on Sun, folding her hands into her own. "You have to find her."

Sun squeezed. "What's your name?"

"Mari. Marianna St. Aubin."

Ah yes. The St. Aubins were transplants as well. They'd been the talk of the town last summer when they moved to Del Sol from the Midwest to start a winery. And they had money. The root of all evil and many abductions.

Sun gestured for Salazar to grab a pen and memo pad. A memo pad that Sun smudged with blood. Her hands were covered in tiny cuts. She wiped one on her pants, winced at the glass shards still lodged in her skin, and continued.

"Okay, who took your daughter? Did you see him?"

"No. He took her last night. I was asleep. I fell asleep."

Someone brought Sun a chair, and she sat in front of Mrs. St. Aubin. The splinters of glass digging into her back stung every time she moved, but she could see to that later. The siren from an ambulance wailed as it neared, which seemed ridiculous to her since the fire station was only two blocks away.

"Mrs. St. Aubin, how old is your daughter?"

"Fourteen."

Same age as Auri. For some reason, that knowledge startled her.

Mrs. St. Aubin spoke between sobs, her voice strained. "She'll be fifteen in three days. Three days." Her eyes rounded again, and she clawed at Sun's hands. "You have to find her. We don't have much time."

Before Sun could ask what she meant, the woman disintegrated into a fit of sobs, her shoulders shaking violently. Sun sent one of the deputies for water as the EMTs rushed in. She showed a palm to stop them and continued her interrogation.

She put a hand on the woman's shoulder to get her attention. "Mrs. St. Aubin, start from the beginning. How long has your daughter been missing?"

The woman blinked, trying to make sense of her surroundings, and said in a hushed tone, "Forever."

Sun called Quincy and one of the EMTs to her office while the other tech checked on Mrs. St. Aubin. She glanced at the new station décor as she passed. A white Mercedes sedan that probably cost more than Canada now graced the foyer. They could do worse, she figured. They could have a statue of the town's founder, a man who looked alarmingly like Lurch from *The Addams Family*.

She thought back, trying to remember exactly what hit where when the car came at her as though laser guided. She remembered ducking, because that made so much more sense than jumping out of the way. Sadly, her reflexes weren't so much catlike as roly-polylike.

The car's bumper must have hit her shoulder. It was enough to send her sprawling back, a fact that probably saved her life if the placement of the tire was any indication. Three inches closer and she'd be in dire need of a face-lift. As in her face lifted off the floor.

Her phone beeped with a text from Auri. The very Auri she'd just left at school not an hour earlier. She prayed the kid hadn't actually cut a bitch this early in the semester. She checked the message and breathed a sigh of relief. It was only their standard check-in.

"Knock-knock," she'd texted.

Sun smiled. "Who's there?"

"Your mama."

A bubble of laughter surfaced. "Sweetheart, I know you're lying. Your grandmother never knocks."

She received a GIF of a dog on its back in a fit of laughter for her efforts. A breathy sigh of relief slid past her lips. She'd genuinely been worried this last week. Not about Auri cutting a bitch. For the girl's well-being.

The tribulations of being a parent, she supposed.

She sent her a row of hearts before restarting the journey to her office.

With no time to spare, she began unbuttoning her shirt before she made it there, but something else drew her attention. She looked across the street to see Levi observing from the gas pumps.

She paused, not because she wanted a better look. Well, yes, because she wanted a better look, but it was his expression that stopped her in her tracks.

When his powerful gaze met hers, he lowered his head and stared a solid minute, his fists tightening around a worn cap.

Concern lined his face. And something akin to knowing, as though the crash didn't surprise him. As though Sun's presence didn't surprise him. Then again, why would it? He'd had to have known she'd won the bid for county sheriff.

He wet his lips, the movement so sexy Sun could hardly see straight. Before she could wrench her gaze away, he turned, climbed back into his truck, and took off, heading north toward his family's land.

"Nope," Quincy said from beside her. "He hasn't changed at all." His tone was teasing, and Sun wanted to punch him in the arm like she had on numerous occasions in high school. "You think maybe we ought to find a missing kid now?"

Sun straightened her shoulders and winced as the fabric of her uniform scraped over the glass in her back. Death by a thousand paper cuts suddenly seemed much worse than she'd previously imagined.

"After we deglass you, that is," Quincy added.

They started toward her office again, the EMT right behind them, when Anita stepped out of the restroom, her hands pressed against her abdomen.

"Mrs. Escobar, are you okay?"

"Please, Sheriff, call me Anita, and I'm sorry about this." She gestured toward the bathroom. "I have stomach issues. Every time I get upset or excited or nervous, I have to, you know, find a restroom."

"That's . . . unfortunate," she said, surprised the woman worked at a sheriff's station. "And you can call me Sun. Or Sunny. Or Sunshine." She rolled her eyes. She really needed to choose one and stick to it. "I need you to get all the info you can on Mrs. St. Aubin. Her daughter is missing."

"Again?" Anita asked. Shaking her head, she started for her desk, but Sun stopped her with a hand on her shoulder.

"What do you mean? Has she gone missing before?"

Anita closed her mouth as though she'd said something she shouldn't have. "Nope. Nuh-uh. Forget I mentioned it." She started for her desk again. "Carry on."

When Sun's questioning expression elicited only a shrug from Quincy, she walked back to Mrs. St. Aubin. An EMT was checking her vitals while she cradled a cup of coffee.

Sun knelt in front of her again. "Mrs. St. Aubin, has your daughter ever run away?"

"What? No. She didn't run away. She just, she was scared. But it doesn't matter now. We don't have much time."

A terrified parent was one thing, but Marianna St. Aubin seemed awfully sure of her daughter's potential fate. Sun's suspicious mind began to work overtime. Maybe that little statement about forever meant something, after all.

"Why?" she asked, her voice taking on a harder edge. "Why don't we have much time?"

Mrs. St. Aubin blinked in surprise, then stumbled through an explanation. "Well, isn't that what they say? The first forty-eight hours are the most vital?"

She had her there. But still. "You said *he*."

"What?" The woman was shaking so badly that hot coffee sloshed over the side of her cup. She gasped and almost dropped it.

"You said, 'He took her.' Who is *he*?"

"No one." She handed the cup to Zee and brought her scalded hand to her mouth. "I don't know. It was just a guess. Isn't it usually a male?" Then she turned, her sense of entitlement taking over. "I don't see what any of that has to do with my missing daughter, Sheriff. Are you going to do your job or not?"

Mrs. St. Aubin's words were just as much defense mechanism as entitlement, so Sun didn't take them too personally. She let the events of the day turn over in her mind before standing and heading back to her office. The deputies were easing the car down the stairs and out of the station as a tow truck waited nearby.

"What are you thinking?" Quincy asked.

"I'm thinking Mrs. St. Aubin isn't being completely honest with us."

"What gave it away?" he asked, his tone dripping with sarcasm.

"But right now, there's a fourteen-year-old girl out there somewhere, and we need to find her."

"Agreed. Are you sure you're up for this? What with it being your first day and all?"

"Up for it? This is why I became a law enforcement officer."

"To save abducted girls?" he asked.

She eyed him a long moment, then said, "To catch criminals."

After an excruciating session in which the EMT begged Sun repeatedly to go the urgent care facility, claiming a couple of her cuts needed stitches, he dressed them the best he could so Sun could don a fresh shirt and she and Quincy could drive Mrs. St. Aubin to her house to investigate the possible abduction site.

She set the deputies on various tasks like calling the school to see if the girl showed up there and getting her phone records, with her mother's blessing.

Mrs. St. Aubin questioned Sun the entire way to her house. "Why aren't you calling in the FBI or the CIA or whatever other organization needs to be notified? Shouldn't you be calling for backup?"

At that moment, Sun just wanted to keep the woman calm. "We need to inspect the site before we call anyone in."

"But we don't have much time." The woman was in a state of near panic, but Sun knew one thing Mrs. St. Aubin didn't. They don't always kill them in the first forty-eight hours. Sometimes they hold them for days.

The site was not what she'd expected. The St. Aubins owned a large vineyard, and their house—scratch that—their *mansion* was proof that it was doing well. They pulled up to a stunning rock-and-glass three-story contemporary with a stone entrance.

Mrs. St. Aubin hurried them upstairs to her daughter's room, where nary a *Beauty and the Beast* figurine nor a Harry Potter book was out of place.

"This is it. Sybil's room."

Sun studied a collection of snapshots that haphazardly lined the mirror of an otherwise impeccable bedroom. Sybil St. Aubin was adorable. She had auburn hair, not quite as coppery as Auri's, that she wore in braids. A smattering of freckles peppered her nose, on top of which sat a pair of round glasses that screamed *book nerd*.

Sun liked her instantly.

But the room hadn't been disturbed in the least. If this was a teen's room, Sun wanted one: a teen that kept her room clean. Auri's room looked like a tornado tore through it on a weekly basis.

"Mrs. St. Aubin—"

"Mari, please."

"Mari," she began again, only to be interrupted a second time.

"See?" Mari said, gesturing wildly. The longer she spoke,

the louder her voice became. "Her backpack is still here. Her bed hasn't been slept in. The clothes she'd set out for school today haven't been touched, and her phone is still on the charger. She's been missing all night." With Quincy's help, she sank onto a chair by Sybil's desk and whispered, "She's out there all alone." Fresh tears ran down her cheeks as Sun and Quincy took in the scene.

Quincy checked the window for signs of forced entry, just as he had when they'd come in the front door. Nothing. Sun looked through a smattering of papers on the desk and nightstand, but nothing looked unusual there, either.

"Mari, are you sure Sybil didn't take off on her own?"

"I'm positive!" Mari jumped up, wringing her hands. "She wouldn't do that. You have to believe me."

"Then why does my admin think she did?"

She slammed her eyes shut and said softly, "Because Sybil left the house a few days ago without telling me, and I panicked."

Mari's behavior once again bordered on the bizarre. Either she took overprotection to a whole new level, or she wasn't giving them everything.

"Did she take her phone with her that time?"

"Yes!" She jumped up and rushed to Sybil's phone.

Quincy stopped her from touching it with a gentle hand on her arm.

She nodded in understanding. "Yes, she did. Her battery had died, and I couldn't get ahold of her, so I dialed 911."

And she got Anita.

"But this time, she left it here. Nothing on earth could separate that girl from her phone barring a natural disaster or an abduction."

Sun had to agree with her on the point. "I'm going to send a team in, Mari. I'll need you to stay out of Sybil's room until they get here, okay? Don't touch anything."

She clutched her chest and nodded.

"Where is your husband?"

"In California on business. I told him not to go. He's on his way back."

"Why?"

"Because our daughter is missing!" she practically screeched.

"No, why did you tell him not to go?"

"Oh. Well, Sybil's birthday is coming up."

"Of course." Sun scanned the room one more time. "Remember, don't touch anything."

"I won't. I'll wait here."

They left by a side door to get a look at that entrance. Again, no sign of forced entry.

"Well?" Sun asked Quincy when they got back into her cruiser.

"If something smells fishy, it's usually fish," he said.

"It is indeed."

Before she left the St. Aubins' house, Sun took out her phone and knock-knocked Auri. This case made Sun more grateful than ever that her daughter was safe and sound. A few seconds later, she received a thumbs-up.

At least Auri's day was going better than hers.

6

With about five minutes of class left, Auri watched as her class-mates performed musical chairs so they could make plans on when to meet to do their interviews. Some cheated and agreed to simply fill out the forms themselves instead of doing an interview and then trading papers before class. Auri hoped her partner wouldn't suggest they take that route.

Since he'd made no move to sit next to her, she was left with little choice but to go to him. He may not have cared about his grades, but she cared greatly about hers, and she was not about to let a grumpy grizzly risk her requisite A.

She took the seat directly in front of him. He watched her. When he made no effort to break the ice with conversation, she took the initiative.

She let her gaze drop, unable to look at him—his gaze was so intense—and got on with it. "Okay, I get it. You don't like me. Join the club. But we have an assignment, and I can't afford a zero, so—"

Before she got another word out, he slid the paper out of her hand, turned it over, and wrote on the back. When he finished, he handed it to her and waited.

She read the phone number. "Is this your cell?"

He nodded, then asked, "Why don't I like you?" His voice was smooth and deep, and it did the same things to her it had before when he was reading the poem.

"Because I called the cops at the lake."

His lids narrowed as though trying to figure her out.

"That's what everyone thinks, anyway."

He handed her his paper. She turned it over and wrote her number on the back, her hand shaking slightly.

"Do I make you nervous?" he asked.

She scowled at him.

For the first time, he let a grin slide across his face. The effect was nothing short of spectacular.

She cleared her throat and went back to writing. Or she would have if she hadn't completely forgotten her address. Panic surged inside her. As did her grasp on reality, apparently.

"Why are you shaking?"

This was getting ridiculous. She lived on Solaris Drive. She knew that much. "Oh, you know. That's what happens when the whole school is out to get even with the narc."

"Ah."

She gave up and handed the paper back to him. "How about I just come to you?"

"You live behind your grandparents' house, right?"

How did he know that? "Yes."

He handed the paper back. "One eleven."

"What?"

One corner of his mouth tilted. "Your new address. It's 111 Solaris Drive." When she gaped at him, he raised a hand in surrender. "I helped build it. You're all your grandparents talk about."

She felt her cheeks warm as she wrote down her address for reasons she couldn't fathom. He knew it better than she did.

"Do you have any afternoons free this week?" she asked. When he didn't answer, she looked up at him.

After a long moment, he said, "Every single one."

The way he said it caused a tingling sensation in her stomach.

"Hi!"

Auri started and looked up at the blonde standing beside them.

"I'm Chastity. We met this summer, but you probably don't remember. That's okay, though. I'm horrible with names, too. I'm much better with faces. I have to do something to associate a name with a face. Like with yours. Your hair is like a sunrise, so now I remember it. Aurora. But everyone calls you Auri. I remember that part without a mnemonic device."

Cruz hadn't bothered giving Chastity even an ounce of his attention. It was all focused on Auri, and she was trying to figure out why. Was this a joke? Was she being punked? He'd been furious with her when the principal came during first period. Why was he being so nice now?

"I remember," was all Auri got in before Chastity started anew. Thankfully, the bell rang so the girl could catch her breath.

When Cruz stood, he purposely blocked Chastity's view of her, effectively dismissing the poor girl. Not everyone had mastered social skills.

Auri stood and slid her backpack over her shoulders, a tad grateful for his intervention. Chastity would take some getting used to.

Some boys passed by and patted Cruz on the back or shoulder, promising to see him later. He barely acknowledged them. It was as though he were an unwilling member of the popular clique. Auri had never seen anything like it. He took her schedule, scanned it, then walked with her to the hall where she saw her newest frenemies.

No, that wasn't true. In order for Lynelle and her group to be called *frenemies*, they would have to have been nice to her at some point. So not the case.

If the glowers from Lynelle and the gang had been bad before, she'd just earned their eternal wrath. Their expressions, especially

Lynelle's, when they saw her walking with Cruz were at first shock and then cold, calculating anger.

Maybe Lynelle had a thing for Cruz, but she had a boy by her side everywhere she went. Liam Eaton. The rich jock who spent his summers in Paris and, according to rumor, had a Porsche waiting for him when he turned sixteen next year.

Maybe Lynelle and Liam were just friends. Either way, Auri had a feeling things were going to get much worse before they got better.

Her phone vibrated. She took it out of her jacket pocket and replied to her mom's text with a thumbs-up. At least her day was probably going better than Auri's.

"She's not in school today," Zee said when Sun and Quincy walked into the station. She had to speak up, as men were boarding up the gaping hole in the front of the building. "And no one called in to excuse her."

"What do we know about them?" she asked her deputies before taking a file Price handed her.

"They're new to the area," he said. "Originally from Chicago. Been here about eight months. The husband is from money. The wife, your typical trophy, was a waitress."

"They only have the one kid?" Sun asked, scanning the contents of what little they had on the family.

Zee chimed in, "As far as we know, but these rich people always have skeletons in their closets."

"True." Sun wondered how much she should pressure Mari St. Aubin. If she knew more than she was letting on, now was certainly the time to come squeaky clean.

Quincy leaned on the desk beside her. "Either Marianna St. Aubin is genuinely distraught, or she is one hell of an actress."

Sun scanned the deputies surrounding her. "I think it's time I hit the streets."

"You mean—?" he asked, surprised she'd go there.

She nodded. "I mean." If anyone had dirt on the St. Aubins, it would be the Book Babes, her mother's book club, a.k.a. a front for drinking wine and gossiping. "They're expecting me, anyway. I promised to talk to them about law enforcement today."

"On your first day of work?"

"Don't start." The things her mother could talk her into. "They're about to get a crash course. In the meantime, you guys keep digging."

Salazar raised her hand. Unnecessary, but effective. "What about an Amber Alert?" She gauged the reaction of her colleagues. "Is it too soon?"

"An Amber Alert is never too soon." If anything, they were usually too late. "Why don't you get that going?"

She brightened. "You got it, boss."

"Price," she said, getting the young deputy's attention. "I don't suppose you have any connections in Chicago PD?"

Price wasn't from Chicago, but Detroit was only a few hours away. He could have friends on the force there. She could get all the official reports on the St. Aubins there were and still know very little about the dynamics of the family. She wanted the gossip. The calls that weren't reported because of their wealth and power.

Was there any history of domestic violence? Alcoholism? Prescription drug addiction?

He tossed her a knowing grin. "I'm on it."

"Good man," she said, hurrying out the door.

"You want backup?" Quincy called out to her.

She snorted, then changed her mind and turned back to him. Interrogating a group of women was one thing. Interrogating a group of women while a man they'd repeatedly referred to as *stupid hot* was another.

"Come to think of it."

Quincy jumped up and followed her a little too enthusiastically. He'd always had a thing for her mom. An affinity thing. A disturbing thing.

"Just keep your hands to yourself," she warned him.

He chuckled. "It's not my hands you need to worry about."

Excellent point.

"So," Quincy said on the way over, "you're going to talk to the nosiest people in town about law enforcement."

"I know," Sun said, deflating. "Just don't let Wanda corner you. That woman's a menace." Wanda Stephanopoulos was a firecracker with the damage potential of a grenade, only less stable. Like a Molotov cocktail.

"I think she likes me."

"They all like you. That's why you're here. You're my distraction. They'll be so enamored with you, they'll answer all my questions without too much fuss."

"Have you even met your mother?"

Sun conceded with a shrug. "It's worth a shot."

"I feel so used." When she raised a brow at him, he added, "Just how I like it."

They pulled into the crowded driveway of Darlene Tapia, one of Sun's mother's oldest friends. It was apparently her week to host the book club. Besides Darlene's small crossover, several cars lined the street in front of the house, including Elaine Freyr's Buick Encore. All sensible vehicles for fairly sensible women.

Wanda Stephanopoulos, on the other hand, drove a shiny red Dodge Hellcat. God help the town. The woman was barely tall enough to see over the steering wheel. It took up most of the driveway. Probably because she couldn't park to save her life.

Elaine ran out to meet them before they could get out of her cruiser. "You're late," she said, a smile on her face and a glass of wine in her hand.

As Sun stepped out, her mother's eaglelike vision locked on to the bandages on her hands.

"What happened?" she fairly screeched, almost spilling the wine. Thankfully, the woman had catlike reflexes when it came to alcoholic beverages. She took one of Sun's hands into her own to inspect it.

"You don't want to know."

"Of course, I do."

"A car crashed through the front of the station, showering me with glass before it ran me over."

Her mother's pretty mouth pinched up at the corners. "Fine, don't tell me." She saw Quincy and brightened.

He walked around and gave her a hug as the other women streamed out of the house to greet them, heedless of the chill in the air. And they'd clearly had wine with breakfast.

Sun got a hug from each of the women present. And all but one had a glass of wine in her hand. Wanda didn't have a glass. She had an entire bottle, and she sloshed the liquid on Quincy's uniform when she did everything but wrap her legs around him during their hug.

Oh yeah, this was going to be great.

Sun let Quincy field questions while she followed one Mrs. Ruby Moore, the muffin maker, to the kitchen to grab a few. She wasn't sure how well muffins went with wine, but at least the women would have something in their stomachs other than fermented grapes.

"Oh, sweetheart," the woman said when she noticed Sun behind her. "We're so excited you're back. Your mother is over the moon."

"I'm glad," she said, trying to think of how to word her inquiry.

The woman, a stout sixtysomething, didn't miss a step as she went about her business.

"Is Myrtle going to be okay?" Sun asked.

When they'd walked into the house, they'd found an elderly woman asleep on the couch, a half-drunk glass of wine dangerously close to tipping over in her hand. Sun remembered her. She'd worked for her doctor for years.

"Oh, she'll be fine," Ruby said with a dismissive wave. "She's drinking grape juice. She always passes out either way. No need to waste the good stuff."

Sun laughed softly. "I wanted to thank you for the muffins you sent to the station."

"Oh, pfft," she pffted. "I love making them. I always wanted to open my own muffin shop and call it Moore Muffins. It's a nice play on words, don't you think?"

"I do. And you certainly have the talent." She gestured toward the warm muffins Ruby was loading onto a tray along with her signature sauce, a sugary butter glaze. Sun's mouth watered just thinking about it. "Why didn't you?"

"Well, you know Theodore," she said as if that explained it.

She didn't know Theodore, not really, but she wasn't going to tell Ruby that. "Can I ask you something?"

Ruby stopped what she was doing and turned to her. "Of course, sweetheart."

Sun cleared her throat, suddenly uncomfortable, then just came out with it. "Are you psychic?"

The woman's expression didn't waver. In fact, if Sun didn't know better, she'd have sworn Ruby purposely froze her face to hide what was going on behind it.

After a moment, she blinked and went back to her muffins with a soft laugh. "You kids. Always joking around."

Okay. She'd bite. "Then how come every time you send a basket of muffins to the station, all hell breaks loose? Or so I'm told."

"I don't know what you mean. I just made too many muffins and decided to share."

If there was one thing Sun had learned first as a police officer and then a detective, it was when to keep her mouth shut. And that's what she did. She leveled a patient smile on the poor woman and waited.

It didn't take long.

"You can't tell Theodore," she said in a hushed voice that startled Sun.

"Ruby, are you safe? Will he hurt you?"

She snorted. "Theo? Oh, good heavens, no. I just . . . well, I promised . . . I mean, he doesn't know . . ."

"That you're psychic?"

She shook her head. "No. He knows that part. He just doesn't know that I use my powers for good. He thinks I gave it all up years ago after this thing with a rattlesnake and a lasagna. It's a long story. Anyway, he doesn't know I still practice."

Sun nodded, almost understanding. She blamed the town. Peculiar things and all.

"You're not going to tell him, are you?" Ruby asked.

"I wouldn't do that."

Ruby rested a grateful hand on her arm. "Do the others know?"

"You mean everyone at the station? Let's just say your muffins have become legendary."

"Oh, well, that's good. I guess." She picked up the tray and walked into the living room.

"It's about time," Wanda said to her, eyeing the muffins. "We're starving."

"The jig's up, guys."

"Already? We just got here."

Ruby put the tray on the coffee table. "No, I mean, she knows."

But Sun's interest rocketed to her mom's best friend, Darlene Tapia. Because when Ruby made the announcement about the jig being up, all expressions morphed into one of mass confusion. All except Darlene's. Darlene went white, and as a gorgeous Latina with sable hair and bronze skin, white was not her best color.

Elaine looked from Sun to Ruby and back again. "What exactly does my daughter know?"

"That I use my powers for good."

The entire room gasped. Well, almost the entire room. Quincy sat in a beige recliner, clearly amused. But Darlene had a different take as well.

Sun knew better than to look directly at her, and she studied the woman from her periphery. When Ruby had announced that *Sun knew*, Darlene went white. But when Ruby commented about using her powers for good, everyone except Darlene gasped. Darlene did just the opposite. She let out a breath, clearly relieved. What did she think Ruby had been talking about?

Quincy cleared his throat, and asked, "So, they're magic muffins? Is that your power?"

He was covering. He'd noticed Darlene's behavior as well and let his gaze flit to Sun for the briefest of moments to confirm the fact that she'd noticed too.

As expected, the ladies laughed at his query. Even Darlene, whose laugh stemmed more from nerves than amusement.

"I'm not magic. I just sort of sense things."

He nodded. "So, you can sense when things in Del Sol are tanking?"

"What did you sense today?" Sun asked, not convinced of Ruby's abilities in the least. But what could it hurt to ask?

"Two days ago, actually. I knew something bad was going to happen, and I just wanted our finest to enjoy a muffin or two before it all went belly-up."

Elaine chimed in then. "I promise you, ladies, our secret is safe with my daughter."

Awww. That was sweet.

She reached over and grabbed a muffin, before adding, "She doesn't believe a word of any of this."

Several sets of eyes landed on Sun in horror.

Oh, well. She needed a segue, anyway. "Actually, I need to know what you ladies have heard about the St. Aubins."

"He's a handsome thing," Wanda said, and Sun could only assume she was talking about Mr. St. Aubin.

The fastest way to get the lowdown was to pass the info along to the Book Babes and see what sprang up. It had been a time-honored tradition since Sun was a kid. "Any dirt? I know they're new, but—"

"There's always dirt," Elaine said. "But Marianna genuinely seems to be in love with her husband."

The others agreed with a nod.

"I think she had a rough life growing up," a dark-haired Book Babe named Karen said.

Sun nodded. "I only know that she was a waitress when she met Forest St. Aubin in Chicago."

"Yes, she was." Karen seemed to know more about the family than the rest. "But before that, well, let's just say she emancipated herself from her parents when she was sixteen."

"Do you know why?" Sun's question took Karen aback, but she needed everything she could get, so she explained, "Their daughter may be missing."

Every face showed genuine surprise, but Karen seemed to catch on the quickest. "And you think Forest and Mari had something to do with it?"

"Honestly, no, but I can't afford to form any opinions just yet. I'm trying to stay open to all possibilities."

When Karen's expression hardened, Elaine added, "As any good law enforcement officer would." Her tone was sharp, and Karen reined in her offended posture immediately.

"I don't know why she emancipated herself," she said, brushing crumbs off her slacks. "I just know that Mari's parents were not nice people, and she divorced them at sixteen."

"Tell her what they've been up to lately," Wanda encouraged, elated with the juicy gossip to which she'd been privy.

"They?" Quincy asked.

Wanda scooted to the edge of her seat. "Mari's deadbeat parents."

"Actually, that's been going on for a while, now," Karen

corrected. "Ever since Marianna married into money, they've been trying to get their hands on it."

Sun tamped down the adrenaline that had spiked within her, and asked calmly, "Trying how?"

"I'm not sure. We've had coffee a few times. Mari is really nice, and she adores her daughter. You have to know that."

"I could tell, hon."

"All she told me was that her parents were always calling up with one sob story after another, needing money for this or that."

"Does Marianna give them any?"

"Never," Karen said, a mischievous twinkle in her eye. "And why should she? They were horrible people. Not that Forest would let her be taken advantage of, anyway, but still."

"Have they contacted her lately?"

Karen's squinted in thought. "The last time we talked was right after New Year's, but she didn't mention them. I know they tried to get some serious money out of them last summer right after their big move here."

"How serious?"

"Hundreds of thousands of dollars. Her father had some new scheme that was going to make them all rich. A sure thing."

"Like there is such a thing," Elaine said, her face lined with concern.

"Exactly. Forest refused, of course, but from what I understand, Marianna's father was furious."

Furious enough to abduct his granddaughter and demand a ransom? It wouldn't be the first time such a scenario came to town.

"Thank you, ladies," Sun said, rising to leave.

"But wait!" Elaine jumped up. "You were going to talk to us about law enforcement."

Sun grinned at them. Every face shone with eagerness. Every face but Darlene's. She seemed relieved that Sun was almost out of her hair. Which was odd enough to tickle Sun's Spidey sense.

"I have a feeling you guys know more about law enforcement than I do."

"Well, we were hoping you could tell us how to get away with murder," Wanda said.

Ruby jumped up, waking Myrtle, the ancient woman sleeping on the sofa, in the process. "You know," Ruby said. "For research purposes."

"Hi, Myrtle," Sun said, waving. The woman blinked at her, then settled back onto the sofa with a sleepy smile on her face. "Ah, well, getting away with murder. That's tricky. In a word, you can't." A unified wave of disappointment crashed into her. "Sorry."

"Can't you just look the other way?" Wanda asked.

Elaine shushed the woman. "She can't do that, Wanda. It would be *unethical*." She'd added air quotes around the word *unethical*, and Sun realized she'd slipped into an alternate universe. One where elderly women, and some not so elderly, plotted murder and her mother used air quotes.

"Well, Elaine, the man needs to die. Who's going to do it if we don't?"

"Just who are we talking about?" Sun asked.

"No one," Elaine said. "We're just thinking out loud."

"Are we killing him or not?" Myrtle chimed in at last.

Quincy snorted, enjoying every second of the conversation.

"Apparently not," Wanda said as though thoroughly inconvenienced.

"Who's the hottie?" Myrtle asked, pointing to Quince.

"You remember Quincy," Elaine said to Myrtle, raising her voice.

"He is fancy, but who is he?"

Wanda, now annoyed, scowled at the poor woman. "How are you not dead?"

"We need to go," Sun said before she had to arrest the lot of them. "But I do have one more question."

Darlene tensed. That time, Elaine noticed.

She cast a worried expression on her best friend. "Darlene, are you okay?"

Darlene snapped to attention. "Yes. Absolutely. I'm sorry. What was your question?" As she spoke, her hands curled into fists, clearly apprehensive about what Sun would ask next.

"Right. Okay, do you guys know who the Dangerous Daughters are?"

After a tense moment in which the ladies exchanged furtive glances, they burst out laughing en masse. Again, Darlene's laughter was a tad more forced than her book buddies', but she did seem relieved.

"The Dangerous Daughters," Wanda said, doubling over. "What's next? Aliens going to high school in Roswell?"

And the laughter began anew.

That was their cue. Sun and Quincy left them in a state of hysterics after Sun made them promise to call her if they remembered anything about the St. Aubins or if they heard anything.

Elaine followed them out.

Sun stopped and addressed them both. "Could this really be a ransom situation?"

"Wouldn't be the first," Quincy said, his posture tense.

Elaine's lids slammed shut.

Quincy rushed to apologize. "I'm sorry, Elaine. I didn't mean—"

"Don't be silly." She gave the giant next to her a hug. "I just feel so bad. A missing persons case on your first day. I'm sorry, hon."

"It's not your fault, Mom." She thought about that and corrected, "Wait, actually it is. What the hell?"

Elaine had the decency to look ashamed, and Quincy gave her shoulders another squeeze.

Wanda yelled from inside the house, "Elaine, for the love of tacos, we have to discuss this danged book!"

Sun laughed. "What book did you guys read this week?"

"Oh, I have no idea. I don't read them half the time. We just drink wine and let Wanda rant. It's entertaining. I'll see what else, if anything, I can get out of Karen. Keep me updated."

"Thanks, Mom."

Sun and Quincy sat in the cruiser a few minutes, trying to digest everything they'd just learned. Especially the parts the women didn't want them to learn.

"Wow," Quincy said, as stunned speechless as his new boss. "Not only are the Dangerous Daughters real, but they know exactly who they are."

Sun nodded in disbelief. "It's like my whole world has been turned upside down."

"Hey, do you think it's them?"

"The Book Babes?" Sun frowned in doubt. "Surely not. They aren't old enough, and my mother isn't even from this area. She was a Vegas showgirl when my dad met her."

"Oh, I am very aware." His face softened in memory. "I've seen the pictures."

"That's so disturbing," she said, lying through her teeth. Her mother was a hottie. Nothing wrong with that. "Maybe it's a post. You know, a position passed down from one generation to the next."

"Maybe."

"Either way, it'll have to wait."

"Let me guess," he said, guessing. "You want me to find out everything I can about Sybil St. Aubin's parents."

"Wow, you're a good guesser." She leaned over to start the cruiser when Anita Escobar, her blond administrative assistant, came through the radio.

"Boss," she said, her voice hushed.

Sun pressed the button on the radio at her shoulder. "Go ahead."

"Yeah, you need to get back here."

"On the way. ETA seven minutes. What's up?"

"There are marshals here. Two of them. They're pretty much taking over your office."

"Like hell they are," Sun said, throwing the cruiser into reverse. "Buckle up, buttercup. It's go time."

She'd never gone to war with a U.S. Marshal, but there was a first time for everything.

7

Del Sol deputies responded to a call claiming that patrons
of the Pecos Street Grocers were being harassed by a man on a
drunken joyride with a motorized scooter from Walmart.
It should be noted that Del Sol does not have a Walmart.

—DEL SOL POLICE BLOTTER

Sadly, Auri's hiatus from the glares was short-lived. Her third class of the day was a veritable cornucopia of narc haters. Yet there seemed to be more furtive scowls than blatant glares. A step in the right direction, perhaps?

She'd made a pit stop between classes at her locker. A janitor was cleaning the red spray paint off it, so she decided to keep her two new books with her. Cruz had looked on curiously, then, realizing what it said, he'd darkened. He dropped her off at her classroom and stalked away as though he'd made a horrible mistake in friending her.

She could hardly blame him.

After repeating the usual routine, handing the teacher her schedule, then sitting in an empty seat, Auri settled herself between a girl in full gang regalia, who could probably kill her with her pinkie, and a guy dressed much the same way, who would look on with delight as she did so. She decided to forgo eye contact and busied herself by taking out a notebook and a pen.

A knock sounded at the door a microsecond after the bell rang. Auri stiffened, praying the principal wasn't after her again. The teacher, a young woman the width of a two-by-four, answered the door and spoke quietly, but Auri couldn't see with whom.

The girl turned around to her and raised her chin. "Hey," she said, her expression both amiable and curious. "What's your name?"

"Auri."

"Right. The narc." She said it with a friendly giggle, and Auri couldn't help but smile.

The kid behind her laughed, too.

"I'm Beatrice, but everyone calls me Bea. And that's Raymond." She gestured to the kid in back.

"And everyone calls me Raymond," he said, leaning forward to take her hand.

They shook as a brunette from the next row leaned over and whispered to Bea.

"Really?" Bea said. She turned to Raymond. "They're looking for that girl in fifth with the braids and the glasses."

"No shit? What'd she do?"

Before Bea could answer, the teacher closed the door and walked to her desk.

"Welcome back, guys. Hope Santa was good to you."

Some of her classmates nodded. Some shrugged. Most ignored.

"We have a new student today."

Auri froze.

"This is Aurora," she said, gesturing in her general direction. "I'd appreciate your best behavior."

A wave of heat washed over her.

"Why?" someone asked. "She'll figure out it's all a lie soon enough."

The class erupted. Well, most of the class. A couple of the

students were still in glare mode, but oddly enough, when Bea turned to them, they suddenly had somewhere else to glare.

Auri considered asking if Bea would be her bestie but figured it was too soon. She didn't want to come across as the desperate newbie she was. And besides, she already had a brand-new bestie, even though she had yet to see Sybil. The girl she'd met over winter break. The girl who wore braids and glasses.

Concern itched the back of her neck, and she used her inhaler again just in case. Why would they be looking for Sybil?

As class went on, Auri heard more and more of the whispers that chained across the room. They were looking for a girl. A girl named Sybil. The principal was going from room to room. That's who was at the door, the principal, asking if their teacher had seen her. She wasn't in trouble. No, she was in trouble. She had run away. She'd been abducted. She was last seen at the park. She was last seen walking north on I-25. They'd put out an Amber Alert. She could be dead.

By the time class was wrapping up, Auri knew only one thing for certain. Sybil St. Aubin was missing.

Risking everything, mostly her phone privileges, Auri took out her cell, angled it away from the teacher's line of sight, and texted her mom. "911. A girl is missing? Mom, I know her. What's going on?"

Then she palmed the phone and waited as panic slowly took hold.

The second the bell rang, and she hurried to the bathroom to call her mom. She locked the stall and dialed her mom's cell.

"Hey, bean sprout," Quincy said. "You're mom's driving. I'm putting you on speaker."

"Thanks, Quincy."

"Hey, bug bite. So, you know Sybil?"

"Yes, I met her at the lake on New Year's. She was supposed to meet me this morning. What's going on? Is she okay?" The tardy bell for fourth period rang.

"Where are you calling from?"

"The restroom."

"Are you supposed to be in class?"

"Yes."

"Attagirl. I never had the nerve to skip my first day, but you go."

"Mom. Sybil."

"I don't know, hon. This stays between us."

"Of course," she said, the statement dripping with *duh*.

"Sybil's mother has reported her missing, but we have yet to find any signs of foul play. Did she say anything to you in the last few days?"

Auri thought back. "I don't know. She said a couple of things that were odd, but I just thought she was like me and saw the world a little differently."

"Nobody is like you, sprout," Quincy said.

She smiled.

"What did she say?" her mom asked.

"Before Quincy showed up and stole all the beer—"

"That wasn't me."

"—we made plans to meet in the front hall. But then she said her birthday was coming up and that she really liked me but we wouldn't have much time and she hoped I would forgive her." Her mom didn't say anything, so she gave her a moment before coaxing her with, "Mom? What does that mean?"

"I don't know, bug. I wish I did."

"Sunshine," Auri said, letting her mom know she was serious. "What aren't you telling me?"

"That you're too smart for your own good?"

"And?"

Quincy spoke up. "It's just that Mrs. St. Aubin was saying something similar. Like we were running out of time."

"Like she knew something," Auri said, thinking out loud.

"Okay, I'm pulling into the station. Get to class."

"'Kay. Will you please, pretty please with cherries on top, keep me updated?"

"I will, sweetheart. Hey, how's your day going?"

"Aside from my missing friend? Peachy." She hung up the phone before her mom could ask any more questions.

"Peachy." Sun looked at Quincy after Auri hung up. "She is not having a good day."

"Damn it. I hate to hear that, poor kid."

"Maybe the narc thing is worse than I thought."

"Or kids are dicks."

Leave it to Quincy to boil every problem down to its basest element. They exited the cruiser and examined an official-looking car parked beside them.

"Marshals," Quincy said, distaste evident in his tone.

Sun tried not to laugh. "Have you ever met a marshal?"

"Yes."

She raised her brows.

"No. But still."

They walked into the building, having to go through two electronic checkpoints. "So, who do you think the Book Babes want to kill?"

"Uh, the former sheriff. Duh."

Surprised, she stopped at the last door and turned to him. "How do you know that?"

"Because he's a dick. Why do you think you're here and he's not?"

"But why? What did he do to them?"

"Well, he's Myrtle's grandson."

Okay, that she didn't know. She also didn't know the poor woman could get drunk on grape juice and had a pretty serious case of dementia, if her inability to remember Quincy was any indication. "And?"

"He's trying to get control of her estate."

"Myrtle's estate? How big can it be?"

He leaned against the wall. "I don't know if you know this, but those Book Babes went in together and invested in a little company a few decades ago."

She eyed him suspiciously. "Which little company?"

"Well, I'll give you a hint. Their logo is an apple."

"Oh, holy shit."

He opened the door for her. "Yeah."

She stopped him again. "Wait, even my mom?"

"Your mom and dad invested first, then the Book Babes pooled their resources when they saw how well your parents did and bought in pretty early, too."

"How do you know this and I don't?"

"Because I used to work for said former sheriff. You hear things."

"So, are they all rich?"

He lifted a shoulder. "Let's just say they won't be hurting for money any time soon."

"Wow. Who knew?"

Quincy and Sun walked into the station like they owned the place, Quincy because he could and Sun because she was ready to take on some marshals. At least she was until she saw them.

Or, well, him.

"Sheriff Vicram." A slim woman with short black hair, large eyes, and elfin-high cheekbones walked up with hand extended.

Beside her stood her male counterpart with skin as dark as midnight and a startlingly attractive face.

Sun took the woman's hand. "Nice to meet you. This is Chief Deputy Quincy Cooper."

She shook both their hands. "Nice to meet you. I'm Deputy Marshal Isabella Batista. This is my partner, Deputy Marshal Vincent Deleon. Hopefully, we'll be out of your hair in no time." When Sun looked in her office, more specifically at the box sitting on her desk, Marshal Batista laughed softly. "Don't worry. We aren't moving in. Do you mind?"

She gestured toward Sun's office, the one she hadn't even unpacked yet, and started toward it.

"I'm sure you're aware that the pen recently lost a few prisoners," she said when Quincy closed the door behind him.

Deleon took the box off her desk and sat it on a shelf while they spoke.

Sun nodded, taking her chair. "I am. Five inmates took over a transport van and put the guards in the hospital. Four of the fugitives have been recovered."

"Exactly." She handed a file to Sun and sat in one of the visitor chairs someone had supplied since that morning. The label on it read *Rojas, Ramses* followed by his inmate number. "We received a call from one of your residents." She scanned her notes. "A Douglas Pettyfer."

Quincy, who'd leaned against a wall by the window, coughed softly into a closed fist.

"Yeah," Sun said, suddenly very uncomfortable. "Doug isn't exactly the best witness in these types of situations."

"We figured that out over the phone," Deleon said, offering Sun a humorous smile. "But his description was spot-on."

"Really?" she asked, surprised. "And you're certain he didn't just see Rojas on television?"

Batista handed her a photo. "This is the picture we have streaming."

The police photograph showed a kid in his early twenties. Shaved head. Slightly crooked nose, probably broken at some point. And every available inch of skin on his arms and hands covered in tats.

"Okay," she said, waiting for the rest.

"That was taken when he was first arrested." She handed her a second photo. "This is his latest photo, compliments of the state pen."

Same face, though thinner. Harder. His hair was a little longer, and he sported a scar that sliced perpendicular through his right eyebrow as well as a couple more tats, a feat she wouldn't have thought possible mere seconds ago.

"And Doug knew about the scar?"

The marshal nodded. "He described it perfectly. Said he saw him out by the lake."

Her lake? That was disturbing AF.

"We just can't figure out why he's here," Deleon said.

Batista confirmed with a nod. "There is a Rojas family in the area, but they don't seem to be any relation. If someone is helping him, it's not a blood relative. Not that we know of, anyway."

"Any known associates in the area?" Quincy asked.

"None that we can find."

"Can I keep these?" Sun asked, handing the photos to Quincy.

Batista nodded. "Of course. We just wanted to check in, see if you'd received any reports of sightings or anything unusual."

"Not that I know of, but I've only been on the job for a little over three hours."

"You've had a busy morning," Deleon said.

"Yes, I have."

"The missing girl," Batista said. "Any chance our guy took her? Is maybe holding her hostage?"

Sun had considered that the minute they'd shown up at her station. If Sybil were taken from her room, Rojas would've had to case the house. He would've known about Sybil and how to get past the St. Aubins' extensive security system. Since his file said he'd been in prison for three years of a seven-year sentence, she doubted he'd know how to disable a latest-and-greatest, top-of-the-line security system.

If he'd been hanging out by the lake, however, he could have formed a connection with Sybil. Become friends. Lured her out of her home and convinced her to meet him somewhere.

"However unlikely, it certainly can't be ruled out," she said. "This says he was in prison for armed robbery. No assaults of any kind?"

Both marshals shook their heads, but Deleon made a good point. "Desperate men tend to do desperate things."

"That they do." Sunshine would be a fool to ignore this turn of events.

The marshals stood to leave. Sun walked them out the side entrance.

Batista shook her hand again. "We'll talk to Douglas first, then we have an appointment with the parks and rec officer. We're hoping he's seen Rojas in the area. We'll keep you apprised either way."

"I appreciate it."

"Any good places to eat?" Deleon asked before leaving.

Sun named off a few. That was a perk of living in a tourist town. Good food.

He handed her his card. "Call if you get hungry and want to join us."

"Thank you," she said, more than a little flattered.

He took her hand and held it a microsecond longer than necessary. Sun let him, then ended up cursing herself after they'd gone. She hadn't dated in over two years. Bad breakup. Apparently, she has commitment issues. Either way, now was certainly not the time to try to resuscitate her love life.

"So," Quincy said from behind her, catching her ogling the deputy marshal, "he seems nice."

"Shut up."

Just as Sun sat at her desk, the same desk she had yet to organize, Anita walked in, her lids wide and her face pale. In her gloved hands was an envelope. A pink one.

"Anita?" Sun said, standing.

The look on her face convinced Quincy to rush to her, but he stopped when he looked at the envelope. "It's addressed to you."

"It's from her," Anita said, moving her fingers so Sun and Quincy could see the return address. "It's from Sybil St. Aubin."

The deputies in residence gathered around her desk as Sun carefully pried open the envelope with gloved hands and a letter opener. According to the postmark, it had been mailed the day before. The handwritten address, with its neat script and rounded letters, suggested it was indeed from a girl. A young girl.

She slid the opener under the flap, cut along the top, and lifted the parchment out.

Quincy slipped the envelope into an evidence bag and sealed it for processing.

Sun unfolded the letter and scanned it. Then she scanned it again before reading it aloud. But only after a quick, confused glance at Quince.

"It's dated two days ago. Postmarked yesterday," she said.

Quincy angled for a better view. "So, she wrote it Sunday but couldn't mail it until Monday?"

"Possibly. It's addressed to me in care of the station, and it just happens to arrive on my first day?"

"She met your daughter," Zee said. "She probably knows who you are."

"True, but it gets stranger," Sun promised, and began reading. "Dear Sheriff Vicram, by the time you get this letter, I will be gone, but I'm not dead. Not yet."

She spared a quick glance at Quincy. His face was tightly drawn in thought.

"You have three days to find me," she continued. "If you don't, it will be too late."

"What the hell?" Quince said, his voice whisper soft.

Price straightened and stepped back as though not sure what to think. As though not wanting to be a party to such events. "Is this a joke?" he asked, just as confused as Sun.

"If it is," Zee said, "it's not a very funny one."

"I agree." Sun kept reading, trying to analyze the strokes of the writing at the same time. As the letter continued, the signs of stress increased. The writing became heavier, like the writer was pressing down harder and harder. And the points became sharper. "I know this is going to sound crazy. Not even my parents believe me, but when I was six years old, I had a premonition, for lack of a better word. It's the only one I've ever had, but it was very vivid, and I knew the minute I had it, it was real.

"It began as a voice. I was standing in our backyard in Illinois, and a presence told me I would be abducted three days before my fifteenth birthday, held in a dark place, and then killed on the day I turned fifteen."

"What does that mean?" Price asked. "What kind of presence?"

"That night," Sun continued without answering him, "I dreamed about the abduction, and I've had the same dream several times a year since. In my dream, I am taken by a man I don't know. I try to fight him, but I can't. For some reason, my arms and legs feel like they're made of sand. No matter how hard I try, I can't make them work right."

Sun paused to catch her breath as a wave of anxiety washed over her.

"We've all had dreams like this," Anita said.

"More like nightmares." Salazar, clearly buying into every word, shivered.

Fighting to keep her distress to herself, Sun continued, "My birthday is important to him. I don't know why, but he wants me to die on the day I was born.

"When my parents told me we were moving to New Mexico, I was so happy. I hoped that by moving to Del Sol, the threat would go away. Instead, the dreams have been getting stronger.

"I started keeping a diary, hoping to get new clues, but I really only see the same thing over and over again. Snow and trees and rocks. I wake up once when he's carrying me and that's what I see, so I think he's keeping me in the mountains.

"I wish I could see his face more clearly. I'm blindfolded most of the time, and I can't focus when I'm not. All I can tell you is that he is thin but strong, and he has dark hair but light skin. And I think I scratched him, so if you find my body, be sure to check under my nails for DNA.

"I'm sorry, I don't mean to be crude, but you need to know this isn't sexual. He never touches me. Not like that. But he calls me *Syb*. Like my dad. Like he has a right to call me by my nickname.

"I can hear water underneath me. He keeps me in a small room like a shed, and it's cold, and I think I'm going to die from the cold, but I don't. I don't die until he strangles me on my birthday. I fight and kick and claw, but he always wins because nothing works right and everything moves in slow motion."

Sun's vision blurred while reading the next line.

"It takes me a long time to die."

She stopped when she realized she was shaking visibly. Quincy knelt beside her, but she pulled away from him, fighting the sting at the backs of her eyes like a cage fighter in a championship match. Her demons were not something her deputies need ever see.

After clearing her throat, she read the last paragraph.

"Please don't be sad if you don't find me. According to my dream, you don't. Nobody does. And I doubt anything will change that, no matter what you do. But I'd be stupid not to try, I guess.

"Sincerely, Sybil St. Aubin

"P.S. Please thank Auri for being my friend for a whole week. I've never known anyone like her. We were hoping we would have at least one class together, like first period, but just in case we didn't, we came up with a way to pass notes to each other like spies sending secret messages. Maybe we can still do that someday. I hope she liked me as much as I liked her."

Sun forgot how to breathe after she finished the letter. It took her a few minutes to remember how again. She kept reading it over and over as her deputies stood or paced or stared at the floor, waiting for her to take the lead. Waiting for orders. Some way to put a stop to this.

"Are we taking this seriously?" Price asked, breaking first. "I mean, doesn't this prove that it's a stunt? No one can predict something like this. Sybil St. Aubin is probably at her boyfriend's house eating pizza and bingeing on Netflix."

Quincy pinned him with a scowl. "We have no choice but to take it seriously, Price. Stunt or not, it's evidence."

"I find it odd that Marianna said something similar," Sun said at last. "She kept saying we were running out of time. We had to hurry. Maybe she does believe her daughter, after all."

"Where do we stand on it?" Quince asked her, his voice tender with understanding.

She filled her lungs in thought. "Too early to tell. Can you make a few copies of this? And bring one with us."

"Where are we going?"

"We're going to talk to Sybil's mom. I have a few more questions."

Since Quincy was the only other person wearing gloves, she handed the letter to him and then made her way to the restroom before she vomited in front of her posse.

8

How to Twerk:
Step 1: Don't

—SIGN AT DEL SOL MIXED MARTIAL ARTS AND DANCE STUDIO

The rest of the morning was like a blur to Auri. Though some of the students did seem to be warming up to her, she couldn't stop worrying about Sybil. She may have gotten her looks from her father, but she definitely got the analytical side of her brain, the curious and driven side, from her mother. A fact that made her tingle with pride.

She thought back to that night at the New Year's Eve party. Sybil had walked up to her and introduced herself, a feat Auri admired. The girl seemed painfully shy.

"You're Auri," she'd said to her right before she'd handed her a bottle of water.

"I am."

Both freckled and bespectacled, the girl held out her hand. "I'm Sybil."

And they sat talking by the campfire the rest of the night. Or, well, until the cops came. Every so often, Auri's gaze would wander to the quiet kid whom she now knew was Cruz De los Santos, but other than that, Sybil had her complete and undivided attention.

She was easy to talk to. Auri especially loved the way her eyes lit up when they discussed astronomy or books or boys. Mostly boys. And she liked how her glasses made her eyes look a little bigger than they actually were. She looked like an American Girl doll.

"You just started this year?" she'd asked her.

"Yep. In August. We moved here this summer to start the vineyards. My dad has a couple in Illinois, but my mom wanted to open a winery in New Mexico, too."

"Why here?" Auri asked, baffled.

"She told me she came to the Balloon Fiesta when she was a kid, and she'd dreamed of living here ever since."

"Weird."

Sybil laughed. They clinked their water bottles and toasted to new beginnings and red hair and boys. Mostly boys.

Sybil St. Aubin was the first girl in Del Sol she'd felt that bond with. That deep connection that told her they'd be more than just friends. They'd be best friends.

And now this. Auri needed to help. She had skill. She'd been investigating certain events of her life since she was seven. Unbeknownst to her mom, Auri had mastered the art of surveillance when she was eight from watching her. From listening.

She'd learned how to investigate. What to take note of and what to discard. She'd deciphered her mom's universal password when she was nine, which wasn't difficult once she realized the woman had had a mad crush on Levi Ravinder since she was, like, two and his birthday was in her calendar. In bold letters. With a tiny heart dotting the *i*.

All that aside, she could be helping with the investigation instead of sitting in class, listening to a lecture on eye color and dominant traits, a concept she'd learned years earlier when she realized none of her coloring had been passed down from either of her parents.

Not only that, who knew teenage girls better than other teenage girls? Who better qualified to search for her friend?

She almost cheered aloud when the bell rang for lunch.

She hurried out the door and texted her mom for an update. But before she could hit Send, someone making a mad dash for the lunchroom crashed into her from behind.

She lunged forward, dropping her backpack and her phone, and plowed into some poor soul in jeans and an army jacket.

Thankfully, that someone had long arms and catlike reflexes. He caught her a microsecond before she face-planted on the tile floor. Then he lifted her effortlessly to her feet.

She regained her balance, her fists curling into the guy's jacket as though her life depended upon it, and raised her gaze until it collided with the scowl voted Most Likely to Turn Innocent People into Stone.

"Cruz," she squeaked, shoving away from him and dusting herself off. "I'm sorry. I didn't—" But when she looked up at him, he had refocused his scowl on the boy in a Seattle Seahawks hoodie running down the hall. "Yeah, he must be really hungry."

He turned back to her, and she noticed the muscles in his jaw flex as though he were grinding his teeth to dust. She also noticed how his jaw looked when it flexed. Like a movie star's, all strong and masculine and—

"Are you okay?"

She hesitated before answering with a surprised, "Yes. Thank you."

After giving her one last inspection, he turned and strode off. Like she meant nothing to him. Probably because she didn't.

She bent down to gather her effects when another thought hit her. She bolted upright and turned full circle to take in the last of the students headed to lunch.

While she'd only met Sybil recently, surely she had some friends who'd known her longer. Maybe even a best friend. One who would know if someone had been following her or sending her messages or, worse, threatening her.

Auri needed to interview Sybil's friends. And she could do something silly and unproductive like ask around willy-nilly, hoping to stumble into one of them, or she could narrow down her search tenfold.

She looked toward the guidance counselor's office, where a student aide readied himself for his turn at the helm, and she formed a plan. Pulling her bottom lip between her teeth, she contemplated her fate should she fail. Should her mom find out.

What would happen if her mom discovered she broke into a guidance counselor's office to steal another student's file? She could check Sybil's schedule. Go to her classes. Find out who her friends were. Surely, she'd made friends in her classes. And who knows? A concerned teacher could've made notes about Sybil. Who she hung out with. Who she ate lunch with.

So, what would happen if her mom found out? Auri would lose her life. Plain and simple. Her mother would seek the death penalty. Of course, there were always worse alternatives. She could lose her phone.

She dropped her gaze to the square piece of plastic in her hands, her wellspring of knowledge and art and communication. The magical instrument around which all life revolved. She could lose it for the next thirty years.

Then again, she pretty much had her mom wrapped around her little finger. If she did lose it, surely it wouldn't take long to win back her mom's favor and her precious phone. Thirty years? Pshaw. She could do it in twelve.

A tiny smile tugged at her mouth as she sized up the student who'd pulled the short straw and got the lunch shift. Twelve years? It'd be worth it.

And that was how Auri Vicram found herself in the principal's office.

All things considered, she couldn't be that upset about her situation. Not when two male teachers escorted two boys into the office, the first boy wearing jeans and a green army jacket, the second wearing a Seattle Seahawks hoodie and a sheepish expression.

Stunned, Auri turned to Cruz De los Santos. Even with his chin lowered in obstinance, the surprise on his face when he saw her sitting in the principal's office was almost comical, though probably no more than the surprise on her own. Had he gone after the boy who'd run her down? *Had he hit him?*

Mr. Jacobs had been talking softly to Corrine. He finished and gave Auri his complete attention, something she'd never craved.

"I'm calling your mom this time," he said to her, almost sadly.

Auri felt the color drain from her face. Of course, he would call her mom. As far as he was concerned, she'd been stealing ACT scores or social security numbers or nuclear launch codes. She couldn't believe he'd caught her so red-handed. She totally needed to sharpen her criminal mind.

"And I'd call your dad," he said to Cruz, "but I'm not sure I can trust you to give him the whole story."

What did that mean? Cruz lifted a shoulder as though baffled himself.

The kid in the Seahawks jersey spoke up. "We were just talking," he said before giving Cruz an apologetic sideways glance.

"What? Between shoves?"

"It was just a misunderstanding." The kid looked at her. "I didn't mean to run you down like that. It's just, it's pizza day."

Auri was partly amused by his honesty and partly stunned. Cruz had shoved him on her account? Her emotions volleyed between elation and horror.

"Yeah, well, Mr. De los Santos seems to have a lot of misunderstandings." He crooked his finger, and the Seahawks fan followed him into his office.

Auri pretended to study her shoes. Instead, she studied Cruz's. He wore a ragged pair of Adidas that used to be white. The strings were frayed, the glue around the soles worn and about to fall apart. She glanced down at her boots, the brand-new ones her grandparents had bought her for Christmas, and suddenly felt uncomfortable in them.

She could tell from her periphery that he had yet to focus on anything but her, but she couldn't tell if he was still angry with her or not.

"I didn't thank you," she said, her voice softer than she'd intended. "So, thanks."

"For what?" he asked.

She lifted a shoulder. She wanted to say, "For taking up for me. For being nice to me. For leaving heat trails when you walk so I can always know where you are." Which wouldn't have sounded stalkery at all. Instead, she said simply, "For catching me."

Mr. Jacobs opened his office door and summoned Cruz with a brusque, "De los Santos."

Cruz's gaze traveled over her face before getting up, his expression part curiosity and part appreciation, and Auri suddenly understood that whole boy-girl attraction thing on a much deeper level.

Before she made a complete fool of herself by asking him to show her the ways of love, she nodded toward the office where Mr. Jacobs stood waiting.

One corner of his mouth slid up, but he obeyed. Auri watched in fascination as said heat trails streaked in his wake, then slowly dissipated. Metaphorically speaking.

Sun walked out of the restroom a new woman. Or, well, a cleaner woman after washing her face and brushing her teeth. Vomit tended to leave an aftertaste.

She set her deputies on various duties, including a thorough background check on the St. Aubins and a preliminary search of the public areas in town.

Her phone rang just as she took the copy of the letter from Quincy. She checked the ID and slid the button to the right, her anxiety spiking again.

"Sheriff Vicram."

Through the miracle of technology, a male voice floated into her ear. "Hello, Sheriff. I thought perhaps you'd like to come talk to your daughter. Explain things to her like how the law works. How breaking and entering is wrong. And how stealing is frowned upon in most cultures."

"Auri?" Adrenaline shot through her, spiraling down her spine and contracting her stomach again. "My Auri? What happened?"

"Look, I know you're having one hell of a day, but maybe you could swing by the school?"

She bit back a curse. "I'll be there in five."

She turned to her deputies to make one final statement before heading out. "He drugged her. And he's keeping her drugged."

Price gaped at her. "You're taking that note seriously?"

Now was not the time. "About as seriously as I take you."

He showed his palms, and she groaned inwardly. What the hell did that even mean?

"Salazar," she said, turning to the young deputy with chipmunk cheeks and doe-like eyes.

"Yes, sir. Ma'am. Sheriff."

She lowered her chin and raised a brow. "Call in the dogs."

The room went silent as Sun turned and headed out the door. Then, in barely contained enthusiasm, Salazar whispered, "I get to call in the dogs."

Quincy chuckled as he followed her. "Want to explain that comment to Price?"

"Want to explain your face?"

"No explanation would do it justice. Let's just say the world needed a hero. I rose to the occasion. Clear-cut case of supply and demand." He herded Sun to the passenger's side of the cruiser. "I'll take this one, yeah? In case you get sick again?"

Mortification swallowed her. "You heard that?"

"The entire block heard that." After he started the SUV, he

paused and sobered. Sober was not Quincy's best look. "You sure you're okay? You're taking this note thing pretty seriously."

"I am, aren't I? And do you know why? Because we're in the crazy capital of the world. I've been trying to tell you since we were kids. Things happen here that don't happen in other towns. Strange things. Unexplainable things."

"Like a regular joe's addiction to chocolate-covered pretzel sticks dipped in red chile powder?"

"Yes," she said, vindicated. "Finally, someone gets it."

He headed toward the high school without her having to tell him. "Any idea what that kid of yours did?"

"Not a clue. But I did come on strong with the Lisbeth Salander talk this morning."

"You have got to cut that shit out, Sunburn. She's going to end up in prison for setting someone on fire."

He had a point. One she decided to ignore.

Instead, she looked out the window as they drove down Main. Much of the town was made up of the old housing the miners had lived in. Rows of small A-frames lined one side of the street while the other side was made up of stucco and wood Pueblo buildings.

Most of the businesses that occupied the buildings were artists of various metal and talent, but there was also a smattering of small restaurants, a grocery store, and a firehouse.

At the end of Main, before the road headed up into the Sangre de Cristo Mountains, sat a biker bar owned and operated by the Ravinders. It was a place Sun imagined she'd be visiting often, considering her new position and nickel-slick badge.

She looked for his truck as they passed. As far as she knew, Levi rarely stepped foot inside his family's pub, but she couldn't keep herself from checking.

"He's not there," Quincy said, reading her mind as usual. "He's probably at the distillery."

"I wasn't looking."

"Never mind," Quince said, craning his neck. "Oh, he is there."

Sun whirled around and saw . . . nothing.

The stucco building was one of the oldest in the town and sported thick wood accents and a plethora of neon signs, but it did not have a truck sitting in the parking lot with a Dark River Shine wrap.

"Asshole," she said, disappointment consuming her. Sun saw this becoming an issue if she didn't get her hormones under control.

Quince accepted her insult with a shrug and a nod. "I've been called worse."

Two minutes later, he pulled into the high school parking lot, threw the SUV into park, then turned to her, doing the sober thing again. "You didn't tell me that."

She shifted in her seat. "Tell you what?"

He scratched at a stray thread on the steering wheel. "You were drugged."

He needn't have explained any further. She knew where he was going without saying another word. "It's so weird. That is at the very top of my Things I Never Want to Talk to Quincy About list."

Though she didn't remember even a tenth of what had happened to her, it was still a violation of epic proportions. There was still a barrier she couldn't quite get past, even with her best friend.

When she turned to get out, he stopped her with a hand on her arm. "I get that, Sunny. I always have. But you were drugged. You went through the same thing Sybil described in her letter. You felt the same. Weak. Disoriented. Scared."

She finally saw the hurt and anger in his deep blue eyes. She so rarely considered what he went through that summer, and it was unfair and selfish of her to leave without an explanation. But now was not the time.

"I'm sorry, Quince."

"I know. Bad timing. But now that we're working together, we are going to talk about it. Eventually."

She swallowed hard, then nodded. "One of these days. Scout's honor." She hurried out of the cruiser before he could question her again, but he caught up with her easily.

In a tone that told her everything was okay between them, he pointed out one pertinent fact. "You were never a scout."

Auri had always thought of herself as a bit of a Goody Two-shoes, a tad uptight when it came to throwing caution to the wind, and when she saw her mother enter the building wearing full sheriff regalia and a frown the size of Texas, she remembered why.

Self-preservation.

She took a hit off her inhaler and sank down in the chair that sat across from Corrine's desk in the main office. And Corrine's desk sat in front of the door to the principal's office, the same principal who was busy eyeing her with a combination of disappointment and humor as he ate lunch at his desk. Corrine was taking her lunch, as well, and the scent of baked turkey and green chile subs from the Bread Basket made Auri's mouth water.

Mr. Jacobs had already let Cruz go. She had no idea if he'd gotten ahold of Cruz's dad or not, but when Cruz left the office, he didn't seem particularly upset.

Then again, not much seemed to ruffle him.

Quincy stepped inside the building with her mom, and Auri's mortification exploded, bringing tears to her eyes. So now both her mouth and her eyes were watering.

Principal Jacobs stood when he saw the law enforcement officers enter, and Auri could only pray that they'd talk about the incident inside his office. The bell was about to ring, and everyone in school would see her being interrogated for breaking and entering.

Sunshine Vicram stepped into the office, her expression completely neutral when she cast Auri a quick glance before addressing the principal. He summoned Auri with a crook of his finger.

Time slowed as she walked past Quincy, ignoring the look of

encouragement he wore—she didn't deserve it—and took a seat in front of Principal Jacobs's desk.

It was good to see Leo again on that very desk. She could only pray Principal Jacobs wouldn't tell her mom about the lion's adventure or the spray paint fiasco. Her mom had enough to worry about with Sybil missing.

Principal Jacobs motioned for her mom to come around to his side of the desk, while explaining, "It seems your daughter broke into the counselor's office and went through her things. I'm just foggy as to why."

Her mom leaned over and looked closer at his computer. Was there surveillance footage? No way was there surveillance footage. And yes, telling herself that made her feel better.

"Of course, after the morning she's had, I'm more than willing to hear her side of it." He left the sentiment hanging, and Auri slammed her lids shut.

"What do you mean?" her mom asked. "What happened this morning?"

While Sunshine's expression and posture remained neutral, Auri could hear the stress in her voice. The edge in her tone.

Auri curled her hands into fists and clenched them tightly. Her mom didn't need to know what happened this morning.

Mr. Jacobs glanced at her in surprise, then pressed his lips together. "I just mean, it's her first day, and the first day at a new school is always difficult."

Quincy had been hanging back near the door to the office when the bell rang. To Auri's horror, one side of the room was all glass, just like the main office, and looked out into the hall. Students filed by, and Auri slid down in her seat.

The deputy maneuvered himself, using his wide shoulders to create a barricade between two bookshelves so the students going by would be hard-pressed to see who sat in the hot seat.

Auri could've kissed him right then and there if it wouldn't have been inappropriate. And a little gross.

"Auri?" Sunshine asked, straightening, the edge in her tone sharpening.

"I'm sorry, Mom. I wanted to help with the investigation. I wanted to help you find Sybil."

All three of them blinked at her.

Sunshine sobered first. "And just how was your breaking and entering going to help us find Sybil?"

Auri hadn't wanted this. She was usually so good at these kinds of things. She could find a needle in a haystack given the right tools. Through all the cases she'd worked—she preferred to call them *cases* as opposed to *favors* since she'd started charging for her services—she'd never been caught. But one day at Del Sol High, and her perfect record had come to an unfortunate and terrifying end.

"I was going to interview her friends, but I don't know who her friends are, so I wanted her class schedule so I'd know where to start, but I knew they couldn't just give it to me, so I needed the password to hack into the system and get it."

The three adults in the room stood for a solid minute, and Auri could tell her mom wasn't sure what to do. Now was her chance to plead her case.

"Who better to investigate a teen than another teen?" she asked. "I mean, I can gather intel here while you're investigating out there."

When Sun finally spoke, the edge in her voice hadn't softened one iota, much to Auri's disappointment. "Aurora Dawn Vicram. You broke the law. And you had plans to break it even more. Since when do you hack into someone's computer?"

The sting in the backs of Auri's eyes caused her frustration to spike even further. "I can help, Mom. I'm very good at getting information when I need to, and Sybil is missing. Isn't that all that matters?"

Sun sat in the chair next to her. "Sweetheart, did Sybil say anything to you?"

"Not directly. That's why I wanted to talk to her friends. She seemed to know something was going to happen."

"In what way?"

"She texted me a couple of days ago."

"When you met up at the Pecos?" The Pecos Percolator was one of three coffee shops the tiny town had to offer.

She nodded. "She was acting strange, saying things like she was so glad we got to be friends, even for just a little while. I didn't understand, but I think someone was following her, Mom. Or threatening her. I mean, why would she say something like that?"

Quincy knelt in front of her. "Okay, bean sprout, did she say anything else? Anything that could help us identify who it was?"

"No. And I didn't push." The wetness she'd been fighting slipped past her eyelashes. She swiped at the trail, annoyed. "Quincy, she's so nice. We have to find her."

Without another word, Quincy pulled her into his massive arms. His hug felt like home. Warm and comforting and oddly constrictive.

Principal Jacobs stood. "Aurora, I need to know you aren't going to try to hack my system again."

Hope blossomed inside her. "I won't try again. I swear."

"Well, then, I don't see why we can't let this slide, considering the circumstances."

While Mr. Jacobs seemed satisfied, the new sheriff wasn't so easily placated. Her expression remained impassive as she scrutinized her daughter.

"Mom?" Auri said, her chest squeezing her lungs until they hurt.

"And," the principal continued, addressing the surly woman in black, "since there's an ongoing investigation, I suppose giving *you* a copy of Sybil's class schedule wouldn't be breaking any laws. If it just happened to slip out of your hand and into someone else's—like, say, a student's—that wouldn't be on me."

Her mom deadpanned him. "You're encouraging my daughter to insert herself into an ongoing missing persons investigation?"

A wicked smile spread across his face. "I try to nurture the talents of all my students. Not just your daughter, Little Miss Sunshine."

Auri almost snorted aloud. Instead, she slammed a hand over her nose and mouth to hold it in.

Her mom cast him a withering scowl. "You know, you got away with that nickname when I was in high school—"

"And I'll get away with it now."

Ignoring her indignation, he walked to his office door. "Corrine, could you print a copy of Sybil St. Aubin's schedule?"

"Of course," she said, stuffing the last bite of her sub into her mouth and swinging her chair around to her computer.

Two office aides had come in to work, a boy and a girl, both of them upperclassmen and each one of them on separate tasks. They both paused and focused their attention when Principal Jacobs walked to the door. But what Auri found interesting was when the principal asked Corrine for the schedule, the guy whipped his head around in surprise.

He caught himself and recovered quickly, bending over a stack of papers he was separating into three mystery piles, but the knee-jerk reaction was hardly subtle.

Auri made a mental note to check him out later. Unfortunately, when she turned back to her mom, she realized she'd made the same mental note.

Auri gestured toward the guy, urging her mom to let her help, to let her question him, but Sunshine fired a warning shot over the bow of her ship. A ship called *In Your Dreams*.

As frustrated as Auri was, she did understand. A girl was missing. Her life was in danger. Auri had to remember that. Not only could she get caught up in a bad situation, she could botch the entire investigation.

But she wasn't born yesterday. She knew the stakes. And she knew how to handle herself. She prodded her mom to let her help with another pleading glance.

As the principal droned on about something her mom had done in high school that involved a training bra and a stuffed monkey, her mom cast her a warning glare, ordering her to stand down.

Auri pursed her lips and lifted her shoulders, pleading.

Sunshine shook her head.

Auri spread her hands in the universal gesture for *why not?*

Sunshine crossed her arms, refusing to budge.

Auri crossed her arms, too, and sank down in her seat, literally pouting like a five-year-old.

Sunshine tilted her head to the side, asking her to understand her position.

Auri turned her face away, refusing to even try.

Sunshine released a long sigh.

Auri kept her gaze averted.

Sunshine softened her expression.

Auri sat up and offered up her best look of hope.

Sunshine caved, and she dipped her head in a barely perceivable nod of approval, but then her expression morphed into a lecture. A long lecture complete with PowerPoint slides and a pop quiz, and she did it all with one ominous glance.

Auri nodded. She understood what was at stake.

"And that's how your mother came to be known as the Masked Potato."

Auri sat beaming, then the principal's words sank in. "The Masked what?"

"Can I have a moment alone with my daughter?" her mom asked him.

"Of course." He grabbed the schedule from Corrine, handed it to the sheriff, and left them alone. Well, almost alone. Quincy was still in the room.

"That was fascinating," he said. "Can all mothers and daughters have an entire conversation without saying a word?"

"Yes," her mom said before leveling another death stare on her.

"I'm so sorry, Mom."

Watching her mom downshift from an enraged law enforcement agent to a worried mom was what she imagined the melting of the polar ice caps looked like.

"Sweetheart, what you did was serious. Mr. Jacobs could press charges in a heartbeat. And this is a missing persons case. A young girl's life is at stake."

"I know, Mom. But I can help."

"And if he comes after you? What then?"

"It doesn't work that way," she said. She considered quoting statistics, but her mom knew them even better than she did. Heck, her mom was the one who usually quoted them to her.

"It doesn't *usually* work that way. We simply don't know what's going on. We can't make assumptions this early in the investigation. If this guy feels like you're a threat—"

"I know. But really, Mom, unless he goes to school here, how would he even know I was helping?"

"And who's to say he doesn't go to school here? Do you think high school kids don't commit crimes?"

"I know they do. That's exactly why you need me on the team. I'm your inside man. Only without man parts." She could tell her mom was coming around to the idea. That meant she was desperate. "I'm your inside girl."

"You're something," her mom agreed, shaking her head. "I'm just not sure what."

Auri jumped up and hugged her. "I'll let you know if I get any good intel."

"Don't even consider missing class for this."

"Never!" she said, running out the door. She was late, yet again, only this time she didn't care. She had a case to solve. What would Mom do without her?

9

"She's been doing this for a while now." Sunshine glanced at the behemoth in the passenger's seat of her cruiser.

"The bean sprout? What do you mean?"

She turned up Cottonwood Drive, sliding in the melting snow as they conquered a steep incline. "I can't be 100 percent certain, but I think she was doing some side jobs for her classmates at the academy."

"Side jobs?"

"I believe she fancies herself a PI."

"No shit? Do you think that had anything to do with her decision to switch schools?"

"I don't know. I'm waiting for her to relax. To get comfortable in her new surroundings. Then I'll take her into an interview room and give her the third degree."

"Good plan. Or you could just ask her over tacos."

"The direct approach? Where's the fun in that?"

They pulled up to the St. Aubin home for the second time that day just as a text came through from Salazar. The dogs were on the way.

Two deputies, Zee and Salazar, sat in a cruiser waiting on them.

"You two start outside," Sun said when they stepped out. "Canvass the area, but keep it light."

"Got it, boss," Salazar said.

She studied the front door, a massive oak with decorative carvings. But before they could climb the steps, Marianna St. Aubin rushed out, her cropped hair unkempt, her clothes, the same ones she wore that morning, wrinkled.

"What happened?" she asked, already breathless when she skidded to a halt in front of them. "Did you find her?"

"Not yet, but I did get a letter." Sun handed Mari a copy of the letter Sybil sent her.

The woman was shivering when she took it.

"Maybe we should go inside."

But Mari was already lost in the letter, her expression full of anguish.

"Mari," Sun said softly, but Mari was gone, drowning in a sea of memories and regret as she ran her fingertips over her daughter's writing.

"She tried to tell us," she said, her voice cracking. "For years, she tried to tell us, but we didn't listen."

Quincy put a hand on her shoulder. "I'm sure that's not true, Mrs. St. Aubin."

She put one hand over her eyes as a flood tide of tears spilled past her lashes. "What have we done?"

Quincy took her by the shoulders and led her inside the house.

Sun gave her deputies a nod to get started. They'd been observing, and by their expressions, they were just as heartbroken as she was.

Inside, Quincy led Mari to a sofa and sat her down before

getting her a glass of water. Sun sat across from her, trying to come to terms with the fact that this could all be real. Sybil could very well have prophesied her own abduction. Her own death.

She knew this town was strange, but come on. Sybil wasn't even from Del Sol. And she just happened to end up in a city teeming with the strange and bizarre?

Despite the fact that most of the stories were just hype, there was always that 1 percent. That narrow margin of the unexplained that left her questioning the world she grew up in.

And now this. She just didn't know what to think, and as the new sheriff, that was not a good place to be. She couldn't be the indecisive schoolgirl anymore, no matter what coming back to Del Sol did to her psyche.

Once Mari had calmed a bit and taken a drink of the water Quincy brought, Sun began. "Okay, Mari, I need to know everything. When did this start?"

"She was six, I think. She'd had a nightmare like all kids do, but this one changed her." She focused a laser-like gaze on Sun. "She was never the same after that. Her whole world began to revolve around her fifteenth birthday. She's told us since she was a kid she would never grow up. Never graduate high school. Never date a boy. We just thought she was being melodramatic." She dropped her face into the wad of tissues in her hands and let the sobs take over.

"Start from the beginning, Mari. What exactly did she tell you that night? I just need whatever you can remember."

Mari's story confirmed everything they'd learned from the letter. Unfortunately, that's all it did. She had no information beyond it. But Sun still had a thousand questions.

"Why didn't you tell me any of this earlier?"

Mari scoffed. "Would you have believed me?" Before Sun could answer, she said, "I wouldn't have. It was my own daughter, and I didn't believe her. Can you imagine growing up like that? With an image of your own death in your head and your parents, the people you are supposed to depend on the most, are the last people on earth to believe you?" She broke down, her shoulders shaking as she sobbed. "What have we done?"

Sun let the wave die down before asking her next question. "Mari, when Sybil went missing a few days ago—"

"She was trying to hide out. She thought if she stayed hidden until after her birthday, the threat would pass. But we found her and dragged her back home."

Sorrow took control again, and Sun turned to Quincy. "Does Doc Finely still make house calls?"

Quincy nodded. "He's mostly retired, but he will take an occasional query."

"Why don't we see if we can get him here." Quince took out his phone, but she leaned closer and added, "And tell him to bring Valium."

"Gotcha." He left the room to make the call.

Sun refocused on Mari. "I don't want you to take our looking into these events as a sign that we are buying this. I need you to be aware of the fact that we must, as law enforcement officers, consider the fact that this is all an elaborate scheme." It didn't matter how much Sun believed the girl; it was her job to follow the evidence. Not her hunches.

At first, Mari started to argue with her, but her own guilt stopped her. Sun could read it on her face.

"Also, just so you know, a wanted fugitive has been spotted in the area. Have you seen anyone hanging about? Perhaps lurking along the tree line?"

Although her eyes were wide with worry, she shook her head. "No. I haven't seen anyone. Do you think—?"

"No. We don't. But we can't rule anything out yet."

She nodded, then her eyes widened. "The diary! She kept a diary. Maybe there's something in there that will help."

That had been next on Sun's list. "Do you know where it is?"

Without answering, Mari rushed upstairs, almost stumbling

in her enthusiasm. Sun followed her to make sure she didn't disturb anything.

She lifted a mattress covered in pink and produced a small journal with hearts on it. "She's been keeping a journal since she was a kid."

After slipping on some gloves, Sun took it and placed it inside an evidence bag. "Once it's processed, I'll go through it. See if there are any clues that weren't in her letter."

"Thank you," Mari said, "for taking this seriously even if you don't believe it."

"I wouldn't go that far. And your daughter seems amazing."

"She is," she said, her eyes tearing up again.

Sun helped Mari to the living room to lie down on the sofa in case Sybil walked through the front door. She'd seen it a dozen times: Parents keeping a constant vigil on doors or windows over-looking the street, hoping for a glimpse of their child coming home. Mari's rest would probably be short-lived, however, with all the deputies and now the state K-9 unit coming in.

"He's on his way," Quincy said. "And he's bringing a seda-tive."

"Thank you." They walked to the front door. "Mr. St. Aubin should be here soon. That should help her. If this is an elaborate hoax, Sybil's mom would definitely take home the gold statue."

He opened the door, and they stepped out into a crisp, sunny day. "I agree, but I'm still not swallowing any of this without a serious dose of reservation. I mean, Sybil could have staged this whole thing for her parents' sake. To pay them back for not believ-ing her."

"True. And we have to take that into consideration, but there's one more angle we haven't considered yet."

"And that is?"

"A self-fulfilling prophecy."

He bowed his head in thought. "In what way?"

"She could believe this so blindly," Sun said, hoping against hope that she would be proved wrong, "that she has somehow caused the events to take place. Somehow provoked her own abduction."

"Do you think she could have, I don't know, convinced someone to kidnap her?"

"It can certainly be done and quite innocently. She could have met someone online, a predator, and mentioned her premonition. He could have convinced her to meet up. Told her he'd keep her safe."

"Escobar is working on her online footprint. Maybe something will come up. But what about the fugitive?"

"Yeah, I need to look into that more. If Rojas is in the area and is in hiding—"

"He could have convinced her to help him."

"Exactly." Sun filled her lungs. "And again, there is always the possibility that she is in hiding like before, hoping to ride all of this out. For now, this is still a missing persons case, and until we hear otherwise, we need to treat it as such."

He nodded. "What next?"

"Let's take a look around, see if Zee and Salazar have found anything."

"It'll be hard with this fresh snow."

"Where is an expert tracker when you need one?"

Quincy smirked at her. Rumor had it Levi Ravinder was the best tracker in the state thanks to spending his summers with his biological grandfather, a Mescalero Apache. He'd been recruited several times to help find lost hikers and the like.

Once the K-9 unit arrived, which included a studly Officer Buchanan and an even studlier—and quite a bit furrier—Officer Bones, the deputies' investigation had to be suspended. They'd found no footprints, but that wasn't surprising considering the snow.

Sun and Quincy looked on as the state police's K-9 unit did

their thing. Admittedly, it took everything in her not to pet the gorgeous German shepherd. How did K-9 cops do it? How could they keep a professional relationship with their fellow officers when all she wanted to do was roll around on the ground and cuddle with them?

One of the mysteries of life, she supposed.

She sent Zee and Salazar to grab lunch so they could get back to guard the perimeter.

"What are you thinking?" Sun asked Quincy as they followed the K-9 unit, searching the grounds for anything out of the ordinary.

When he spoke, his breath fogged in the air. "That I'm cold. And hungry. And that I'm in the wrong business. I need to join the K-9 unit."

"Right? I'd be horrible, though. I'd call my partner Princess and let her sleep with me."

"Sheriff?" the officer called out.

They hurried through the snow to where Officer Bones was sniffing the ground excitedly. "Did you find something?"

"Not sure." He called the dog back and let Sun poke around.

"Here," Quincy said, brushing snow away with a gloved hand. He lifted a pink button off the ground. It had a tiny blue flower painted on it with brown flecks.

"Is this what he detected?" Sun asked the officer, but he needn't have answered. The dog barked when Quincy held it out.

"There might be blood on it," he explained. "Bones is a cadaver dog."

Quincy dropped the button into an evidence bag, and they combed the entire area more thoroughly, but Officer Bones found nothing else of interest. To him, anyway. Sun found a receipt under a tree a few yards from the house. Thanks to the cover of trees, the ground beneath it was wet but snowless, and the receipt sat under a clump of leaves.

But it was recent enough that the ink hadn't faded completely despite the weather conditions. It was a receipt from the Quick-Mart convenience store for an energy drink, paid for with cash, and while the date had faded, the receipt number hadn't. She hoped the store could look up the transaction based on that number and give her an exact date and time.

Sun sealed it in a bag and went inside to speak with Mari before they left.

The woman had lain down on her sofa, and the doctor was checking her vitals.

"Is she okay, Doc?" Sun asked.

He glanced at her in surprise. "Sunshine Freyr."

She smiled. "It's Vicram now."

"Oh yes, that's right. You're our new sheriff." He finished checking Mari's blood pressure and put the stethoscope away. "Congratulations."

Raj Finely had been her doctor since she was a kid. She'd loved him ever since she'd caught a raging fever and he'd stayed up with her all night, soaking her in cool washrags. His frailty did nothing to diminish her crush.

"Thank you." She knelt down and placed a hand on Mari's shoulder. "How is she?"

"*She's* fine," Mari said from behind a wet towel over her face.

"I'm glad to hear it. Can you look at something for me?"

She lowered the towel as the doctor busied himself by putting away his things.

Sun lifted the evidence bag with the button. "Is this Sybil's?"

She squinted, then nodded and sat up straight, hope evident in her expression. "Yes. Where did you find that?"

"What's it from?"

"Oh," she said, rubbing her temples. "I think it was on a backpack she used to carry. It had buttons. You know, decorative. But she hasn't carried that backpack in, oh gosh, probably a year or more. Do you think she has it with her?"

"I don't know, hon. We found this under a window outside,

but on the opposite side of the house from her bedroom." She pointed down a long corridor. "What's at the end of this hall?"

Mari was having trouble concentrating. Whatever the doc had given her seemed to be working. "It's, um, the laundry room. That's the only room on that wall with a window. The other door leads to the garage."

Sun looked at Quincy, but he was already headed that way. She jumped up and followed him.

"Do you think we've been processing the wrong room?" he asked when she caught up.

They opened the door to what looked like the aftermath of a tornado.

"Holy shit," he said. He got on his radio and called in a team to process the room as Sun looked around.

"I don't see any blood," she said, her voice soft with relief.

"It's no wonder Mrs. St. Aubin didn't hear anything. She was on the opposite side of the house."

Sun walked carefully to the window, stepping over strewn clothes and towels. "If nothing else, this gives us a strong indication that Sybil was taken."

"I agree," Quincy said. "I find it creepy as hell, and it has me questioning everything I've ever known, but I agree."

He was right. The letter—the premonition—was hard to explain.

When her deputies got back, Sun sent Zee to question the neighbors. If this guy was staking out the place, one of them may have seen him. Then she set Salazar to watch the St. Aubin home.

"You know who could really help with this investigation?" she asked Quincy as they headed back into the house.

"Who's that? We've called in everyone."

"Not everyone. I still haven't seen hide nor hair of Bo."

"Who?" he asked, beginning the game anew.

She rolled her eyes so far back into her head she almost seized. "This again?"

He cleared the three steps to the front door in one giant step.

Sun thought about doing the same, but she didn't feel like falling on her ass just then.

"What again?"

"Quincy," she said, her tone brooking no argument.

He turned to her, the picture of innocence. "Sunshine."

"Where is Lieutenant Bobby Britton?"

"Oh, LT? Why didn't you just ask? He's probably still out on a call." He started inside, but she grabbed his arm.

"There haven't been any calls besides the one we are on."

"Oh, right." He chuckled and started inside again.

"I swear to God, Cooper, if you don't tell me where Bo is—"

"Who?" he asked as he headed for the living room.

Sun welded her teeth together and drew in a deep, calming breath. She would get to the bottom of this if it was the last thing she did as sheriff of Del Sol County. Which, if the mayor had her way, could be pretty soon.

After checking with Mari about the energy drink, a beverage no one in the house drank, Sun and Quincy headed back to town to grab a bite and check in. The closer they got to town, the louder Quince's stomach growled.

"Sorry," he said as they pulled into the Shed, an amazing breakfast-and-lunch place that served the best breakfast burritos this side of the Pecos. And they served them all day. Ish. They were only open until 3:00 p.m.

"I know what I'm having," she said, suddenly ravenous despite the upset state of her stomach.

"I know what you're having, too. You really need to switch it up every so often. Be more adventurous. Like me."

She pursed her lips. "You order the same thing every time we come here. You have since high school."

"You've been gone a long time, sweet cheeks."

"Oh yeah, Mr. Chicken Burrito Smothered in Green?"

"Yeah, Miss Green Chile Breakfast Burrito with Extra Salsa on the Side."

"Okay, fine, what else do you order?"

A smile stretched across his handsome face. "A chicken burrito smothered in *red*."

Sun snorted.

"Oh, it gets better."

"No," she said, waiting with bated breath, the anticipation killing her.

"Yep. Sometimes I go crazy. Sometimes I order a chicken burrito Christmas-style."

Sun gasped playfully, the conversation proving to be the salve they needed after such a strenuous morning. "You know what you are?" she asked, keeping up the game.

"A chile connoisseur?"

"I was going to say a chile slut."

That time, he gasped. "Who told? Was it Wanda Stephanopoulos from the Book Babes? I knew I shouldn't have let that woman hump my leg."

They burst out laughing as Sun let the levity of the moment overtake her. It felt good. Just like the image of that tiny lady wrapping herself around the massive deputy. The Book Babes were nothing if not entertaining.

They stepped inside the Shed, a miniscule place that always had more customers than chairs. Thankfully, Sun and Quincy were ordering to go. The crowded room went silent when they walked in, and all eyes landed on the law enforcement officers. Quincy, they were used to. Sun, not so much.

The pair stepped to the counter to give their order when an older man walked up, took her hand, and slapped her on the shoulder. "Congratulations on the win, Sheriff."

"Thank you," she said, more than a little surprised.

And the floodgates opened. Each patron stood and took a turn to offer her a hardy congrats before sitting down to their food again. Everyone seemed pleased and hopeful with her win. Everyone except the former sheriff, who sat seething in a corner booth.

Baldwin Redding had a thick body and thin hair, and both of those adjectives could describe his mental state.

Sun chose to ignore him and turned back to the waiting server. But when he stood as well, the room fell silent again. The server stepped back as though afraid. After everything Sun had heard, she couldn't blame her.

"Sheriff," he said when he stepped within earshot. He gave her a once-over, his face distorting as though on the verge of laughter.

"Former Sheriff," Sun said in return.

The reminder wiped the smirk off the man's face. "I'd hate for your election win to be called into question."

"Not as much as I'd hate for your terms served to be called into question, but we all have our burdens to bear."

He bit down, then let the smirk reemerge as he said, "I hear you're having a really bad first day."

"On the contrary. I'm glad I can actually be of use in these types of situations. I'm not sure what you could have done."

"Keep telling yourself that."

"Okay," she said, adding a healthy dose of pep.

He gave her one more leisurely appraisal, as though that would unnerve her. Clearly, he'd never been a woman walking past a construction site. After he'd finished, he tipped his hat and then sauntered, actually sauntered, out the door.

"Tootles," she called after him.

Quincy leaned into her. "Honestly, who names their son Baldwin? It's like they set him up for failure from the get-go."

Sun nodded. "Or, at the very least, male-pattern baldness."

Quince snorted, then rubbed his own head, suddenly worried.

"Speaking of which, thanks for the backup."

He laughed softly. "Yeah, like you need my help with the likes of that pile of shit."

He had a point.

They got to the station just in time to eat one-tenth of their food before a call came in. A very interesting one.

Dispatcher Anita Escobar, the pretty blonde with masses of unruly hair pulled back into a thick ponytail, rushed into her office as they ate, almost bursting at the seams with the news. And yet she said nothing. She waited for Sun to address her, which took a moment because she'd just taken a huge bite.

"Yes?" she asked after swallowing.

"I don't want to bother you."

Sun chuckled. "Yes, you do. Spill."

"We got a call from Mr. Parks. You might remember him? He owns the feedstore just off 63? Anyway, it seems a red-haired girl fitting Sybil's description has been seen hanging out with that Ravinder boy. The young one with autism. Jimmy."

Sun stilled. Jimmy Ravinder was Levi's nephew. Though a few years older than Auri, he was born with a disability. From what Sun's mother had told her about him, he was fairly high-functioning but would probably need at least a little assistance for the rest of his life.

She looked at Quincy, who knew how high the stakes had rocketed without her saying a word. Because there were few things members of the Ravinder clan liked less than a law enforcement officer questioning them about one of their own. Unless it was two law enforcement officers. No way was she going out to the Ravinder compound without backup.

10

Soup of the Day: Whiskey

—SIGN AT THE ROADHOUSE BAR AND GRILL

Auri had lost count as to how many times she'd entered a classroom late that day, so when she stepped inside her sixth-period classroom, late yet again, the students turned and watched her walk to the teacher's desk with schedule in hand.

American Sign Language. She'd finally arrived. She'd been looking forward to this class for weeks, and it was all Jimmy Ravinder's fault.

When they were younger, Jimmy had had a difficult time talking, so his mother and his uncle Levi learned some ASL to help him communicate. And Jimmy taught her. She didn't know much, but whenever Jimmy got flustered, he'd use sign to talk. And she'd been fascinated ever since.

But the school year was half over. To get into the second semester of ASL I, she first had to catch up on the first. She'd spent her entire break learning the signs, classifiers, and grammar—which, in ASL, was mostly on the face—so they'd let her into the class.

Mrs. Johnson, a pear-shaped woman with short red hair and purple wire-framed glasses, signed her schedule and handed it back to her along with a book and workbook. Then, without a word, she gestured toward a desk in the middle of the room.

Auri ignored the eerie silence and slid into her seat as quietly as possible, only to find Mrs. Johnson finger-spelling in the air while reading from her computer screen.

She would pause and look up at a raised hand, and then repeat the whole thing again and again, and Auri realized she was taking roll. Panic began to rise inside her when she found herself unable to understand a single thing she spelled. It was all so fast, the teacher's hand a blur of motion, and yet every time she paused, a student would raise his or her hand.

She'd made a mistake. A huge one. When she felt a trickle of perspiration slip down her back, she followed it, sinking farther down in her chair.

The teacher stopped and looked up as though confused. She looked at her screen again and then back at the class. Then she stood, put her hands on her hips, and said aloud, "Mr. De los Santos, what are you doing in my classroom?"

Like the rest of the class, Auri turned to see Cruz hunkered down in the back row.

He lifted an indifferent shoulder and said, "Have to have two years of a foreign language. ASL counts."

"Yes," she said as though struggling for patience, "but why are you in this class?"

"I don't like the French teacher."

She rolled her eyes. "No one likes the French teacher." The entire class erupted in laughter, but she continued, "But that doesn't explain why you are in my class."

Clearly, the teacher had a problem with Cruz, but Auri was getting defensive. If he needed the credit, she couldn't stop him from getting it, could she?

"Two years. There are only two classes. ASL I and ASL II. I don't have a choice."

Mrs. Johnson crossed her arms over her chest and leaned back against her desk. "You know very well that you could test out of this class and take the next one. You could test out of that one, too, if you really wanted to."

Auri straightened her shoulders in surprise.

"So, once again, why are you in my class?"

He lifted that same shoulder and let his gaze land on Auri. "I like the company."

The class laughed again, and Mrs. Johnson went back around her desk, but before she sat down, she signed something to Cruz, her movements so fast, Auri only caught one word: *help.*

Cruz nodded as though agreeing to something, but that wasn't the interesting part. He'd understood her. Every word. As though he knew ASL as well as he knew English, because another student raised her hand, shook her head, and signed *understand.* She didn't understand either and was asking for clarification.

Mrs. Johnson spoke aloud again. "I just asked Mr. De los Santos if he would consider helping out in class every so often, and he agreed."

The female student flashed him a smile, clearly as impressed as Auri, but he didn't seem to notice. Nor did he seem to notice the seven other girls vying for his attention. But he did notice Auri. He had yet to take his eyes off her.

Auri faced the teacher again before she lost control of her own inane smile, but she burned with a million questions for him, not the least of which how he seemed to know ASL so well. Hopefully, she'd find out when she interviewed him for their history assignment.

When the teacher passed out a worksheet, Auri opted to check out Sybil's schedule instead. As luck would have it, she shared not one, not two, but three classes with Sybil, and one of those was their seventh-period class, athletics.

After obsessing over Cruz and the fact that he knew ASL like the back of his hand through the entire class, Auri refocused her energy twenty minutes later on investigating the elusive St. Aubin girl. So far, no one in her seventh period knew that much about her. Nor did they know of any friends she may have had.

But surely Sybil hung out with someone in PE. There was safety in numbers in such a class.

As luck would have it, Chastity was in the class, too. The only person in school ridiculously happy to see Auri rushed up to her after they dressed out. Auri was assigned to the bleachers since she had yet to purchase the requisite uniform, which was basically shorts and a tee in the school colors, red and gold.

Still, bleachers as opposed to slamming her face into someone's elbow during basketball? New-girl perk.

"Hi!" Chastity said, sitting beside her on the bleachers while the teacher, a curvy brunette, took roll. "I have an extra pair of shorts and a tee if you want to dress out."

"I'm good," Auri said with a grin.

Chastity laughed. "Right. Sorry. So, you and Cruz seem to be getting along well."

"Um . . . thanks?"

"Oh, you're welcome. Remember that summer Miller Thomas almost drowned and Cruz De los Santos jumped in and dragged him out, doing that lifeguard hold while the lifeguard just kind of stood on the pier with his mouth hanging open? That was so crazy. And then he got a medal for bravery and—"

"That was Cruz?" Auri did indeed remember that summer, but she didn't remember Chastity being there or the fact that Cruz was the one who'd saved that kid. They were only nine.

Cruz was only nine years old and had saved a kid from drowning. She could barely walk and chew gum at the same time when she was nine, and he was saving lives.

She was learning all kinds of new things about Cruz De los Santos, but why now? Perhaps because he'd only recently shown up on her radar? But that wasn't true. She'd had a bit of a crush for years, she just didn't know his name. And she was always too shy to actually talk to him. Who did that?

But she remembered the very day she'd first noticed him. It was exactly three summers ago, and he'd sat on a boulder reading while the popular kids tried to get him into the lake. He ignored them. Completely.

Maybe his saving Miller did have an impact on her, she'd just never made the connection. She liked how he just sort of hung back and let others take the spotlight even though he was clearly popular. Everyone seemed to respect him, and the girls definitely showed interest even when he didn't.

And while all of that was fine and dandy, Cruz was not the one she needed to be gathering intel on.

"So, do you know Sybil?" she asked Chastity as the girl tied her gym shoes.

She sat up. "The missing girl? Sure."

Finally.

"She's so nice, and she has this really cute jacket, and she likes to read. A lot. And this one time—"

"You were friends?"

"Well, I tried to be. She didn't talk much, though. Really shy."

She was at that, and yet she'd come up to Auri at the New Year's Eve party. She'd introduced herself. Struck up a conversation. Something even Auri had difficulty doing.

"I get it, though. It's hard to be the new girl. She just moved here this summer. But it could've been me. I'm a bit much sometimes. I tend to scare people away."

"Really?" Auri asked, pretending to be shocked.

"I know, right?" She laughed, and Auri loved that she could do that. Laugh at herself. Many people couldn't. Where was the fun in that? "You know, she looks a little like you."

Auri raised a brow. "You think?"

"I mean, she's not quite as pretty but, you know, the hair."

"Oh, right." They did both have red hair.

"Except yours is richer. I've never seen hair quite that color."

She reached out and took a long strand, totally invading Auri's space bubble. A bubble she was quite fond of. "It's copper."

Auri laughed. "It's okay. You can say it. It's orange."

She joined her. "Kind of, but it's also gorgeous."

"Thank you," Auri said, genuinely flattered. "So, do you know who Sybil's friends were? Who she hung out with?"

"Wait a minute." Chastity leaned closer, her brown eyes glossing over. "Are you helping your mom with the investigation? Because I could help, too. I'm great at talking to someone so much they give up and tell me everything they know. I'm considering a job in the FBI."

"You'd be great," Auri lied. "So, Sybil?"

Chastity bowed her head in thought. "I don't know. I just don't remember seeing her hang out with anyone. Isn't that weird? I mean, everyone hangs out with someone."

Not necessarily. A sadness tugged at Auri's heart. Sybil was adorable. And very likable. Why would a girl who'd started at a school four months earlier have no friends?

The teacher called the class to the floor. That was when Auri noticed Lynelle Amaia and her goons dressed in gym clothes. Lynelle turned to her, held her fingers up in the shape of a gun, and pretended to pull the trigger.

Great. She'd have this to look forward to all day every day. Lynelle in both her first period and her last. Lynelle bookends. Just what she'd always wanted.

But Auri was once again struck with the fact that there had to be more to Lynelle's animosity than just the raid. She would eventually have no choice but to confront her.

And her investigation was failing miserably. She had yet to uncover a single ounce of information that might help her mom find Sybil.

She needed to talk to the one man she could confide in. The one man she'd always gone to when she felt the world turning against her.

Oddly enough, it was a man she'd never met. A man she'd only seen pictures of and dreamed of and whose voice she longed to hear.

It was time she paid a visit to her father.

Before Sun and Quincy could leave to question the Ravinders about Jimmy, a task Sun was not looking forward to, an official-looking man in an official-looking jacket walked in the front door. An older man with graying brown hair, he had strong enough features to command a room with a single glance. Or perhaps it was his confidence. The way he stood. The expression he wore.

"And who do we have here?" Quincy asked as the guy spoke to Anita.

"He screams FBI," Sun said.

"Because he's wearing a parka with the letters *FBI* on the left side of the chest?"

"Yes. Also, he looks like FBI, don't you think?"

Quincy gaped at her. "Are you checking him out?"

"What? No. But so is every other female in the room."

"And women complain about men in the workplace."

Damn it. He was right. But it was seriously impossible not to notice the guy. "He's just so chiseled. Wait, he's coming over." Pretending to be busy, she picked up an empty box. No idea why.

"Of course he's coming over. He probably needs to talk to you, what with you being the sheriff and all."

Sun considered jumping behind the human refrigerator but thought better of it. She had to remain professional even in the face of such comeliness.

He walked straight up to her and held out his hand. "Sheriff, I'm Special Agent Carter Fields."

A jolt of electricity shot through her. Even his name was sexy. "Sunshine Vicram." She dropped the box. "Sheriff. The sheriff. Of Del Sol. The county." She decided to stop while she was ahead.

He paused as though trying to figure her out, then refocused on Quincy.

"Chief Deputy Quincy Cooper."

"Sorry we're meeting under these circumstances."

"And what circumstances would those be?" she asked.

"Ah. You weren't informed of my arrival."

"No, sir."

"The governor asked if I could take a look at the St. Aubin case."

Of course the St. Aubins knew the governor. Why wouldn't they? They weren't even from New Mexico, and they had an in with the freaking governor. "Well, we certainly won't mind an extra pair. Of eyes. A pair of eyes. A set, as it were."

Quincy coughed into his hand.

The agent nodded. "Thank you. I hear you have a lead?"

Quincy shrugged into his jacket. "We're heading out there now. You're welcome to come along."

"Don't mind if I do. Do you have a copy of the file I can peruse on the way?"

"Of course." Sun grabbed her copy and handed it to him. "Anita can make you a copy, but you can look at mine for now. Shall we?"

Sun had worked with the FBI before, naturally, but she wondered exactly when Marianna called the governor. "So, exactly when did Marianna St. Aubin call the governor?" She looked at her passenger in the rearview as they drove north, but he was studying the file.

"First thing this morning, as far as I know. I don't think it was the wife, though. I think the husband called him. Is he back in town yet?"

"Not yet. His plane should be landing now."

They discussed the evidence they had thus far, which wasn't much.

"Any thoughts?" she asked him.

"I'm fairly certain this will be solved quickly."

"How's that?" Quince asked.

"It's clearly a hoax, but when the governor says *jump* . . ."

Sun knew he'd think that. Any sane person would. But he didn't know Del Sol like she did.

They drove up a freshly paved road that led to the Ravinder compound. It used to be dirt. And the compound used to be part dilapidated mobile home park and part junkyard. When Sun drove past the entrance gate, she slammed on the brakes.

The place was gorgeous. Several houses sat on the Ravinder land. Land that had been in their family for three decades.

"Has it changed much?" Quince asked, his voice tinged with humor.

"I'd say so."

"Business has been good."

"What business is that?" Agent Fields asked.

"Levi Ravinder has a world-famous corn whiskey distillery."

The man nodded in understanding.

"Maybe you've heard of it?" Sun asked. "Dark River Shine?"

He let out a soft whistle. "I have. It's good stuff."

For some reason, pride blossomed inside her chest.

"According to rumor," Quincy said, "the Ravinders had been part of the Dixie Mafia. They'd headed west in the early '80s, when the organization decided to set up shop in California."

"The name sounds familiar."

"It should." Sun proceeded up the drive slowly. She didn't know which of the sprawling rustics or multiple outbuildings to go to, so she decided on what looked like the main house. "They'd sent the five Ravinder brothers and their families." They consisted of Levi's father and four uncles, but Fields didn't need to know that. "They were on the way there when the big raid happened."

"The big raid?"

"The FBI launched a massive raid of the organization, and

they designated the entire Harrison County Sheriff's Office in Biloxi, Mississippi, a criminal organization."

"Oh yes. I do remember reading about that. It's a famous case."

Quincy spoke up. "It set a new precedence in dealing with organized crime and basically left the Ravinders hanging." He gestured to their surroundings.

"And they ended up here?" Fields asked.

"They'd apparently been taking back roads, scoping them out for future reference. And one of their vehicles broke down just over the pass."

"They've lived here ever since," Sun added. "I guess they couldn't go back."

"I wouldn't think so. You have any problems with them?" he asked.

Sun shrugged. "Not as much as you might think. Not anymore, anyway. But it's only my first day on the job."

"No kidding?" The man smiled in surprise.

"No kidding."

"And that would be thanks to Ravinder," Quince said. "The drop in complaints. He'd been trying to get them to go legit for years. To break all ties with organized crime. It took him a while, but he may have finally succeeded."

"Ravinder? I thought they were all Ravinders."

"They are, but oddly enough, the title has gone to the youngest male in the family, Levi. All the others just go by their first names. It's a status thing, I believe."

Butterflies decided to come out of hiding in her stomach and shift into attack mode when Quince said Levi's name. Also, it hit her that she was going to have to deal with the Ravinders as a whole. The entire lot of them, and there were many. None with whom she had a great history.

"You okay with this?" Quince asked, knowing she'd suffered through the same punishment from the Ravinder cousins as he had growing up.

"I'm just praying Hailey isn't home."

Fields leaned in. "Hailey?"

"Hailey Ravinder," Quince said. "They don't get along. She tried to stab Sunshine in the face with a stick."

"Only once," she said defensively. "Though it did make an impression."

"When was this?" the agent asked.

"We were still drinking from sippy cups."

"Ah." He laughed softly and sat back.

"But she's bullied her ever since."

"Just be careful around her," Sun said, hoping to steer both of them away from the woman. "She's basically harmless. Like a mountain lion. Or a rattlesnake. Or a drug lord. You leave her alone, she'll leave you alone."

"Yeah," Quince said. "You don't and she'll slice through your jugular."

"She's never had the best impulse control, but I like to think she's grown both as a mother and a human being."

The snort from Quincy cast a substantial amount of doubt on her theory.

Hailey was Levi's little sister by a couple of years, even though she'd always bossed him around like she was older. She'd had the man wrapped around her little finger since she was in pull-ups.

And she'd been Sun's mortal enemy since preschool, when Hailey broke all of Sun's crayons on the first day of school.

She could still smell them. Forty-eight crayons stacked to exquisite perfection in a bright cardboard box. The uniformity a thing of beauty. The tapered ends cut with laser precision. And all of them destroyed by a three-foot monster with blond hair and a demon's soul.

Ever since then, the chick had gone out of her way to make Sun's life miserable, and Sun went out of her way to make sure Hailey knew how happy she was despite the girl's pitiful attempts to ruin her existence.

Of course, a lot had changed since preschool.

"Strange thing is," Quince said, turning around to Fields, "no one knows how the Ravinders got this land. There's no record of sale. It was just suddenly in their name one day and that was that."

"Interesting," he said, and Sun could almost see the gears in his mind working overtime.

They pulled up in front of the main house, a stunning ranch with a massive log porch that wrapped around the entire building.

Fields whistled when they stepped out. "At least crime paid for someone. Where's the distillery?"

Quince gestured past the house. "It's farther down the road."

He nodded, and they started for the front door when a truck, a huge black truck with a wrap that read *Dark River Shine,* slid to a halt beside them.

Sun froze. Well, they all froze as they waited for the aggressive driver to get out, but Sun froze for a different reason. The bones in her legs had once again vanished as the epitome of male perfection climbed down from the truck and stabbed each and every one of them with an expression that would liquefy a lesser law enforcement officer.

She tried not to stare at him, but she couldn't help a few quick glances at his spectacular frame. Wide shoulders. Lean waist. Dark hair with an auburn glint in the sun and an even darker red five-o'clock shadow framing his full mouth.

Her mind rocketed back to the first real encounter she'd had with the Ravinder gang. With Levi in particular.

In hindsight, she realized she'd simply made an easy target, but at the time, she'd wondered what she'd done to upset the entire clan. Why they hated her so very, very much. A theme that would continue throughout middle school and into high school until she put the town, and everyone in it, in her rearview.

She was twelve when she got her first taste of the Ravinders as a unified whole. Not just the trite tribulations of her tormentor,

Hailey, but the entire lot of cousins and second cousins that made up Del Sol's public menace number one.

She'd been riding her bike home from the lake like she did almost every day in the summer, an ice cream cone in her left hand. She saw them riding their own bikes to the lake, a gang of seven Ravinders with only one girl in the bunch.

Their bikes were bent and rusted and squeaked when they got closer, and Sun's damnable empathy kicked in. But these were the Ravinders. The emotion would be wasted on them.

Hoping Hailey would ignore her for once in her life, she put her head down and pedaled faster, trying to hurry past. But two of the boys slid sideways to cut her off, and the rest surrounded her.

She had to stop so fast she almost fell, skidding to a halt in a cloud of dust. This amused them. Well, most of them.

Levi Ravinder sat on his bike a few feet from her, stone-faced, his gaze locked on to her as though he were contemplating inviting her to dinner. Or cooking her for it.

She never forgot the dynamics that day. The youngest boy of the bunch, Levi, who was taller and slimmer and darker than any of the others, seemed to wield the most power.

The gang stayed on their bikes, none of them saying a thing as they stared.

Her ice cream had melted over her left hand. She'd been struggling with it, anyway, but in the heat of the moment, she'd crushed the cone, and cold butter pecan oozed out of the wafer cone and slid between her fingers.

She dropped it in the dirt when they got off their bikes and closed in on her. All of them except Levi and, surprisingly, Hailey.

She tried to back her bike up to go around them, but one of the boys caught her rear wheel.

Her lungs stopped working, and the sun beating down overhead made her dizzy. "What do you want?"

"Your bike," Hailey said. Her dirty blond hair hung in strings over her eyes, and she brushed it back with painfully thin hands.

"No," Sun said. Her parents had given her that bike for her birthday. She wasn't giving it up without a fight.

The boy who had a death grip on her back wheel sneered at her. "Then maybe we'll just take it."

She turned to him. "You can try, I guess."

Everyone oohed and aahed at her bravado, but she was shaking so hard she could barely speak. Her voice came out breathy and weak, and her cheeks heated even more.

She made sure to keep one leg on the ground and one on a pedal in case she got the chance to take off. She wasn't stupid. But now they knew she was scared.

She looked back at Levi and kept her gaze there. She knew who he was. Everyone knew who he was. He was the boy mothers warned their daughters about.

Even at fourteen, he was built like one of those guys in the movies. Tall and lean with muscles that cut across his stomach and chest. A chest bared to the golden sun overhead.

He wore only a pair of faded orange swimming trunks that looked a little big on him and an old pair of sneakers. He sat deathly still on his bike, one foot on the ground, and let his glistening gaze travel the length of her. It was dark and intense and made her stomach tighten in response.

The boy holding her wheel broke the spell Levi had her under. "You know how we like to have fun in the sun?" he asked the other kids, an eerie smirk slanting across his face. "We could have a lot of fun in *this* Sun."

Levi's cousins laughed, all five of them sizing her up.

Hailey, tiny for a twelve-year-old, dropped her bike, walked up to Sun, and ripped the chain from around her neck. The one that had her house key on it.

She tried to grab it back, but Hailey was too fast. She walked backward, swinging the chain back and forth like a hypnotist, her smile evil as she stopped beside her brother. Then, without warning, she turned and dropped the key down the front of Levi's shorts.

Since they were swim shorts, the key must've caught in the fishnet lining, because they didn't fall through and land on the ground like she was hoping.

"Why don't you come get it?" Hailey said, probably hoping Sun would get off the bike so she could take it.

The others jumped back on their bikes and whooped and hollered as they rode around them in circles, stirring up dust, waiting to see what would happen next.

Levi had yet to move, as though his psycho sister did that kind of thing all the time. As though it were normal.

The cousins yelled really helpful suggestions like, "Get it!" and "We dare you!"

"Come on," another said. "Don't be a chicken. Get the key."

Hailey crossed her arms, the challenge in her expression blatant. Almost as blatant as the crazy.

Sun gave in. She drew her leg over her bike, grossing out at the stickiness between her fingers, and dropped it on the ground. Hailey's eyes glistened as Sun walked toward Levi.

Without waiting a second longer, Hailey ran to the bike, hopped on it, and took off, but the boys stayed for the show. They all stopped riding and watched, their eyes just as hungry, just as greedy, but for a very different reason.

He didn't let go of his handlebars when she reached over and put her right, non-sticky hand on his stomach. But his muscles did tighten. His breath did still as he watched her.

She bit her bottom lip and slipped her fingers down the waistband of his shorts.

His skin was hot and smooth. His stomach hard. When her hand slid lower, he licked his lips.

"Come on, Levi," one of the boys said, craving more. Craving violence. "Throw her down. Show her what you're made of."

Her heart beat so fast and so hard, she could hear her blood rushing in her ears, but she still didn't feel the key. She slid her hand even lower down his abdomen, so low another couple of inches and she'd be between his legs.

"Yeah, Levi," another boy chimed in, his voice soft as though mesmerized. "Get her on the ground. We can take care of the rest."

Her fingertips dipped farther until he wrapped a hand around her wrist, the movement slow and calculated, effectively putting a stop to her exploration. He lifted out her empty hand then he reached down his shorts and brought up the key himself.

She reached for it, but he pulled it toward him. Not to be mean like Hailey, but to study it, his dark hair with sun-streaked, coppery-blond locks falling over his face. He was the kind of boy summers were made for.

"Can I have that back, please?"

He ignored her, took the broken link, and re-clasped the chain so she could wear it again. Then he lifted it over her head, put it around her neck, and examined his handiwork.

She didn't know what to do. Thank him? She'd had her bike stolen. She'd been threatened with physical violence from a pack of jackals. And she'd touched, for the first time in her life, the boy she'd been in love with since forever.

Emotion threatened to spill over her lashes. The last thing she'd wanted was for him to see her cry. This perfect boy who came from a perfectly broken home. A home that had been broken for generations.

With back ramrod straight, she turned and walked home, mortified and humiliated and more in love than she ever imagined possible.

She didn't see him again that summer. She'd heard from other kids around town that Levi spent most of his summers on the Mescalero Apache reservation, but they didn't know why.

Sun did. Thanks to her parents, she also knew he almost died because of it. His mother hadn't been so lucky.

Levi's gaze finally landed on her and he paused, his expression incredulous, the sinew in his arms straining as he flexed. "Really?" he asked, the edge in his voice razor sharp. "On your first day?"

Quince started to come to her defense, but she couldn't let him. She needed to set the precedence for their interactions from here on out. "There's a girl missing," she said, her voice just as sharp. "We got a tip that she's been seen several times with your nephew, Jimmy. We need to talk to him."

If Sun had told him she was going to burn down his world and kill his family, she doubted he could have become more enraged. He stepped toward her, and both men closed in. Fields held up a hand, warning him to keep a safe distance.

The passenger got out of the truck. She couldn't be certain, but she thought he was one of Levi's cousins. A shorter, stockier cousin like they all were.

Levi took note of the FBI agent at last, his expression a blatant confession of just how unimpressed he was.

"What are you doing here?" the cousin asked.

Before she could ask Levi where his nephew was, an older man came out of the front door with Levi's sister, Hailey. She screeched to a halt when she saw the officers, but then she ran to Levi, her eyes like saucers.

"Did you find him?" When Levi didn't answer, hysterics took hold. "Levi!" she shouted.

"What are you talking about?" Sun asked.

Hailey finally noticed Sun specifically, and her face morphed into one of disgust. "What the fuck is she doing here?"

"Hailey," Sun began, but the woman lost it.

She bolted toward her and was only held back by her much larger brother.

Sun kept one hand on her duty weapon, but showed a palm in surrender with the other. "We just need to talk to Jimmy. He's not in trouble."

She tried to fling herself at Sun again, but Levi held her back.

"They think Jimmy's been hanging around with that missing girl," Levi said to her.

And Hailey went ballistic. She clawed and scratched at him, trying to get to Sun. "How dare you!" she shouted. "He would never hang out with a St. Aubin. Those kinds of girls wouldn't give my son the time of day. But maybe that's why you're here." She stilled as shock took over. "You think he took her."

"We don't think anything, Hailey." Sun worked hard on keeping her tone soft but confident. "We just need to talk to him."

Hailey fought Levi's hold again until he pulled her against him and spoke into her ear.

She whirled around and gaped at him. "What do you mean?"

Levi let out a long breath, then said, "I lost his tracks in the snow. He's still up there."

Hailey plastered both hands over her mouth as fresh tears fell down her cheeks. She looked like she'd been crying all morning. "He'll freeze to death in those mountains."

"He knows that rock better than I do. I'll find him, Hails," Levi promised as the older man came forward and put an arm over her shoulders.

She stiffened and shook him off before heading back inside the house. Just before she closed the door, she looked at Sun and said, "Get that piece of shit off this property."

It was nice to see nothing had changed. Sun was still hated for no reason whatsoever, and Hailey was still a hellcat. At least she knew where she stood.

The slam echoed against the surrounding buildings, and Sun turned to Levi. "What's going on?"

"We just came back for dry clothes. Dipshit over there fell in the river." He gestured toward the dipshit.

"You're searching the mountain. For whom?"

He tilted his head to the side as though stunned she would dare talk to him, his annoyance crystal clear.

When they were growing up, he'd seemed to like her. Well, *like* may have been a strong word, but he didn't hate her. They'd even started talking. He was three years older, but after he'd graduated high school, she'd see him around here and there. It always made her day.

But in high school, Sun was involved in . . . an accident. She spent a month in the hospital in a coma. Afterward, Levi kept his distance, even going so far as to ignore her when she called out to say hi. It was bizarre, and she didn't deserve his indifference, so she grew bitter and he grew bitter, and before she knew it, they were at an impenetrable impasse.

"Or I can bring you in for questioning," she said, her threat as clear as his corn whiskey. "If that would make this easier."

He kept his dark, unwavering gaze trained on her face for a solid minute before he answered, "Jimmy didn't come home last night."

Sun released a disappointed sigh. Of course, she'd guessed instantly who they were talking about, but she'd needed confirmation. "Levi, I have a missing girl, and now a boy who's been seen with her is missing, too?"

Fury sparked in his whiskey-colored eyes. He leaned closer, putting Quincy on edge enough to step between them, and whispered just for her, "Fuck you," before stalking into the house.

The cousin laughed, the sound strangely high-pitched like the jackals she'd considered Levi's relatives to be.

"Wow," Quincy said softly at her side. "He really dislikes you."

"Thanks for the reminder."

"No, seriously, what did you do?"

"Hey," she said to the cousin before he could follow Levi inside.

He grinned. "What is it, little girl? You think I'm going to give you information when Ravinder wouldn't?"

Even the other family members called him *Ravinder.* "Why do you call him that?" she asked. He flipped her off and tried to walk away again, but she asked, "How long has he been missing?"

The guy turned back, and she could tell his concern was real.

"Since yesterday afternoon." He looked back at the house, checking to see if anyone was watching. "We think he went out and got caught in the storm yesterday."

"You should have called us."

"Yeah," he said, chuckling. "Because the law enforcement officers of Del Sol have always been such peaches to work with."

She lifted a shoulder. "New regime. You could do something crazy and give me a chance."

He wore the very definition of a shit-eating grin before he turned and followed his younger cousin inside.

With little choice, Sun climbed back into the cruiser. Quincy followed, but Fields stayed back.

"You're just going to let this go? It's the only lead you have."

"I have no intention of letting it go, but I know the Ravinders. The more we push, the more belligerent they become." She gestured for him to get inside the cruiser. Once he was inside, she asked Quincy, "How fast can you get into civvies and get back out here?"

He smiled. "Depends on how long it takes you to get back to the station, Grandma."

"Do they know your vehicle?" she asked him.

"Yep, but they don't know the Yellow Jacket."

"You still have your mom's junker?"

"Junker?" he asked, thoroughly offended. "Well, okay. But you have no idea how much action that old pickup has seen."

"Um, ew?"

"Jealousy is so unbecoming."

Fields leaned forward. "May I ask what we're doing?"

"Wait," Quincy said, cutting Fields off. "You *are* jealous, right?"

"Levi Ravinder just happens to be the best tracker in the area," she said, ignoring her BFF. "Probably the entire state and quite possibly the entire country. If he's tracking Jimmy and the only lead we have connects Sybil St. Aubin to him, we're following up on that lead."

Quince urged her to drive faster, gesturing with his hand. "It won't take them long to change, eat, and get back out there."

"I'm hurrying," she said, trying to stay on the slippery road.

She didn't want to say it out loud, not with Fields there since he was such a pessimist concerning the note, but according to Sybil, there was a strong possibility the girl was being held somewhere in the mountains as well. Since that covered thousands of square miles, she'd stick with Levi.

"We just need to know where they're concentrating their efforts. We can get the search party started from there."

"How long will it take to get a search party going?" Quincy asked, already stripping.

"For now, it'll just be us. If you're up for it, Agent Fields."

He nodded. "Of course. I have a change of clothes in my car."

"It's too late to get a large party going. It'll be dark in two hours. Tomorrow, we can call in the volunteers and get an early start. And you might want to invite your sister. She's amazing."

"That she is."

"His sister?" Fields asked.

"Twins," Sun said. "Wait until you meet her. You can hardly tell them apart."

She and Quincy laughed softly, and Fields apparently decided not to go there.

The minute Sun stepped inside the station, Anita handed her a file with everything they'd found at the St. Aubin house.

"No blood," Anita said, filling her in as Sun examined the construction crew installing temporary wood panels at the front of the station. Which would certainly help with the heating bill. "But they did find a partial fingerprint. Price is bringing it in now. And they sent over a description of what Sybil was wearing the day before she disappeared. Mrs. St. Aubin can't find those clothes, so she could still be in them."

"And the photo? It looks like an ad off the internet."

"It *is* an ad off the internet. That's the backpack the button came from. She could have it with her."

Sun studied the list and the photo. "Anita, you are a god among mortals. Get this out to everyone."

Anita lowered her head, unused to such compliments, then turned to Fields as he scanned the file over Sun's shoulder. "Mr. St. Aubin is home. He wants an update."

Her words seemed to irk the agent if the straight line across his face where his mouth used to be were any indication. She could hardly blame him. Mr. St. Aubin was used to getting his way because of his money. That wouldn't get him far with a hardworking field agent.

"Would you mind calling him for me, Anita?" He took his clothes and followed Quincy to the locker room.

"What should I say?"

"Tell him I'll call him when I have something."

Anita shrugged and went back to her desk to make the call.

Sun watched him go. Chiseled features. Assertive personality. Penis.

All qualities she liked in a guy.

11

Suspect arrested for shoplifting a travel-sized
toothpaste and for murdering his neighbor.
The incidents do not seem to be related.

—DEL SOL POLICE BLOTTER

Before they headed out, Sun checked in on her inquisitive daughter. "Knock, knock," she texted.

After a few seconds, her phone vibrated. "Who's there?"

"Mrs. Are you staying out of trouble?"

"Mrs. Are you staying out of trouble who?"

Sun giggled. "Mrs. Are you staying out of trouble because if you're not, you'll be grounded for the rest of your life and your grandmother is going to pick you up after school."

"That is the longest name ever. Have you heard anything?"

"Not yet, hon, but we may have a lead. Anything on your end?"

"Nothing substantial."

Sun swelled with pride. How many kids used the word *substantial* accurately in a sentence?

"Sybil is nice and smart and cute, but she keeps to herself, and I have yet to find a single student who really knew her. One she opened up to."

"That's okay. At least you tried. I'll be home late."

"Can I help?"

"Yes. You can go to your grandparents' house and do your homework. And don't con them into ordering pizza."

"Okay."

"And when you do con them into ordering pizza, at least make sure there's a vegetable on it. Somewhere. Or a fruit. Pineapple is good, I hear."

She could almost see the eye roll when her daughter texted back, "Fine."

Quincy came out in civilian clothes.

Sun gestured him closer as she looked past the guys doing construction and pointed. A rust-colored rooster rushed past, much like the roadrunner in the Wile E. Coyote cartoons. "Isn't that Puff Daddy?"

"The chicken?" he asked.

"The rooster. And, if I'm not mistaken, that's Mr. Madrid chasing him."

A man with more bandages than a six-year-old left alone in a doctor's office stumbled past the front of the station. The two plodded through the snow. The rooster with relative ease. Mr. Madrid not so much.

"Bold of him to give a station full of deputies front-row seats to his criminal activities."

"Okay, now we have to arrest him."

"For what?" she asked. "Technically, poor Mr. Madrid does not have possession of Puff Daddy."

Quincy snorted. "Not for lack of trying."

"True. But we have work to do."

"Fine. I'm heading home to get my mom's pickup." He wore a khaki jacket, denim jeans, black-framed glasses, and a baseball cap low over his brow. "They'll never recognize me in it."

The Ravinders were painfully private people. They would never let Sun or her deputies on their land without some kind of warrant, but Sun needed to know where Levi was searching. Once they had a location, they could get a warrant to assist. If, and only if, Quincy wasn't spotted on their land.

If it were up to Levi, Sun liked to think he'd be sensible and allow them access. But she couldn't take the chance. If Sybil was up there, they needed to know sooner rather than later.

"Thanks, Q. Keep me updated."

"I'll let you know where they're searching."

He started for the exit, but Fields called out to him, "I'm going with you."

Quince lifted a shoulder. "I'm just getting a location."

"Yeah, from what I've seen, if they spot you following them, you'll need more than that thin disguise."

"Thin?" He gestured to himself as they headed out. "There is nothing thin about my disguise."

"Other than the fact that there is?"

"I'll have you know I played the lead in *Oklahoma!*"

Sun laughed softly, wondering, as Fields probably did, what the hell that had to do with anything.

She waited three more minutes, told Anita she was going out, then headed out the side door as well. After making sure they were gone, she walked around the small detention center and down the alley, careful of the shaded areas where the snow was still high and packed hard enough to be hazardous.

Then again, even butter knives could be hazardous in the wrong hands. Like hers. She'd never been accused of being agile.

Her phone had dinged on the way back to town with a message from Daisy Duke. It simply said, *15.* That was twenty minutes ago, so Sun hurried.

She opened the back door to the latest and greatest coffee shop Del Sol had to offer, Caffeine-Wah, and stepped into a dark storeroom. The smell of espresso almost dropped her. She hadn't realized her levels had plummeted so low.

A small blonde came out from behind a stack of shelves

overflowing with coffee of all makes and models. She glanced around, her eyes red and swollen, making sure no one was with Sun, then ran to her.

Sun wrapped her in her arms. "Sweetheart," she said when Hailey Ravinder began sobbing. "Are you okay?"

"No." She let another round of sobs quake through her, before saying, "My baby is gone."

Sun sat her at arm's length and smoothed back her hair. "Hailey, why didn't you call me? Holy cow."

Despite her emotional state, her expression went flat. "Sun, my big brother is the best tracker in the state. What else could you have done?"

She had a point.

Even so, there were about a thousand reasons she should have called her, but there was no sense in going into it now.

"And even if Jimmy knows that St. Aubin girl, he would never hurt her. I know every parent says that, but he's a gentle giant. He is the sweetest kid on the planet, Sunshine."

"But you've never seen them together?"

"No. Never. He walks to the lake a lot and hangs out, but nobody talks to him." Sun could see the pain that realization caused in her. "Not that I know of."

"Has he gone missing like this before?"

She lowered her head. "He gets lost in the moment sometimes. Wanders too far. But we've always found him. He's never been out all night."

One of the two proprietors, a.k.a. two of Sun's best friends ever, stepped into the dark storeroom and spotted them. He glanced over his shoulder to make sure no one was looking, then hurried to the pair and threw his arms around them both.

"Is everything okay?" he asked into their hair. "What's going on? Ricky and I have been worried sick."

Sun and Auri had lived above Richard and Ricky's garage—a.k.a. remodeled loft of luxury—in Santa Fe for several years. She'd even officiated their wedding, both men decked out in killer tuxes with their own special brand of flair.

But they weren't just fashion savvy. They'd started the most successful coffee chain in the city. When they'd heard Sun was moving back to her hometown, they'd jumped at the idea of opening yet another coffee shop there. They loved the area, swearing artists were their people. They were certainly in the right place.

"Is Jimmy okay?" Richard asked Hailey, his spiked black hair a glorious mess.

Before she could answer, Ricky, an Asian god who knew eyeliner like nobody's business, rushed into the storeroom, presumably between customers, and grabbed a hug from both women before hurrying back to the bar.

It was sad that these were the only two people in the entire town Sun could completely trust with her and Hailey's secret. There were plenty of people she trusted, but not when it came to her former nemesis's life. Or her son's.

In a bizarre twist of fate, one that left Sun baffled to this day, she had been working with Hailey on an investigation for months, even before Sun won the election.

The hot mess of a woman had reached out to her while she was still in Santa Fe, and they had become very close in the months since, a fact that boggled Sun's mind even more than it had Hailey's. Funny what the common ground of motherhood, and protecting one's own, could do for a relationship.

Sun would never forget the first time they met up in a dive halfway between Santa Fe and Del Sol. Hailey had walked in with her tail tucked between her legs, so to speak.

"I'm sorry. For everything we did to you, but mostly for what happened. For the . . . accident."

Sun shook her head. "It was a long time ago. I hear you have a son."

Hailey beamed at her. "I do. He's gorgeous, Sunshine. Just like your daughter."

The mention of Auri had surprised her at the time.

"I've seen her," Hailey explained. "When she stays with your parents over summer breaks." She leaned in. "What a beauty."

And just like that, all was forgiven. As though the woman hadn't been her worst nightmare for years. As though she hadn't tried to kill her once and maim her twice. As though she hadn't been part of the reason Sun left Del Sol in the first place.

But Hailey had sought her out for a reason. Her uncle Clay had been trying to worm his way back into the Dixie Mafia. That wouldn't be a big deal, but he wanted to use Levi's business as a means to get back in.

"My brother has worked his ass off for that business," she'd told her on the first meeting. "And my dumbass uncle wants to use it to launder money for the DM."

Fury and indignation for Levi flooded every cell in Sun's body. "Surely, Levi would never allow your uncle to do something like that."

"You don't understand." She leaned closer and took Sun's hands into her own. "Even if Levi refuses, which he will, once the DM sees the potential gold mine of Dark River Shine, they'll do everything in their power to take control."

The image sliced through Sun's thoughts like a straight razor. "Would he ever give in to them?"

"Levant Arun Ravinder? Hell no. He'd go to his grave first, and they will have no qualms about putting him there."

"What about your uncle?"

"Please, he'd help them dig the grave."

"Son of a bitch," Sun said, chewing on her fingernails. "Have you gone to the sheriff?"

"Sheriff Redding? I would, but since he's in on it . . ."

"Sheriff Redding?" she asked, stunned. She knew the guy was an asshat, but . . .

Hailey nodded. "They're involved in several *business ventures* together. And there's a deputy, too, but I can't tell which one. I've never seen his face."

"Would you recognize him from his build?"

"Maybe. He looked big. Wide shoulders. But that could've been the jacket he wore."

The blood drained from Sun's face. Quincy was the tallest deputy Del Sol had at the moment. And he had the widest shoulders by a mile.

"Ever since Levi legitimized the family business, my uncles have been trying to come up with a way to knock him off his pedestal."

"Of course. He can't do better than they did."

"Never."

Never underestimate the devious nature of a family drenched in crime and blood. "The only thing I can suggest is that we go to the FBI."

Hailey jerked back as though Sun had slapped her. "I can't do that. If they find out . . . No, it has to be you. Once we gather enough evidence against my uncle, then you can go to them."

"Hailey—"

"No. No, Sunshine. I can't risk my son's life. Or Levi's."

Sun understood more than Hailey could ever know. "If your uncle finds out you're doing this, he'll kill you, Hailey."

She raised her chin a notch and pasted on her brave face. "Let's make sure he doesn't find out."

That was months ago, and she still worried about Hailey's uncle finding out she'd been gathering intel for her. And she worried about the Dixie Mafia taking over Levi's operation.

Since then, Sun had been investigating each and every one of her deputies. Well, before they were hers, that is. Even Quincy. Her face-to-face meetings with them served two purposes: to get to know them and to get an initial impression.

None set off any alarms for her, so maybe the elusive Lieutenant Bo Britton was the deputy in cahoots with former Sheriff

Redding. He'd been with him the longest. If one of her deputies was corrupt, he or she was an excellent actor. Then again, they'd have to be.

"Okay, enough." Richard was tearing up even though he had no idea what was going on. "I have to get back. You girls just be safe. Promise me."

"We promise," they said in unison.

He got to the door when Sun remembered another promise, one the couple had made to her.

"You still have to teach me that trick with the eyeliner!" she whispered.

"And you still have to teach me how to get away with murder!" he whispered back. "I got people to kill, damn it."

It worked. Hailey laughed softly.

"Do you know where they're searching? Where Levi found Jimmy's prints?"

"It's over by Dover Pass."

While Sun knew a few of the names for places in the mountains—like Dover Pass and Strawser's Holler—she had no idea where any of them actually were. It wasn't like they were on a map. Not most of them, anyway. But leave it to a family of bootleggers to come up with names and landmarks to navigate the mountain range, because no native New Mexican would ever name anything a *holler*.

She wrote it into her notepad, anyway. Quincy might know.

"Hailey, what happened to the rest of your uncles?" Sun only knew that Hailey's mother had died when she was young, and her death was rumored to be about Levi. Their father never believed Levi was his, and Levi's coloring, so unlike the rest of the Ravinders', would seem to support that.

If her parents were to be believed, Levi's father was a Native American. A Mescalero Apache, to be exact, which was why he spent much of his summers on the reservation with a man believed to be Levi's paternal grandfather.

But then Hailey's father died about a year later in a car accident, and Levi and his sister were raised by a slew of aunts and uncles. None of them were what anyone would call *upstanding*.

"I mean, you had four, and now you're down to the one?"

"Two, actually. Uncle Clay is here, as you know. And Uncle Wynn is in prison in Arizona."

Right. Sun did know about that one.

"Uncle Wes died. Cancer."

She did not know about that one.

"And Uncle Brick ran off to California. Nobody's heard from him in years."

"Really?" she asked, surprised. She also had no idea why they'd called him *Brick*.

Hailey nodded, and if she hadn't bitten her cheek and looked away, Sun may have believed her. As it stood, she knew more about that uncle than she was letting on.

But she also knew Hailey was a good person. Motherhood had changed her. Jimmy was all she cared about, and she was clearly willing to go to great lengths to keep him safe.

"Hailey, don't you think it's strange that all of this is happening my first day on the job? Do you think your uncle knows we're onto him? Do you think he had anything to do with any of the disappearances? Whoever took the St. Aubin girl knew how to get past their security system. Knew how to sneak her out without anyone hearing. Had a solid plan and executed it with laser-like precision."

"A solid plan? Laser-like precision?"

"Yes."

She chuckled, the sound void of humor. "Yeah, my uncle had nothing to do with it. Trust me."

"What about Redding?"

Her mouth thinned. "He's definitely smart enough. And more than capable."

Sun nodded and took Hailey's hands into hers. "I have to get back. Please keep me updated."

"You'll do the same?"

Sun nodded. Before she left, she turned back to Hailey and asked, "How is he?"

"Oh, hell no." The blonde crossed her arms over her chest, adamant. "I'm not doing that."

"What?"

"If you want to know how my brother is, you'll have to ask him yourself."

Sun scoffed. "Like that'll happen. Like he would answer me, anyway. That man hates my guts."

That time, Hailey scoffed. "Right. That's why he named the distillery after you."

Sun gaped at her, then shook her head. "Dark River Shine?"

"Shine," she said, heading for the front for a coffee. "He's always called you *Shine*."

Shine, as in Dark River. The thought boggled Sun's already rattled little mind.

She checked in with the marshals, who were traipsing about her town in search of escaped fugitive Ramses Rojas. They had two possible sightings thus far, both promising, but they couldn't zero in on a location or figure out who Rojas would be staying with.

With Auri taken care of for the evening, Sun set Anita on the task of communications with the mission coordinator, the person who organized the search party starting at 7:00 a.m., then she took Zee and headed to the trailhead to meet up with Quincy and Fields.

"So," Sun said to Zee as they drove back through the mountain pass toward Ravinder land.

Zee's hair had been pulled back into a tight bun, emphasizing her wide eyes and shapely cheekbones.

"We've known each other for a while, right?"

"Yes, ma'am," she said, her tone wary.

"So, don't take this the wrong way, and I apologize if this sounds sexist, but with your looks and your body, why did you become a sniper for the Bernalillo County Sheriff's Office when you could have been a supermodel?"

Zee laughed out loud. "I could ask you the same thing, Blondie."

"Please."

"I don't know. It was just something I'd always wanted to do."

"Kill people from a safe distance?"

Another chuckle. "Keep people safe from a safe distance. I wanted to be the one they called in when all else failed, you know? I'm not sure you would have hired me had you known this, but when I started, I wanted to be a hero."

Sun understood that all too well. She pulled down her visor when they turned into a low-hanging sun, only a couple of hours away from dipping under the horizon. "What happened?"

"What do you mean?"

"Everyone in law enforcement has their reasons for signing up. For many, it's a desire for control. For power. For some, it's a desire to solve a puzzle. To bring bad guys to justice."

"And for you?" she asked.

Sun cracked a sly smile. "I wanted to keep people safe, too."

"Okay, then what happened to you to make you want to keep people safe?"

"Hmmm, that would be a story for another day."

They pulled in behind the Yellow Jacket, which was an ancient pickup the size of a remote-control car.

"Are we going up?" Zee asked, wondering if she should change into her hiking boots and parka.

"It doesn't look promising." She stepped out of the cruiser.

"Hey, sis," Quincy said. He'd been leaning against the Tonka truck.

Zee waved, and Fields just stared.

"Did Levi see you?" Sun asked Quincy.

Fields shoved him. "Like he was a lighthouse on a clear night."

Quincy raked a hand down his face. "That man is not normal. He spotted a deer mouse under a patch of leaves at ten yards. Then went on to tell us it was too small and what that meant for the area and how it was responding to its environment and the deforestation happening a few hundred miles to the north and how it was all tied together."

"His family cooked hooch in these mountains for decades," Sun said. "They had to know that kind of thing."

"Well, he's up there with that cracked cousin of his. I don't know how, though. It's slick and steep." He lifted his boots and checked the tread as though that were the problem.

Fields scanned the area, craning his neck to check out the clouds overhead. "We're going to have to wait until tomorrow. We tried to get a helicopter in here, but the storm's coming in. It's supposed to clear out by midnight, though, and warm up in the morning. Might melt some of this snow."

Sun agreed reluctantly. "In the meantime, there's a teenage boy wandering around lost." It broke her heart.

"Not to mention a teenage girl," Zee said, "possibly kidnapped and being held in these woods."

"We can look if you'd like, boss," Quincy said. "I'm game."

"No. You go home. Get some rest. We have a couple of dozen volunteers showing up first thing tomorrow morning. I need you fresh and warm and"—she stepped closer to her near-frozen chief deputy—"less blue."

Zee laughed and punched him on the arm. They would make beautiful babies someday if Quincy didn't fuck it up.

"I'll get back in time to pick up Auri from school, drop her off at the empty nesters', then head over to the Quick-Mart."

Quincy gave her a thumbs-up. "Fingers crossed their security cameras actually work."

She grabbed a pen and paper out of her cruiser and walked to Levi's truck. It was locked, of course, and the storm would probably make the ink run, but she left a note on the windshield, telling him about the search party and to let her know if they found Jimmy.

After walking back to the cruiser, she turned to look at the mountain. She should have found the snow-covered trees beautiful, the sun glistening through them stunning, but today, she found the scene treacherous. Deadly. An obstacle she didn't want to take on.

12

*One shot of our espresso, and you'll
be able to thread a sewing machine.
While it's running.*

—SIGN AT CAFFEINE-WAH

Sun pulled into the parking lot later than she'd hoped. Most of the kids had already gone home. Those that hadn't were standing around, waiting for their rides or bus, shivering. A fresh helping of snow had been promised, but it was getting colder. Almost too cold to snow.

She put the cruiser in park, then looked across the smattering of students for a head of bright copper. Having no luck, she texted her offspring. "I'm in the parking lot. I got back earlier than I thought I would, so I'm here instead of Grandma. Did she pick you up, anyway? After I texted her that I'd be here? Because I wouldn't put it past her."

When she didn't get a response, she started to worry. Not bad. Just a faint uneasiness in the back of her mind.

She grabbed her phone to text again when a knock sounded on her window.

She lowered it to a pretty blonde with a round face. "Are you Auri's mom?"

The faint uneasiness catapulted into near panic. "Yes," she said, making sure her interior turmoil did not leech to her exterior.

"Hi!"

Sun flinched at the girl's enthusiasm but kept her cool.

"I'm Auri's friend Chastity. We have athletics together. But there were some girls teasing her in class."

Sun's calm exterior evaporated. "Teasing her?"

"Yeah. Just being jerks. You know the kind."

"Unfortunately, I do."

"She took off down the street." Chastity pointed past the school and toward the center of the village, which was the opposite direction of their apartment.

Then it hit her. Damn. It meant Auri had had a worse day than she'd expected.

"Thank you, Chastity."

The girl beamed at her. "No, ma'am. Thank you."

Having no idea what the blonde was thanking her for, Sun threw her cruiser into drive and headed toward Town Square.

She pulled into the parking lot and up to the memorial that sat in front of city hall. Auri sat on the side of a memorial fountain. A fountain dedicated to Samson Elio Vicram, Auri's father for all intents and purposes, as well as other soldiers the town had lost in military combat, some going all the way back to World War I.

But the memorial itself was mostly in memoriam of Samson.

Sun sat beside her daughter, who'd cleared off a spot for her on the fountain when she saw her walking up.

"Hey, Mom," she said as though she hadn't a care in the world.

"Hey, bug bite. I was worried your grandmother forgot and picked you up, but then this extremely happy blonde—"

"Chastity."

"Yes, Chastity told me you'd walked toward Town Square."

"Yeah, I just wanted to get out. Get some fresh air."

"Thirty degrees is pretty fresh."

"I guess."

"How bad was it?"

"What?"

"The teasing."

Auri wilted. "Not bad. I'll probably never live it down, and I'll need a lot of therapy, but all in all, not bad."

Sun nodded, wondering how she of all people had raised such a horrible liar.

"How's your dad?" She turned and looked at the gorgeous memorial the town had put up after Sun's husband was killed in Afghanistan barely one month after they got married.

The artist had carved an image into the sandstone pillar, three circles interlinked. Underneath was a bunch of gibberish about Samson being a son of Del Sol even though he hadn't been from the town, and then a list of all the sons Del Sol had lost. Legitimate sons. Sons who deserved the monument much more than her husband had.

Sun had barely looked at it during the dedication. Hadn't even noticed the image when it was first erected, and only took note after walking to and from the courthouse for this reason or that.

But Auri had come here often. Sun's parents had told her that Auri would come to the memorial several times each summer and talk to her dad. It both warmed her heart and weighed it down.

"He's good. He says hi."

She laughed softly. "Well, tell him hi back. So, everything is okay?"

Auri shrugged. "Of course."

"The whole narc thing just blew over?"

"I guess. Nobody's said anything about it."

"You know, you could tell me if they did."

"My boots are ruined," she said, changing the subject. She picked up one foot. It had mud on it from her walk.

"Oh no." Sun inspected the boot and then said, "I don't think three tiny spots of mud constitutes ruination, but we can have them cleaned."

"No, it's okay. I'll see what I can do."

Sun drew in a deep breath. It was back. The wall Auri constructed whenever she worried she was becoming a burden. Most kids loved being burdens. Reveled in it. Counted on it to get their way on multiple occasions. But not this little morsel of moxie. Nugget of nerve. Princess of pluck.

It was the red hair. Sun knew it down to her bones. That red soaked into her brain and set it on fire. And Sun would have it no other way.

"Well, if you're done shivering, you ready to go to Grandma and Grandpa's?"

"Can I order pizza?" she asked after a quick hit off her inhaler.

"As long as it has something with an actual vitamin on it."

"Cheese has vitamins."

Sun laughed and walked her daughter to the cruiser arm in arm.

She dropped Auri off and gave her mother the signal. The look she only gave her when Auri was in a bad place but didn't want anyone to know. They'd been through a lot with her when she was younger. They'd perfected that look and the many devious ways in which to send it with Auri none the wiser.

Elaine's lids rounded, but Sun followed up the look with the shake. A quick, almost imperceptible shake of the head that let the other one know to stay quiet. For now.

Elaine pursed her lips, but complied.

After a quick trip to the apartment to change into something more comfortable, basically still her uniform but a khaki shirt and jeans with her badge attached to the belt, she donned her official bomber jacket and headed out. She grabbed a burrito from the Kachina Kitchen and headed back to the station.

Salazar had procured the surveillance footage from the Quick-Mart for the date of the receipt Sun had found under the tree. She was impressed. These situations could get sticky. It was amazing how much a regular joe did *not* want to assist in an investigation, especially if it consisted of them getting off their stools behind the cash register and hunting through surveillance footage.

Sometimes it took a little extra assertiveness to convince them to do their civic duty. Threats also worked. But Salazar was about as threatening as a bunny rabbit dressed in pink.

With the swing shift in full force, Sun sat down at her desk and reviewed the footage. An older male, judging by his gait, tall and painfully thin wearing a dark jacket, baseball cap, and sunglasses. And he bought an energy drink. He paid cash. It was a nail-biter. A real edge-of-the-seater. Then he walked out.

Unfortunately, the cameras outside were not working, so they didn't get a description of the vehicle he drove.

She checked the records they sent over for every gas purchase in case the guy filled up and wrote down the names for Anita to cross-check with the parameters set.

"Burrito," Zee said.

"Want some?" Sun asked, inviting her into the office with a wave.

"Nah. Just signing off. What do you got?"

"Surveillance footage."

"Fun." She stepped closer. "Want me to run those names?"

"Nope. I need you fresh tomorrow, too."

"I don't mind."

Sun grinned at her. "I know." Zee started to leave, when Sun stopped her. "Are you sorry you took this job yet?"

"Please." She waved a dismissive hand. "I love this weird little town. And I'm thinking about asking Doug out."

"The flasher? I heard he's a great kisser."

"I bet he is."

"So," Sun said, hedging a subject that did not need to be hedged, "you and Quincy."

"Ew. We're siblings. Twins, even. How can you . . . ? Why

would you . . . ? He is cute, though." Her dark skin practically glowed with appreciation.

"He is, and he's one of the good ones, but if you tell him I said that, I'll seek revenge. I'm not above threatening you with a grapefruit spoon."

"They make spoons for grapefruit?"

"They do. They're really cool. Serrated."

"Nice. Welp, off to get my beauty rest."

"Wait," Sun said, leaning closer to the computer screen.

"Okay."

The problem with surveillance cameras were they usually had horrible resolution. This footage was no exception, so it took a minute to figure out what she was seeing. "Check this out."

Zee leaned down. "What are we looking at?"

"Okay, this is the guy who bought the energy drink."

She raised her brows in surprise. "Wow. Older than I'd thought."

"Right? It would have taken someone younger to pull off the abduction. Getting a fourteen-year-old through a window without making a sound?"

"He had to have drugged her, but even with that in mind—"

"Exactly," Sun said. "It would have taken a lot of strength to get her out of that window and to carry her to a waiting vehicle, which had to be out of range of the St. Aubins' cameras."

"True, and look." Zee pointed. "He's limping."

"He could be faking it, but I don't think so. Look what he does next."

In the corner of the screen, almost out of camera range, the man tossed the receipt into the trash can.

Zee stood back. "No way. Our one and only lead was planted?"

"Son of a bitch." Sun wanted to say much worse, but held back. "Anyone could have accessed that trash can. We need the footage of it for the rest of the day, until it was dumped."

"Even then, they could have gotten it out of the Dumpster out back."

"Motherfucker," she said, going for the gold. "Price!"

The bespectacled deputy Lonnie Price appeared at her door instantly.

"Get over to the Quick-Mart. I want the records of every single purchase made in that store for the last two days, starting after this one." She handed him a copy of the receipt. "And I want all the footage."

"You got it, Sheriff."

He left, and Zee sat in the seat across from her. "You okay?"

"We're being played, I just can't figure out what's real and what isn't."

"The letter?"

She nodded. "It's Sybil's handwriting. I checked it against the diary."

"Do you think this is all a ploy of some kind?"

Sun sat back and raked her fingers through her hair, dislodging thick locks from her already frayed French braid. "I wish I knew, but we certainly can't let that doubt taint our investigation."

Zee stood to walk out.

"Right, sorry," Sun said, having kept her. "Thanks, and I'll see you in the morning."

After a soft laugh, Zee shrugged into her jacket and said, "Oh, I'm not leaving. Well, I am, but I'm going to be right back. Caffeine-Wah. Place your order now, or I'm coming back with an iced caramel almond milk macchiato."

"Oh, god no." When Zee grinned at her in question, she said, "Real milk. And make it hot."

"You got it, Sheriff."

Under the guise of changing clothes, Auri went to the apartment and, well, changed clothes. But she also snuck onto her mother's computer and logged on to the sheriff's database. A place she definitely should not be logged on to.

She ran checks on everyone she knew for certain was in Sybil's life, including her parents. Well, at this point, pretty much only her parents. Besides a couple of speeding tickets—Mrs. St. Aubin liked to go fast—nothing in the couple's past would indicate any type of abusive behavior.

That didn't let either off the hook completely, but it went a long way in helping Auri feel better about their possible involvement in her disappearance.

Before she logged off her mother's computer, she decided to do one more check. She'd promised Principal Jacobs she wouldn't try to hack their system again, but she had no intention of trying. She had every intention of succeeding.

"Auri?" Her grandmother opened the front door.

Auri shot out of her mother's room carrying a sweater. "Found it! Mom is always stealing my stuff," she said, pulling it over her head as she walked. "Now if I could just find my other boots."

Elaine exchanged a knowing look with Auri and giggled. "Your mother did the same thing to me. Pizza's here when you're hungry."

"Thanks, Grandma!" she said, dropping to her hands and knees and pretending to search under her bed.

"Don't be too long. It'll get cold."

"Okay." Poor thing had no idea it was better that way.

The older woman left Auri to her guilt-ridden thoughts—she hated lying, especially to her grandma—and hurried back to her mother's computer.

"Bingo," she whispered when she made it in successfully. Her success had nothing to do with the fact that, while she was trying to steal Sybil's records, she'd accidentally stumbled upon the password. Nothing whatsoever.

Biting her bottom lip, she typed in the name she'd been burning to know more about: Cruz De los Santos. His school records popped up instantly, and his picture . . . a picture that was nothing short of breathtaking. Full, mischievous mouth. Straight, defined nose. Black eyelashes thicker than her mom's oatmeal. So, really thick.

If they'd had a printer hooked up, she would've printed a copy. Because that wasn't creepy. Or underhanded. Or frowned upon in most states.

His grades were pretty much what she'd expected. Bs and Cs for the most part with a few As sprinkled in for good measure. He was more than smart enough to get straight As. At the same time, he didn't seem particularly interested in impressing anyone, so why not squeak by?

But she wasn't looking for his grades. That was none of her business, she told herself after she'd scoured his entire public-school career. She only wanted his address.

She'd tried texting him several times since she'd gotten home, but he'd never answered, and they had a report to do. Or so she told herself to justify her despicable behavior.

She jotted the address down, cleared the search history, and logged off. There was one more component to all this snooping. If her mother just happened to see what times she'd logged on and realized she hadn't logged on at that particular time, but what were the odds of that?

Thirty minutes and four pieces of pizza later, Auri looked at her grandparents as they watched the news. They were really, really into the news. She swallowed her last bite and said, "So, I have a school project."

They both gave her their full attention. They were kind of awesome that way.

"And I have to interview another student and do a report."

"Really? Who?"

"Oh, you don't know him. His name is Cruz. Cruz De los Santos."

The couple cast sideways glances at each other as though in cahoots over something. "We know his dad," her grandma said. "Such a great guy."

"He's a mechanic," Grandpa said, like that explained everything. "Guy could rebuild a Hemi in a hurricane."

"He certainly sounds talented. So, I was wondering if I could take the car to his house to work on our project."

They stared at her a minute, then burst out laughing. "And just when did you get your license?"

"You used to let Mom drive when she was almost fifteen."

"Sweetheart," Grandma said, not patronizingly at all, "there is a difference between our letting her take the car and her taking it. Your mother didn't actually have permission the one time she decided to wreak havoc on society before she actually had a license to do so."

A wave of shock vibrated through Auri. "My mother broke the law?"

Grandpa chuckled. "Stole that sucker right out from under our noses."

"Our sleeping noses," Grandma corrected.

Auri clasped her hands together over her heart. "This is the best thing I've ever heard all day."

They laughed out loud. "Now, don't go getting us in trouble," they said, almost simultaneously.

"Never."

Her grandpa lifted a shaggy brow. "That being said, if you're game, I can drive you over."

Her emotions skyrocketed. She jumped up, ready to go. Almost. "Thanks, Grandpa! I'll get my things and meet you in the car!"

She heard her grandmother say, "I think she's in a hurry."

"I meant to tell you," she said, growing anxious, "I'm not actually sure he's home. I can't get ahold of him. We have the rest of the week to do this project, but I wanted to get a jump on it."

Cruz didn't exactly throw her a kiss goodbye when they'd parted ways after sixth period. He'd looked at her oddly. Then again, he looked at her oddly all the time. She could never tell what he was thinking.

"No worries, sweetness. It's not like it's a long drive."

He was right there. They found the place in about four minutes, a white house with blue trim.

She drew in a deep breath and got out of the car.

Her grandpa got out as well. "I'll just make sure it's okay, then you can call me when you're ready to come home. I'll be here in a jiff."

"Thanks, Grandpa."

He looked up at the ever-darkening sky. "That storm is going to hit soon, so you might hurry."

"I will. I'm sorry to do this to you."

Her favorite grandpa in the world stopped and turned her to face him. "Your grandmother and I are beside ourselves with excitement that you two moved back here. I will drive you wherever I can whenever I can. You just say the word. I am now the official Auri Vicram chauffeur. I am yours to command." He did a silly bow that made Auri giggle.

"Can you drive me to my next mani-pedi?"

"When do we leave?"

She laughed again and wrapped her arms around his chest. He drew her into a deep hug, then they walked to the porch arm in arm and rang the bell. A light blinked off and on inside the house, and Auri couldn't fathom why.

A thin wood door opened, and Cruz stood on the other side. He didn't seem at all surprised to see her. Or happy about it.

"Hey," she said.

He nodded a greeting, then looked at her grandpa.

"Oh, this is my grandpa, Cyrus Freyr."

Cruz opened the door wider and took his hand. "We've met. This summer. And my dad works on his car sometimes."

"He sure does. Guy could rebuild a—"

"—Hemi in a hurricane," Auri finished for him.

Cruz chuckled softly. "Yes, he can. Want to come in?"

"Oh no," Grandpa said, "I'll just leave Auri here while you work, if that's okay?" He glanced at her. "You can call when you're ready for your mani-pedi?"

Auri suddenly realized they didn't actually make plans. She didn't actually get permission to crash Cruz's life. "If you're busy, we can—"

"I'm not busy," he rushed to say. "We have to do it. May as well get it done."

At first, Auri soared with his willingness to spend time with her, but with his next words, she wondered if he wanted to get the project finished to be over with her. "Okay, well great." She turned back to her grandpa. "I'll call you?"

"My dad could take her home if you don't want to get out again. It's up to you."

"Only if it's not a bother."

"I'll call either way," Auri said.

He gave her another quick hug and headed to his crossover while Cruz ushered her inside.

The house was cozy and warm with a lit fireplace and throws on the sofa and love seat.

"This is nice," she said.

He offered her a playful smirk. "No, it's not. But it works."

A man walked in then, carrying a plate of food and a beer. Tall like Cruz and almost as handsome.

"Hi," she said softly, holding out her hand even though his were full. "I'm Auri."

He put the beer down, took her hand and smiled, then turned to Cruz.

Cruz signed what she said, finger-spelling her name. She recognized that much. And humiliation washed over her. Cruz was fluent in ASL, and the lamp flickered when they rang the doorbell. It didn't take a genius to figure out someone in his family was probably deaf.

When she realized her cheeks had warmed substantially, they warmed even more and she worried they'd catch her hair on fire. Hair engulfed in flames was not a good look for anyone.

"Hi," Cruz said, interpreting for his dad. "I'm Chris. You're new, right?"

She smiled. "Yes. We just moved back."

"Your mom is the new sheriff. I was so glad she won," Chris said as Cruz interpreted, making the most charming face. "I voted for her."

Auri beamed at him. "Thank you."

"We have a school project to work on. Is that okay?"

The man narrowed his eyes on his son, then agreed. He signed something really fast, and Cruz said, "Okay, fine."

They walked past him and to Cruz's room.

"What did your dad say?"

Cruz was busy picking up clothes and tossing them into a hamper. He moved a pile of books so she could sit at his desk. "He told me I'm still grounded until the stars burn out."

"Oh. Wow. That sucks. What happened?"

"Nothing. A fight. Not even a fight. An almost fight. It's all good."

"An almost fight? Who'd you almost fight?" Then she remembered the kid in the hall. "Oh yeah. That kid from this morning. You weren't suspended."

"The kid told Jacobs we weren't fighting."

"Were you?"

He shrugged and sat on the edge of his bed. He'd been watching TV in his room with the captions on.

"Do you always watch TV with the captions on?"

He lifted a shoulder. "I got used to it. Dad thinks it helped me learn to read at such an early age."

"Really? How old were you?"

"Is that part of the interview?" He seemed almost as uncomfortable as she was.

Embarrassed, she took out her notebook. "It's a great hook. Especially with how incredible your poetry is."

"You a writer or something?"

"I want to be. Or a detective like my mom. Or a brain surgeon."

He didn't smile when she said it.

"I'm just kidding. The last thing I want to do is play with people's brains."

"So, no zombie apocalypse for you."

She giggled as the tension in the room eased. "I'm sorry I didn't call first. I mean, I tried."

"Yeah, still grounded."

"Oh." She shook her head. "I thought—"

"That I was ghosting you?"

"Something like that." Of course, one had to be dating or in some kind of relationship prior to being ghosted to actually be ghosted, but she didn't point that out.

He got up and walked out of the room, only to come back with a bottle of baby oil.

She gaped at him. "Um, I don't know what you think is going to happen here, but—"

"You have pizza sauce."

Once again, her cheeks heated to the red-hot level of habanero salsa.

He took a tissue and poured some baby oil on it, then leaned in, his face barely inches from hers, and wiped at the corners of her mouth.

She closed her eyes, both humiliated and intrigued, and let him. While his touch on her face was gentle, soothing, it was his other touch, his left hand on her knee, that sent tendrils of electricity lacing through her body.

He pulled the tissue back and showed her the red streaks. "All gone."

"Um, thanks, but why baby oil?"

He shrugged. "Pizza sauce is very acidic. And your lips are already chapped."

Embarrassed yet again, she covered her mouth with a hand, but he didn't notice. He got a clean tissue, poured another couple of drops, then lifted it to her face again. When she didn't lower her hand, he tugged it off her face and ran the tissue over her lips, the act feather soft.

His coffee-colored eyes studied her as he did it, and a warmth she hadn't expected flooded every cell in her body. Then she noticed a scar on his arm.

She took his hand to maneuver his arm for a better look.

He pulled it back, and said softly, "Stop."

She leaned away from him. "I'm sorry." She stood and grabbed her backpack. "I'm . . . I should go."

He stood, too, and put a hand on her arm. "Please, don't."

"Look, if you're mad at me, just say so."

"Mad? Why would I be mad at you?"

She really had no answer. "Be . . . cause."

He stared at her a long moment, spending an inordinate amount of time on her mouth, before saying, "Great reason."

"I thought so."

"Look," he said, sitting on the bed again, "I don't always have the best social skills. I was raised in the deaf world. Their cultural norms are a little different from the hearing world's."

She sat at the desk again. "That is the coolest thing anyone has ever said to me."

Smothering his confused expression, he asked, "Their cultural norms are a little different?"

"No, that you were raised in the deaf world. That's just so cool."

He cast her a soft scowl of doubt.

"Of course, that's easy for me to say. As an outsider looking in. It must be challenging."

"In some ways, it is."

"Is your mom deaf, too?"

He stood and grabbed his backpack off the floor beside her. "No, she was hearing."

"Was?"

"Yeah, she died a few years ago."

"I'm so sorry, Cruz. I didn't know."

"And I'm sorry about your dad."

"Thanks," she said, genuinely appreciating his thoughtfulness.

Cruz tossed a notebook on the bed beside him along with a couple of textbooks and an unopened box of pens.

But it was the notebook she was most interested in. "So, any poetry in there?"

Without even looking at her, he took the notebook and put it on a shelf behind him. "Nope."

"Can I read some?"

He stopped unpacking his things but still kept his gaze averted. "I don't think that would be a good idea."

"Why? You're incredible."

"I'm a hack. Just like everyone else at Del Sol."

She held out her hand. "Can I be the judge of that?"

He chewed on his lower lip, then said, "No, but if I ever get to that point, you'll be the first I tell."

Disappointment washed over her, but she understood. It took courage to open yourself up to criticism. "Deal." Then, to lighten the mood, she brought out the homework assignment. "Okay, do you or have you ever stolen a candy bar from a grocery store?"

"No," he said. "It was gummy bears, and it was at a gas station."

She laughed, and thus the interviews began.

13

*Several callers complained about thongs
hanging from an eighty-five-year-old female's apple tree.
When questioned, she explained,
"It was either the apple tree or the azalea bush."*

—DEL SOL POLICE BLOTTER

While Price was out collecting the information from the Quick-Mart, Zee brought Sun her macchiato, then went to her desk to study every inch of the footage they had thus far.

Sun studied the letter. Again. Like she didn't have it memorized. Then she opened the diary and started on page one.

Sybil was so innocent. Too young to prophesy her own death. No wonder she was so shy. So withdrawn. She didn't know who to trust.

There were entries other than her premonition, as well. She liked a boy named Chase in the fifth grade. She loved *The Big Bang Theory* and wondered why people couldn't mention *Star Wars* and *Star Trek* in the same sentence without infuriating a certain percentage of the population. And she loved—

Sun looked closer. She loved a girl named Auri like a sister for making her feel seen. In a sea of invisibility, Auri made Sybil feel special.

Sun's chest swelled.

She went back to Sybil's accounts of the dream. "Come on, Sybil. Give me something new. Anything." But the girl had been right. It was just more of the same. The dream never changed. She never saw the guy. Never knew why he took her. She only knew how she would die. And when.

Sun made notes about any changes in the girl's story, no matter how subtle. But they were mainly expansions in her vocabulary. She began calling it an *abduction* instead of a *kidnapping*. And using the word *male* instead of *man*. *Caucasian* instead of *white*.

A male voice drifted to her from her office door. "Nobody told me you talk to yourself."

She looked up at U.S. Marshal Vincent Deleon. "Nobody told me you eavesdropped, but here we are."

He chuckled and stepped inside. "That the diary?"

"You've heard about it?"

"Who hasn't?"

"Great," she said, wielding sarcasm like she was born to. "It'll probably be on the news tomorrow."

"Not necessarily. Your deputies are pros."

"True. How was your day?"

He gestured toward one of the chairs across from her. "May I?"

"Of course."

He sat and stretched before answering, "Two possible sightings. One was from a cat lady who swore he was living in her attic."

"Oh no. Mrs. Fairborn?"

"The one and only. We got excited for all of five minutes until we realized she didn't have an attic. Her Pueblo-style house had a sparkling new pitched roof, but not enough of a pitch for an attic."

"And it took you five minutes to realize that?"

"What?" he asked, defensive. "We were desperate."

"Don't feel bad. She's the town sympathizer. Tries to help out where she can. She confesses to everything from shoplifting to murder, because she's worried the sheriff's office won't be able to solve the crimes and she doesn't want us to look bad."

"How do you know? You just started."

"She's been doing it since I was a kid. I caught on when she claimed to be the hijacker of a Piper pilot's plane who took off and never came back."

"What happened with the case?"

"His wife finally hunted him down. He was in Fiji with his girlfriend. But Mrs. Fairborn was bound and determined to take credit for that one. Said she'd gotten into the drug-running business and she forced poor old Larry, the owner of the plane, into the thug life." Sun burst out laughing. "Her words. I swear."

He put a hand over his eyes while he laughed, then sobered and said, "Makes a mean cup of tea, though."

"That she does. And the second?"

"We thought we had a legitimate sighting from some kids who'd been playing at the lake."

"With their parents, I hope."

"Yeah, I guess they were ice-skating."

"That lake doesn't get a thick enough ice cap to skate on. Those parents should know that."

"Well, we knocked on their door, but the mother said she'd never seen him. And that her kids tended to embellish."

She took a moment to admire his strong jaw and warm eyes. He let her. "Most kids do. So, nothing solid?"

"Other than the guy who called it in, no." He stood and closed the door, and Sun grew a little wary. Zee was the only other deputy in the station at the moment. Price was still at the Quick-Mart. "It's strange," the marshal said.

"Your face? It's not that bad." She said it before realizing what she'd done. Had she flirted? Actually flirted? She never flirted with other law enforcement officials. It was the one rule she'd never broken in all her years as a patrol officer and then a detective.

And boy, did she get flirted with. She just never returned the favor and had proudly earned the title of Ice Queen. Because women who didn't succumb to men's whimsy were obviously cold, heartless bitches.

He raised his brandy-colored gaze to hers, the one that held both surprise and appreciation. "Well, thank you, but no. A couple of the residents we talked to were lying."

It was her turn to be surprised. "How do you know?"

His expression went flat. "Really?"

He had a point. "Okay, who was lying?"

"I got a weird feeling from the mom, and she wouldn't let me talk to the kids directly, which I found odd."

"Agreed."

"And then there was another woman who almost fainted when we showed her the picture and asked her if she'd seen Rojas."

Concern prickled along her skin.

"She said her name was Wanda Oxley?"

Wanda Oxley. The Book Babes had a Wanda Stephanopoulos who was in love with Quincy and a Karen Oxley who was, well, also in love with Quincy, but there was no Wanda Oxley that she knew of.

"I don't know a Wanda Oxley. Can you describe her?"

"Yeah, about yay high." He held up his hand, but the height he indicated was much taller than Wanda or Karen. "Curvy. Hispanic. Hair done up nice like in a beauty salon."

Darlene Tapia. She'd gotten a strange vibe from her that morning, too. That time, alarm shot through her. Could the fugitive be staked out at her house? Was she in trouble?

But if that were the case, why would he have let her go to the book club meeting?

"Sorry," Sun said, chewing on her bottom lip. "I'm not sure who you're talking about."

He sank down in the chair and watched her. "Isn't there one decent liar in the whole town?"

"I beg your pardon," she said, taken aback. "I have played poker with champions. I can lie. Trust me."

"Did you win?"

"So not the point."

He chuckled. "You going to tell me what's going on?"

She ran her pen over her mouth in thought. "Can I get back to you on that?"

"Sheriff, I don't think I need to remind you—"

"You don't. I just need to check into something."

"Okay, fine. I can let it slide for the moment, but I want the story in return."

Sun raised a brow. "The story?"

"The one about how you single-handedly brought a killer to justice. I want the real story."

"Please. It's like I always say, nothing in law enforcement is single-handed."

"Pulling the modest card?"

"I'm not that kind of girl."

He steepled his fingers. "Okay, here's what I've heard. You ignored your captain's orders and continued to work a murder case you'd been taken off of. Even though her body was found outside of Santa Fe, you believed she was killed in Albuquerque, where she was going to school."

"I did believe that, yes."

"You had a hunch, so you went back to what you considered the true crime scene, even though the body was found in another city entirely, and questioned the students in the dorms one more time."

"That part's true, too. But in my defense—"

"And you just happened to ask the right guy the right question on the right night, when he was least expecting it, thus catching him off guard."

"The guilty always show their hand eventually. Also, I was dressed like a sorority girl during rush week. He wasn't expecting to be interrogated."

"Was it rush week?"

"No. But he wasn't the fraternity type. He had no idea."

"And then, what? You could tell by his reaction he'd killed the girl?"

She let out a long, annoyed sigh. "Yes. I could tell by his reaction he'd killed the girl."

"The next part gets a little murky. You hit him first or he hit you?"

"Dude, are you with IA?" That was the last thing she needed. A run-in with internal affairs.

"Please. They wish I was with IA. Who hit first?"

"He did. He panicked. Apparently, you were right. My poker face sucks. He figured out I knew he'd killed his classmate about a split second after I realized it myself. But what did he do?" She stood up and began pacing. "Did he slam the door and lock it? Did he run? No, he dragged me inside his dorm room to kill me, too." She gaped at him. "I mean, who does that?"

Deleon laughed softly, then asked, "So, you got the upper hand—"

She sat back down. "Only because he'd been chopping vegetables and he'd just cut himself pretty bad, so he was already wounded."

"—kicked his ass up one side and down the other—"

"Only because he just kept coming back for more. I would've stopped otherwise."

"—and ended up handcuffing him to you and dragging him to the nearest police station."

Sun thought back. "Yep. That pretty much covers it."

"So, you dragged an unconscious man five blocks instead of taking him to campus PD?"

"I'd just been in a bar brawl, metaphorically speaking. I wasn't thinking clearly."

He doubled over laughing. Sun watched him. Still annoyed.

"What did the desk sergeant say?"

"I don't remember exactly, but he put in his report that we

were both so bloody, we looked like we'd just stepped out of an '80s horror film."

"I bet," he said, wiping his eyes. "I gotta ask. You know I have to ask."

She raised a brow, waiting with bated breath.

He leaned closer to the desk and said, "What was the question?"

She crossed her arms. "I'm not sure you're worthy."

"Oh, I'm more than worthy. Would you like me to prove it? Maybe over drinks?"

Taken aback for the second time that evening, it was her turn to recline in her chair and give some thought to the situation at hand. But before she got too far, a knock sounded at the door.

"Come in," she said, straightening in her chair.

Agent Fields stepped inside, took one look at the marshal, and asked Sun, "Are you busy?"

"Nope. Join the party."

He grinned. "Have you eaten?"

"I just had a burrito."

"Good." He walked in carrying a bottle of moonshine and two glasses. "You do not want to drink this on an empty stomach. I can get another glass, if you're game," he said to Deleon.

The man let out a long sigh, then said, "Nah. We're helping with the search tomorrow, since we're in town and our fugitive could be involved." He turned to Sun. "See you then?"

"Sure. Sleep well."

He started to leave, but just couldn't do it. He turned back to her. "I gotta know."

She grinned. "I looked past him and asked him if he didn't know Sherry Berkley, why did he have her underwear hanging from his mirror."

He chuckled, waved to Fields, and took off.

"That sounded interesting," Fields said when Deleon was out of earshot.

"Not really." She returned to the diary.

"Good job today."

She stopped reading, this time to admire the sharp angles and steely gray eyes of the almost-silver fox in front of her.

He poured two fingers into each glass.

"Yeah," Sun said, wary again, "no offense, but that stuff is 100 proof. If I drank that much, you'd have to carry me home."

The humorous grin that spread across his face stopped her heart. For a few seconds, anyway. "That can be arranged."

"And what did I do that was so special? Besides get run down by a Mercedes, that is. And get threatened by a mayor who hates me. And eat muffins I'm pretty sure were cursed."

"Well, you found several pertinent clues in a missing persons case. You managed to figure out we are being toyed with by someone who knows what he's doing, thus you came up with a basic profile of our suspect. And you believed a girl who wrote a letter predicting her own death when no one else would've given it a second thought, which either makes you a genius detective or just as loopy as the girl."

"Since you put it that way." She took the glass, clinked it against his, and took a cautious sip. Then promptly coughed into her hand, and said in a strained voice, "That's . . . really smooth."

He chuckled and sat in the chair Deleon had warmed.

"Oh, I forgot. I don't know if you're aware of this, but there's a bona fide moonshine named after you."

She scoffed lightly. "I've heard. But I have to disagree."

"Okay, but it's hard to deny it." He turned the bottle until she could read the label. It was definitely one of Levi's. It had the Dark River Shine logo, a skeleton cleverly disguised in the clouds of a New Mexico landscape, but the name of that particular recipe was called Sun Shine by Dark River.

She sat bewildered for a few seconds, then laughed it off. "Not likely. The guy who started the company is not a fan."

Fields watched her for a minute, then said, "That's not what I hear."

It took everything in her, every ounce of strength she possessed, not to jump over her desk, grab him by the collar, and beat more information out of him.

First off, it would've been horridly unprofessional. Second, getting her hopes up only to have them crushed by the devastating realization that Levi did, in fact, despise her would be just a bit much to bear at that moment. She'd had a rough day.

But if she were honest, she'd been glued to her phone, hoping he would use the number she'd written on the note she put on his truck and call. To tell her he'd found Jimmy, yes, but it was more than that, and she knew it.

"Okay," he said, downing the last of his drink, "I'm going to take off."

She raised a brow. "On foot, I hope."

"Absolutely."

She put the lid on the bottle and handed it to him.

He held up a hand. "You keep it."

"Oh no, that's—"

"No, I insist. But look a little closer at the label."

When he left, she turned the bottle into the light, not really sure what he was talking about. Then she saw it. A face. A profile, actually, of a blond woman, her hair covering most of her face as she smiled.

The image was so transparent as to almost be nonexistent. Yet it was there. And she recognized it. Rightfully so, since it was an image of her.

Quincy had taken the photograph in high school as part of an art project called Friends. He'd put it in a collage but then drew the collage on watercolor board and painted it, and it won a blue ribbon at the state fair. Soon after, however, the actual collage from which he'd created it went missing.

Sun ran her fingers over the image. It was like she was a ghost.

Is that how he felt about her? A ghost from his past? Not that they'd ever really had one, but . . .

Either way, the use of that image was illegal on several levels and employed with a callous disregard for her privacy and mental well-being.

She loved it.

She grabbed her cell and looked up the number of an old flame. Well, an old flame in her eyes. She'd been in love with him since she was ten. But since he was married at the time, and the sheriff of Del Sol, any relationship with her would've been frowned upon. And resulted in prison time.

"Hey, handsome," she said.

He let out a loud sigh. "I knew you'd hunt me down eventually, gorgeous, but on your first day?"

Royce Womack was a burly biker in his sixties who'd run this town with an iron fist and a deep laugh. He was sheriff for decades until he retired and a man named Herbert Kornel took over the post, much to Royce's dismay. He currently spent his days running an incredibly successful, all things considered, rehab center called RISE.

Sun had fallen in love with him the first time she'd met him, probably because he'd pulled her out of the lake after she'd decided to swallow half of it. There was something about a man saving her life. Carrying her to the banks in his arms. Pumping her stomach until twelve gallons of water came out. It left an impression.

And he was there when she woke up in the hospital seven years later, even though it was well out of his jurisdiction. He'd held her when she cried. For three hours.

"I know. I know," she said. "But it's been a busy day."

"It's okay. Happens every time."

"Oh yeah? What happens every time?"

Sun could tell by the tone of his voice he was about to hand her an overflowing load of BS. "Every time a hot, young sheriff blows into town, digs in her heels, and swears to clean up the place, she falls in love with me. Every damn time."

She didn't even try to fight the grin that commandeered her face. "And how many hot, young sheriffs blow into town? You know, ballpark."

"Thus far, just the one, but that one proves my point. One hot, young sheriff blew into town, and one hot, young sheriff fell in love with me. It was inevitable, I guess. Numbers don't lie."

She nodded, keeping her eyes on the bottle of moonshine in front of her. "You might want to read this little book called *How to Lie with Statistics*. Numbers, my friend, *do* lie. And the fact that you find me hot is a little disturbing."

"And just who the hell said I was talking about you?"

"You were talking about Redding?"

"Hell no." He made a blubbery sound as though he were trying to shake off the image. "I was talking about the sheriff before him. What was that guy's name? Little fellow with glasses and a deviated septum."

Ah, Kornel, a man who was older than dirt, straight as an arrow, and about as hot as the green chile crop that year. Too much rain. Ruined the promise of a good autumn roast. "Why, Royce. I had no idea you two were a thing."

"That's what you get for thinking."

"I was wondering if maybe you could help me with something."

"Isn't wondering a form of thinking?"

"Darlene Tapia might have a fugitive in her house," Sun said, ignoring his implication. "Can you find out if she does? And if so, can you keep an eye on her? Find out if he's threatening her or just hanging out, eating her chips, and watching *Jeopardy!*?"

"Why not put your boy on it?"

He'd always called Quincy *her boy.* "Because Darlene knows Quincy. I don't want her suspecting we're watching her, and you're the stealthiest guy I've ever met. Stealth isn't really Quincy's strong suit."

He laughed. "You'll know by tomorrow morning."

"Thank you so much, Royce."

"You got it, Sunny Girl. Anything else you need since it's thirty below and I have nothing better to do than babysit a noob coming down off fentanyl?"

"Yes. I've had a bad day. Can I come live at the rehab with you?"

"You are aware that this is a men's rehab?"

"My favorite kind."

He laughed, the sound deep and smooth.

She drew in a breath and reveled in the sound. "I love you."

"See? You keep proving my point."

"Let me know what you find out."

"I love you, too. Always have, Sunny Girl."

She was just about to hang up when she asked, "Wait, did you vote for me?"

"Hell no. I voted for Phillip Usury."

"Didn't he die last year?"

"Ah, that's probably why he didn't win."

"Oh, wait again!"

"Keeping me on the phone. Are you tracing this call?"

"Do you know what's up with Bo Britton?"

"Who?"

Really? "Lieutenant Bobby Britton? Of the Del Sol Sheriff's Posse? Has worked here for almost twenty years? Was the best man at your second and third weddings?"

"Oh, Bo! Twenty years, huh? I bet he can retire soon."

"I'm sure he can if he so chooses, but I have yet to see him. Do you know where he is?"

"Who?"

It was a conspiracy.

Sun welded her teeth together. Though she did hang up feeling much better about herself than she had five minutes earlier. But she really needed to find Bo.

14

Autocorrect has become our own worst enema.

—SIGN AT DEL SOL CELLULAR

As Zee and Price went through the footage from the Quick-Mart, Sun decided to call Auri to check in. It took her a few rings to pick up.

"Hey, bug bite. Are you at Grandma's?"

"No, I'm at a friend's house doing a homework assignment. We have to interview each other."

"Oh, okay. Do they know who it is?"

"Yeah, Grandpa brought me over. He knows his dad."

"His?" Sun asked, suddenly very interested.

Auri giggled. "He's just a friend. We have English together and got assigned the project."

"I see. Well, are you okay to get home?"

"Yep. His dad is going to take me, or Grandpa is going to come back."

"The roads are about to get bad again. You might want to wrap that up."

"Okay. We're almost finished. I just asked him the last question about what he wants to do after graduation. How do you spell *gigolo?*"

Sun snorted. "You're funny. I need you to sleep at Grandma's, okay? I don't know what time I'm going to be back."

"Okay."

Thankfully, the kid still had her own room there. A fact Sun knew would come in handy at some point, just not this early in the game.

"Love you, bug. Sleep well."

"Love you, too, Mom."

With Auri taken care of for the night and Zee and Price going over the footage, Sun decided she couldn't wait any longer. She had to check on Levi. See if he found any sign of Jimmy. Or Sybil, for that matter.

She drove out to the search area just as the snow started falling. Levi's truck was still in the same place, her note still on the windshield. They were probably camping on the mountain instead of coming all the way down.

It was freezing. She should have been doing exactly what Levi was doing. She should've been out there, on that mountain, searching for Hailey's son, blizzard or no blizzard. Instead, she sat in a warm cruiser with heated seats and ambient lighting.

Guilt assaulted her fast and hard. Oh yeah. She was going to make a great sheriff.

Despite her inability to do anything even remotely resembling productive, she stayed put, waiting and hoping Levi and his cousin would come back with Jimmy. And even Sybil. The winds howled, and sleet pelted the truck from all directions.

It was no wonder. The forecasters had predicted this was going to be the worst storm the county had seen in a decade.

Sun kept the cruiser on for a while but ended up turning it off to save gas. And she waited, mulling over her day. Only one word seemed to sum it up and tie a nice bow on top: *clusterfuck.*

Or was that two words?

She huddled inside her coat to stay warm, and her lids grew heavy. Before she knew it, the digital clock read 1:00 a.m. She needed to get home, but hope won out again. She watched the mountain like a mama bear watches her cubs, looking for any sign of them, until her lids staged a rebellion and refused to cooperate any longer.

Slowly freezing to death, Sun tried to climb out of a snowdrift in the wake of an avalanche. Wind whipped around her, and she wondered how she'd gotten there. How she'd been buried neck deep in ice and snow. But she couldn't remember getting out of the SUV. Or the avalanche cascading down the mountain. Or the gentle crackling of water as it solidified into an ice block around her body.

Before Sun could open her eyes and make sense of her sur-roundings, a loud crash jerked her awake. She bolted upright and looked around, trying to figure out how she'd gotten back in her cruiser.

She turned to her left and saw someone short and stocky standing at her window, wearing coveralls, a face mask, and gog-gles. He lifted gloved hands and motioned for her to roll down her window. She shook her head. Then another sound caught her attention. Someone was at her passenger window, but this guy she recognized. Somehow, through all the layers and survival gear, she recognized him.

Levi Ravinder motioned for her to open the door. He also wore a face mask and goggles, but he looked far less ridiculous than his cousin for some reason.

He opened the door, and Sun realized the rocking in her dream had been caused by the wind rocking her cruiser. Levi climbed inside and closed the door with some effort before re-moving his face mask and lifting his goggles to the top of his head.

"You're turning blue," he said, breathing hard. He tossed her a blanket. "It's as cold in here as it is out there."

She jutted out her chin, the one underneath her chattering teeth. "I look great in blue." Even with all her bravado, she shook out the blanket and wrapped it around her.

"Right." He motioned for his cousin, who was still standing

outside her window, to get to the truck. He gave a thumbs-up, then did as ordered, stumbling twice before he managed to get inside the massive vehicle.

Sun leaned forward, turned on the cruiser, and amped up the heat. Then the reason she was there hit her, and she gasped, wide-eyed, and asked, "Did you find him?"

Levi shook his head, his disappointment evident in the set of his shoulders.

"Oh, my god, Hailey must be sick with worry."

The ice in his hair had started to melt. He wiped moisture off his face with a large hand, the act so everyday and yet so sensual. "Since when do you care about Hailey?"

"Since never." God, she was going to make such a great sheriff. "Of course I care about her; I just don't think she cares much for me."

They'd sworn a pact to keep up the pretense no matter what, but she did want to tell him that she cared very much for his little sister. That she had grown to love the woman. A woman who, like Levi, grew up in a horribly broken home.

But she didn't dare. Doing so could put Hailey in danger, as well as Jimmy and Levi.

"You'll be able to leave in a few minutes. We called out the crew to clear the road to town."

"You can do that?"

"When it's your crew, yeah."

"What are you going to do?"

"We're going back to the house to change again and get back out there. There's a trail where we can take our ATVs up."

"Levi, does he know what to do? How to survive?"

"Yes." He bit down and looked out the window. "I'm just worried he panicked and went too far into the forest. He knows how to make a shelter and start a fire, but this is more than even most experienced hunters could manage."

She tried to swallow the turmoil wreaking havoc on her chest. "Can I go out with you?"

He studied her a moment, a long, tense moment, then shook his head. "You'd only slow us down."

Sun didn't take offense. He was right. He knew this area and knew how to cover it quickly. If he had to watch out for her while doing it . . .

It was the first time she'd ever truly been alone with him, and the circumstances were the worst kind imaginable. But it was nice to hear his voice.

"I wish I could do something."

"You can. Go home so I don't have to worry about finding a Sunshine Popsicle on my next pass."

"Okay, but I'm leaving under duress and against my better judgment."

"Yeah, well, your judgment was never that great."

What was that supposed to mean? "What's that supposed to mean?"

If perfection manifested into human form, it would look exactly like the man sitting in her passenger's seat. The one with the annoyed look on his face. "What it means, *Vicram,* is go home." He said her name like it was something he would spit out if he were starving.

Before she could argue the point again—and take up more of his precious time—he climbed down from her cruiser and slammed the door. Then he pointed, telling her to lock it.

She obeyed almost faster than his cousin had. There was something about the way he gave an order. She felt that ignoring it would be risky.

But he hadn't replaced his face mask and goggles. She waited and watched as he trod back to his truck, his hair whipping about his head, until he was safely inside. Then she released the breath she'd been holding.

Yet not five seconds after he got inside, he opened the door again, reached over his windshield, and pulled off her stupid note, the one that the storm had surely melted the lettering off. Humiliation burned through her.

He looked at it, the wind almost ripping it out of his hands. Then he looked back at her and let it go, the blizzard carrying it into oblivion before climbing back into his truck.

She rolled down her window and shouted, "That's a five-hundred-dollar fine, mister!"

A backhoe drove past then. Levi turned the truck around to head back to his house, but he waited for her to do the same, for her to follow the backhoe. She did, and when they arrived back at 63, Sun and the backhoe went one direction while Levi and his cousin went the other.

Just like she and Levi always seemed to do.

Auri couldn't sleep. She knew it would be an issue the next day, what with her coloring and the fact that dark blue circles just didn't look good under her hazel eyes. But it didn't matter.

Cruz's dad had taken her home just as the winds picked up and the sky started dumping snow like it was a Christmas in Denver.

She enjoyed talking to Cruz's dad—with Cruz interpreting, of course—on the short drive home. He was a nice guy and made a killer hot chocolate. The real stuff. Not the powdered stuff in a can.

Cruz walked Auri to the door when they got to her grandparents' house.

"Do you like it?" he asked, gesturing toward their apartment in back.

"Are you kidding? I love it. Which part did you work on?"

"See that wall closest to the alley?"

She grinned. "Yes."

"I built that. Among other things."

"That's my favorite wall."

"Really?"

"And my bedroom."

"Oh."

He kept his gaze steady until she asked, "Hey, why did you work construction when your dad's a mechanic?"

"I work for my grandfather in the summer. On my mom's side."

"Oh. I didn't know that." The wind had picked up so that even in the covered porch, Auri's hair was being flung about. "Thanks for working on this with me."

"Of course. We're partners."

The smile that spread across her face couldn't have been stopped if Moses himself had commanded it. Jesus, maybe, but Moses didn't have quite enough clout to dampen her joy.

"Guess I should go before my dad freezes to death."

"That would suck."

"Yeah, it would."

He turned to walk away, and she'd thought of him almost nonstop all night. And Sybil. And the students at Del Sol High she was going to have to face today.

She took one last glance in the mirror and considered her options. Not about her coloring. Nothing to be done about that. But about the students at Del Sol. The mean ones, anyway.

The way she saw it, she had three. Options, that is. She could face the students at school and be mocked and ridiculed for being a narc once again. She could beg her mom to let her help with the search. Or she could run away, change her name, and become a Vegas showgirl like her grandmother had been.

Decisions, decisions.

She grabbed her backpack and walked out to steal a gulp of her mom's coffee.

"Hey, bug bite. How'd you sleep?"

"Great. Kind of. I don't know. I kept waking up." She noticed the patient smile on her mom's face and grew wary. "What?"

"Who was the boy?"

"What boy?" The delicate arch of a single brow convinced Auri not to try to scam her mom. She plopped her backpack on a chair with a huff and dropped into the chair beside it. "I think I'm in love."

Was that it? Was it her feelings for Cruz that had her so hesitant to face the day at Del Sol High? She'd never liked anyone so much she was afraid of losing them. Well, besides her mom.

That very woman had been taking a sip of coffee when Auri had professed her love, and she sipped and gasped at the same time. Then she spent the next ten minutes hacking up a lung. It would have been hilarious if Auri's insides weren't being eviscerated by shards of glass.

"Mom. Stop," she said after an eternity. "This is serious. I need to skip school."

Her mom sobered, but it would take her voice a little while longer to recover fully. "Sorry. That had nothing to do with you. I just swallowed wrong."

"Right. So, can I skip school?"

"Absolutely not."

"I can help with the search party. She's my friend."

"Still thinking absolutely not. Not only would you be more hindrance than help—"

"Mom!"

"—but your asthma has been sketchy lately. We can't risk an episode."

"But I feel fine."

"All the more reason to keep you healthy."

"Oh, wait," Auri said, flattening a palm on her chest. "I think you're right. I think I'm having an episode." She gasped, then coughed for good measure.

"Good try, kid. What's his name?"

Auri sank against her chair. "Cruz." She ducked her head. "Cruz De los Santos."

"Really?" she said as though impressed. "Is that Chris's son?"

"Yeah. I met Mr. De los Santos last night. He's super nice."

"Yes, he is. And as soon as a I run a complete background

check on this kid, including his credit report and his immuniza-tion history, you can go to Caffeine-Wah and have coffee with him."

"And have your spies report our every move to you?" she asked, the betrayal cutting deep. Ish. Not like a gaping chest wound or anything. More like a really painful paper cut. Then she thought about the owners of Caffeine-Wah and melted. "How are Richard and Ricky? Have you seen them yet?"

"Saw them yesterday. They send their love."

Auri drew in a deep breath, crossed her fingers, and asked, "The eyeliner trick?"

Sun's shoulders sagged. "Not yet."

Auri wilted right along with her. "You're just going to have to bring them in on charges of mail fraud and conspiracy to commit murder. Then you can force them to show you."

"That's a great idea. Nothing like abusing my position for personal gain."

"Exactly. Why else be a sheriff?" she asked with a snort.

"Are you sure you're okay after yesterday?"

One shoulder rose of its own accord. "I'm okay. Another day, another dollar."

Her mom's brows did a squiggly thing. "And how does that apply to this situation?"

"I don't know. It just sounds light and carefree, like I'm going to be today. Nary a care in the world. No skulking in the shadows for me."

After putting her cup down, Sun put a hand on Auri's arm. "You know, you don't have to pretend to be okay, sweet pea. Not ever."

Discomfort prickled along Auri's spine. She didn't like it when her mom worried about her. She did everything in her power to make sure that didn't happen. "I know. Can I at least help with the search after school?"

"How about you help your grandma and the rest of the Book Babes hand out coffee? If you get your homework done first."

"You're trusting Wanda Stephanopoulos to hand out coffee to a bunch of law enforcement officers?" When her mom nodded, Auri's jaw fell open. "Mom! You know what uniforms do to her."

"I know. It couldn't be helped. If she does impede the search in any way—"

"Like wrapping herself around Quincy?"

"—I'll have to ask her to leave."

"No. You'll have to take her away in handcuffs."

Her mom laughed at that. Hard.

"Mom, this is serious. Wanda could give the whole town a bad name."

She wiped a tear from underneath her eye. "You are such an old soul."

"Yeah, yeah. So, what time did you get in?" she asked, putting her mom in the hot seat for once.

"You do not want to know."

She looked at the map her mom was poring over.

"Why are you searching for Sybil there?"

"Didn't your grandparents tell you? Jimmy Ravinder is missing, too, and we got a tip that he's been seen hanging out with a girl who matches Sybil's description."

Alarm rocketed through her. "Jimmy Ravinder? How long has he been missing?"

"Since Sunday afternoon." She stopped and focused on Auri. "Why?"

"Who said he's been seen hanging out with Sybil?"

"Not Sybil, but a girl matching her description. And with them both going missing around the same time . . ." Her mom caught on. "Come to think of it, you match Sybil's description, too."

Auri sank into her chair. "It's me." She said it so softly, she was worried her mom didn't hear her, so she said it again. "It's me. The girl Jimmy's been hanging out with."

She had been friends with Jimmy since she was seven, but with the way her mom felt about the Ravinders, she'd never told her. While her mom worked, she'd spent the summers with her grandparents. She'd gone to the lake, taken up hiking the trails of the Sangre de Cristo Mountains, and hit up all the coffee shops almost every day with Jimmy. That was why she'd never really gotten to know any of the local kids.

She spent all her time with her grandparents or with Jimmy.

The color drained from her mom's face. "All this time, we thought we had a solid lead, and . . ." She focused on her daughter again. "Honey, why are you hanging out with Jimmy Ravinder?"

"He's my friend. He's smart. And he's nice."

"He's nice?" she said. "He's a Ravinder."

The way she said the words cut Auri to the bone. No paper cut this time. Her mom wielded a machete. "So, that's how we decide who to hang out with? We look at their last name? What about the color of their skin? Does that count?"

Sun gave her an admonishing glower. "That's not fair. I've told you, they're a crime family. A criminal organization unto themselves. And they're mixed up with some very heavy hitters who make mincemeat out of little girls and—"

"I know. I know. Eat them for breakfast."

She leaned into her. "Sweetheart, it's not that Jimmy is a bad guy. It's that his family is, and you could get caught in the crossfire."

"Jimmy wouldn't let that happen."

"Jimmy? What can he do against an entire family of criminals?"

"He's gone legit with his uncle Levi. Everything about Mr. Ravinder's operation is legal. He's made sure of it. He's trying to get his family out of that life, Mom. No more crossfire."

"Yes, but there are members of the family who don't want out of that life. Those who want back in, no matter the cost. What then?"

Auri folded her arms over her chest. Not to be belligerent, but to silently protest her mother's position. Sun had always worried about the Ravinders. If she knew what they'd done for her, what they'd done for Auri, she wouldn't be so quick to judge.

Besides, the woman was so in love with Jimmy's uncle Levi, it was ridiculous.

Auri suddenly realized the larger implications of all of this. "Mom, does this mean you don't have any clues as to where Sybil might be now?"

"I don't know anymore. Just because you match Sybil's description doesn't mean he isn't with her."

"Mom, you can't actually suspect him of taking her!"

"I'm not saying he took her. What if they were walking and got lost? What if one of them is hurt? We can't rule out his involvement."

Auri ignored the worry gnawing at her stomach. "He's not involved with this, and Sybil is okay. I'll find something, Mom."

"Oh, honey, even if you did—"

"No. She's still alive. She has to be. We only just met."

Sun tilted her head, her expression full of warmth and appreciation, but Auri didn't understand why. "Leave it to my daughter to give the sheriff a pep talk."

"I'm just worried about them. Both of them."

"I am, too, bug bite."

"Please let me help with the search. He's been out in this weather. He'll be scared and disoriented. And he knows me. He trusts me. He would come if I called to him."

"Sweetheart, it's just too cold in the mountains. I promise I'll let you know immediately if we find him."

She pursed her lips. It was better than nothing. Besides, she had a couple of students to interrogate.

15

Go ahead! Try starting your day without coffee!
Our deputies need a few more arrests to make their quota.

—SIGN AT CAFFEINE-WAH

Her mom dropped her off at school, this time with no flashing lights, and sped off to get ready for the day and then join the search. The search Auri would have killed to be at. Still, she did have another fun-filled day planned with the Lynelle clones. She could only imagine what the day might bring.

But first, she needed to interrogate one Mr. Aiden Huang, the boy who was in the office the day before and who was surprised when they talked about printing Sybil's schedule.

He knew something. Auri could feel it. So she waited by the front doors for him, even though she didn't look up his schedule. He could have first period in another building.

Of course, she also waited for Cruz, and she was only a little disappointed when Aiden showed up first. She made eye contact as he walked past and tried to wave him down, but he only walked faster. So she followed faster.

She may be short, but she was determined. She could outlast him if it came to that.

He stopped at his locker and started when he looked over his shoulder and found her standing there.

"You're the new girl," he said, making small talk.

"Don't even pretend to care. What do you know about Sybil St. Aubin?"

It took him several tries, but he got the locker open. "Sybil who?"

She stepped closer, and his lids rounded. Only he wasn't looking at her. He'd looked over his shoulder at the kid towering over her and paled.

"What's going on?" Cruz asked.

"Nothing. I swear," he said, way more nervous than he should have been, and Auri was beginning to see a pattern.

She turned to him and asked, "Cruz De los Santos, are you a bully?"

His expression flatlined, then he said, "He's getting away."

She whirled around and watched Aiden rabbit. "Damn it," she said, practically running after him. When she caught up, managing to only take out one or two other students, she grabbed his collar and pulled.

He made a strangling sound and faced her. "What? I didn't do anything. And I don't know the girl."

"Then why the reaction yesterday?"

"What reaction?"

"You do know who my mother is, right?"

He paled even further, but Cruz had walked up again, and she didn't know if it was due to the threat or due to his presence. She needed a control group when she did stuff like that.

"I could get in serious trouble," he whispered, his voice hissing loudly.

"I don't care," she said, hissing back. "What's going on?"

He led them to a corner, glanced in both directions, then said, "She wanted me to do something for her. Said she'd pay me."

"Really? What did she want?"

Cruz crossed his arms and leaned against the wall beside Aiden. Aiden started panting as though he were having a panic attack.

"Better hurry," she said. "The bell's about to ring. If I don't get an answer, I'll go to Jacobs."

He scraped a hand through his hair. "Okay, it was before winter break. She wanted a schedule, too. Asked me to print it out."

"Whose?"

He licked his lips, then said, "Yours."

"But I wasn't going here before break."

"Yeah, but you had registered. They'd already given you a schedule. She didn't say why she wanted it."

"How much did she pay you?"

"I can't say. I'll get in trouble."

"Seriously? I was just curious. Now I'm really curious."

Cruz stepped closer, presumably to intimidate him. It worked.

He gave in, exhaling sharply. "A bottle of wine from her family's winery."

"Really? Wine? Did you drink it?"

"Every last drop. A Moscato. Fruity and sweet. Light and yet surprisingly full bodied. How is that even possible?"

Curious about the mechanics of the transaction, she asked, "She brought it to school? Like, in her backpack?"

He nodded.

"Wow, so why did she want my schedule?"

The bell rang. "Dude, I don't know. She didn't tell me. Just said she needed it for a project. Can I go now?"

He asked Auri but looked at Cruz, who raised his brows in question at her.

"I guess," she said, liking the power a little too much.

They headed to class, but Auri needed the little lionesses' room, so she took a quick pit stop.

Unfortunately, Lynelle had the same idea. She walked in, smirk firmly in place, and walked straight up to her. Something told Auri it might be a good idea to start recording their interactions. Evidence for when she ran her over with her first car, a '65 poppy-red Mustang with white GT 350 stripes and a honeycomb grille, later.

"What do you have going on with Cruz?"

Auri was busy applying lip gloss. "For someone who hates me, you sure spend a lot of time trying to get my attention."

Lynelle acted like she'd slapped her, she was so taken aback.

She recovered quickly, though. Vampires often did. "My aunt went to school with your mother."

"Good to know."

"It's amazing what you can learn with just the right questions."

"I suppose it is."

She let a grin that spelled out the word *evil* spread across her face. "Have a good day."

"Yep. You, too. And remember," she said as Lynelle walked out, "it's never too late to seek help!"

Lynelle ignored her. It was bound to happen eventually.

She hurried out and tried to beat the tardy bell with Cruz. They failed, but only by a couple of seconds. Mrs. Ontiveros was just taking roll. Auri hurried to her seat and slid into it, then gave a quick wave to Chastity. Cruz strolled in like he owned the place, like he hadn't a care in the world.

"Nice to see you could make it," she said to them. "But that's strike one for the semester. Don't let it become a habit."

Auri shook her head, swearing to never be late again as long as she drew breath on this earth. Cruz nodded an acknowledgment, and she sat in awe. She'd had no idea coolness like that actually existed. She'd thought it was only in books and superhero movies.

"Can I ask you a question?" Mrs. Ontiveros said to Cruz when she'd finished the roll.

He didn't say yes, but he didn't say no, either.

"Could you read your latest to the class?"

"Yeah!" Chastity practically yelled, her enthusiasm contagious, because two other girls agreed with her.

"Please," one of them said.

His latest? How did Mrs. O. even know there was a latest? Cruz wouldn't let Auri even peek at his work the night before, but his English teacher had front-row seats to his latest?

He shook his head. "That's okay."

She didn't push it with him, but she did ask, "Then would you mind if I read it? I sent it into the contest, barely making the midnight deadline, but it's just so beautiful, Cruz. I would love for the class to hear it."

He seemed to be growing tenser by the moment. "I guess. But I wrote it really fast. It's stupid."

The teacher grinned knowingly. "I don't think you could write anything stupid if you tried." She took a sheet of paper off her desk and stood in front of the classroom. "Okay, class. I want you to really think about the words here. What is the author saying? What is he feeling? Who is he talking about?"

Cruz's head whipped up when she asked the last question, but she didn't notice. She cleared her throat and began.

MELICACENT: *A Love Story*

She was something other
The girl
Something not entirely human
A song perhaps
Created to be sung, not touched
Heard, not looked upon
But listened to as a series of notes that twist your spine
That crack your skull and bleed your feet
That hum with every breath you steal from her world
The only constant keeping her in check
Keeping her from shredding the flesh from your bones
Is the rhythm she dances to

The pulsing beat of your heart
A heart she would gladly stop
Should you dare look away
And then she would laugh
And set the galaxy on fire

Mrs. Ontiveros filled her lungs and then folded the paper and looked at the class. Auri would have as well, but she was too busy being hypnotized by his words.

After a long silence, the class erupted in applause. Most of the class, anyway. The boys that could reach him pushed and slapped him on the back, because that was what boys did. But the girls seemed just as impressed as Auri.

Lynelle, however, only had eyes for her. She sat with her arms crossed over her chest, her dark hair styled to red-carpet perfection, and her gray eyes set to stun as she stared at Auri.

But Auri couldn't seem to find the strength to care. She watched Cruz, his head bowed, clearly unused to receiving such praise, and realized her heart was so very, very much in danger for the first time in its life.

Sun planned her day all the way to the station, so for about three minutes, after she dropped off Auri at school. As the county sheriff, she needed to get out to the search site and make sure things ran smoothly, but she also needed to interview Forest St. Aubin, Sybil's dad, about his daughter.

She needed to know his whereabouts when she went missing and his list of possible enemies. If she absolutely had to, she could let Agent Fields handle the interview alone, especially since their strongest lead was Jimmy Ravinder.

The fact that both kids went missing on the same day at the same time pushed her tolerance for coincidence way over the line, despite what Auri said about her being the girl he'd been seen with. It was simply a lead she couldn't dismiss.

The search had to take precedence that morning. Once she made contact with the state police field coordinator of the SAR team and made sure everyone was where they needed to be with safety the top priority, she would think about going back to town and sitting in on the interview with Mr. St. Aubin.

She parked her cruiser and walked into the station. When she saw Quincy's face, however, she stopped and looked herself over. If she forgot her pants again, she was going to be livid.

She patted her legs. Nope. Pants were a go. She'd even showered and French braided her hair, but apparently, it hadn't been enough.

Quincy eyed her, then handed her a cup of coffee without saying a word. Good decision.

"Okay, guys, the SAR team is already on-site. Let's get out there. And be safe."

Price walked up before she could head out. "Hey, boss. Mr. Hughes didn't see anything suspicious."

"That's too bad. Who's Mr. Hughes?"

"The guy in the surveillance video? The one buying the energy drink at the Quick-Mart?"

"Right. The receipt found at the scene. Do you think he was targeted? Specifically set up?"

"We can't rule it out, but I really think this guy just took the opportunity to throw us off his trail. To keep us busy with a wild-goose chase."

Sun agreed.

He handed her a report of what he'd found, which was basically nothing wrapped in another layer of nothing. "According to the clerk, Mr. Hughes goes in every day about the same time and buys the same energy drink."

She perused the report quickly, then grabbed a photocopy off her desk and handed it to him. "You gave him a ticket. Do you remember him?"

Surprised, he scanned the photocopy. "Seventy in a fifty-five."

He looked at the photo of Mr. Hughes again and thought back. "Wait, I do remember him. He'd just gotten off work. Said he was in a hurry to get home because his wife was making his favorite. Lasagna."

"I can hardly blame him, then," she said with a grin.

"Right?"

"Did he seem sketchy in any way when you asked him about the receipt? Evasive?"

"Not at all," Price said. "He seemed genuinely surprised. Said he always throws his receipts away in the same trash can."

"Okay, good job on this."

Price gave her a curt nod, clearly unused to compliments.

"So, why the new look?" Quincy asked.

She looked herself over again. "What new look?"

He gestured to indicate her overall appearance. "Hell in a handbasket."

"Gee, thanks. I didn't sleep well."

"Yeah? Anybody I know?"

"Quincy, not everything is about sex. I slept in the cruiser."

He stopped and gaped at her.

"I went back out to the search area."

His expression morphed into one of extreme concern. "What the fuck, Sunny?"

"I didn't actually search. I didn't even get out of the cruiser. That blizzard was brutal."

"Worst we've had in twelve years, according to the hot meteorologist on channel seven. If you didn't search—"

"I went out there to wait. Levi's truck was still there, so I waited to see if they came off the mountain."

"Of course Levi Ravinder would be involved. Did he? Come?" He waited just long enough to make sure his not-so-subtle innuendo was understood, then added, "Off the mountain?"

"Funny. And yes, but they didn't find Jimmy. He went back out there in the middle of that melee."

"He's got spunk. That's for damned sure."

"Spunk? That's what you call it when someone risks his life to save his nephew?"

He shrugged. "I don't like the guy, okay? Never have."

Levi had always been a sore spot for him. "Why?"

"He's not good enough for you," he said matter-of-factly while checking his phone.

Anita walked into the office before Sun could question him further. "There's someone here who'd like to talk to you, Sheriff."

"About what? I really need to get out there."

"She said you're friends and that it'll only take a minute. A Melody Hill? She seems pretty desperate."

"Most of her friends are," Quincy said.

Sun smiled. "You're my friend."

"Most," he said with a wink. "Not all."

She just happened to look past Quincy to the lobby. A man was sitting there covered in bandages. "Is that Mr. Madrid?" she asked, shocked.

"Oh yeah," he said, chuckling. "I think the chicken is winning."

"Rooster. And I have to agree. What does he need? Besides an ambulance?"

Anita looked at the exit longingly, then faced her duties like a champion. "He wants to file a complaint against Mrs. Sorenson. Says she's harassing him about her rooster, because, and I quote, he didn't take the god-danged thing, end of story."

Sun tried to feel sorry for the guy. She failed. But she did feel sorry for the rooster. "Poor Puff Daddy. Caught in the middle of all this."

"I think he's the only sane one," Anita said. "Do you want me to send the woman back?"

"Yes, thanks, Anita."

Quincy grabbed his jacket. "Want me to wait?"

"No. Will you meet up with the field coordinator? Make sure we're good to go?"

"You got it."

Anita showed in Melody Hill, a sweet girl who was a year ahead of Sun in high school. She'd grown into her curves, her attire much more attractive than what she'd worn in school, but Sun figured that was due to her mother's constant reproach of her. The fact that the poor girl had been on a diet every day of her life couldn't have helped her self-esteem.

"Melody," Sun said, surprised to see her. She rose to shake her hand, then gestured toward the chair.

"Sunshine. I can't believe you're the sheriff. I totally voted for you."

Sun offered her a grateful smile. "Thank you. What's up?"

"Oh, right, I'm so sorry, but I didn't know what to do. Who to tell."

That sounded serious. "Who to tell what?"

"Okay, first I want immunity."

Sun smothered a grin. "If you've killed someone, I'm afraid I can't grant that."

Melody burst out laughing, but it was one part humor and two parts nerves. Then she sobered and said, "No, really. I don't want to be prosecuted for lying to a U.S. Marshal."

Ah. Deleon had said a woman lied to him when he was doing his interviews. Two, actually, but Sun was about 110 percent positive one was Darlene Tapia. She'd know for sure once the intrepid Royce Womack reported back to her.

"All right. I promise not to prosecute you for lying to a U.S. Marshal. Tell me what's going on."

She breathed in deeply through her nose, gathering her courage. "Well, someone told the marshals that I had seen that boy who escaped from jail."

"And had you?"

"Well, I think so, but I may have lied to the marshal."

Sun's adrenaline redlined. So, they were right. The fugitive really was in the area. She took out a notebook to take some notes, but it was really just for show. Sometimes when people were confessing to a crime, they didn't want anyone looking directly at them. It was a psychological thing. "Okay. Can you tell me why you lied?"

"Well, I'm not positive I did. He may have not been the same boy."

"Gotcha. Why did you possibly lie?"

"Because, if it's the same guy, he saved my daughter's life."

Sun looked up. "How?"

Melody closed her eyes and pressed a tissue to her mouth. "I was part of the cleanup crew at the lake a couple of days ago. Everyone was heading out for the day, but I wanted to check a few more areas. Sure enough, someone had tossed trash behind Soda Rock."

"Always," Sun said, shaking her head.

"Exactly. Anyway, I went to get more trash bags out of the car, and even though I'd threatened their lives, my kids got on the lake."

Alarm paralyzed Sun's lungs. It simply didn't get quite cold enough to create a thick enough barrier between air and water to hold people. Too many sunny days in New Mexico, even in winter.

"My baby—" Melody's voice cracked, and it took her a moment to recover. "My baby fell through, Sunshine. My baby girl."

The mere thought pressed against Sun's chest and stole her breath.

"And he saved her. The boy."

"The man the marshals are looking for? He saved her?"

"I don't know. It all happened so fast, and he took off as soon as he handed her to me."

"He pulled her out of the water?"

"Pulled her out? No, Sunshine. He jumped in after her. He was on the cliffs, and he jumped in after her. He could've broken both his legs, but he didn't care."

The lowest cliff looking over the lake was thirty feet. The tallest almost eighty-five. The thought of him jumping from any of them onto solid ice made Sun's legs hurt.

"The ice broke with his fall, and he swam under the surface until he found her. All the while, I was screaming and my boys were screaming. I ran out onto the ice, too, but it started to break. That was when I saw them surface out of the hole she fell through. Oh, my god, Sunshine, she would have died. I know in my heart that if he had not been sent to save her, she would have died."

Sun sat stunned, not sure what to think. It was one thing to be a violent criminal who preyed on those he saw as weaker. But for this guy to jump into a frozen lake to save a little girl?

"So, there you have it." She raised her chin. "Do what you have to do. I won't be telling the marshals anything, but I thought you should know, since it's your town."

"Thank you, Melody. But why wasn't I told about the incident? I've read all the reports up to date."

"I took her to the hospital in Santa Fe. They must not have reported it to you."

"All that matters is that your little girl is okay. I have one of those, too. They're pretty great."

She laughed through a light sob. "They are, aren't they?"

Sun saw Melody out and got ready to head to the search site when she got a text from Royce, the other, older love of her life.

"No news yet. Will call soon."

"Sheriff?" Anita said from across the room.

Sun walked over to her as she pulled on her jacket. "What's up?"

"The mayor would like you to call her with an update."

"Oh, okay, can you take down a message for when she calls back?"

"Yes, ma'am."

She made sure her badge was securely fastened to her belt, then said, "Okay, it's three sentences."

Anita nodded, pen at the ready.

"Bite. My. Ass."

The poor girl actually wrote down all three words before looking at her questioningly.

"I know it's a bit cryptic, but she'll figure it out."

Anita's eyes had rounded, but she nodded without hesitation. "Yes, ma'am."

16

*Two elderly sisters reported a man in the house
across the street watching them for hours at a time.
Deputies ID'd the man as a cardboard cutout of Captain America.
The sisters grew distraught when they found out he wasn't
real and were transported to the Del Sol Urgent Care Center for
observation.*

—DEL SOL POLICE BLOTTER

A helicopter flew over the search area as Sun stepped out of her cruiser and went to find the incident commander. She heard dogs barking in the distance, the ground pounders already hard at work.

The snow wasn't much deeper than it had been. Small blessings. Though the chill was still razor sharp, apparently a hot meteorologist had promised sun and lots of it. Hopefully, it would warm up as the day wore on.

"Commander," she said as she stepped up to a very tall and very busy state officer holding a clipboard. Commander William Ledbetter stood as tall as his position would imply.

He glanced down and took her hand. "Good to see you, Sheriff."

"Thank you for getting this going so quickly."

He surveyed the surroundings. "Yesterday would have been better. Wish we'd known earlier in the day."

"How much time do I get to keep you before you have to pack up?"

He dropped his gaze as though afraid to give her the bad news. "I can't imagine we'll find this kid alive, Sun. Two nights exposed to these conditions? If he weren't disabled, maybe, but . . ."

"I know," she said, turning her face away. "But he's smart, Will."

"I'm giving it two days, and then we'll have to pack it in."

She nodded but decided to press her luck with every ounce of strength she had. She knew how much these things cost. Budget was always a concern in New Mexico, and when weighing the cost against the odds, the cost usually won.

"I'll tell you what. You give me four and I'll give you a home-cooked meal."

"You cook?"

"Hell no. But my mom is a savant."

The soft laugh was promising. Sun held her breath as he thought about it. "Three. It's the best I can do, but you have to keep a woman named Wanda away from me."

Sun chuckled. "Deal. Thanks, Will."

"My team doesn't need to worry about that escaped convict, does it?"

"Not even a little. I'm going to head back to town, but I'll join the search in a couple of hours."

He nodded. "Stay alive. I'm going to be hungry later."

Apparently, Levi had already talked with the field coordinator and the incident commander, letting them know which areas he'd covered. She looked up just as a search team took off on horses, their breaths fogging in the air.

Sunshine walked into the station just as Agent Fields was finishing up his interview with Mr. and Mrs. St. Aubin.

He motioned for her to join them and welcomed her with a handshake. "Sheriff."

"Agent Fields. Mari." She held out her hand to Mari's husband. "Mr. St. Aubin. I am so sorry to be meeting you under these circumstances."

"Forest, please."

They took seats in the conference room so she could go over what they'd discussed and ask any questions of her own.

Forest St. Aubin was younger than she'd expected, especially since he was so successful running a vineyard and winery. The only clue to his age was his salt-and-pepper hair, which placed him in his early forties, but he looked more like late thirties when she focused on his face. In fact, he looked a little younger than his wife.

"Have you heard anything?" he asked her, and she couldn't miss the agony on his face.

"I'm sorry."

"What about that Ravinder kid? Jimmy? Do you suspect him?"

"We aren't ruling anything out at this juncture. We have a search party looking for him right now."

"Do you think . . . do you think she's up there with him?"

"She'll freeze to death," Mari said from behind closed fists.

"We don't know. But if she is, we'll find her." Her words did absolutely nothing to ease the couple's distress. She looked at the agent beside her, then back to the man on the verge of tears. "Did you guys come up with any other possibilities?"

Mari wasn't on the verge of tears. Her cheeks were soaked with the things, her dark hair in a state of turmoil, her nose red.

"Like I told Agent Fields," he said, "I can't think of anyone who would do this. Or why anyone would do this." He pressed a thumb and index fingers to his eyes.

She gave him a moment. No need to ask his whereabouts. She could read Fields's report. His people had probably already checked his alibi. Sun was more interested in the man's thoughts on Sybil's prediction.

As though he read her mind, he said, "I guess you know about Syb's premonition?"

"I do. What do you think about it?"

He scoffed, the sound bitter and resentful. "I think I'm an asshole."

Not the direction she'd expected. "Why do you say that?"

He drew in a deep breath to steady himself, then explained, "All those years, all those times she tried to talk to us about it, and we just dismissed it. Like it meant nothing. Like her fears meant nothing."

"I'm sure she doesn't think that."

"She has to. It's the truth."

"But you believe her now?"

A light sob escaped him. "How can I not?"

His phone rang, and he checked it. When he didn't recognize the number, he looked between her and Fields. The agent pressed a button on the digital recorder and nodded to him.

The man swallowed, then answered on the fourth ring with a shaky, "Hello?" He frowned at them when no one spoke. "Hello? Do you have my daughter?"

Sun leaned over to the agent's laptop as he tried to locate where the call originated from. Because the number had come up on the caller ID, he could put it in the program and track it with GPS.

"Who is this?"

Mari pressed her hands over her mouth to squelch a sob.

"Mr. St. Aubin," Fields said softly, the lines on his face hardening. "It's coming from your house."

Without even a hint of hesitation, Fields took the phone, and the two officers scrambled out of the conference room.

"Quincy—*Deputy Cooper*," she corrected, "follow us with the St. Aubins."

"You got it, boss." He grabbed his jacket as she and Fields ran for her cruiser.

Sun skidded to a halt in the St. Aubins' drive, careful not to disturb any fresh tire tracks. Snowy footprints on the walkway led to the front door, but the St. Aubins entered and exited through their garage. The tracks were definitely not theirs, though there were any number of law enforcement agents they could have belonged to.

With gun drawn, she walked through the yard alongside the pathway while Fields flanked her, and Quincy went around the back of the house.

She gestured toward the front door with a nod. "There's something on the porch."

Fields nudged her arm, wanting to take the lead. He was more old-school than she'd imagined. But she had this. It didn't look like an explosive device from the size of it. Too small. And pink. Very pink.

They took up positions beside the front steps and waited for Quincy to come around the other side of the house.

He jogged up behind her. "Back door is locked. Doesn't look like anyone has tampered with it."

"Is that a phone?" Fields asked.

"It is." Sun took the steps, checking the windows as she went. A burner phone sat on a small child's jewelry box in the snow. The kind that played music when opened.

Quincy checked the front door while Sun put on a pair of gloves.

She pried open the box. A little ballerina starting spinning to a chimed version of "Greensleeves."

The St. Aubins walked up then, following Sun's footprints to avoid contaminating the scene.

"Is this Sybil's?" she asked Mari.

The woman's face morphed into astonishment. "Forest bought that for her on the day she was born."

"We lost that years ago in a move," he said, his voice cracking. "She was what . . . nine?"

"Ten," Mari said. "When we moved into the house on Stanford."

"Right. What's inside?"

Sun pulled out a long lock of red hair, and Mari broke down.

"We'll process this," Fields said. "You get back out to the search."

"Thank you. Call me if you find anything."

"Of course."

After dropping off Quincy's patrol car at the station, Sun and Quincy headed back to the search-and-rescue efforts that were already under way. They did the better part of the journey in complete silence. Quincy broke first.

"Someone is fucking with us," he said.

"I know."

"It could be her."

"I know."

"We can't rule it out."

"I know."

Even Sun, with that gut of hers that was never wrong, the one she had to ignore and follow the evidence no matter how it conflicted with her instincts, had to admit the bizarre set of coincidences surrounding Sybil's disappearance were hard to dismiss.

Two items from Sybil's past showing up now? This guy had to have stalked her for years. Stalked the family for years. That kind of patience took incredible dedication and discipline. Talk about holding a grudge.

"Do you want to talk about it?" Quincy asked.

"No."

"Brainstorm?"

"No."

"Spitball?"

"No. And ew." When he didn't ask again, she gave in. "Okay, fine. Let's say Sybil stashed all this stuff from her past, made up a story about a premonition when she was six years old, and then planned this elaborate scheme to make it look like she was abducted? For what? Why would she go to such lengths for years?"

"Attention. What else? Her father travels all over the world. Her mother reads romance novels all day. She feels abandoned."

"If that were true, if she were really just in it for the attention, why stick to her premonition story when nobody believed her? Her story never wavered. Not once in nine years."

"Kid's smart," he said. "Smart kids can do anything. You of all people should know that."

She ignored the compliment. "And if it were her, the abduction would've been more obvious. More staged. There would have been signs of a struggle in her room. Not the laundry room. And then she what? She planted that receipt to frame poor Mr. Hughes for buying an energy drink?"

Quincy held up his hands. "I'm not arguing with you. It's just all very convenient."

"Yeah, well, so are handkerchiefs, but you don't see me carrying one around."

They parked on the side of the road to the search site, and Sun walked to the command tent.

"Crazy," Quincy said when he took it all in.

"You or me?"

"This whole situation."

Dozens of vehicles, both civilian and emergency. Over a hundred people scouring the mountain.

She put the coffee her mom had handed her on the way in on a folding table and looked at a couple of maps they'd laid out.

Quincy pulled a pair of official coveralls over his uniform, then accessorized with matching boots and gloves, ready to do his part. "It's new to me."

"Yeah, I've only been directly involved in one other search and rescue. Got to know the incident commander." She pointed at him. "See? Networking. Get to know your fellow law enforcement officers."

"What if I don't like them?" he asked as he slipped on a ski cap.

They emerged from the tent, ready to face the mountain. Sun

had brought her best spiked boots, wiggled into thick black cover-alls with her credentials on them, and pulled a knit cap over her ears.

"I got us an ATV," Quince said. "The IC is sending us over that hill."

"Sounds good to me." She greeted the Book Babes as they handed out coffee, her deputies that were on-site, and the marshals before getting onto the ATV.

"What did Melody want?" he asked, shouting over the sound of the motor.

Sun explained about the possibility that the escaped fugitive, Ramses Rojas, may have saved her daughter's life. Not just saved it, but risked his own life, his legs, and his freedom to do so.

They bounced over the hard-packed snow, grateful for the snow tires someone had thoughtfully provided, and searched as deep into the forest as they could before they had to get off and walk. She could hear other searchers, including many of the townsfolk, calling out Jimmy's and Sybil's names, and she wondered where Levi was. She'd heard he'd closed the distillery and now had several of his cousins and employees searching as well.

One would think with that much manpower they'd find Jimmy quickly, and hopefully Sybil. But there was just too much forestland for it to be that easy. Hundreds of square miles, and much of it mountainous. The Sangre de Cristo Mountains were the southern tip of the Rockies. Just as beautiful. Just as hazardous.

The meteorologist had been right. Thank goodness, because Sun didn't want to think the woman was all beauty with no brains. The sun came out of hiding and warmed the place to a comfortable sting. Just enough to keep their cheeks cold but not frozen solid. Like a lettuce crisper with the temp set a little too low.

"Nothing like a brisk stroll through the forest," Quincy said.

Every few feet, they stopped, yelled for Jimmy and Sybil, and then waited for a response before continuing. Quincy checked in with their location every half hour.

After a couple of hours of trudging through the snow, Sun began to worry that three days would not be enough.

The radio squawked, but the helicopter made a pass overhead, and they didn't catch what the IC said.

Quincy pressed the Talk button on the radio. "Say again, command."

His voice came back over the speaker. It had a somber tone, and Sun's heart stopped beating to better hear his message.

He said quietly, "We have a body."

"When did you write that?" Auri asked Cruz as they filed into the hall.

He made the smallest effort humanly possible to shrug, probably to conserve energy should the apocalypse happen. "Last night."

"What? After I went home?"

Another energy-efficient shrug. "Mrs. Ontiveros wanted me to enter one more poem in some contest she helps coordinate, so I told her I'd write her one. I do it all the time." He offered her an equally energy-efficient grin where only one side of his mouth tilted up. "She loves that shit."

"I love that shit, too. That was stunning."

He lowered his head, clearly unused to praise.

"How do you do it? How do you write such beautiful imagery?"

"My imagery is rarely called *beautiful*. Did you miss the part about the shredding of flesh?"

She laughed softly. "No, but it was still beautiful. So, you gonna tell me? How you do it? How you think like that?"

"I don't know." He stuffed his hands in his pockets. "I don't really think in English, if that makes any sense. I think in pictures. In signs. I signed way before I could talk, and I've thought in signs ever since."

She gaped at him, but only a little. "Okay, I take back what I said last night. *That* is officially the coolest thing I've ever heard."

He flashed a set of blindingly white teeth. "See ya later."

Before she could say goodbye, he took off.

Auri watched him walk away, then she looked around, astonished that the students had pretty much accepted her. She wasn't getting nearly the number of glares as she was yesterday, and nobody had spray painted her locker or tried to frame her for theft. The day was definitely looking up.

She turned a corner to get to her next class and saw the L&Ls, Lynelle and Liam with Aiden Huang, the kid she'd interrogated. Liam had Aiden Huang by the collar while Lynelle read him the riot act, poking his chest with a razor-sharp fingernail.

The kid looked more annoyed than scared at first, but then Lynelle said something, and he paled before her eyes.

He held up a hand in surrender and took the USB she handed him.

She fired off one more threat before Liam shoved him away and they walked off into the sunset together. Or the glare from the plate-glass windows at the front of the school. Either way.

It was a classic love story. One that would be repeated for generations to come.

Girl asks first boy for a favor. First boy refuses. Second boy grabs first boy by the collar. Girl threatens first boy while second boy shakes him like a rag doll. First boy finally agrees to said favor, and girl and second boy fall in love.

A tad dysfunctional? Yes.

Would it last? Not unless they found themselves riddled with bullets like Bonnie and Clyde did before they could realize they weren't as compatible as they'd originally assumed and spent the next ten years breaking up and getting back together and breaking up again, bringing strife and misery to everyone they came into contact with.

Fingers crossed.

Auri sat in her second-period class, Lynelle and Liam completely forgotten as her thoughts traveled once again to Jimmy Ravinder and Sybil St. Aubin.

Her mom had a good point. They both went missing around the same time. It would be a hard stretch to convince anyone it was a coincidence, but it had to be. Or at the very least, there had to be a good a reason for it.

First, Sybil and Jimmy didn't know each other. Auri spoke to Jimmy often. They hung out. They'd been close for years. The fact that she'd had to keep it a secret from her mom was ludicrous on several levels, but her grandparents knew and supported their friendship. They had a special place in their hearts for Jimmy.

But what they didn't know was that Jimmy had saved her life when they were kids. Jimmy and one other member of the Ravinder family. No way would she abandon him just because her overprotective mother said the whole lot of them, every single Ravinder, was more trouble than they were worth.

She couldn't help but wonder if that carpet diagnosis applied to the Ravinder her mom was in love with.

The tardy bell rang, and a few seconds later, a television powered up in class. A weekly student news program popped on.

"Good morning, Lions!" a peppy brunette said from behind an anchor desk. A desk that looked like it had been made from cardboard, but that fact only added to the charm. "Welcome back! This week, we have a special investigative report brought to you by the Journalism Club. Roll it, Aiden!"

The screen went black, then Lynelle Amaia popped into the frame holding a microphone and standing in front of the sheriff's station.

Auri's palms slickened instantly, and she fought the urge to reach for her inhaler.

Lynelle wore a million-dollar smile as she took over the spotlight. "Thanks, Callie. We have a special story for all of you Lions out there. If you didn't already know it, we have a new sheriff." She gestured to the lettering on the building.

Auri glanced around, becoming a little concerned. What was Lynelle doing? Besides being really, really perky?

"So, we decided to check her out—to dig into her past, so to speak—and see what we had to look forward to for the next four years. After all, we got a brand-new lioness in the deal. Aurora Dawn Vicram? Welcome to Del Sol High!"

Auri froze. This was not happening. Dig into her mother's past? There was no way they could've found out the truth. It was buried along with the Ark of the Covenant, Jimmy Hoffa, and her pent-up emotions.

"Liam?"

The camera cut to Liam Eaton in front of the monument the town put up in Auri's pretend dad's honor, and the edges of her vision grew dark.

"Jimmy's uncle found him!"

Sun practically jerked the radio out of Quincy's hands, because whomever shouted that Jimmy had been found didn't seem distressed.

"Did you find Jimmy?" she asked. "Or a body?"

She recognized Deputy Salazar's feminine voice saying, "Um, both?"

"No," Sun whispered. Quincy put a hand on her shoulder to steady her.

"We found Jimmy, but I guess they found a body, too?"

She slammed her eyes shut and braced herself. "Sybil?"

"Not a girl," she said.

Sun almost dropped the radio. "Where are you? I need your location."

"Okay, we are by the command center. Levi Ravinder just brought Jimmy down from the mountain. He's half-frozen, so the EMTs are taking him now."

Closing a hand over her mouth, Sun looked heavenward and let the light soak into her.

A male voice came over the radio then. Sun could hear dogs barking in the background. Cadaver dogs. "We have a body about half a mile north of Estrella Pond. Male. Decomposition would suggest it's been here a long time. Possibly years."

"What the hell?"

Sun shook out of it and nodded to Quincy. They sprinted back to the ATV, which, in the snow, was so much harder than it sounded. She had no signal, or she would have texted Auri that they'd found Jimmy. Then again, if he didn't make it . . .

She decided to wait.

"Where to first?" Quincy asked.

"Let's check on Jimmy first." She gave orders to cordon off the area where the body was found, and they made it back to base camp in record time.

Sun spotted Levi accepting a blanket around his shoulders as an EMT checked his vitals. Or tried to. He was not being the most cooperative of patients. But he looked tired. His face raw from the elements. His lips cracked and bleeding. He'd been searching nonstop for almost forty-eight hours.

His cousin trudged down the mountain, gasping for air. Apparently, Levi had carried Jimmy down and left his cousin eating his dust. Or his snow flurries.

When Levi spotted her, he frowned, but that could have been because the EMT was trying to put an oxygen mask over his face. He looked like he'd lost ten pounds. In all honestly, he'd probably lost more than that.

Sun took a step toward him, but Quincy tapped her shoulder.

Outside of a second ambulance, Hailey had thrown her body over Jimmy's as emergency personnel tried to load him into the vehicle. She wailed and kissed and hugged. He smiled back at her and tried to pat her face.

Sun almost cried. She walked over to them, very aware of the need to keep up appearances, but she had to question Jimmy. Time was running out.

She cleared her throat, then asked, "I'm glad you're okay, Jimmy."

Hailey looked up at her wearing the face of a banshee ready to attack.

Sun held up her hands. "I just have a couple of questions."

"He almost died," she said, her voice a hiss of emotion, and Sun knew beyond a shadow of a doubt that she was not acting this time. She was a pissed-off mama bear, and Sun was on the verge of taking one step too close to her cub, but she had no choice.

Making sure no one could see her face but Hailey, Sun offered the woman the best apology she could muster, infusing her expression with sympathy and remorse.

Hailey seemed to snap out of it. She turned away, but kept herself wrapped over him while the EMT got an IV started.

Sun stepped closer, gaining the interest of Jimmy's uncle Levi, and not in a good way. "You are the bravest boy I've ever met," she said to him.

He smiled from behind the mask and gave her a thumbs-up. The sixteen-year-old had blond hair like his mother, but darker. It was wet and plastered to his head, and his cheeks were bright red. That, along with the glassy eyes, had Sun worried he had a fever.

She could hardly blame Hailey. She wanted to throw herself over him, too. But for now, she needed to hurry.

"Jimmy, how on earth did you survive?"

With that, he flashed her a nuclear smile, and she finally saw a little of Levi in him. He pulled down the oxygen mask and said, "I made a snow cave. Like the rabbits."

"Oh, my god, aren't you the clever one? Can I ask you how you wandered so far out?"

"A deer," Hailey said, shaking her head.

"It was hurt. I was trying to help it."

"You were following an injured deer?"

Pride practically burst out of him when he nodded, but then he caught sight of the needle headed his way.

She could tell it scared him, and she almost laughed. "Let me get this straight," she said, eyeing him with disbelief, "you just survived two days alone in the mountains with snow and blizzards and wild animals, and you're scared of a needle?"

He nodded.

She leaned down. "Me, too. You know what helps?"

He shook his head.

"Panting." When his expression turned dubious, she demonstrated. "Like a puppy." She showed her tongue and breathed in and out in rapid successions. In other words, she panted.

He laughed softly.

"Don't knock it until you try it, Daniel Boone. Come on. Stick out your tongue."

He stuck it out but kept smiling.

"And now pant. Breathe in and out really fast."

Hailey laughed as her son panted like a dog, but the needle had gone in before he'd even started. He never felt a thing.

"Guess what?" she said, leaning closer. "It's done."

He looked down wide-eyed at the IV in his hand and then back at her.

"Told ya," she said, blowing on her nails and polishing them on her coveralls.

When he smiled like he'd single-handedly won the state championship, she took his other hand in hers. He was on fire. She needed to wrap this up.

"Jimmy, can I ask you a question?"

"We need to go," the EMT said.

"Just one more. Jimmy, do you know Sybil? A girl a little younger than you with red hair and freckles? Did you . . . did you see her?"

He frowned. "No. Not Sybil. She's not my friend. Only Auri's. But everyone likes Auri, so it just makes good sense."

"But wait, you know her?"

"No. Auri told me she's her friend. I'm Auri's friend, too, but mostly Sybil is her friend because she's a girl and Auri's a girl and they talk about girl stuff. It's gross."

Sun snorted, as did Hailey.

The driver climbed into the ambulance and started it up.

"We're going," the EMT said.

Hailey followed the stretcher in and sat beside her son as the EMT shut the doors, and Sun prayed that he would be okay. She turned to Levi, worried for him, too.

"How is he?" she asked his EMT. She would've done it when Levi wasn't looking, but he hadn't stopped. He was annoyed with her, probably for questioning Jimmy.

"Dehydrated." After another minute, he added, "And cantankerous."

Levi leveled a scowl on the guy that could remove automotive paint.

"No fever?" she asked as Levi shifted the scowl to her. That was okay, though. She didn't exfoliate that morning.

"No fever. He should be fine, but he definitely needs to rest for a few days."

"Yeah. I'm sure he's on top of that."

"I'm right here," Levi said.

"I'm very aware," Sun answered. She took out a notebook and started writing.

"What are you doing?"

"Giving you a citation for littering. I saw what you did to the note."

"The wind got it."

"Mmm-hmmm, tell it to the judge."

Quincy walked up, rubbing his hands together. "Okay, we should get out to that body. They've cordoned off the area, and we should be able to take the ATV all the way out to the site."

"Great," she said, folding her notebook without actually giving Levi a citation. Mostly because it was the wrong book. "I take it you know where we're going?"

Quincy winced. "I was hoping you'd know the way out there. I haven't been to Estrella Pond since I was a kid."

"Me neither."

"Why go to a pond when you have a lake?"

"Exactly. So . . ."

They turned in unison to Levi. When people said he was known for his skills in tracking, they weren't talking about a race-track. The guy new the land better than anyone in the area. He may have spent his summers on the Apache reservation, but when he came back, he put what he learned to use here.

Levi worked his scruffy, dark auburn jaw before saying, "I can take you there."

17

She believed she could, so she did.
Now she needs bail money.
We are here to help!

—SIGN AT DEL SOL BAIL BONDS

He was so tired. Sun could tell. The emotional drain as well as the physical exertion of searching a mountain range for two days had to have taken its toll on him, but Levi stepped up and took them out to the incident site.

He rode his ATV in front of Quincy and Sun's, almost losing them in the thick, snow-covered brush on numerous occasions.

"I think he's enjoying this," Quincy said over the roar of the motor.

Sun couldn't take her eyes off Levi. He had stripped down to a lighter jacket and ski cap. His wide shoulders and long arms crossed the terrain with effortless ease, whereas she and Quincy struggled with every bump.

That being said, she could see the appeal. These things were probably a blast if the riders weren't searching for missing persons or hunting dead bodies.

They crested a large hill and looked down upon a small iced-over pond in the valley where three mountains converged. The winter scene was breathtaking. Levi pulled to a stop and pointed.

Sure enough, the team had already set up a tent to preserve what they could.

Sun got off the ATV and took in the surroundings. She turned to Levi. "Thanks. You have to be exhausted."

He kept his gaze on her, but with the ski cap, the scarf covering his mouth, and the dark glasses, she couldn't gauge what he was thinking.

"I'm so glad you found Jimmy," she added.

"Me, too, man," Quincy said. "That was kind of amazing."

Levi didn't even acknowledge their compliments. Instead, he turned back to the investigative scene, and Sun could see why he and Quincy didn't get along. Quincy was a social genius. He could charm the skin off a snake.

Levi didn't care enough to be charming. If someone didn't like him, he would find the strength to carry on.

If someone didn't like Quincy, he would do everything in his power to find out why. It would drive him crazy. Which was way more fun than it might seem on the surface.

Sun glanced at Levi, wanting so very much to pull down the scarf and run her fingertips over his shapely mouth. "You can go home if you'd like to."

"I'm good here."

"Here?" she asked, surprised. "You're not going home? The EMT said—"

"This is my land."

"Well, technically—" Quincy began, but Levi interrupted again.

"This is my land."

She understood. While the mountain range butted up against his land, he'd spent his life exploring it. Of course he would consider it his.

Quincy started the ATV, and they headed down while Levi stayed up top. She looked back at him. He sat like a cowboy on a horse surveying the landscape. Or, possibly more accurate, like a Native American. An Apache, to be exact, though according to her mother, he was only about one-quarter Apache. The rest was all South. Kentucky, Mississippi, Alabama. A culture all its own.

"Sheriff," Jack, the medical investigator from the OMI in Albuquerque, said when they walked into the cordoned-off area.

Sun was taken aback. "Jacqueline, wow. What—? How—?"

"Oh," she said with a light chuckle, "I volunteer with the SAR team when I can. Gets me off the slab, if you know what I mean."

"I do."

Jacqueline Baumann performed many of the autopsies Sun had to go to. She'd helped Sun get over the nausea and gave her some tips for future reference that Sun had used ever since.

"How're the puppies?" she asked.

The young woman's face morphed into that of a proud mom. "So wonderful. The little one, Sheila, is ball of fire. She's discovered her tail, but she's just too round to get to it."

"Awww." Sun melted, but reanimated herself when a state police officer, who'd been in the search party, walked up. "Officer," she said in her best sheriff voice.

"Sheriff. We have one DB. Medium height. Dark blond hair. Forty-four years of age."

She looked at the shriveled, mostly skeletal body wearing a plaid shirt and denim jacket, both of which had seen better days. "You can tell his age?"

"We can when we have his ID." He presented an evidence bag holding a driver's license, a key, and some cash. "One Mr. Kubrick Ravinder."

A soft gasp escaped her before she could contain it.

"Did you know him?" the officer asked her.

"Uncle Brick. That's what they called him. He left years ago and never came back. So I've been told."

"Well, judging by the decomposition," Jack said, "he didn't get far."

"How long ago was this?" Quincy asked her.

Sun shrugged. "Fifteen, sixteen years ago. I'm not sure. I just found out. The family didn't consider him missing so much as up-and-left."

"So, no missing persons report?" the officer asked.

"None that I know of. What are we thinking?" she asked Jack. "Natural causes? Exposure? Worse?"

"I'll know more when I get him back to the lab in Albuquerque. For now, all I can say is it looks like his larynx may have been crushed. But he's been out here a long time. An animal could have done that postmortem."

Sun leaned over to look at it.

"It looks like he was dragged here from another location. See all that dirt?"

Sun nodded.

"He may have been buried at some point. If so, he was dug up. He's missing several bones. I will, of course, do the usual workup. But as an initial point of note, there's an awful lot of blood on his clothing for all of it be postmortem, which would be the case if he did die of natural causes or exposure."

"Homicide?"

"Wouldn't rule it out just yet. I'll let you know my findings, unless you want to be notified when I'm starting."

"Maybe. We're working a missing persons case."

"Another one?" she asked.

"The girl. Sybil St. Aubin."

"Oh yes. Okay, well, keep me updated, and I'll text you either way."

"Thanks, Jack. Brick," she said softly. "What more can this family take?" she asked Quincy, who was standing back, not particularly interested in the particulars, but the minute she did so, she noticed a bolo around Brick's neck with a silver slide.

Quincy scoffed, though, and when she questioned him with quick glance, he said, "I'd bet my last dollar the same family you are worried about is the one who put him out here."

She couldn't argue that. Levi's uncles were ruthless.

The bolo, made of dark braided leather and a slide with matching metal tips, looked handmade. And expensive. The fact that he still had both it and the cash in his pocket could rule out robbery, unless he'd been carrying something else more valuable.

The day grew brighter and warmer with each passing moment. The snow started melting off. The warmth felt good against her face.

Sun looked past Quincy to see if Levi was still on the hill. He was, and she shook her head. He had to be almost falling over.

Search and rescue was probably already packed up and heading out. She needed to check on the Book Babes, make sure they'd made it down the mountain okay, and get back on Sybil's case.

She had her deputies canvassing the entire town, asking questions and showing Sybil's picture. They were running the images on the news every hour as well. And they were still waiting on the partial print. Unlike in the movies or on TV, that kind of thing took time. Time she didn't have.

Before she could get to the ATV, she caught sight of a small building sitting even farther down in the valley, just past the next hill.

"What is that?" she asked Quince.

He cupped a hand across his brow. "Huh. No idea. I've only been up here once, and that was a long time ago."

She started toward it.

"Want to check it out? I'll get the ATV," Quincy said.

"No, it's okay. It's not far. I'll just walk."

"I'll go with you."

"Or you could help them pack up here."

He pointed to the forensics team. "They're still working. What can I pack up?"

"The DB, for starters."

He made a face, and Sun tried not to laugh. She only slipped twice on the way down the hill. The closer she got, the more she realized the small shed would be almost invisible on the ground.

She only saw it because of her vantage point, but she had to navigate a copse of trees to get to it.

It sat lopsided. A tree had grown into the side and was pushing it to the left. The effect was strange and haunting. It had been whitewashed at one time, but the color had almost completely faded, and in its place sat a pale gray.

The door had been busted off the hinges. It barely hung on and creaked with the light breeze. She couldn't imagine how it had survived the storm the night before.

Sun eased open the door, afraid it would fall off completely. Two small windows on either side of the building let in just enough light to illuminate the dingy room and reveal a filthy mattress on the floor of the building.

Nothing else. Just a mattress, a broken lamp, and a smattering of debris all covered in a healthy dose of an arachnophobic's worst nightmare: thick curtains of spiderwebs.

She pushed one aside and stepped into the building, the ground beneath her feet tilting slightly as she noticed a metal loop bolted to one of the exposed beams in the unfinished walls.

A sharp sting burned against her temple, but it was the scent that had her reeling. She recognized it. Lantern oil? Gasoline? She couldn't tell. She spotted an upended can of thick black liquid and knew it was the source of the smell.

Her abdomen seized, and she felt the burn of bile as it rose to the back of her throat. She bolted to get out and tripped on her own two feet, slamming her head on the door and falling into the snow outside as the world spun around her.

She remembered that scent. She remembered the thin stripes in the mattress. The brown stains on the floor. The spiders crawling across her face when she could do nothing about it.

She'd been here. The memory and the knowledge doubled her over.

She grabbed her radio and pressed the Talk button. "Quince, get down here."

"What happened?" he asked in alarm.

"Nothing. It's empty, but I want this entire area cordoned off and processed. Do not let that team leave until every inch of this valley has been photographed, bagged, and tagged."

"I'm on my way," he said, and she could hear him running. Then she heard the ATV speeding toward the copse of trees, and she lay in the snow, her vision blurry, her stomach on the verge of emptying its contents right then and there.

She'd had the same reaction to Sybil's letter. The same feeling of helplessness. Of darkness. Of fear.

And the blood. There was blood everywhere. Hers? She couldn't remember. But she did remember it on her hands. The sticky liquid drying in her nose and between her fingers.

The ATV slid to a halt in the snow just as her stomach did what it'd warned her it would. Coffee rushed up her throat, and she heaved it onto the snow as a booted foot came into her periphery.

But it wasn't Quincy's boot.

"Thanks, Lynelle," Liam said, the screen too bright and the voices too loud.

Auri watched in horror as the story unfolded. As *her* story unfolded. "The town of Del Sol has spoken, and we have a new sheriff, but what do we really know about her?"

Her mom's senior picture popped onto the screen. "Sunshine Vicram was born Sunshine Blaze Freyr to a military intelligence officer and a Vegas showgirl. She grew up in this sleepy town where the coffee is hot and the people are cool."

"She loves Del Sol," an interviewee said into the microphone. An interviewee named Quincy Cooper. He smiled into the camera. "She couldn't wait to come back."

"And we're glad to hear it," Liam said. "But what drove her away in the first place? We have uncovered a dark secret the Freyr family has spent a fortune to keep under wraps, and we feel the citizens of Del Sol have a right to know."

"That's right, Liam." Lynelle walked onto the screen to join Liam in front of the monument. "You see, a little over fifteen years ago, the woman we know as Sunshine Vicram met and married a man who, according to public records, never existed."

"That's right, Lynelle. We followed up on a tip we received while trying to get to know our new sheriff better and discovered that her claims of marriage at seventeen, only to have her husband shipped out the next day and later killed in action in Afghanistan, are completely fabricated."

Lynelle gasped. "Liam, how is that even possible?"

"That's what we're trying to find out, but we visited the county clerk's office. There is no record of a marriage between a Sunshine Freyr and a Samson Vicram. In fact, there's no record of a Samson Vicram at all." The camera zoomed in on his face. "Because Samson Vicram never existed."

The teacher was on the phone, ordering the person on the other end to stop the broadcast, but Auri sat frozen, so stunned she couldn't breathe. So shocked she couldn't look away. She felt wetness streaming down her face and dripping off her chin, and yet she was too dumbstruck to move.

The camera cut to Lynelle. "In fact, the only record we did find with our sheriff's name on it was a petition to change her surname from Freyr to Vicram mere weeks before this memorial went up in Town Square. It was created to honor the fallen soldiers from Del Sol. And at the top of the list?"

The camera zoomed in on the first name.

"Samson Elio Vicram."

"But, Lynelle," Liam said, gesturing toward the monument, "what about all the soldiers who did die in action? What does this callous disregard for their sacrifice say about the woman who is supposed to serve and protect this great town for the next four years?"

In the back of Auri's mind, she registered appalled glances from her classmates, but for the most part, she just stared.

"Exactly." The camera zoomed in on Lynelle. "These reporters want to know why our new sheriff deceived the entire town. We want to know what she's hiding."

"And we want to know if this deception has anything to do with Sheriff Vicram's five-day disappearance that resulted in a hushed pregnancy."

"Where is my remote?" the teacher asked, tearing through her desk to find it.

The shot of the sheriff's station popped onto the screen again, and the camera panned back to Lynelle. "Del Sol is teeming with rumors. Some say the sheriff ran off with a drummer who dumped her at a gas station in Truth or Consequences."

"Others say she was kidnapped and held for ransom by a depraved predator," Liam said with way too much enthusiasm.

"Whatever the case may be, we will stop at nothing to uncover the truth about our new sheriff, but for now, we must stress that none of this is poor Auri's fault. Whether her mother is a law enforcement officer or a con artist."

"Whether her father was a war hero or a violent criminal, we all need to welcome Auri Vicram with open—"

The broadcast stopped, the TV went black, and the only sound Auri could hear was the rush of her own blood in her ears. A sea of faces stared back at her. Some sympathetic. Some mortified. Some triumphant, relishing the moment.

"Auri," the teacher said, rushing toward her. "I'm so sorry. Those televisions are controlled by the AV department and the plug is in the ceiling and I couldn't find my stupid remote. I couldn't just turn it off."

Auri pushed off her desk and stumbled toward the door, her vision blurring so much she couldn't find the handle. Her fingers finally curved around it. She shoved open the door only to fall onto the tile floor in the hall.

A man was running toward her, Principal Jacobs, but her stomach heaved. She was going to be sick. She scrambled to her feet and fought the darkening of her vision to make it to the girls' restroom.

She felt nothing but the vise around her chest, cracking her ribs and squeezing the air out of her lungs.

She closed the bathroom door and wedged the doorstop underneath it to keep him—no, everyone—out. After falling twice, she managed to get to the last stall. She locked the door, dropped to her knees, and emptied her stomach into the toilet.

Her body expelled the coffee and breakfast cereal she'd had that morning, but she hardly took note. She was numb. She couldn't think. She couldn't process what had just happened.

As though she were a thousand miles away, she wiped her mouth with toilet paper, flushed the commode, then wedged her body between it and the wall. She felt more tears and pressed her palms over her eyes to stop the flow, like putting pressure on a wound.

Noises drifted toward her from the hall, and a deep sob echoed off the walls. Then another, and another and she finally realized they were hers.

Which was odd because she didn't realize she was crying.

A sharp thud sounded at the bathroom door followed by three more until the door opened and crashed against the wall. She heard steps. Breathing. Then another loud bang as the stall door almost flew off its hinges.

But she was still applying pressure. She had to stop the onslaught before she flooded the bathroom.

She felt hands wrap around her legs. They slid her out of her haven. She considered fighting, but if she released the pressure, the floods would start again.

At that precise moment, back in the clearing, Sun felt hands on her shoulders. She thought about fighting them off, but that would take effort, and she worried she would vomit again.

Auri felt herself being lifted.

Sun felt herself being lifted.

When another sob racked her body, Auri heard a soft shushing sound.

When she tried to push out of her rescuer's arms, Sun heard a warning growl.

"You're okay," Cruz whispered in her ear as he cradled Auri against his chest and carried her out of the bathroom.

"You'll be okay," Levi said as he lifted Sun into his arms and carried her to his ATV.

And the next few moments were a blur of backpacks and trees and kids' faces and law enforcement officers and arms. His arms. Wrapped around her in the best way possible.

Sun sat in the back of the ambulance that had been waiting to transport the DB to Albuquerque, still reeling from her rather humiliating experience.

Levi had carried her to his ATV and sat her on it. After being awake for over forty-eight hours and conducting a search-and-rescue operation in freezing weather and blizzard conditions for much of that, he picked her up and carried her.

She'd wrapped her arms around him and buried her face in the crook of his neck, letting go of herself for just a minute. He smelled like campfire and snow and felt like warm steel all around her.

When he sat her down, she reeled herself back in and gulped huge rations of air to calm down.

"Slowly," he said, kneeling beside her in the snow.

"I've been there," she said, gasping. "I've been in that shed."

"Lots of people have."

"Not by the looks of it."

"Yeah, well. I guess it's been a while."

She forced herself to calm down and took a moment to look at him. To appreciate the work of art he'd grown into. The amber in his eyes mesmerized her, and she could have stared at him all day, but she had cases to solve, and they were, as her father used to say, burning daylight.

She swallowed and delivered the bad news. "It's your uncle, Levi. Your uncle Brick."

His lashes narrowed. "How do you know we called him that?"

"I just heard it, I guess. I'm sorry, your uncle Kubrick."

He let his gaze slide past her toward the incident site. "Are you sure?"

She nodded. "He had a driver's license in his pocket."

He nodded, then looked down at the hand she'd unconsciously moved to his arm.

She pulled it back just as Quincy skidded to a halt beside them and jumped off the ATV. "What happened?" he asked, leaning down to her.

Sun shook her head. "Just get me out of here."

Quincy helped her off the ATV and onto his as Levi stood back.

"I'm sorry for your loss, Levi."

He shook his head. "Save it for someone worthier."

Twenty minutes later, Sun was sitting in the back of an ambulance, being grilled by her bestie.

"What happened back there?" Quincy asked when the technician left her to her own devices. A dangerous place to just leave her willy-nilly.

"I don't know." She shook her head, trying to loosen the cobwebs.

"Well, can you try to figure it out, because damn. You passed out."

"I didn't pass out."

"First you threw up, then you passed out."

"I didn't pass out. I don't think. I don't know. I kind of lost touch with reality there for a minute."

"Okay. That's a start. So why are we processing a scene that hasn't had a visitor in a decade, by the looks of it?"

She moved the ice pack to the back of her head. "Damn door."

"They can be such dicks. The scene?"

After taking a quick glance around, she leaned in and said, "That's where I was held."

If she had slapped him, he wouldn't have been more surprised.

"I remembered. The minute I walked in, I remembered the smell. The filthy mattress. The tiny windows where the sun would only stream in at certain times of day."

He picked up his jaw and gaped at her. "I thought . . . I mean, your head injury."

"I know. I've had dreams. Nightmares, really. But I honestly thought I'd just made them up."

Quincy looked outside, then closed the doors for total privacy. "Okay, no more bullshit. Start from the beginning, or I swear to God, I'm quitting right here and now and becoming an opera singer."

She smiled despite herself. "You can't sing."

"Which is why it would be tragic." He leaned closer and took her hand. "Look, I get it, Sun. You don't like to talk about it, but all I know is that you were abducted in high school and held for almost a week. Then you magically ended up in the ICU at St. Vincent's in Santa Fe with a traumatic brain injury. A month later, you woke up from a coma with retrograde amnesia. Oh, and a bun in the oven. So, mind filling in the blanks?"

"Quince, you know almost as much as I do."

"Bullshit." He curled his hands into fists and sat back in the paramedic's seat. "I see how you go off into space sometimes. The look on your face when you come back is not nothing. You're remembering something. Tell me I'm wrong."

She blew out a breathy laugh. "It's just, I don't want my parents to know."

"Like I'm going to tell them."

"Please, my mother has you so wrapped around her little finger, it's a wonder you can walk in a straight line."

He shook his head. "Wrong. It's the other way around. I have her wrapped around this finger right here." He lifted his middle finger, sending Sun a message in crystal-clear Technicolor.

"Ah. Well, she wanted to know if you could take a look at her carburetor."

He sat up straighter. "Really? Is tonight okay?"

She chuckled. "You're so whipped. Does she even have a carburetor?"

He bit back a curse. "I can't help it. I'm in love with her. And it's more than that pitiful crush I had on her when we were kids."

"Had? And what about my father?"

A patient smile spread across his face. "I know what you're doing."

"What?" When realization dawned, she shrugged. "Maybe. It's just hard to talk about."

"Well, get the fuck over it. Tell me everything, or I walk."

She knew he wouldn't, of course, but he did deserve to know what she knew. He'd stood by her every second of every day and never questioned any of her decisions, though he wasn't very happy about her initial exodus.

Anita came over the radio for her. "Sheriff, what's your 10-20?"

"We're at the SAR site."

"Copy that. We have a 10-39 at the high school. Sheriff, it's your daughter."

They looked at each other for 2.4 seconds and then tore out of the ambulance and headed for town.

18

Auri curled her fingers into Cruz's hair in something akin to a death grip. They were sitting on the cot in the nurse's office, her legs draped over his lap, as she sobbed until her chest hurt.

How would she face her mother now? How could she?

With her world collapsing around her, Auri contemplated the penultimate of last resorts again. She'd done it before, but it had been years.

And Cruz—tall, gorgeous, charismatic Cruz—was letting her slobber into his jacket. Why? Didn't he see the broadcast? Didn't he realize what she was?

He tucked a strand of hair over her ear and ran his fingertip over the outer edge. He felt good. Soothing. Wet.

She pulled back, suddenly mortified. Well, more mortified than she had been five minutes ago. His jacket was wet from her sobs. She reached over, grabbed a tissue, and tried to pat it dry.

He caught her hand in his and held it to his chest.

Then she realized she was sitting on him and tried to wiggle off. He caught her legs and pulled her even closer to him.

She let him, but did feel the need to protest. "I'm too heavy."

"Please," he said with a scoff.

"I can't believe that just happened."

"Sadly, I can."

"You don't have to wait with me." She dragged out her inhaler and breathed in two pumps before continuing. "I'll understand if you need to go."

"Good for you."

She turned to face him. "No, really. It's okay. You don't have to hang out."

He cocked his head to one side. "And why wouldn't I want to?"

She shifted away. "You saw the video, Cruz."

"What the hell is that supposed to mean?"

"It means, I don't know, you saw the video." She began feeling defensive.

"Okay, so, I'm supposed to be scared of you now?"

"No. Not scared. Just . . . All I'm saying is I'll understand." Just then, she noticed his hands. His scraped and blood-covered hands. She leaned away from him. "Cruz, what happened?"

He examined them. "Something that's going to get me grounded for a very long time."

Her lids rounded, but before she could ask him about it, Principle Jacobs walked in. "Auri, your mother is here."

And the world fell out from under her. She covered her face with her free hand, unable to face her, as the sobs started anew.

"Auri!" she heard her mom say. She felt arms fly around her as she was practically plucked off Cruz's lap and held close by her mom. "Auri, sweetheart, you're okay. You're okay."

There were some things in life that a person just could not handle, no matter how hard she tried. No matter how cheerful the spin she put on it. It was different for everyone. Maybe it was the loss of a loved one. Or being abandoned by a parent. For Auri, it was the fact that she'd single-handedly ruined her mother's life.

She had to know it. Her mom. She'd never said it out loud, but there was simply no other way to look at it. She was at the root of everything bad that had ever happened to her mother. And now, her mom would know that she knew.

She'd tell Auri she was wrong, of course. She'd tell Auri that she was all that mattered and that her life would have been so different without her.

And she would be right. But what she wouldn't say, because Sunshine Vicram was not that kind of mother, was that she'd had plans. She'd had dreams and aspirations. Her grandparents had slipped once and told Auri about her mom's childhood dream of becoming a jet pilot in the navy. How it was all she'd talked about. All she'd ever wanted to do.

And Auri had ruined that. Her mere presence had changed the course of her mother's destiny, and there was simply no getting around that. No sugarcoating it.

"I'm taking her home," her mother said.

Mr. Jacobs nodded, then turned to Cruz. "Cruz, your father is here. I've called in an interpreter."

Auri's gaze flew to him.

"That serious, huh?" Cruz said.

The principal offered him a grim smile. "We can wait for the interpreter and discuss it then."

Sun led Auri out, and once again, Auri couldn't help but feel she'd just ruined someone's life. That was apparently her thing.

Sun and Auri drove home in silence with Quincy in the back seat. Sun held her daughter's hand, refusing to let go even when Auri gently tugged.

When they pulled into the drive, Auri asked in the softest voice Sun had ever heard from her, "Did Mr. Jacobs tell you what happened?" She looked so small, so hurt, Sun had to swallow down a lump in her throat.

She was in shock for the second time that day. First the shed where she'd been held for five days, then the video. "Let's go inside, okay?"

Auri's lower lip quivered like a child being chastised, and Sun pulled her across the console and into her arms. She broke down, sobbing uncontrollably. Sobbing so much Sun had started, too.

Break her heart. Break her arm or her leg. Break her will. But leave her daughter alone. Those kids crossed a line, and Sun would make sure they knew it. She'd tried to arrest them right then and there, but Quincy stopped her, saying they needed to investigate first. And she needed to cool down.

The fact that he was right didn't help.

Quincy leaned forward and put a large hand on each of their heads.

Auri glanced nervously at him. "Did you see it, too?"

He nodded, and Sun was surprised by the wetness in his eyes as well.

"We need to talk. About everything. And Quincy needs to know, too."

"I'm okay if you aren't comfortable with my being here, bean sprout. I will not be offended in the least."

Auri's breath hitched in her chest, and the sobs began again. She jumped between the seats and into Quincy's arms, and Sun's head spun from the grief coursing through her veins.

She'd never told her. Clearly, she should have. For her to learn the truth about . . . everything like this . . . it was too much.

They went inside her parents' house where Elaine and Cyrus were waiting with coffee and hot chocolate at the ready. They scooped up Auri and held her tightly as the girl broke down again.

Before beginning, Sun checked in at the station. No new updates. Sun needed to get back to work as soon as humanly possible, but this was not something that could wait. Her deputies were competent on every level, and they also had Fields's help.

She told Anita if they found anything, no matter how small, to give her a call. Then she put her phone on vibrate and turned to face her family. Auri was still crying, and something hit Sun.

Something she hadn't considered before. Something she hadn't dared.

But the more she thought about it, the more she realized Auri's reaction wasn't quite on par with what it should have been had that information in the video been new.

Sun sank down onto the sofa and said softly, "Oh, my god. You already knew."

Auri whirled to face her, the guilt so evident, Sun stopped breathing.

"Auri, how? When? How long have you—?"

Auri sat on the coffee table in front of her as her parents sat beside her on the sofa. Quincy took a recliner, barely sitting on the edge and clasping his hands in front of him.

"Auri, you knew?" her mother asked.

The sobs that had been wreaking havoc on her daughter's body were taking their toll. She could barely breathe.

"Where's her inhaler?" she asked her father.

Cyrus jumped up and found a spare in a kitchen drawer. He came back and handed it to his granddaughter, the love in his eyes heart-wrenching.

"Sweetheart," Sun said after Auri breathed in the Albuterol. She looked like a child. Like she had when she was in elementary school, her chest hitching every few seconds. Her eyes and mouth swollen.

She dropped her gaze, and with her chin trembling, whispered, "Since I was seven."

Elaine gasped softly, but Sun just sat there, stunned speechless.

Auri wiped at the deluge on her cheeks again while Sun gathered herself.

She finally asked, "How is that even possible?"

Auri took hold of the cross she wore around her neck. She did that when she was nervous.

"Auri, you're not in trouble. You understand that, right? You could never be in trouble for this. For any of this. It all happened long before you were born."

"I know. I just don't want to get anyone else in trouble."

Sun slid to her knees in front of her and took Auri's hands into her own. "Who could you possibly get in trouble?" When Auri still didn't answer, she brushed Auri's hair back and forced her to look her in the eye. "Auri, you can tell me anything. You know that, right?"

"I know. It's just . . . I overheard Grandma and Grandpa talking when I was staying here one summer. I've known ever since."

Sun couldn't help it. She turned and gaped at them.

Cyrus's head dropped into a hand, and Elaine's mouth hung open, as round as her eyes.

But then the truth hit Sun like a nuclear blast. "Seven," she whispered, gaping at her daughter. "You've known since you were seven. That was the summer—"

Elaine's hands shot up to cover her mouth as Cyrus sat seemingly paralyzed.

"That was the summer you . . . you contemplated taking your own life." Sun ended the sentence with a sob of her own, her chest seizing as she tried to talk.

Auri covered her face with her hands as though humiliated. "I'm so stupid."

"No," Sun said, grabbing her and wrapping her arms around her. "Don't you dare say that. Not ever." She was crying freely now, as was Auri and her parents.

Even Quincy had to clear his throat and wipe his eyes.

She put her at arm's length. "Auri, is this why? Because . . ." She struggled for the right words. "Because we don't know who your father is? Is that why you considered . . . ?" She couldn't even say the words again.

With all the therapy and all the intervention, none of this had come out. How had this poor child kept it locked inside her? Why would she even do such a thing? Was she so horrified? So disgusted?

"What?" Auri said as though offended. "Why would you say that?"

Sun shook her head, just trying to understand. "Then why, baby? Why would a seven-year-old even consider such a thing?"

Auri's chin trembled, and she said so softly, Sun almost didn't hear her, "Because I ruined your life."

Sun struggled to see past the tears. "You what?"

"I ruined your life," Auri said, louder that time. "Not only did that horrible thing happen to you, but then I came along and"— she gasped for air—"you had to deal with me, a constant reminder of what happened to you." Her sobs shook her shoulders as she continued, "I try to be good. I try not to be a burden to you so you won't regret keeping me."

Quincy stood and walked into the kitchen, scraping a hand down his face, while Sun sat in stunned silence, her chest so tight around her heart she could hardly believe it was still beating.

She swallowed the lump in her throat and took Auri into her arms again. Her parents joined them.

"You are everything," she said into her ear. "You are my world."

"Mom," Auri said, trying to pull back. "You don't have to say that."

Sun jerked away from her. "What do you mean?"

"You don't. It's okay. I know I'm not like a kid you would've had with a husband. With someone you loved. It's okay."

Sun covered her mouth with her hands. A sharp pain bored into her chest. "Auri, how can you say that? How can you think that?"

"Mom, you were raped. You can't love me like normal parents do. And that's okay. I understand."

After a long moment, Sun lifted herself back onto the sofa and looked into her daughter's eyes.

"Quincy, will you please explain something to my daughter?"

He walked back in, barely able to contain his composure. "Anything."

"Will you tell her what happened when I read the note?"

Auri blinked. "What note?"

She lifted her chin. "The note you wrote but left in your nightstand."

"You found that?" she asked, horrified. "I didn't think you found it."

"Oh, my god, Auri, that was the worst two hours of my life."

"Your mom went crazy," Quincy said. "She had every law enforcement officer in the state looking for you. I've never seen her like that. I think if you had done it, if you had gone through with it, your mom would have been next."

"No," Auri said, surprised.

"And then you strolled in two hours later," Sun said. "Like you hadn't a care in the world. I had no idea at the time what a good actress you were. I've since corrected that mistake."

"I'm so sorry, Mom. I just . . . I want you to have the life you dreamed of before I came along."

"The life I dreamed of?" Sun stared, unable to wrap her head around the inner workings of her daughter's brain. "Auri, you are my life. I can't live without you."

"But I'm annoying and expensive and frustrating."

Sun settled a stern expression on her daughter. "Aurora Dawn Vicram, you are also amazing and talented and brilliant. I can't keep up with you. You're always two steps ahead of me, no matter how hard I try."

"So, I'm not frustrating?"

"No! Well, yes, but all kids are. You're supposed to be. It's, like, your job. How else are we adults going to pay for our raising?"

"All kids are frustrating? You promise?"

"What?" Quincy asked, a smirk tilting one corner of his mouth. "Did you think you had a corner on the market? Because if you want stories about your mom, we can talk later."

She laughed and then asked, "Why didn't you tell me you found the note?"

Sun took her daughter's hands into hers. "I wanted you to tell me. To come to me. When you didn't, your grandparents and I agreed to put you in therapy, just so you'd have someone to talk to. I spoke to the therapist. Told her what happened. She said you were a little depressed but that you weren't exhibiting any suicidal tendencies." Sun leaned closer. "You are really good if you fooled even her."

Auri shrugged. "No, she just wasn't that great of a therapist."

Sun tackle-hugged her. The duo soon became a dog pile when Elaine and Cyrus joined them, Elaine tickling her granddaughter while Cyrus held her down. Then Quincy decided to play, and the whole melee went downhill from there.

"All right," Sun said a half hour later as she tried to decide if she needed to be taken to the hospital for internal injuries. She'd gotten the brunt of the brute's weight. "No more secrets. What do you want to know?"

She was asking Auri, but Quincy spoke up. "Everything. And I mean it this time, or I'm walking." When everyone stopped to look at him, he stood his ground.

Or he was about to, until Sun asked, "Walking where?"

They burst out laughing, and Sun asked Auri, "Is that what you want? The whole story? I can tell you everything I remember, which honestly isn't much. But no more secrets. You can ask me anything."

Auri sat on the floor and leaned against Quincy's legs. How a guy could make a huge fluffy recliner look small with him in it was beyond her.

Auri looked up at Sun, the deep caramel and green in her eyes breathtaking. "Yes. I want the whole story."

Sun looked at Elaine and Cyrus, then began, "Okay, when I was seventeen, I was abducted and held for ransom for five days

before someone dumped me at a hospital in Santa Fe. I had a traumatic brain injury and was in a coma for over a month."

Auri's lashes formed a perfect circle as she listened.

"The authorities believed someone drugged me at a restaurant
in Santa Fe. I guess I'd met a friend for dinner? I must've pulled
over when I was driving home."

"We found the truck on I-25," Cyrus said, appearing to get
lost in the story. Haunted by it. "She'd probably passed out while
driving. She'd scraped the guardrail."

"It's a wonder it wasn't any worse," Elaine said. Then she got
up to make sandwiches. They had yet to eat lunch, but Sun could
tell the story was taking a toll.

"When I woke up, I'd lost several weeks of time. I couldn't
remember anything about the abduction or about a month or two
leading up to it."

"Retrograde amnesia," Elaine supplied from the kitchen.

"It made the investigation even more difficult, because I
couldn't tell the authorities if anyone had been following me or
threatening me. If I'd noticed anything out of the ordinary."

"She could barely remember her own name when she first
woke up," Cyrus said. "She's come a long way."

Sun leaned into him and gave him a playful shove before saying to Auri, "And that's basically it, sweetheart. That's pretty much
my whole story. Besides waking up in the hospital and finding out
a month later I was pregnant."

"Did you ever get your memory back?"

"Not much about the days I was held, but I did get some of
the weeks I'd lost before the abduction. A few glimpses, anyway."

Auri picked at stray fibers on the carpet. "Mom, why did you
keep me?"

"Oh, honey, I was in a coma for a month, and then I didn't
find out you were percolating inside me for another month. By the
time we found out, you were a part of me. I couldn't let you go at
that point." She turned to her mom and dad, gratitude swelling

inside her. "And your grandparents supported my decision. Without question. They were so amazing."

"And you really, really, really don't regret it?"

She leaned over and put a hand on Auri's face. "I never have, and I never will. Unless you turn out to be a serial killer. But even then . . ."

"But, Mom, if you were held for ransom, what did he ask for?"

"Two million."

"Dollars?" Auri squeaked.

Sun laughed. "Yes. Somehow, the man found out about the nest egg your grandpa had built up. He's a shrewd investor. And some guy decided he wanted it."

"Is that why you didn't call the cops, Grandpa?"

"It is. He said if we did, he'd kill her. And to this very day, I think he would have. I'm not saying we made the right decision, but if I had to do it over again, I don't think I would change anything."

"So, you paid it and he took her to the hospital?"

"No. We waited for instructions on the day we were supposed to drop it off, but none ever came."

"We were worried sick, sweetheart," Elaine added. "We thought something went wrong."

"We thought he'd killed her," Cyrus said, his voice flat. He looked away, and Auri's expression softened on him.

"That's when we decided to risk it," he said. "We called in the sheriff at the time, Royce Womack, and told him everything. He got the state police involved instantly, but before anything came of it, we got a call from Santa Fe PD."

"Someone had dropped your mom off at the hospital," Quincy said.

"Who?"

Sun shrugged. "We don't know. He didn't stick around. We have footage, but it's grainy and impossible to make out a face. It was like he knew where to look and where not to."

"What could you tell about him? Was he short? Tall? Big or skinny?"

Sun smiled. "He seems young in the video. Very young. He wore a hoodie and a baseball cap and, if I'm not mistaken, he was injured. There was a huge dark stain on the hoodie, and one of the nurses said it looked like blood."

"It wasn't yours?" Quincy asked.

"It could have been, but he was really favoring his left side, like he'd been hurt. And there was a ton of blood."

"He carried her in," Cyrus said, "put her on a gurney, called out to a nurse, then ran before she could get close."

"Why would he take you to the hospital before he got the money?"

Elaine started assembling the sandwiches. "We think your mom was injured and he was worried she wouldn't make it."

"But if all he cared about was the money, and he'd threatened to kill her anyway . . ."

"Welcome to my world," Sun said, her daughter every bit as inquisitive as she ever was. "I've watched that footage over and over. I just have no clue who it is. I can't see a face when I get my glimpses of that time, either, but somehow I feel like the kid in the video doesn't fit the face in my head."

"What glimpses?" Cyrus asked, alarmed.

"Right. No more secrets." She looked at him. "You nailed it, Dad. I have been remembering bits and pieces. It feels a lot like Sybil's dreams. I see images but can't make sense of anything."

His mouth thinned into a straight line. "I was worried about that. You've seemed—"

"Worried? Because I did win an election I never entered."

"Is the stress of all this causing more memories to surface?"

She took his hand. "Dad, no. I've been getting glimpses of the abduction for years now. Just images, really. I've even remembered a couple of things that have happened before the abduction that I'd forgotten. Just silly little things, but it's something."

"And?" Quincy asked.

"And what?"

"Oh, I'm sorry." He sat back in the recliner. "I thought the whole no-more-secrets thing applied to the present tense as well."

She frowned at him. "It does."

"This morning?"

She crossed her arms. "I was getting to that."

"Mm-hmm."

"What happened this morning?" Auri asked, her voice hurried. "Besides finding Jimmy. I'm so glad, Mom."

"Yeah, well, that was all Levi."

"Man's a machine," Quincy said.

Sun hid the pleased smile from him, then she looked at Elaine. "Mom, can you come in here?"

"Of course." Elaine put down the knife, picked up the sandwiches, and joined them, but Sun could tell she was a little nervous.

"During the SAR mission, I found a crumbling shed near Estrella Pond. I didn't think much of it, but it did grab my attention. I went to check it out and . . . I remembered." She drew her bottom lip in through her teeth. "That's where I was held."

The surprised looks on her parents' faces left little to the imagination.

"I remembered the smell most of all. But also the tiny windows. And the mattress. And the spiders."

"Spiders?" Auri asked, horrified. "There were spiders?"

"Yes, but I barely remember. You have to think of what I do remember as more like a snapshot than an actual event. I'm still missing so much, but I know I was held in that shed and that's where we found a body."

"I heard that," Elaine said. "At the search site."

"Do they know who it is?" Auri asked Sun.

"They do. It was Kubrick Ravinder."

"Brick?" Cyrus said. "That snake?"

"The one and only. He's been up there a while. I'll know more in a few days, but he could've been up there this whole time. No one's seen him in over a decade."

"Oh, good heavens," Elaine said. "He could've been the one who took you."

"Yes. I just wanted you to be aware."

Auri bit her bottom lip, indicating something weighing her down. "Can I ask one more thing?"

"Auri, yes. Now and always."

"Okay, for now, can I ask why you faked a marriage?"

It was a question she'd asked herself occasionally. Was it worth it? Did it work? Did any of it matter in the long run? But then she would look at her beautiful daughter and the answers to those questions were always yes.

"Did you know it was fake?" she asked her. "Before the broadcast?"

"Yes. I'm sorry."

All those years, all those questions swimming around in her head, and Auri had no one to talk to about it. No one to turn to. Sun imagined the shooting pain that pierced her heart was similar to what a heart attack would feel like.

"Oh, my god, Auri. I'm the one who's sorry. I was going to tell you, but the time just never seemed right. And then when you got depressed, it really didn't seem right."

"I understand, Mom. I really do. I'm just not sure why you did it in the first place."

Cyrus agreed. "You have to understand. We were scared to death. We still didn't know who took your mom. We didn't know if he would come back, and we didn't want him knowing you were his."

"Because in our eyes, you weren't," Elaine said. "You were 100 percent ours. End of story."

A soft hue blossomed over her daughter's face.

"I feel like you were my reward," Sun continued. "My prize for making it through the whole ordeal. I have no idea what I went through, but I do know there were chains and a traumatic brain injury. I deserved you, damn it."

Auri perked up at that, and Sun couldn't believe that after all this time, the truth was coming out. And all because of a bunch of bullies whom she had every intention of arresting for obstruction of justice. As far as she was concerned, they'd released details from an ongoing investigation.

"And the monument in his honor?" Auri asked.

"Twofold." Her dad held up two fingers, just in case no one in the room knew what *twofold* meant. "First, we wanted to make sure he saw it, whoever he was, and believed it was real. We needed him to think that you were the daughter of someone other than him. Anyone other than him. And second, next time you're there, look closer at the circles."

"Closer?" she asked as did Sun herself.

The circles? What was up with the circles?

"Okay, but how did you keep it a secret?"

"The memorial or the fake marriage?" her dad asked.

"Well, both, I guess."

"Family," Elaine said. "There are several core members of this town who are like family. In fact, the fake marriage and the memorial were actually their ideas. To throw the abductor off our scent, so to speak."

The delicate arches of Auri's brows knitted together. "So, most people in town think you really married a man named Samson Vicram and that he died in Afghanistan?"

Sun nodded, almost ashamed. But they'd done it for a good cause. A beautiful cause named Aurora Dawn Vicram. She wouldn't change a thing if she could.

Elaine remembered she'd made sandwiches and handed Auri one. "Auri, I am so, so sorry. I don't know what you overheard, but it had nothing to do with you."

"It wasn't your fault, Grandma. I was the one eavesdropping, though I don't think I meant to."

Unplaced, Elaine looked at Sun. "She could have died because of us. We just keep messing up."

"Are you crazy? You guys stuck with me when I wanted to keep her. You didn't even question my decision when most parents would've tried to lock me up and throw away the key." Sun stood and hugged first Elaine, then Cyrus, and then she stole a sandwich.

"So, this is it," Quincy said as he took a bite of a ham and cheese. "No more secrets. I like it. I have questions. So many, many questions."

"If you even think of asking my mom about her showgirl days . . ."

"Wait, why is that off-limits? No secrets means no secrets. Did you know the Rat Pack?"

Cyrus choked on his sandwich.

"Good heavens, I'm not that old, Quincy Cooper."

His shoulders sagged in disappointment.

Auri was studying her sandwich when Sun asked, "Anything else you want to know?"

"No. I mean, maybe. It's just, if we're going for no more secrets, you might want to know one other thing."

Sun put down her sandwich. "Okay." There was simply no telling what would come out of her daughter's mouth, and from her expression, it looked serious.

"I did plan to take my life that day."

Sun forced herself to remain stock-still, to show no reaction. As a law enforcement officer, she was an expert, but Auri's revelation pushed her ability to its limit. She had her daughter talking for the first time. She didn't want to blow it now.

Auri tucked her chin and said softly, "I was going to jump off the cliffs at the lake."

Elaine pressed a delicate hand over her heart, but Sun forced herself to suppress her reaction.

"I'd climbed up there and was standing at the very edge, working up the nerve to jump, when a man talked to me."

Sun struggled to breathe, but only on the inside. Her outside was made of steel. "Who?"

Auri chewed her lower lip. "He talked to me like we'd known each other forever. He called me Red. He asked me how the water looked and if I thought it was going to rain and was I looking forward to the next school year."

"Auri—"

"Mom, he knew." She looked at Sun with pleading eyes. "He knew what I was going to do. I don't know how, but he did."

Sun's cool façade crumbled. She sat with her mouth hanging open before asking, "What did he say?"

"He told me he'd thought about it once, too, but then he realized that no matter how messed up his life was, there was always someone with a more messed-up life than his."

Sun held her breath as her daughter spoke.

"He was with a boy," she continued. "His nephew. He walked right up to me and took my hand because he said I was making him nervous and that if I jumped I could die. I told him that was the point, but he told me to quit being stupid. Nobody wanted to die in August. It was too hot for a funeral."

Then it hit her. "Auri, was it Jimmy?"

She nodded. "And Levi. He saved my life, Mom. He saw me up there, and he ran up the mountain to stop me. He just knew. And you always talk bad about him and his family, but I know you're completely in love with him. I can see why. He's so handsome and kind. He looks after Jimmy when he doesn't even have to. And I know his family is bad, but he saved my life, and I love him. I love him and I love Jimmy."

Sun put a hand over her mouth as fresh tears cascaded over her lashes. Levi Ravinder. Of all the things she'd expected to learn that day, the fact that Levi Ravinder had saved her daughter's life was not one of them.

She swallowed and thought back to all his uncles and cousins and cousin's cousins. To his abusive father and his murdered mother. He'd been through so much.

"Thank you for telling me that, bug bite." She hugged Auri again amid protests of a squished sandwich.

"Mom," Auri said into Sun's shoulder, "can you check on Cruz? I think he may have done something silly. Like defend my honor."

Sun sat back. "I gotta tell ya, kid, I like him."

Auri blushed again and went back to her sandwich, and Sun had never felt so blessed in all her life.

"You know, you don't have to go to school tomorrow. You don't have to go back to that school ever again."

The look Auri gave her was one of absolute resolve. "Mom, what would you do? Because you wouldn't run away. So, what would you do?"

Sun tilted her head. "I'd show them that while they may be able to put a hairline crack in my heart, they could never, ever break me."

Auri smiled. "I guess I'm more like you than you'd thought."

"Oh no, I had a strong inkling."

Auri giggled, the sound like champagne bubbles bursting in the air.

19

Deputy Salazar responded to a report of a woman stopping
at mailboxes and going through residents' mail.
Upon further investigation, it was the mail carrier.

—DEL SOL POLICE BLOTTER

Sun dropped Quincy off at work with the promise of meeting him
at the St. Aubin home later, but not before she gave him a little hell.

"Really?" she asked as they were leaving the house. "You let
them interview you?"

He flushed. "You know how reporters are. They tricked me."

"They're high school students."

"They're sharks in a town full of minnows." After a minute,
he said, "I am so sorry, Sunny."

She wrapped an arm around his waist and squeezed. "I know.
What line did these sharks feed you?"

"That it was for a 'Getting to Know Our Community Leaders'
post for their news program."

"And you fell for that?"

"Apparently."

She let him hug her, then left him on the street and made him
walk half a block in the snow. Served him right. Sun had almost
fainted when she'd seen him in the video.

With him taken care of, she had a mission, and after making

some calls, she found herself at the Ravinder home in the early afternoon. She didn't know what to expect. If there would be family
with them or if word had yet to get out about their uncle Brick's
death.

In a surprise twist, Sun found out Hailey had come home to
gather some things for her son. Jimmy had received a clean bill of
health. They'd feared frostbite, but somehow the kid managed to
keep all his fingers and toes, a fact Sun found astonishing. But they
were keeping him overnight for observation.

She knocked on the door to the main house.

Hailey opened it and almost growled at her. "What the hell
are you doing here?"

"I came to see your brother. Is he here?"

She looked around and then smiled at Sun. They kept their
distance while talking softly, but Hailey broke the rules and said,
"Thank you so much for everything you did, Sunshine."

"Sweetheart, Levi found him. He's amazing."

"I know. He's asleep, but you can go up."

Sun took a step back. "Oh no, I couldn't."

Hailey pressed their luck further by grabbing her arm. "Don't
chicken out on me now."

"Hailey, if someone sees you being nice to me, it could get
back to your uncle Clay."

"I know."

"Is Jimmy okay?"

"Yes, thank God. Now go talk to my brother . . . bitch. But he'll
never tell you a thing."

Sun realized someone must have walked up. She turned to see
another of the Ravinder uncles, the one they were investigating,
slink onto the porch. Clay stood behind her, looking her up and
down.

Like most of the Ravinder clan, Clay looked like a six-foot man
in a five-foot-six-inch body. They had a scrunched-up look to them
with dishwater blond hair, thin mouths, and patchy stubble.

Sun knew Levi had a different father from his sister, but she was beginning to wonder if Hailey was a true Ravinder as well. Either the scrunched Ravinder look skipped the women in the family, or she was just as illegitimate as Levi. Neither of them had that *je ne sais white supremacy* that the rest of the clan enjoyed.

"You'd better git if you're going before my uncle kicks your skinny ass off this land," Hailey said.

"Thank you." Sun walked past her and up the stairs.

"First door on your right."

"Unless you want a real man," Clay said, smacking his lips as he checked her out. "Then it's downstairs. Second door on the left."

She opened the first door on the right without even knocking. Levi could just get mad, but she was not about to endure Clay Ravinder's ogles any longer than she had to.

With the curtains drawn and all the lights out, the room was completely dark. Of course it was dark. He'd been up for two days straight. He needed a nap.

She took her phone and turned on the flashlight, but made sure to angle the beam downward. Poor guy didn't need to be blinded on top of everything else.

"Levi?" she whispered, tiptoeing into the room. She didn't want to wake him, but if he just happened to be awake, she wanted to thank him.

Right? Wasn't that what she wanted?

To be honest, she wasn't sure how she felt about him saving her daughter's life and not telling her. The state of her daughter's well-being hung in the balance and he'd kept it to himself?

She heard soft breathing coming from deep inside the cavernous room and followed the sound. The whole area smelled like soap and sandalwood. He'd probably taken a steaming-hot shower to warm up after his ordeal, eaten, then gone straight to bed.

His bed. In his room. And she was in it. The closer she got, the faster her heart beat. He'd saved her daughter's life, and she'd treated him like a leper?

Then again, she didn't treat him any differently from how he'd treated her all these years. In fact, he was much worse. Like he'd had a vendetta. Like she'd wronged him in some way.

She thought back. Could he be angry with her about Auri? Maybe he'd thought she was somehow responsible for her daughter's depression.

By the time she got to the bed, her heart was beating so fast she feared she was having another a panic attack. Levi was lying on a massive oak bed, a thick blanket covering his lower half. Nothing, absolutely nothing, covering his torso or the various appendages associated with his torso.

She focused the beam on the ground. The light radiating outside the stream helped her see just enough get closer to the bed without tripping on something, like the boots and pair of jeans that littered the ground. She stepped over them and took in the glorious image before her.

Except for the soft rise and fall of his lean stomach, he was a bronze statue. One her fingers ached to touch. How could they not?

A capable hand with long fingers rested on his side. A sinuous arm led up to powerful shoulders, a wide chest, a strong neck, a square jaw, and open eyes.

She started and jumped back. "What are you doing? Why are you awake?"

"Because I have an intruder." His voice sounded thick and sleepy, and guilt washed over her.

"You most certainly do not. Your sister sent me up."

"She has the strangest sense of humor." He had an arm lying across his forehead. He lowered it to cover his eyes and said, "Get in bed with me."

"What? No. I just . . . I wanted to thank you."

"For what?"

She stepped closer, feeling a bit like a fair maiden stepping closer to a sleeping dragon. "For what you did seven years ago."

"And what did I do seven years ago that would ingratiate the impenetrable Sunshine Vicram?"

"You saved my daughter's life." Despite all efforts to the contrary, her voice cracked with emotion.

He raised his arm and looked at her from beneath thick lashes. "She ratted me out?"

"Did you tell her not to?" she asked.

"Why would I do that?"

Frustrated, she sat on the edge of the bed. Even the thought of Auri contemplating suicide liquefied her legs. The knowledge that she was in so much pain, that she was in such a dark place, stole her breath away. "Did you know what she was planning?"

After a loud sigh, he turned onto his side to face her, then crooked an arm to use as a pillow. "Of course I did."

She bowed her head in thought. "You should have told me."

"Like you tell me anything."

"What?" She studied his expression but couldn't tell if he was serious. "What would I tell you?" Now, she could. Yep, he was definitely serious. In fact, the term *deadly serious* came to mind.

He'd stilled, and his caramel irises glistened as an emotion startlingly similar to rage seemed to take over. But when he spoke, his voice was dangerously calm. "Are you fucking with me right now?"

She twisted around to better face him. "Are you fucking with me?"

He continued to stare as though weighing his options.

She continued to stare, definitely weighing her options. After a moment, one of them called dibs. He'd saved her daughter's life. He could be angry and grumpy and curmudgeonly all he wanted. He could argue and belittle and look down upon her until the stars burned out. Bottom line, Levi Ravinder saved Auri's life.

Without thought, she put a hand on his bristly jaw, bent over him, and placed a soft kiss on the corner of his mouth.

He let her, and when she raised back up, he asked, "What was that for?"

"For saving my daughter's life."

"You should thank the rest of me, too. It was a group effort."

Her stomach flip-flopped. In its defense, it'd had a difficult day. "You need to rest."

"Chickenshit."

She gasped. "I am not. You know what? You're delusional from being out in the elements for two days and almost freezing to death."

"I didn't almost freeze to death."

"You're dreaming all of this."

"If this were a dream, you'd be naked."

"This is all in your"—she waved her hands in the air— "deranged imagination."

"The only thing deranged is you if you think I'm going to forget this."

She stood and hurried for the door, but she hadn't expected him to throw back the covers and follow her. She hadn't expected him to brace a hand against the door and hold it closed when she tried to open it. And she certainly hadn't expected him to press the length of his body into hers. To wrap his long fingers around her throat from behind. To scorch her skin with his nearness.

He was everything she'd ever craved. Every fantasy. Every lascivious thought. All wrapped up into one, powerful predator.

He bent until his mouth was at her ear. His warm breath fanned across her cheek when he spoke, but it was his words that caused the molten lava to pool in her abdomen.

"The next time you come into this room and sit on that bed, you need to plan on staying a while."

Then he took hold of the doorknob and opened the door for her. A door she couldn't get through fast enough.

She hurried past the threshold and down the stairs, every inch he'd touched burning. Every molecule in her body begging her to go back.

When she looked up from the bottom of the stairs, the door was already closed. She took a deep breath and patted her scalding face just as a hand shot out and grabbed her arm.

It whirled her to face its owner, Clay Ravinder, and the smirk he wore cemented her very low opinion of the man.

"Looks like you and the Apache had fun."

She set her jaw, then dropped her gaze to the fingers wrapped around her upper arm before raising it back to him.

He let go and showed his palms in surrender. "Cold as ice, you are."

Without answering him—any form of acknowledgment would only encourage—she walked to the front door and opened it. The wind splashed an icy gust on her face, but it felt good. It was what she needed. A metaphorical slap to snap her out of her fantasy world.

Because Sunshine Vicram and Levi Ravinder?

Not in this lifetime.

Auri took a short nap, a ritual she'd loathed since she was a kid almost as much as she'd loathed ketchup on hot dogs. She was beginning to change her stance on both practices, however.

She did feel better. A little groggy, maybe. A little grumpy. Probably because she had no way to contact Cruz. No way to thank him.

Since he was grounded from his phone and from leaving his room possibly for the rest of his life, she considered walking to his house but thought better of it. It had warmed up significantly, but not enough to tromp through the snow at dusk.

She decided to do some research instead and checked out Sybil's online presence. Or she tried to. She couldn't find a trace of the girl. No social media accounts. No tags. No mentions. The girl was a ghost.

Perhaps she was trying to be invisible on purpose, to thwart whomever she knew was coming after her.

Auri couldn't imagine what it must have been like for her. To know that she was going to be kidnapped and murdered years before it actually happened. What had Sybil gone through? What damage could something like that knowledge do?

And then for no one to believe her.

Thirty-seven pages deep into her Google search, give or take, she finally came across a picture taken on a crisp fall day of a young girl with red hair, round glasses, and freckles. Her name, Sybil St. Aubin, had been spelled wrong in the caption, but it was her, all right.

Sybil was only about ten in the picture. Her cheeks a bright peach from the cold. Her olive-green eyes glistening with life.

She was posed with a boy around the same age. Dark hair. A grin full of mischief.

They were hugging, their smiles a mile wide.

Hopefully, the person who posted the picture had spelled the boy's name right. Auri finally had a lead.

She scrambled to look him up on social media. On a hunch, she put his hometown as Chicago and hit Enter. He was fourth on the list, which surprised Auri since his name, Mads Poulsen, seemed so unusual. Now she just needed some contact info.

Her phone dinged with a message from her mom. She was checking up on her with a "Knock, knock."

Auri put down her coffee and texted back. "Who's there?"

"A little old lady."

She knew this one but went along with it, anyway. "A little old lady who?"

"Oh, my god! All this time, I had no idea you could yodel!"

After an involuntary snort, she texted, "That one's older than I am."

"They're all older than you are, sweetheart. How are you holding up?"

"I'm okay. Promise. But can I say that I'm working for the Del Sol Sheriff's Office so that I can do some digging into Sybil's case? I have a lead."

The way Auri saw it, no more secrets meant no more secrets. She would tell her what she'd been up to at the academy and what she was doing now. Mostly because her mom had some wicked resources. And she would do anything to help find Sybil.

"No," she replied, and Auri slumped in her chair.

"Please?"

"Well, okay. But if you get busted and go to prison, I don't want to read your memoir in ten years telling everyone it was my fault."

"Okay!"

Auri put her phone on Do Not Disturb before her mom could change her mind. She'd never seriously give a fourteen-year-old permission to impersonate a law enforcement officer. Though her mom did send her on an undercover assignment once. She had to order fried chicken from an outdoor vendor. She could've died that day.

After impersonating a sheriff's deputy, a police officer, and a detective at various businesses and organizations in the Chicago area—Chicago PD, for example—she finally had a cell number for the guy. And possibly a warrant out for her arrest.

She made a mental note never to visit the Windy City, then dialed the number. It was later in Chicago than in Del Sol, but still too early for school to be let out. She called Mads, anyway. And crossed her fingers.

A boy picked up. "Hello?"

Auri almost fell out of her chair. "Hi. Hello. Hey, there. Is this Mads?" God, she was good at this.

"Depends," he said, his voice wary.

"Well, my name is Auri, and I'm looking for a friend of a friend. Do you know a Sybil St. Aubin?"

"What's this about?"

"Sybil is missing. She's been abducted, and we're looking for some insight into her background."

After a long pause, he asked, "What's your name again?"

"Sorry. It's Auri. Auri Vicram. My mom is Sheriff Sunshine Vicram of Del Sol County, New Mexico. It's legit. You can look it up."

"And you're working with the sheriff's office?"

"Yes." The lie made her stomach cramp. "I'm helping with this case. It's urgent that I find someone, anyone, who was friends with Sybil in Chicago."

"We're cousins, actually. But, yeah, I probably know her better than anyone."

Mads was in the awkward stage where his voice couldn't decide if it wanted to be a tenor or a bass. He was probably a freshman or a sophomore.

"Her cousin? This is fantastic. Do you know about her premonition?"

"Sure. The whole family does. Not that anyone believes her. Besides me, of course."

"Why do you believe her?"

"Because Sybil doesn't lie. Ever. So, it really happened? No one told me."

"She was taken, yes. We're trying to find any clues as to who could have taken her. Something she may have left out of her journal or something she only told her closest friends and relatives."

He unleashed a heavy sigh that didn't sound promising in the least. "I wish I knew something. I've been trying to call her for two days. I should have known it happened. I should've been there."

"Did you ever see anyone following her? Anyone acting strange? Call and hang up?"

"Not really, but there was something that happened a couple of weeks after they moved to New Mexico."

Auri straightened in her chair. "Really?"

"Yeah. I told Aunt Mari I'd clear the limbs that had fallen in her yard after a storm here in Chicago. She gave me forty bucks."

"Sweet."

"Right? I went over there and started picking up branches so I could rake, and this guy walked up. He said he was with the gas company. He had a clipboard and a uniform with his name embroidered on it, so I believed him. But he started asking me all these questions about my aunt and uncle. When they moved. Where they went. Stuff like that."

"And if he was with the gas company," Auri said, "he should have had that information already."

"Exactly. So, I started getting suspicious, especially when he walked up to their house and looked in the windows. Almost like he didn't believe me."

"Did you get his name?" Auri asked, not really hopeful. If it was their guy, any name he would've given would probably have been fake.

"I did, and that's when I got even more suspicious."

"Yeah?"

"Yeah. The name on his shirt read *Penny*. When I asked him about it, he said it was his last name. John Penny."

"Sure it was. Did you tell your aunt and uncle?"

"I did. I called Aunt Mari, but she didn't seem concerned. She said it was probably innocent and it would only fuel Sybil's fears, so I didn't say anything to Sybil. I didn't want to stress her out, you know?"

"I do. Can you describe the guy?"

"He was pretty unremarkable. Average height. Fairly fit. Brown hair and glasses. But I don't think I could pick him out of a lineup if you paid me to. And I'll pretty much do anything for money. But this happened months ago."

"That's okay, Mads. You have been so helpful. Did my number come up on your cell?"

"Yep."

"Can you call me if you remember anything else? Anything at all?"

"Of course. Can you keep me updated? Please? My family is . . . difficult."

"Absolutely."

When she took her phone off Do Not Disturb, her mom had texted her again.

"You know I was kidding, right?"

"About what?" she asked, giggling just a little. Then she texted, "He may have been keeping an eye on Sybil in Chicago. If so, he's average height, semi-fit, brown hair, and glasses."

Her mom texted back. "How did you—? Never mind. She didn't mention that in the letter or her journal."

"This is from a cousin in Chicago. He always believed her."

"At least someone did. How many laws did you break getting this information?"

"How many are there?"

When her mom texted back, "Aurora Dawn Vicram," Auri fought a giggle before hopping up and running into the kitchen.

"Hey, Gran, I need to make a quick run to the apartment."

"Okay, sweetheart. I made tortillas and green chile stew."

Auri's mouth watered instantly. "It smells divine. I'll be right back. Don't start without me!"

She threw on her jacket and hurried across the backyard to the new apartment. The one she loved and had planned on spending the rest of her life in. She'd never felt home, really home, until they'd moved back to Del Sol. Like it had been calling to her. Waiting for her.

Then Lynelle Amaia happened.

She punched in the combination to unlock the door right as a hand closed over her mouth.

20

Caller reported man at Del Sol Lake
forcibly baptizing the children swimming there.

—DEL SOL POLICE BLOTTER

Sun drove back to the station still trembling. Not from Clay's attempts at intimidation. That pervert couldn't make her tremble if he rented a tree shaker.

Nope. Levi Ravinder had been making her tremble in her boots since they were kids, but they'd had a rough history and were having an even rougher present.

While he'd never been what one would call flirtatious, they did have a moment in high school. Sun, a freshman at the time, had snuck out for the first time in her life. She and Quincy wanted to go to their first high school party. They'd talked about it all through middle school, but by the end of the night, all Quincy had was a raging headache and all Sun had was a memory of Levi Ravinder she would cherish forever.

They'd walked into the clearing, thrilled by all the upperclassmen and the bonfire and the red Solo cups full of any number of alcoholic beverages.

Someone handed her a cup of beer. Since she hated the stuff, she only pretended to drink. Quincy, however, did not pretend. He would later come to regret that decision.

As she wandered around, taking in all the playful flirtations and heated flirtations and downright X-rated flirtations, she saw him. Levi Ravinder. He'd clearly had too much to drink and had passed out under a tree away from the melee.

She couldn't help herself. She strolled closer. At first, she just wanted to see if he was really sleeping. But as she got nearer, she realized he was actually watching her through hooded lids, his lashes making it almost impossible to see his shimmering irises.

She started to back away. "Sorry. I thought maybe you were passed out."

"Not yet," he said, watching her like a mountain lion watches its prey.

"Right. Well, if you're okay, I'll just—"

"Want some?" He lifted a small jug off the ground.

"Um, I have this," she said, holding out her cup.

"You mean the beer you haven't taken a sip of?"

"How did you—? Maybe. I just don't like the taste."

"You'll like this." He lifted the jug again, as though inviting her to get closer. To taste what he had to offer. As he lay sprawled on the ground, his shirt had ridden up. She could see his rock-hard abdomen and even the tops of his red boxers.

She stepped closer, and he held the jug up to her, his hold shaky at best. Since she couldn't quite reach it, she knelt beside him and reached over him.

"What is it?"

"Sunshine," he whispered, a playful grin lighting up his agonizingly handsome face.

But just when her fingers brushed across the jug, he moved it out of her reach.

She laughed softly and leaned farther. "Don't you mean *moonshine*?"

"No."

He moved the jug out a few more inches, and she barely kept her balance, almost falling on top of him. But he wasn't going to let her off that easily. He wrapped an arm around her and caught her to him. She landed on top of him, and humiliation burned her cheeks until she realized he'd done it on purpose.

"You're drunk," she said, trying not to giggle.

"Not yet, but I'm getting there."

He pulled her down to him, and even though she'd never kissed a boy in her life, she knew instinctively to put her mouth on his. To drink. To savor. He tasted like alcohol and cinnamon and fire, because that was what rushed through her veins and burst inside her.

She gasped from behind the kiss, and he grinned. Pulled her closer. Angled his head and slid his tongue deeper inside her mouth. She was so lost in the heady sensations washing over her, she hadn't noticed his hand sliding down her back. Cupping her buttocks. Slipping between her legs.

She stilled and he stilled and it almost became awkward, until he asked, "Is this okay?"

Is this okay? Was he serious? All her schoolgirl fantasies were coming true in one fell swoop. Hell yes, this was okay. But she didn't want to seem too eager. Too zealous. Too inexperienced.

She cleared her throat softly and whispered, "Yes. It's okay."

He kissed her again, then parted her knees with his to give himself more access, and she sucked in a sharp breath when he began to massage her through her jeans. Waves of pleasure crashed into her and around her and through her, the feeling so intense she feared she would climax right then and there.

"Wait," she whispered against his mouth.

He stopped and squeezed her ass before resting his hand on it to give her time.

While she lay panting in a sea of desire like she'd never known, he seemed to barely be fazed. "Will you remember this in the morning?"

"Depends on how far we take it." He said it with a wicked smirk, but she also saw a warmth in his eyes. A teasing sincerity. And something else. Hope?

"You Sunshine?" a boy asked. He stood over them wearing a red-and-gold letterman's jacket.

Sun scrambled off Levi and smoothed her clothes. "Yes. Why?"

"Does he belong to you?" He pointed to Quincy.

"Oh no." She ran to him. He was leaning against a tree, puking his guts up.

By the time she got him in the car, he'd passed out, and she almost groaned aloud. Her one chance, and Quincy had to give beer a try for the first time in his life, though certainly not the last.

She looked past the bonfire at Levi. He sat against a tree and took a huge swig of the moonshine. Then he looked back at her and raised the jug as though in salute.

She sought him out the following Monday at school. As a senior, she rarely saw him, so it took some effort to hunt him down. Not that she didn't know his schedule by heart.

She saw him standing with a group of upperclassmen and gathered her courage. Taking it one step at a time, she walked right up to him, but he only spared her the briefest of glances before looking away. As though he didn't see her. As though she were nothing to him.

She stopped mid-stride, humiliation rushing over her like a wildfire. He hadn't remembered. Or, worse, he remembered and was hardly impressed.

From that moment on, she did everything in her power to avoid him, both her heart and her confidence shattered.

But that was a long time ago. In the two years after the kiss and before her abduction, they'd adopted somewhat of an antagonistic attitude toward each other. Hers was a classic defense mechanism. His was much simpler. A complete and utter lack of interest.

Shaking off her feelings for him, she walked into the station with a text from Royce Womack. She could only hope he'd have news on the nervous Book Babe, Darlene Tapia, and why she was behaving as though she were trading government secrets for knitting yarn.

She was just about to call Royce when Quincy walked into her office.

He leaned against the desk she sat behind. "You know, we've talked almost every day for the past fifteen years, and yet we've never talked about . . . it. About what happened."

She put her bag in a desk drawer and turned to him. "And that's why we've talked almost every day for the past fifteen years."

"Good to know. So, no hits on the partial print."

"Damn. Any tips at all?"

"Just the usual BS. Poor Anita is fielding most of them. Price was helping, but he got called out to a possible break-in."

"Where?"

"Well, they've mostly been taking the calls in dispatch, but they get up and walk around every once in a while. Get some coffee. Hit the head." When her expression changed from deadpan to an even deader pan, he said, "Out near the Hudson's on Route 4."

"See? Was that so hard?"

"How's the sprout?"

Sun leaned back in her chair. "I think she's going to be okay. You?"

"I'm good. Thanks."

She blinked, letting the fact that she was not impressed shine through in stunning Technicolor.

He got the message. "I agree. I think she's handled all this really well, all things considered. So," he said, blatantly hedging, "Levi Ravinder. Didn't see that one coming."

"Me neither. Not in my wildest dreams."

"Did you find out why he never said anything?"

"He said I never tell him anything, so why should he tell me?"

Quincy stood and strode to the window. "That's a great reason. I should arrest his ass."

"On what charges?"

"On the charge of being an asshole."

She chewed on a fingernail, letting everything she knew thus far simmer. "I feel like there's something else going on."

"Okay, an asshole and a prick."

"Like, maybe he really cares for her."

"Then why keep something like that from you?"

"I don't know, Quince, but right now, we have to find Sybil. I shouldn't have spent half the day on anything else." After scanning the station, she asked, "Anita is awfully young. Are you sure she's experienced enough to be fielding calls?"

"Nope. She's just writing everything down and giving it all to Price."

"Well, that's good. What about his connections in Chicago? Anything strange about the St. Aubins I should know about?"

"You aren't going to believe this." He sat across from her and leaned in. "They are squeakier than the front wheel on a rusted tricycle."

"That clean, huh? You talk to the father yet?"

"Forest St. Aubin is so racked with guilt for not listening to his daughter all these years, he's like the weave in a basket case. The governor has called twice, wants you to call him back."

"You probably should have led with that."

"They sent a couple of staties to help out Fields."

"Probably a good idea. Two heads and all."

She leaned back in her chair again, frustration coursing through her. "I'm missing something." She took her copy of Sybil's letter and read it for the hundredth time. "Oh, how's the sweep of the shed at Estrella Pond going?"

"Good. They're almost finished. And then all of that is going to have to be processed."

"Yep."

"Were you still looking into it?"

"What?"

"Your case. Your abduction."

"Nah. What was the point? There were no leads."

"Until now."

"Until now," she echoed.

He got up to leave but stopped at the door and said, "So, the no-more-secrets thing doesn't apply to me?"

She looked up in surprise. "What do you mean?"

"I'm not stupid, Sunny. One of these days, you'll figure that out."

When he turned again, she jumped up and stopped him with a hand on his arm. She closed the door to her office and gestured for him to sit down.

He released a lungful of air, then sat.

"Of course I'm still working the case, but it's very sporadic. I haven't had a lead in years, and I'm just flying blind, but I am working it."

"Then why lie to me about it?"

"Because you're my best friend, and I didn't want to lose you."

He stood and went to the window again. "What the fuck does that mean? How would your working the case—"

"You think I don't know?"

Sun could read her best friend like a paperback, so when he stopped breathing, she knew he was growing worried.

He gave an indifferent shake of his head. "What do you mean?"

She walked around her desk and rested against it. "Quincy, I could tell every time I brought the abduction up how uncomfortable it made you feel."

"That's bullshit. I've been trying to get you to talk about it for years."

"Yes. To talk about what I can and cannot remember about my abductor. About where I was being held. About how I showed up at the hospital. But there were always certain aspects of the event that made you uncomfortable."

His look morphed into one of incredulity.

She ignored it. "At first, I thought it was the whole pregnancy thing. The rape. I mean, I get it. You're a guy, and unless you're actually a rapist, talking about that kind of thing should not give you the warm and fuzzies."

"Especially when it's you," he said with a whisper.

"I know." She walked to him and lifted her hand to his cheek. He wanted to rear back. She could tell. But he stood his ground. "And I understand that."

"So, then, what are you talking about?"

She lowered her hand but stayed close. "Quince, do you understand that none of that, nothing that happened to me, was your fault?"

"My fault? Of course. How could it—?" When she offered him her best sympathetic smile, he stopped and turned back to the window. "How long have you known?"

"Took me a while to figure it out. Alarming, since I'm in law enforcement and we speak almost every day. But I've known for a couple of years now."

He scoffed. "Years."

"And if I do say so myself, I'm amazing at reading people. You're good."

"Fuck that." His voice cracked.

She walked around him, leaned against the wall, and waited for him to get it off his chest. It didn't take long.

"It wasn't like I didn't want you to find out. Once I realized it could actually help the investigation, once I knew a little more about what it takes to solve crimes, I was going to tell you, but it had been so long."

"Sit down."

"I'm okay."

But she led him to a chair anyway and sat in the one next to him. "Quincy Lynn Cooper, I hereby absolve you of any wrongdoing, not that there's anything to absolve, but I want you to know that none of that was your fault, no matter how much your machismo tells you otherwise. I'm only bringing it up now because I can still tell how much it eats at you."

His blue eyes shimmered with emotion. "I wasn't there."

"I know."

"I was supposed to be."

"I know."

"I bailed on you to go out with Kristen Ulibarri."

"I know. And really? Kristen Ulibarri? She was a little above your pay grade at the time, don't you think?"

"And . . . wait, you knew it was Kristen?"

Sun smiled until he figured it out.

"Holy shit, that's how you found out."

"I'd suspected for some time, but she confirmed a couple of years ago. She was in town and invited me to lunch. It was like this weight she had to get off her chest. She had to apologize for dragging you away from me that night. For making me go into town alone. It all made so much more sense once I knew that."

He lowered his head into a hand. "I'm so sorry, Sun. If I hadn't bailed, you never would have been taken."

"That's where you're wrong."

He raised his gaze to her. "What do you mean?"

"This is just like Sybil's case. He'd been planning it for a while. Why else ask my dad for a ransom? He knew he had money and how much. Like almost to the penny. This was not random and would have happened either way. But your not being there that night was a coup for us, trust me."

"How?"

"I don't think the guy was planning on taking me that night. I think he had a much better plan, a much solider plan, but he was getting impatient, and with you not being there, I think he saw an opportunity and took advantage."

"And how is that a coup?"

"Because it was a last-minute decision. And he made mistakes."

"What kinds of mistakes?"

"I think he was going to take me in the parking lot before I drove off, but someone must've interrupted him. Why else let me get into Dad's truck and drive off if I'd been drugged? I could've wrecked and died and ruined the whole plan."

"I wondered about that, too."

"He had to have been watching me for weeks. Maybe he followed me there and saw his opportunity. Seriously, how often were we apart?"

"True. If we were out in public, we were out in public together."

"We were inseparable. Even my mom said so. I think your bailing on me has given us more clues than we'd hoped for."

"Like?"

"Like he had to get me out of the truck before someone pulled over to help, right?"

"Yeah, sure, but forensics went over that truck—"

"I'm not talking about the truck. I'm talking about the guardrail I hit. Because he had to let me get in the truck and start to drive home, I hit the guardrail. Because I hit the guardrail, he had to pull over and get me out. And because it was all so unplanned, he didn't have the opportunity to wait the requisite time for the drug to take affect before he pulled me out."

"Okay, I'm following you. I think."

"I've been remembering things. Like a dream, but still remembering them. When I pulled over, I don't think I put the truck in park."

"Well, you were passing out. It's easy to understand."

"Exactly. I remembered the truck creeping forward, scraping against the guardrail, and someone screaming. Then I have an image—a grainy, blurry image—of a man trying to wrap his hand with a towel or something. It's like I'm in the back seat of a vehicle and he's driving and cursing up a storm and trying to wrap his hand. And it's red."

"His hand?"

"No. Well, yes, but the inside of his car. I remember thinking at least the blood wouldn't show up too badly because it would match."

"So, when the truck crept forward, his hand got stuck between it and the guardrail?"

"Yes. I think."

"You know the likelihood of finding DNA evidence at this point."

She did, sadly.

Zee knocked on the door, and Sun waved her in. "We got a preliminary on the DB, Sheriff. There were definitely two distinct blood types on the clothes. They've sent them off for analysis."

"Good. Did they say what the types were?"

"The first one, O positive, matches that of Kubrick Ravinder."

"O positive?" she asked, one theory shot to hell. She took a moment to absorb that, to contemplate what that meant. "They're certain?"

"As far as I know."

Sun sat back in the chair. She'd so hoped to have some answers.

"What?" Quincy asked.

"I thought maybe he . . . you know. Maybe he was the one. I mean, the timing is perfect, and I have no doubt I was held there."

"Well, he was found near Ravinder land. Maybe an animal dragged him there. But how do you know he's not your guy?"

"The blood type. I'm B negative."

"Oh yeah, I remember your blood type is really rare, right?"

"Very. But Auri has an even rarer type. AB negative. Only 1 percent of the population has it."

"Wow. So, that tells us?"

"That means in order for Auri to have AB, her . . . father, for lack of a better term, had to have either A or AB. Trust me, I've done the research."

"Then this certainly fits," Zee said, scanning the report.

"Really?" A tingling ran up Sun's spine. "What was the second type?"

"AB negative."

Sun stood and took the report out of her deputy's hands. "Are they sure?"

"I'm assuming they know how to type blood."

"So, Kubrick didn't abduct me?"

Quincy stood and studied the report, too. "Not necessarily. He may not be Auri's biological father, but he could have been in on the kidnapping. Maybe he had a partner."

"In all actuality," Zee said, "they both . . . you know, could have."

Quincy nodded. "But only one could get you pregnant."

Sun closed the file and handed the report back.

"I'm sorry," Zee said. "That was callous."

"It was not. You're being methodical and honest. And a good deputy. I appreciate all three."

"Thank you." Zee started to leave, then turned back. "One more thing. Jack called. Kubrick's larynx was definitely crushed at the time of death, possibly in a struggle, but the actual cause of death was not strangulation. He was stabbed through the heart."

"Wow," Quince said, "he had all kinds of a bad day."

"And she said they found some kind of ID bracelet in his hand, a metal one with a leather strap. It must have broken off in the struggle."

"If he ripped off the ID bracelet of his killer and died with it in his hands, I'm buying the next round."

"It's very likely, but the name is worn off. They think they can recover it with some kind of chemical compound they use."

"Well, tell them to hurry." Sun's phone rang, and she grabbed it off her desk. "I need to take this."

They left her alone with none other than the infamous Royce Womack, the man she had surveilling Darlene Tapia and her possible connection to the escaped fugitive Ramses Rojas.

"Hey, Royce," she said, sinking into her chair.

"You sound exhausted."

"Long day. Anything to report?"

"Well, yes and no. How well do you know this Darlene Tapia?"

"Fairly well. She's one of my mom's best friends."

"You were right about the chips and the *Jeopardy!*, but that was all Ms. Tapia. Woman can end a bag of Ruffles faster than I can. By the way, is she married?"

"Royce!"

"Sorry. She's a very attractive woman."

"I know, but I thought you were saving yourself for me."

"Oh, Sunny Girl, don't even tease me."

She laughed softly. "So, no fugitive?"

"Now, I didn't say that."

Sun sat at attention. "You saw him?"

"I didn't say that, either."

"Royce," she said, asking a Higher Power for patience, "what exactly are you saying?"

"I'm saying things are just a little too mundane at the Tapia residence."

"What do you mean?"

"I mean, she's making an appearance at the window every few minutes. Almost as though she knows she's being watched and she wants to make sure she continues to be watched."

"Do you think she saw you?"

"Hell no. But I do think she saw the U.S. Marshal watching her from the unmarked government vehicle across the street. That woman needs to learn more about surveillance."

"No way, really?"

"Yeah, but I have a feeling the marshal wanted her to know she was being watched. Perhaps to make her slip up. Either way, it wasn't a total bust. Like I said, she's not behaving naturally."

"I know. That's why I wanted you to check her out. Could someone be in the house holding a gun on her and telling her to act naturally?"

"While that can't be ruled out completely, I'm going to say no. She's not nervous enough for something like that."

"So, what? She knew she was being watched and . . . no clue."

"Well, she was probably keeping the marshal's attention while the kid in the basement got away."

Sun shot to her feet. "What kid? The fugitive? I thought you didn't see him."

"No, I said I didn't say that I saw him. You were getting ahead of me."

She hurried into the deputies' room and snapped her fingers at Quincy.

He frowned at her.

"Royce Womack." She snapped again and mouthed, "Call the marshals." Then into the phone, she said, "He could be getting away."

"Could be? He already did."

"What? Well, where'd he go?"

"Hell if I know. You said to watch Darlene."

Sun did the universal signal for *dead* across her throat, canceling the order. "Was it Rojas?"

"No idea. A hoodie and a semiautomatic rifle obstructed my view."

Her "What!" came out more as a screech than she'd planned.

"Just kidding. You need to learn to lighten up, or that job's gonna kill you. Of course it was Rojas. But he's probably long gone by now. I tried to get ahold of you this morning."

"Oh, damn. I was out of cell range."

"I heard, but good news on the kid, huh?"

"Yes. Very. Okay, I have to find a missing girl today if I can."

"Any leads?"

"No solid ones."

"Chin up, Sunny Girl. You'll get there."

She hoped his faith in her was not unfounded.

21

A sweet voice Auri loved more than coffee whispered into her ear, "Hi, Auri. Don't scream, okay?"

She giggled and turned to see Jimmy Ravinder standing on her porch. In boots, a winter coat, and a hospital gown.

"Jimmy!" she shouted.

He slammed a hand over her mouth again. "If you scream, your grandpa will come out and make me leave."

"Okay," she said, but it was muffled because his hand was still covering her mouth. She peeled it off. "Jimmy, what are you doing here?"

"I escaped."

"Clearly. And you turned into a Smurf."

"Really?"

If one didn't know about his disability, Jimmy would seem like a normal kid taking a walk in a hospital gown. He didn't talk any differently, really. He just had routine issues. He did not like his routine messed with, so the hospital thing was probably freaking him out.

Jimmy looked like most Ravinders—besides his uncle Levi,

of course—except his eyes were a little too far apart. His nose a little too wide. But he had the requisite dirty-blond hair and boyish features of the Ravinder clan.

Hints at his autism were subtle. He had to think a little harder to get out what he wanted to say, and eye contact was a constant challenge, but the kid could play chess like he was born on a chessboard.

"You are very blue. It's concerning."

He laughed as she opened the door.

"Come in, and I'll call your mom."

"No way, OJ. She'll make me go back."

"Because that's where you need to be." She took off her jacket, tossed it onto the couch, then turned on him. "What were you thinking, anyway? Why would you go that far into the mountains alone?"

"There was a hurt deer."

"Then you get your mom or your uncle Levi. You don't go that far alone."

"I'm sorry. Are you mad?"

"Completely." When he didn't catch on that she was teasing, she grinned.

After a moment, he grinned back.

"Okay, let's call your mom."

She took out her phone, but he practically tackled her for it. They landed on the sofa, her giggling, him yelling, "Noooooooooo!"

"Okay, fine. I'll call your uncle."

"Not him, either. Mom said I almost killed him, and he's at home resting. Do you think he's mad at me?"

They sat up on the sofa. "Of course he's not mad at you."

"My mom said you got upset today at school. That someone was mean to you. You aren't going to try to jump off the cliff again, are you?"

"No, sweetheart. That was a long time ago. I would never do that again."

"Can you come live with us? My mom said it's okay."

"I would love to," she said, smoothing back a lock of hair. "But who would take care of my mom?"

"She can come, too."

Auri threw her arms around him.

He let her hug him for all of eleven seconds, then pushed away from her. Not in a bad way. Not to be rude. But to survive. He could only handle so much affection and Auri knew that.

"That was good," he said, showing her the wrapper of some kind of fruit bar. "Do you have any more?"

She giggled. "I have no idea where you got that, but—"

"He got it from me."

Auri swirled around to a male voice. A male voice coming from her bedroom. Or, more precisely, her bedroom window. She stood and crept toward the door to her room. The light was on, and she saw Cruz De los Santos standing at her open window.

"Cruz!" She rushed forward. "Did Jimmy open the window for you? Why didn't you just come to the door?"

"You tried to kill yourself?" he asked, his expression guarded.

It surprised her. "You heard that?"

"Please answer."

She lowered her head and nodded. "I'm sorry. It was a long time ago."

"Fuck you," he said softly. He stepped away from the window, raked a hand through his hair, thought a minute, then came back. "Don't try it again."

She held up her pinkie. "Pinkie swear."

"This isn't funny. After that shit with Lynelle and her cronies today—"

"Cruz, I'm okay." Without thinking, she took his hands. His glacial hands. "Oddly enough, this was one of the best days of my life."

He stared at her in doubt, but his fingers threaded with hers.

"How did you get here? I thought you were grounded."

"I was. I rode my bike. And I am, but my dad also understood my side of things."

"And what side would that be? Did you get in a fight with Liam?"

He looked at their fingers. Ran the pads of his over the length of hers. It caused warm, tingling sensations in the strangest places. "Sure. We'll call it that."

She took a hit off her inhaler then crawled onto her window seat. Jimmy walked in and sat on her bed.

"Would you like to come in?" she asked him.

"Nah. I don't want to get you in trouble. I just wanted to make sure you were okay."

"Oh, right. No phone. When will you get it back?"

"I have it back. I just wanted to make sure you were okay in person."

If fireworks had burst from her chest, she wouldn't have been the least bit surprised, her elation was so powerful. "You know, you're making my room ice over."

"I know. I have to get back, anyway."

"You have to go?" She rose onto her knees.

"Yeah. I promised my dad I'd only be gone thirty minutes. Can I come by tomorrow when you get out of school?"

"Yes. Please do. How long are you suspended for?"

"Don't know yet. We'll find out tomorrow."

"Okay. Let me know."

"Will do," he said, still studying their fingers.

She leaned closer. "Thank you. For today."

He shook his head as though embarrassed. "I'm so sorry for what they did to you."

"I'm not." When he looked at her in surprise, she said, "It was really a setup to reveal who my true knight in shining army jacket was."

"Ah. So, it was a setup."

"Yep. Sorry I had to go to such extreme measures."

"Was it worth it?"

"Every bit and then some." As her grandpa always said.

"Are you guys gonna kiss now?" Jimmy asked. "I can leave."

Laughter erupted out of both of them, but before she could change her mind, Auri leaned out the window and brushed her lips across the corner of his mouth.

He let her, then ducked, got on his bike, and took off.

"That was a good kiss."

She giggled and turned to Jimmy. "The best I've ever had."

Sun was on her way home with a boxful of file folders and reports—she was going to go through every tip and every piece of evidence herself—when her phone rang.

"It's Mom," Elaine said.

"Yes, I figured that out when your title popped onto the screen."

"Right, well, you should know there's a boy at Auri's window. What do I do?"

"Are you kidding me?" She groaned aloud. "Okay, tell Dad to go to the kitchen—"

"Yes."

"—grab a steak knife—"

"Yes?"

"—and make you a sandwich, because holy cow, Mom. I don't care if there's a boy at the window. Now, if there's a boy inside the house, yeah. That's when you take the steak knife and pay the guy a visit."

"Oh, well, there's one of those, too."

"What?"

"Do you want me to keep an eye on them?"

"With every fiber of my being."

Elaine breathed a sigh of relief. "I'm on it."

Hell yes. Definite advantages to living in your parents' backyard. Auri didn't stand a chance, poor kid. Sun couldn't have stopped the giggle that bubbled out of her if she'd tried.

"Oh, wait, the boy at the window left. And the boy inside is wearing a hospital gown."

"Jimmy Ravinder."

"Oh yes. He's so sweet. Shouldn't he still be in the hospital with that gown and all?"

"I'm thinking yes. I'm stopping at the Roadhouse, then I'll be home."

"Okay. I made stew."

"Thanks, Mom. You know you don't have to cook for us."

"Stop it. Take your time. I'll keep an eye on them."

Sun couldn't help it. She texted her daughter. "Knock, knock."

"Who's there?"

"A boy at your window."

After a long—very long—pause, Auri called. "Grandma?"

"Grandma."

"He's gone now."

"Great. What about the one in the house?"

"Mom, don't get mad."

"Auri . . ."

"I'm putting you on speakerphone. It's Jimmy."

"I actually figured that part out. The hospital gown gave it away."

"Oh, my god, does she have binoculars?"

"Eagle eyes, baby. She sees all. Also, the house is probably bugged. You have to remember your grandfather was in military intelligence. Now why is Jimmy there? In a hospital gown?"

"He escaped."

"I figured. Does his mom know where he is?"

She heard Jimmy yell in the background, "No, she doesn't!"

"I've texted her," Auri said, then she lowered her voice. "Have you heard anything?"

"No, sweetheart, but I'm on my way home. I'll be there in a bit."

"Okay."

"Love you."

"Love you, too," her daughter said, followed by Jimmy, speaking way louder than necessary.

"Love you, too!"

She laughed before hanging up and going inside the package store for a bottle of wine. It had been a long day and promised to be a long night, and she didn't keep alcohol in her house as a general rule.

An older man was working the counter. Tall. Lanky. He'd clearly lived a hard life. There was no one else in the package store, but there were two young men who looked barely legal in the hall that led to the cantina. They were waiting for the restroom as she was perusing the tall shelves for just the right bottle of Moscato when she overheard them talking.

"Hey," one said to the other. "I've decided to go to the sun. Want to come?"

"Dude, you can't go to the sun. It'll burn you alive."

"No, no, no. You don't get it." He chuckled and leaned forward to whisper to the guy, but a drunk whisper sounded strangely similar to a shout. "I'm going at night."

Sun walked past them and into the cantina to seek out the bartender.

Twelve civilians, including two males, sitting at opposite ends of the bar.

The bartender just happened to be a gorgeous American Indian with long black hair and biceps that rivaled the statue of David, if the tight tee were any indication. Not that she was looking.

"Hi there."

He lifted his chin in greeting as he wiped down the bar. "What can I get you?"

"Nothing for me. I just want to make sure you've stopped serving those two."

He scoffed. "Like three hours ago. They must've snuck in some booze. Happens all the time. I hear you found a dead body."

"Well, not me personally, but . . ."

He stopped wiping and regarded her with a serious demeanor. "You can't talk to it, can you?"

"I'm sorry?"

"The dead body? You can't talk to it, right?"

"The . . . the dead body."

"Yeah. I knew a chick who said she could talk to dead people. She was crazy. I worked at a bar her dad owned, but things got really weird. That's when I decided to move here. You know, peace and quiet. Less conversing with the dead."

"Wow," she said thoughtfully. "If only I could. Can you imagine how much easier my job would be?"

"You'd think, but that chick was bat shit. And trouble followed her like a fly follows, well, bat shit."

"Sorry to hear that. I'm Sunshine."

He held out his hand. "I'm Donnie."

"Awww," the male sitting at the end of the bar said. "Ain't that sweet."

She thought about ignoring him completely, but that could cause an even bigger scene. She turned to Clay Ravinder, acknowledging his existence.

"The Apache's never gotten over you." He tapped his temple with a dirty index finger. "Don't got no sense. No marbles where it counts."

From what Sun could tell, Levi was one of the few Ravinders who did have marbles, especially where they counted. He and Hailey gave Sun hope for the whole family. With Levi at the helm and Hailey by his side, they could break the chain of abuse and criminal behavior that probably went back generations.

She decided to take advantage of the situation and ask Clay

about his brother Kubrick, the DB they'd found on the mountain. "When was the last time you saw your brother?"

"'Bout an hour ago." He walked closer and took the seat she was standing beside. "Ain't never seen quite so much of him, though. Little disturbing, a bear chewing on him and all."

"Why didn't anyone report him missing?"

He leaned in and winked. "Maybe 'cause no one missed him."

"Ah. Well, that would make sense. Nice to meet you, Donnie."

The hottie nodded, and Sun turned to leave, but alas, it was not going to be that easy.

"Why don't you stay? Keep an old man company?"

"I have work, but thank you for the offer."

"It was more of a demand than an offer."

Donnie stilled.

Sun did not. "Yeah, not happening, Clay."

When he reached out his hand, she did the unexpected and stepped closer to him. So close they were nose-to-nose when she spoke again, her voice even. Nonthreatening. Her words were a different matter.

"I know exactly one hundred nine ways to take you down from this position alone, thirty-seven of those involve breaking your thumb before you get a chance to touch me."

Anger exploded in his eyes, but he didn't move. As badly as he wanted to, he didn't. And here Sun thought Levi and Hailey had hoarded all the intelligence in the family. Maybe she'd underestimated good ole Uncle Clay.

"Clay," came a warning voice from a dark corner of the room.

They both turned to see Levi Ravinder sitting in a corner booth, a glass of whiskey in his hand.

She'd missed him. How did she miss *him* of all people?

Then again, it had been dark when she'd walked in. Her eyes hadn't adjusted. She was going to add him to her warm body count, but she completely forgot her original count when he stood and walked toward them.

The look on Clay's face suggested he hadn't been aware of his nephew's presence, either.

Levi leveled a look on him that was part warning and part *Go ahead, I dare you.*

Clay strummed his fingers on the bar a moment, his annoyance crystal clear, then got up and switched seats without another word.

So, what now? She didn't want to be the girl who needed saving, and she didn't want to be the girl who stubbornly claimed she didn't need saving even when she did because those girls always came across as shallow and ignorant as opposed to the first group who just genuinely did not want to be the girls who needed saving. They wanted to be the girls who lived in a world where they didn't need to be saved from the Kubricks and the Clays and the Liams. They wanted to be the girls who lived in a world that deserved them.

And yet here he was. Her knight in shining, majestic, rugged, panty-melting armor.

She decided to change the subject.

"Your nephew is at my house."

The once-over he was in the middle of performing from underneath thick lashes paused at her hips. "Jimmy?"

"The one and only."

"Shit." He grabbed his jacket. "He escaped again?"

"He's done this before?"

"Yeah, he doesn't like hospitals."

"He must like the gowns. He stole one."

"He does that, too."

"Wait! My Moscato!" she said as he started for the door.

He made a U-turn and waited for her to buy her precious Moscato even though it clearly irked him. Oh yeah. Definitely a knight in shining, majestic, rugged, panty-melting armor. Damn it.

22

It's all fun and games until
Russia tries to hack our queso recipe.

—SIGN AT TIA JUANA'S FINE MEXICAN CUISINE

Levi followed Sun to the apartment where the kids awaited their return. Only they were in her parents' house eating green chile stew and homemade tortillas. Those things were worth the price of admission right there.

Levi took the box she was carrying and held it as they went inside.

"Hey, Mom!" Auri said, thankfully because anyone else saying that would have been awkward.

"Hey, bug bite."

Auri beamed at her for a half second before her jaw dropped to the floor. She'd spotted him.

"Uncle Levi!" Jimmy shouted. "You found me again!"

Levi put the box down and opened his arms. The boy, who was almost as tall as Levi, ran into them, but only for a second. He stepped back and asked, "Are you mad?"

Levi frowned. "Mad? About what?"

"About that you have to find me."

"I'm not mad, but your mom is probably really worried."

Sun's parents had also taken note of their visitor. Her dad stood and offered his hand. "Levi, good to see you."

"You, too, sir." He nodded to Elaine. "Mrs. Freyr."

"Mrs. Freyr," she said as though indignant. "Call me Elaine, and sit down. You've had quite a day."

"Thank you." His gaze landed on Auri, who was still gaping.

Without another word, she jumped up and threw her arms around his neck. He lifted her off the ground and let her feet dangle as he held her, and the emotion that hit Sun like the shock wave from a nuclear blast stole the breath right out of her lungs.

He'd saved her life. It was the one thought that she'd repeated all day over and over. He'd saved her life, and she'd never even known.

"How are you, Red?" he asked into her hair.

"I'm good. Better now."

Sun had of course entertained the idea of a father figure, and the consequences of the lack thereof, throughout Auri's life. But it had never hit her quite so hard as now.

Had it been selfish of her to focus so much on her career? Should she have at least tried to find a suitable match so that Auri would not miss out on the everyday normality other kids had?

Not all kids, of course, but there was no denying the immense advantages for a kid with two supportive parents in the home.

Hailey showed up about five seconds later, and because of their supersecret pact, could not stay for dinner. Levi, however, could. Hailey thanked her parents and Auri and then whispered a soft thank-you to Sun before taking a very disappointed Jimmy back to the hospital.

"You stay put, mister man," Auri said to him. "And I'll come see you first thing tomorrow morning."

He brightened at that, and Sun was struck with just how wonderful her daughter was. A daily occurrence, yes, but one she cherished.

They sat down to eat, and Sun was so distracted by the god sitting at the table, as one is when gods sit at tables with mere mortals, that she didn't even notice when the same daughter she'd just praised, the same one she'd just gushed over, snuck off to look at the evidence she'd brought home on the Sybil St. Aubin case.

While her parents made small talk with Levi, asking him about the business and the world of moonshine, Sun downed about half the bottle of Moscato and enjoyed every ounce. Staring into her glass helped her not stare at Levi. Helped her not dwell on how he'd looked in bed that morning. Or what he'd said to her when she'd left.

She was contemplating all the excuses she could come up with to invade his sanctuary again when Auri walked into the kitchen holding a copy of the letter Sybil sent.

"Mom," she said, her eyes like saucers.

"Auri, you can't have that." Sun jumped up to take it from her, knocking her wine over in the process, but the expression on Auri's face stopped her. "What is it, sweetheart?"

"Why didn't you show this to me earlier?"

"Auri, you can't have that. It's part of an ongoing investigation."

"But I think there's a message in this letter."

"What do you mean?" She hurried around to her, and they looked at the letter together.

"Remember when I told you how I met Sybil and how we hit it off and talked about everything from boys to school?"

"Yes."

"Okay, her letter says, 'Please thank Auri for being my friend for a whole week. I've never known anyone like her. We were hoping we would have at least one class together, like first period, but just in case we didn't, we came up with a way to pass notes to each other like spies sending secret messages. Maybe we can still do that someday. I hope she liked me as much as I liked her.'"

"I was going to tell you that part, honey. With everything going on, I just—"

"No, it's okay, Mom. But I found out something today." She sank into the chair next to Levi, and if the room had suddenly exploded and blinded her, Sun would still have noticed the arm he put around her daughter's shoulders.

She melted into a quivering puddle of emotion, but she snapped out of it when Auri continued with, "So I had to practically threaten this kid today."

"You had to what?"

"Remember the boy? The office aide at school who was very interested in the fact that we wanted Sybil's schedule printed out?"

"I do," she said, thinking back. "Average height, Asian, glasses, probably no more than a hundred pounds soaking wet. Hundred ten at most."

Auri chuckled. "Yes. Aiden Huang. He told me he'd reacted that way because he'd printed out a schedule for someone else, and he thought he was getting into trouble. It was Sybil, Mom. She negotiated a trade with him to print out a schedule before winter break. My schedule."

"Yours?"

"Yes. Mom, she already knew my schedule. She knew it before the New Year's Eve party."

Sun sank beside her. "Okay."

"So, first off, she struck up a conversation with me, something that, according to everyone at school, she never did. Ever. She was painfully shy. Second, she already knew my schedule when we met at the lake and if we would have any classes together. She'd gotten it from Aiden."

"Okay. What does it mean?"

"This might sound crazy, Mom, but I think she left a note for me. At school."

Sun once again marveled at her daughter's gray matter. Kid would go far. "What do you suggest we do?" she asked, tossing out the bait to see what she would do with it.

"We go to the school."

"Sounds like a plan, but why not just tell you? Why go to all this trouble?"

"I wondered about that, too." She crossed her arms in thought. "I think it's because no one believed her. I think she was worried what I would think. If I would see her as a freak who didn't want to hang out with her."

"If she was worried about what you thought of her, she really did want to be friends. That says a lot."

Auri flashed a timid smile, then said, "We have to get to that school."

"Yes, we do." She picked up the phone and called Quincy.

"Quince, who's the security guard at the high school?"

"Gary Woods. Why?"

"Do you have his number? We need to get over there. Auri caught something in the letter we didn't see."

"Figures, the little firecracker. But don't call Gary. Holy shit. We have a key somewhere. Or call Jacobs."

"Why can't I call Gary?" Sun found it odd that even Auri was against the idea of calling the security guard, their school liaison.

Auri was waving her arms, shaking her head and mouthing, "No, no, no, no, no."

"You remember Barney Fife?" he asked.

"Really? He's that bad?"

"Oh no. You misunderstand. He makes Barney Fife look like Sherlock Holmes."

"Ouch."

"I'll call Jacobs and meet you at the school."

"Okay, and Quince," she added hesitantly, "radio silence on this, okay?"

"Ten-four."

Levi stood and followed them to the door.

"Thank you again for everything," Sun said to him.

He looked at Auri, winked, and then walked out with them,

only he didn't go to his truck. He went to her cruiser. He looked over his shoulder and said, "Shotgun."

Auri laughed and got in the back seat.

"Um, what are you doing?" Sun asked.

"What does it look like I'm doing?"

"You can't go with us. This is an official investigation."

"Yeah, I don't know if you know this, but I'm a bona fide, sworn-in deputy."

"The hell you are."

"The hell I'm not. Ask your boyfriend."

"I don't have a boyfriend."

"Cooper," he added.

"We are not—"

"He was there when I was sworn in for a special assignment."

She narrowed her eyes. "What kind of special assignment?"

"I'm not sure that's within your pay grade."

"You know what?" she asked, frustrated. "It doesn't even matter. You can't go. You could be the kidnapper, for all I know."

"I'm a suspect?"

She glared at him. "Everyone is a suspect until they're not."

"Well, un-suspect me, because I'm going."

"Why?"

He leaned over the hood and said, "Because you are taking Red into a potentially dangerous situation, and I like her."

Sun blinked when he got in the cruiser and closed the door. When it took her a moment to get in, he leaned over the console. "Want me to drive?"

"No, I do not want you to drive." She got in, slammed her door shut, and jerked her seat belt on. He made her sound like a bad mother. She'd only sent Auri in undercover the one time. She wasn't a monster.

"You said she traded something?" she asked Auri in the rearview instead of railing at the man in her passenger's seat.

"What?"

"Sybil. You said she traded something with Aiden for your schedule."

"Oh, right. Wine from her family's vineyard."

"Figures."

"Why radio silence?" Levi asked her.

"I don't need to explain myself to you."

"Humor me."

"He's clever, this guy. And good with technology. Surely, he's keeping tabs on the investigation. I'd like to keep my daughter safe, too."

"I never doubted it."

But he did. She could see it on his impossibly handsome face. Either that or she was projecting her own guilt onto him. It happened.

Sun watched as Auri practically sprinted for the faculty entrance when Principal Jacobs opened it and gestured for them to come inside.

"First period," she said to him, hurrying down the hall.

Sun and Levi followed her, Levi's presence like an armed nuclear missile with a clock counting down: sweat-inducing, worrisome, and impossible to ignore.

Auri stopped in front of a classroom and checked the doorknob. Finding it locked, she turned and waited for what Sun could only imagine seemed like an epoch, her impatience dancing through her as she shifted her weight from leg to leg.

Quincy emerged from the same hall Jacobs had come from. "You okay, sprout?" he asked Auri when he walked up.

"Yes." She gave him a hug. "And I'll be better when we find Sybil."

"Me, too."

Quincy acknowledged Levi with the barest hint of a nod. Levi didn't return the favor. It was a rivalry they'd had since they were kids, and it was ridiculous.

It was also her fault. She should never have told Quincy about the kiss. About the petting. About her heart breaking when he'd ignored her afterward.

Her BFF could hold a grudge until the stars burned out.

Principal Jacobs opened the door, and Auri tore inside, sliding under the desks until she found the one she was looking for.

"Here!" she shouted, and Sun didn't even have to tell her not to touch anything. Auri knew better.

Sun and Quincy kneeled and looked at the underside of the desk. There was a note taped to it addressed to Auri.

They turned the desk over and carefully removed the note by cutting around it with a pocketknife. Then she handed her daughter a pair of gloves.

Auri filled her lungs, took the blue gloves, and slipped them on. With some help from a chuckling Levi.

"Okay, sit here, hon," Sun said.

Auri sat at a desk and took the note. After Sun gave her the okay, she unfolded it. But it wasn't a note. It was a drawing.

She squinted as she tried to figure out why Sybil had drawn her a picture of Auri's name, graffiti-style. Underneath the pencil drawing was a short note.

"This is the only thing I see clearly. I knew when we met it was all real. I hope you find this. If not, please don't be sad. I'm just grateful we got to be friends."

"Mom," Auri said, her eyes watering, her voice pregnant with panic. "I don't understand what this means. What if we don't find her?"

Sun sank to her knees beside her, but so did Levi. He put a hand on Auri's shoulder and turned her face toward his. "Deep breaths, Red. Remember what we talked about."

Auri drew in a deep breath as she gazed into his eyes. Sun sat back on her heels in surprise as Auri and Levi breathed together. Sun could see a calm wash over her daughter. She visibly relaxed, and Sun sat more than a tad stunned.

"Okay," he said, his voice as soothing as cool water on a hot day. "Take another look."

She nodded and took the picture in, turning it this way and that. Then she ran her fingers over not her name but the background of the picture.

"It's textured," she said. "Like stucco. Or . . . or cinder block."

Her eyes widened, and she gasped when recognition finally kicked in. She plastered a hand over her mouth, tears already threatening to spill over her lashes. Her words were muffled when she screamed from behind her hands, "I know where she is!"

The bond that Auri and Levi had was so much deeper than Sun had ever imagined. She'd been struck dumb when he'd averted Auri's panic attack, something she was only successful at about 50 percent of the time. But the way he looked at her, the warmth in his expression, the knowing grins he cast her way made a tightness form in her chest.

Who was this man, and where could she get one of her very own?

Logic would suggest *Levi Ravinder* and he was *right the fuck in front of her,* but things in the real world were not quite that black and white.

And yet, there they were. Levi leading a team across a frozen field, his tracking skills undeniable since no one, not even Auri, really knew where the well house was.

She'd only been there once when she was in the sixth grade, and Jimmy was the one who'd taken her, but after they made a quick pit stop, Jimmy couldn't remember where it was, either. He only remembered it was near a spot the kids call *the clearing.*

While at the well house, he and Auri had found an almost empty can of spray paint, and she'd graffitied her name onto a cinder block wall of the tiny room. Sun couldn't believe she'd do that, but thank God she had.

Sun dropped her back at her parents' house and told them

that under no uncertain terms was she to go back to the apartment alone. She would stay the night with them.

They stopped by the station for supplies, picked up Zee and Special Agent Fields on the way, and headed out, all while maintaining radio silence. They could not tip this guy off.

The minute they got close to the clearing, Levi picked up tracks. Human footprints in the snow and ground. They followed them until the well house came into view.

"Okay," Sun said as they huddled in the trees nearby. "He's probably in there with her now."

"The freshest prints would suggest otherwise," Levi said.

"What do you mean?" Fields asked.

"They're leading away from the shed. If I had to guess, he came to check on her, then left while the sun was still out and hasn't been back."

"Someday, you're going to have to tell me how you do that," Sun said.

"Someday," he promised.

Quincy drew in a deep breath. "Okay, let's do this. I'll take point."

Sun nodded. Surprisingly, Fields let her take the lead and followed her commands accordingly. "Zee, how is your visibility from here?"

"Great, except there are no windows."

"If you see anyone walking up, press the Talk button a few times."

"And then?"

"Can you get a nonfatal shot out of that?" Sun asked.

"With Beth here, I can."

Hoping Beth was Zee's gun, she said, "Then blow his ass away. Just try to keep him alive."

Levi armed himself with a hunting knife that could double as a sword on *Game of Thrones*.

Quincy held up a palm. "Hold up there, buddy."

"Really?" he asked, unimpressed. "This again?"

"I don't think our insurance would cover—"

"I have my own. Let's get this girl and go home."

They ducked down and hurried across the field, Quincy in the lead and Levi at their six.

They got to the building and pressed against it. The only door sat on the side opposite them. They had no way to see inside, to make sure no one was in there with her. She couldn't risk it. They needed another plan. If Levi was wrong—

"I'm not," he said beside her.

"What do you—? How did you know what—?"

"There's only one suspect. Male, size ten shoe, one fifty to one sixty. No one else has been out here, and he is gone."

"Do you know what he had for breakfast?"

He grinned down at her. "Go get your girl."

She tapped Quincy on the shoulder. He unfolded his tactical knife, slid it into his belt, and raised his semiautomatic to advance. Sun had only drawn her gun twice in the line of duty, but she'd never shot anyone. This would be her third draw. She hoped her record would continue.

Quincy got to the door, listened, then shook his head, indicating no sound. Sun and Fields crept to the door, and after a three-count, Quincy and Fields kicked it in together.

Quince raised his rifle and yelled, "Del Sol sheriff! Hands up!" The light on his rifle showed no other people in the room. "Sheriff!" he said.

Sun rushed inside and found a tiny, shivering ball of a girl wedged as far into a corner as she could get.

She knelt down. "Sybil? Sweetheart? I'm Sheriff Vicram. I'm Auri's mom."

Her eyes were huge circles on an elfin face, but even in the light, her pupils were dilated. She raised her hands to defend herself. Good girl. Never stop fighting.

"What did he give her?" Quincy asked.

"No idea. Possibly morphine or Rohypnol."

Fields knelt down and found a clear vial. "Rohypnol."

"I think it's time," Quincy said to her.

"Call them in."

As Quincy called in a rescue team, forgoing radio silence to get Sybil to the hospital, Sun tried to reach the girl. "Sybil, you did it. You led us straight to you. You and Auri. Such clever girls."

She finally blinked and tried to focus. "Auri?" She pointed.

Sun turned to see Auri's name in graffiti on the cinder block. No wonder she could see it in the windowless room. The paint was glow in the dark.

"Auri," Sybil repeated, nodding as though wanting Sun's approval.

"Yes. Auri."

Levi took off his jacket and wrapped it around Sybil while Fields called in a report.

"You and Auri." Sun drew her into her arms, and while one might imagine she would break down, she was simply in too much shock from both the ordeal and the cold.

"We can't wait," she said to Levi.

He nodded and lifted her into his arms.

"Zee, you and Quince get the ATV."

"On it," Zee said.

"Quincy, we don't know if this guy is out there. Stay sharp."

Quincy gave Sun a curt nod and took off in the direction from which they'd come, rifle at the ready. Levi carried Sybil, and Fields took point as they followed her team out. Levi's role was as transparent as the rest of theirs. He was the knight.

State police escorted them to the small Del Sol Urgent Care Center. Levi sat in the back with Sybil. She clung to him, her dirty fingers and broken nails digging into the flesh at his neck. He didn't seem to mind.

Emergency vehicles in every size and shape were waiting for

them when they arrived. A medical crew had a gurney at the door as soon as they showed up. They didn't know yet if they'd have to transfer Sybil to Albuquerque or not.

The mayor was there, speaking to news crews. They called to Sun, but she strode past and inside the UCC.

She watched the medical team work as she called Auri.

"You found her!" Auri cried when she picked up.

"You've seen the news."

"You found her. Thank you, Mom."

"Thank you, bug bite. I didn't do it alone."

"You have to tell me everything when you get home."

"No, because you will be in bed asleep."

"Tomorrow, then. Promise me. Everything."

"Remember that whole no-more-secrets thing?"

"Yes."

"I'm pretty sure it applies here."

Sun hung up and looked around for Levi. He was gone.

She'd been dealing with doctors and family and reporters. The mayor gave her a semi-approving nod. The St. Aubins were rushed in among a flurry of camera flashes and hugged their daughter for days. And the doctors agreed Sybil would be fine despite her state of near hypothermia and dehydration.

Never one for the spotlight, however—even when it came to promoting his own company—Levi vanished before she'd gotten a chance to thank him.

"Around the clock?" Quincy asked before checking out for the night.

"Around the clock," she said. With the kidnapper still out there, they'd have to keep a very close eye on the little ginger with olive-green eyes. In the meantime, Sun would contact some of her friends in the SFPD to see if they could borrow a safe house, although the St. Aubins might just want to take her somewhere safe. "Who's up first?"

"Your call," her chief deputy said through a yawn. "Not sure I could keep my eyes open, but I can take point first thing tomorrow morning."

"Thanks, Quincy. I'll stay tonight and work on getting her moved somewhere safe. You get some rest."

"You got it."

He started to walk off when she added, "You know who would be great right about now?"

He turned back. "Who?"

"Lieutenant Britton. We could really use him, don't you think?"

Quincy frowned at her and said, "Who?" before doing an about-face and walking away.

Expecting nothing less, she gave his back a sassy thumbs-up, swearing to get to the bottom of that fiasco. As soon as she had time to breathe, that is.

After grabbing a cup of coffee, she sat across from the state trooper who'd joined her on the night watch. There were only a couple of hours before dawn when help was due to arrive. She just hoped she could stay awake that long.

Of course, the fact that a tall, ebony-skinned hottie with an authentic U.S. Marshal's badge sat down next to her would definitely help. He handed her a sandwich, then stretched out his legs, clasped his hands behind his head, and closed his eyes.

"Come here often?" she asked him as she took a bite of the turkey club.

"Every chance I get."

She moaned, having had no clue how hungry she'd been. "I don't think you understand what carbs do to my ass."

"Nothing I wouldn't like to do to it, I assure you."

A sharp tingle jolted through her, and she had to stop and count the days since her last visit from Shark Week, because what in the actual fuck? Was she ovulating? She was currently in the throes of drooling over not one, not two, but three men. It was very unlike her.

It had to be Levi's fault. Every time he looked at her, every time he got near, she felt like her girly bits had started their own reality TV show called *Hormones Gone Wild*.

"Do you mind?" the trooper said, pointing toward the vending area.

"Not at all. We'll hold down the fort."

"Thanks. Be back in ten."

Sun took another bite, then balanced her coffee cup with her sandwich and massaged her neck with her free hand.

"I can do that for you," Deleon said, though how he knew what she was doing mystified her. He had yet to open his eyes.

"Have at it."

A calculating grin slid across his face. "Not here."

She lifted a brow in question. As though he could sense her inquiry, he gestured toward an empty room.

She scoffed, shook her head, then took a page out of his playbook. She leaned her head against the wall behind them and closed her eyes.

But all she could see was that man. That infuriatingly exquisite man she'd loved for as long as she could remember. The way he carried Sybil through the snow. The way she'd clung to him.

And he'd let her. Cradled her. Whispered words of encouragement into her ear every few yards.

The clang of metal crashing onto the floor startled her out of her thoughts. "What was that?"

When she didn't receive an answer, she turned to Deleon, but he was gone.

"Marshal?" she called into the empty hall. "Hello?"

Another sound whirled her around. It came from one of the empty rooms. She put her sandwich and coffee on the chair Deleon had vacated and walked toward the noise, placing one foot carefully in front of the other. The lights flickered, enveloping her in absolute darkness for a few seconds at a time.

Not creepy at all.

She called out. "Are you okay in there?"

When she still didn't get an answer, she drew her duty weapon and held it down and to the side with both hands.

"Marshal? If that's you, respond if you can."

Could the kidnapper have come after Sybil? A hundred scenarios flashed in her mind. None of them good.

OD'ing on adrenaline, she eased closer and closer to the door. "This is Sheriff Sunshine Vicram. I have my weapon drawn. I am giving you one final warning to identify yourself."

She heard rustling and the sound of paper ripping when she inched the door open, only to find Levi Ravinder sitting on the hospital bed, shirtless with his shoulders hunched, trying to wrap his ribs with a blood-soaked bandage.

"Levi?" She holstered her weapon and hurried over to him. "What happened?"

He glanced at her from over his shoulder, and the glare he gave her should have sent her up in flames. "Don't you remember?"

What the hell? Blood leached through the bandages from three distinct wounds at an alarming rate. She covered them and applied pressure, but it only seeped through her fingers.

"I'll—I'll get a doctor."

He caught her wrist to stop her. "It's too late."

"What?" She didn't understand.

The lights flickered again. When they came back on, his entire demeanor had changed. He seemed lost. Mesmerized. Quite possibly drunk, though she didn't smell alcohol. He let his gaze wander the length of her.

"Levi, you're hurt." She looked down, but the bandages were gone. In their stead was the wide chest and rock-hard abs she'd dreamed of more times than she could count. "I—I don't understand."

He wrapped a hand around the back of her neck and pulled her closer. "You have to remember to understand," he said.

Her gaze wandered past the expanse of his chest to the fullness of his mouth. The very one that sent tiny quakes shooting through her body like a freak electrical storm every time he was near.

He bent his head and pressed his lips to hers, parting them with his tongue to explore her more fully.

She sank against him. Wrapped her arms around his neck. Let her head fall back when he seared her throat with kisses.

When he pulled her onto the bed, she tried to protest. Not very hard, but still.

"Wait," she said, panting into his hair. "We can't do this here."

He lifted her shirt and trailed scalding kisses over her midsection, before saying, "Where should we go?"

The heat of his mouth was something she never wanted to lose. "Never mind. Here's good. Should we close the door?" She tried to raise onto her elbows, but he pushed her back down and spread her knees with his shoulders.

"Hush. I'm concentrating."

The sound of his voice created a warmth that rushed through her veins and pooled in her abdomen. And while she should have been wondering what happened to her pants, she was instead marveling at the sensations rocketing through her.

His mere presence did things to her. Things she only dwelled upon when she was very much alone.

Only she wasn't alone. At least she hadn't been.

She looked into the empty hall. "Where did Deleon go?"

"I need these off." He tugged at her underwear.

"Oh. Okay." She lifted her bottom so he could slide her panties off. "You know, there are nurses up and down these halls all night."

"They'll have to wait their turn."

It made perfect sense at the time. As did his tongue on her clit.

Her gasp echoed down the hall, and she covered her mouth with both hands, but only for a moment before she grabbed his hair. His tongue stroked the most sensitive area of her being. The feather-light touch caused wave after wave of unimaginable pleasure that soaked into her like rain on a parched desert.

"Who am I?" he asked.

She caught her breath, confused. "What?"

He climbed on top of her. Balancing himself on an elbow, he pushed two fingers inside her. "Who are you with?"

She caught his wrist and sucked in a lungful of air. "I don't understand."

"Sure you do." He pushed his fingers deeper, rubbing her clit with his thumb, the friction spiraling through her. "Who am I?"

"Levi," she said breathlessly. "Levi Ravinder."

"Good," he said with a smirk. "Wouldn't want you to forget again." His lashes dipped as he studied her, then he wrapped a hand behind her knee and lifted her leg, sliding back down and reapplying himself to the task at hand. His efforts were valiant. His tongue sent tiny quakes of delight shuddering to her core.

She twisted her fingers in the blanket underneath her as the pressure in her abdomen grew. Like a rising tide, the promise of orgasm pulsated and swelled until it exploded and flooded her entire body in sweet, sharp spasms of unimaginable pleasure.

She couldn't help it. She cried out, riding the waves crashing into her until she jerked awake. Coffee spilled over her hand, and she'd dropped what was left of her sandwich.

"Crap," she said, bolting to her feet. But the orgasm was still rocketing through her. She stilled and let the climax run its course. When the currents subsided, she turned to see both the state officer and Marshal Deleon watching her with something akin to shock and awe.

"Sorry," she said, but they both shook their heads.

Deleon stood to steady her. "I don't know what you were dreaming about, but I'd like to place my order now."

She tried to laugh it off. She failed. "I have to get this cleaned up. Be right back."

"Sheriff," Deleon said, stopping her with a hand on her arm. "Go home. We've got this. You've been up for days."

"It's okay. I won't be going back to sleep."

And she wouldn't. She'd had that dream before. Maybe not with that particular setting, and the wound and bandages were new, but Levi Ravinder in her bed? His fingers inside her? His mouth on her clit? Oh yeah. She'd dreamed that scenario countless times.

One aspect of this dream was certainly new, though. Despite the fact that she'd been dreaming, she'd climaxed. In her sleep. That had never happened before.

Sun got home just in time to grab a shower and take the wee one to school. "When can I see her?" Auri asked as she stole a huge swig from her coffee. Again.

She was dressed in a cute button-down with a floral tie that matched her hairband.

"Let me check with the St. Aubins. See how Sybil is doing before we throw her a welcome-home kegger."

"But I already bought the balloons," she said, whining. "And hired the male revue. How did she look?"

"Scared, sweetheart. Terrified." There was no reason to lie to her. The real world could be a scary place. "I need to get everything situated with our little Houdini, and then I need to find a child abductor."

Auri smiled. "You will."

23

Not all Mondays fall on Monday.
Stop in for a pick-me-up any day of the week!

—SIGN AT CAFFEINE-WAH

Auri sat in the hall while her mom and Principal Jacobs duked
it out in his office, mortified she'd decided to go to school today.
What had she been thinking? What must these kids think of her
after the news broadcast?

She cringed when the yelling coming from the office broke the
sound barrier yet again. There was a lot of pointing and gesturing
and gnashing of teeth. But some of that could be attributed to the
interpreter they'd brought in for the suspension meeting.

Thank God Cruz sat beside her to take her mind off all the
ways the day could go south. He was looking over his shoulder
and interpreting the events for Auri.

"Your mom is furious. The broadcast news team is getting off
scot-free. They aren't even taking them off the news crew. Their
parents are screaming censorship and threatening to go to a real
news channel to plead their case as well as sue the school if any
action is taken against their children."

Auri gaped at him. "Are you kidding me? They are doing
nothing to those . . . those—"

"You can do it," he encouraged.

"Those assholes?"

"Not bad. And nope. Not a damn thing." His voice sounded neutral, but the line of his jaw hardened.

There was still one thing she didn't understand. She crossed her arms over her chest and glared at him.

"Hey, shortstop, don't kill the messenger."

"Why are you friends with them, Cruz? They treat you like you're one of them, but you don't even seem to care."

"I don't."

The dynamics of the school as a whole versus the enigma that was Cruz De los Santos puzzled her to no end. "Then I don't get it. You're nice to them. You hang out with them."

He lifted a shoulder. "It's more of an understanding. They don't mess with me. I don't mess with them."

That was helpful. "What do you mean?"

He filled his lungs as though he didn't want to talk about it, but she raised a brow. A single, unrelenting brow, just like her mom taught her. It totally worked.

"Okay," he said, sitting up a little straighter. "When we were in second grade, there was this kid who was pretty much known as the school bully."

"Why is there always a bully?" she asked.

"Right? So, he was messing with everyone, picking on different people every day. You get the idea."

"I do, unfortunately."

"Then one day, he decided it was my turn."

She stilled as a sickening feeling washed over her. She tamped it down, not wanting to risk interrupting him. To risk not getting the whole story. "He went after you?"

"He tried to. I guess I didn't know how to play the game right. He pushed me down and tried to take my backpack."

The image gave her a stomachache. "Cruz, I'm sorry."

"It's okay. I just got up, took this girl's crutch as she walked by, and beat the shit out of him."

She blinked in astonishment. "Wow. You were only, what, seven?"

"Something like that. Suddenly, everyone wanted to be my friend, and it's been that way ever since."

"It's because you're not afraid of anything. And you don't care what anyone thinks of you." She looked down to study her shoes, adding, "You're kind of amazing."

He seemed surprised. He studied her a long moment until she asked, "What happened to the girl?"

"What girl?"

"The one with the crutch?"

"Oh, she fell."

A bubble of laughter escaped despite her best efforts. He was dead serious. And utterly charming.

"You beat up Liam Eaton yesterday, didn't you? Lynelle's BFF?"

He lifted a shoulder. "Only a little. He deserved worse, but he's shitting himself now, I guarantee it."

"He's scared of you?"

He lowered his head. "Everyone's scared of me. They're only my friends because they think it keeps them safe. It's not like I go around beating the crap out of people every day."

She ran her fingertips along the scabs on his knuckles. "I'm not scared of you."

Without looking at her, he said, "You will never have to be."

Before she could say anything else, like a marriage proposal, her mom stormed out of the office and into the hall. "No way," she said, livid.

The principal followed her. "What am I supposed to do, Sunshine?"

She took one look at Auri and Cruz and got that look on her face. The one that said someone was about to be very unhappy.

"Fine, Jacobs. Go ahead and bow down to the elite in this town. To the pricks and the ass-kissers."

"And the superintendent. You know, my boss?"

They were drawing a crowd. Students stopped and either laughed behind cupped hands or gaped. Either way, it was a good show.

"I get it, but if nothing is going to happen to those privileged little fucks—"

Auri gasped. Her mom just didn't do that. Not in public, anyway.

Her mom looked past him toward the secretary, a.k.a. Lynelle's mother, before she continued, "Then nothing will happen to Cruz."

"Now, Sunny—"

Cruz's dad and the interpreter came out. The interpreter looked flustered just trying to keep up with the conversation.

"Don't even," she warned Principal Jacobs.

Auri had never, in all of her fourteen-going-on-fifteen years of existence, seen her mom that mad. She gaped at her wide-eyed while Cruz looked on approvingly.

"Nothing happens to these kids." She pointed to both Cruz and Auri. She turned to Cruz's dad. "Mr. De los Santos, it was a pleasure to meet you."

He took her hand and nodded a thank-you.

She turned to Cruz. "And you . . ." She bent down and kissed his cheek. "You are a rock star."

"Come on, Sunny," the principal said. "Don't encourage him."

"And you . . ." She knelt down in front of Auri and took her hand. "You give 'em hell, bug bite. And remember, it's okay to stab a bitch in the face with a pencil."

She heard a unified gasp.

"Sometimes you have to use what's in your environment."

"Um, Sunny," Jacobs said. "I'm not sure—"

"If you have no other choice, resort to hair pulling. It isn't pretty, but it's effective."

Auri's mouth thinned into a huge smile. "WWLSD?"

"WWLSD."

Her mom stood then and strode out of the building like she owned it. And in a way, she did. Auri prayed she would have an ounce of her strength, her flair, when she graduated high school. Her mother set the world on fire. She wanted to at least light a candle in it.

"Quincy, don't laugh. You didn't see me. It was like Sunshine had left the building and something evil had taken over her body. I went crazy. In front of the entire student body. Or, well, a fraction of it, anyway."

"Let's just pray there's not a new viral video in a few hours."

"Oh, holy crap." She sat down at her desk.

Price came in, looking more disheveled than usual. "Hey, Sheriff."

"You okay, Price?"

"Yeah, I'm good. Dogs got out. I chased them all night."

"Oh no. I'm sorry." He had a nasty scrape along his temple. "Is that how you got that?"

He touched his temple, including what looked like a small cut, but there were no visible signs of injury surrounding it. "Probably. Freaking bushes attacked me."

Sun laughed. Price had only been on the force for about six months and came highly recommended by Detroit PD. He had probably been in line for detective, but he told Sun during their get-to-know-each-other lunch he just wanted to see that yellow bright orb in the sky more often. To feel the warmth on his face instead of the ice-cold wind that blew in from the Great Lakes.

She could understand that. Even with the snow, the sun shone almost every day of the year in New Mexico. The fact that he'd chosen Del Sol made her wonder about his gut instincts, but his former lieutenant swore by him.

"I just wanted to congratulate you." He shook his head, impressed. "Stellar work last night, guys."

"Thanks. Anything on the man who brought us all together today?"

He offered a grim smile. "Sorry, Sheriff. Nothing is panning out. But we're still looking into a couple of the tips from the hotline."

"I was going to go through those last night but didn't get around to it. Nothing with the surveillance footage from the Quick-Mart?"

Sun found it sad that their only lead at that moment was a receipt from the Quick-Mart for an energy drink. A receipt that someone apparently lifted out of a trash can to plant at the scene of Sybil's abduction.

This guy was nothing if not thorough.

"No, ma'am. He must've waited until they dumped the trash and then stole the receipt out of the bin behind the store. No witnesses to that, either."

"Of course not. Keep looking."

"Will do. If you need me to take a turn on guard duty—"

"I think we're covered. Agent Fields is getting some state officers to take a shift, too."

"Good. Well, just let me know."

Zee walked into her office then, her face the definition of concern. "Hey, boss."

"What's up? How'd you sleep?"

"A little better now that we've found her, but he's still out there."

"We'll get him, sis," Quincy said. "Then you won't have to look so haggard all the time."

She rolled her eyes.

"Whatcha got there?" Sun asked, looking at the file in her hand.

"A report. Jack called from the OMI about the DB from yesterday."

"Great. What does she have for us?"

"Well, they cleaned the ID bracelet with acetate and looked at it under a microscope to get the name off it."

"Finally, some good news. And?"

"It's just, you know, with everything going on, I thought maybe we could put this aside until we have more time and man-power to focus on it."

"Or we could do both. I've heard some law enforcement agencies do that."

"We could. But I think we should wait on the DNA analysis to get back and then—"

"Zee, I have a child abduction case to solve."

"I know, it's just—"

"Zee . . ."

"It's your guy."

She blinked. "I don't have a guy."

"But if you did."

Every muscle in her body went still. "If I did?"

"The name on the bracelet is *Levi*."

Quincy straightened in his chair and took the folder out of her hands. "Are you shitting me?"

"Levi?" Sun sat stunned.

"Okay," Quincy said, holding his hands in the time-out position, "this doesn't have to mean what it looks like on the surface."

"That Levi killed his uncle?"

"Think about it. It had to be self-defense, right?"

"That he had something to do with my abduction?"

"Sunny, we can't possibly make that kind of assumption at this point."

She forced her resolve to the forefront. "Bring him in."

"Absolutely, for the possible homicide. But to assume he had anything to do with your abduction, I don't know, Sunny."

"Quincy," she said between gritted teeth.

"No, Sunny. Take a step back and look at this. Why? What reason would he have?"

"That doesn't matter. We don't look at motive until afterward. First, we follow where the evidence leads us."

He nodded in agreement, but added. "Okay, let's check his DNA before we ask for the electric chair, though. Yes?"

Tears burned the backs of her eyes. "Fine. Just get him in here."

She walked to the restroom and leaned against the cool door. Three days on the job and she'd had at least two panic attacks and had behaved stunningly unprofessionally in front of a group of kids.

She thought back, trying to figure out how many panic attacks she'd had before moving back to Del Sol.

Oh yeah. None.

She could not do this. It was the town. The crazy, erratic, messed-up town that she'd loved so much growing up. And she could keep telling herself that until the stars burned out. It still wouldn't be true.

It was him. Her emotions went haywire anytime he was near, like he emitted some kind of electromagnetic field that kept her and her alone off balance.

And now this? Would he . . . *could* he do something that heinous?

This was not going to work. She'd known it since she'd first stepped foot into the station. This whole thing, her being the sheriff, them moving back. None of it was going to work.

Auri would be devastated, but she could not live here. Not anymore. Maybe the old saying was right. There was simply no going home. And the town deserved a sheriff that didn't have a panic attack every five minutes or throw hissy fits in front of children.

At least the mayor would have plenty of ammunition when it came time to have her position rescinded.

Sun would have to figure out how to tell everyone eventually, but for now, she had to solve this case. It was right there in front of her. The pieces of the puzzle were there; she just had to link them together. She was missing something. Some oddly shaped piece that would make the whole picture make sense.

She forced herself to calm down. To breathe slowly. To take control.

If Levi was innocent, he had nothing to worry about.

If not, well, he was about to have a very bad day.

"I think I'm in love with your mom."

Auri gaped at Cruz, pretending to be appalled. Then she gave up. "It wouldn't be the first time my boyfriend fell in love with my mom. Nor the second. Sadly."

"So, I'm your boyfriend?"

She sucked in a sharp breath and turned to him. "What? No. I didn't mean—"

"It's okay. But if the position opens up, I'd like to put in my application."

Her mouth imitated a goldfish for a few seconds before she caught herself. She unfolded from the chair and started for first period. "Okay, well, what are your qualifications?"

Cruz said goodbye to his dad as the principal explained how the school would not be suspending his son due to extenuating factors. "I'm good at hitting things with rocks. And I can write with a pencil and a pen, but not at the same time."

She winced. "That's kind of a deal breaker."

"And—"

Auri was enjoying the conversation so much, she didn't realize he'd stopped both talking and walking. She turned back to him, then pivoted around to see what he was looking at. The hall was lined with students three kids deep on either side, all gazes locked in her general direction.

Her eyes rounded, and she looked behind her. No one. They were definitely looking at her.

For a moment, she'd forgotten where she was. Del Sol High. Land of the Vicious and the Depraved.

Humiliation burned through her as Cruz gestured for her to go first through the throngs of students. Was she about to be tarred and feathered? Because she'd heard that sucked.

As they passed, however, the kids offered her their hands or patted her back or flat out introduced themselves.

"I'm Jeff," one kid said, shaking her hand.

"I'm Auri."

He laughed. "Yeah, we know."

Another girl held out her hand. "I'm Heather."

And another. "I'm the other Heather. The cool one."

Then someone patted her back and said, "Welcome to Del Sol High, Auri."

"We're glad to have you."

"Is this like a Del Sol thing?" she whispered to Cruz, who was receiving his fair share of high fives.

He whispered back, "No, this is like an Auri Vicram thing."

"I'm Sarah."

"I'm Caleb. We have geometry together."

On and on. Student after student. Until she had to keep her mouth pressed together to keep her chin from trembling.

"I'm Sammy."

"I'm David. I look forward to getting to know you better."

"Hi, I'm Carla, and you and your mom are kind of amazing."

Auri took her hand and laughed softly through a sob. Some faces looked familiar. Most didn't. But all of them, each and every one, now held a special place in her heart. She totally took back the vicious-and-depraved thing.

She hid her face when they came to their classroom. The hall went silent, then in one uproarious cacophony, they erupted with applause and cheers.

Auri tried and failed to smile, as she asked Cruz, "Why are they doing this?"

"Because it needed to be done."

She managed the barest hint of a smile before realizing the halls had fallen completely silent. Row by row, the students turned and faced the walls, and Auri was completely lost until she saw Lynelle and Liam walking toward the classroom.

The students turned their backs as she walked past. Every. Single. Student.

Auri took in a sharp breath, watching Lynelle as she turned up her nose and walked like a model at fashion week. Liam lagged behind her. At least he had the decency to look ashamed.

Lynelle strode past them and into the room. Liam followed suit, and the students stayed in their positions even after the tardy bell rang. Teachers had to come out of their classrooms to usher them inside.

Auri turned to Cruz, her top applicant and career hopeful, and she hugged him.

He hesitated, then hugged her back. His long arms wrapped around her and pulled her tight, and he buried his face in her hair. They hugged until someone, a teacher perhaps, cleared her throat.

Auri pulled away and hurried into the classroom. The kids were standing. They greeted her, too, each one introducing himself or herself and welcoming her to DSH. Besides Team Lynelle, that is.

She sat at her seat just as the room fell completely silent. That was when she got a good look at Liam. He sported several bruises and a swollen eye.

Lynelle had raised her hackles, her defenses on DEFCON 1, when she glared at everyone and turned in her seat. "Please. Like I care what you hacks think."

The teacher began taking roll when slowly the students started turning their desks. The legs scraped along the floor, the sound making as much of a point as the action. By the time all the chairs had been moved, not a single student faced Lynelle or Liam. They'd all turned their backs on them.

Lynelle stood and ran from the room as Liam sank down in his chair.

Auri sat dumbfounded. And confused. And grateful.

God, she loved this town.

"Now, Ravinder, just hear me out."

Levi Ravinder tore into the sheriff's station with a bone to pick. Or a bone to break. Either way, he was testy.

The way Sun saw it, he could just be mad. He was her number one at the moment for a homicide—and possibly more—and he could not deny the evidence that put him there.

Admittedly, the bracelet was thin. No DA in the world could get a conviction on such circumstantial evidence, but it was a starting point.

Even after this, however, her feelings toward him hadn't changed. She could read people to an almost eerie degree. Well, everyone but her own daughter. But Levi threw her off balance. Her sixth sense was what had kept her alive and moving up the proverbial ladder in Santa Fe. It was legendary and had never let her down.

Until now.

She was beginning to wonder if she'd lost it in the move.

Quincy led him back, and Levi went straight for her office. Quincy followed to stand between him and Sun should he need to intervene.

Levi stopped short in front of her. "You think I'm a murderer now?"

She glared at Quincy.

He showed his palms. "I said nothing."

"He didn't have to." The fury on Levi's face was only part of the picture. She sensed something else. Pain, perhaps. Homicidal tendencies? It was hard to tell. "You think I'm an idiot? You find my uncle's body and now you want my DNA?" He stepped closer.

"Fuck you. Get a warrant. And don't ever drag my ass in here again unless you talk to my lawyer first."

"We found evidence that places you at the scene when he was killed."

"Bullshit."

"And we found a secondary source of blood on his clothes."

"So it must be mine."

"Prove me wrong. Give me a sample, and we'll have this cleared up in a matter of days."

"Like I said, get a fucking warrant."

"People only say things like that when they're guilty."

He almost came unglued. He stepped even closer, and Quincy stepped even closer, and the whole situation got up close and personal real quick.

"You know, if you'd finished what you started yesterday, you wouldn't need my DNA. You'd already have it."

"What'd you start yesterday?" Quincy asked.

"We were going to rule you out, but if you don't want that . . ."

"How many times can I say *fuck you* before you get the picture?"

"Levi, he was holding your ID bracelet. The leather one you used to wear."

He scoffed. "Holy shit, that's what you have? A bracelet my uncle took from me after my name had been worn off because he liked it and that bastard stole anything and everything he could from me? That's your evidence?"

She smiled. "Don't forget about the blood."

He smiled back. "You know what? Let's do this. My DNA is your DNA."

"Really?" When he only stared down at her, she grabbed the swab kit, took it out of the box, and lifted it to his mouth.

"Just remember what happened when Pandora opened that pretty little box."

"What does that mean?"

He didn't answer. Nor did he open at first, preferring to glare at her instead. Then his lips parted, just barely, and he waited.

She didn't dare ask him to open wider. She was about to get his DNA without a warrant. Score one for the home team.

When he refused to give her better access, refused to part those sculpted lips any farther, she took hold of his chin and gently lowered it. She inserted the swab and ran it along the inside of his cheek.

He never took his eyes off her, and she began to tremble, but why? Why in God's name did Levi's nearness make her tremble? Did he really affect her so powerfully?

He could, she supposed, if she were twelve. She didn't want him to be the one. To be Auri's father. Because that would mean the worst thing in the world. It would make him the worst kind of person in the world.

But he wasn't. She'd seen his kindness again and again.

The thought that he could do something so savage made no sense. Yes, he was a Ravinder, but he was so different from the others.

A scream came from the lobby. "I did it!"

Sun looked out and saw Hailey at the front desk.

"Please, I need to speak to the sheriff. I did it."

"Son of a bitch." Levi raked a hand through his hair.

"What is she talking about?"

"Nothing. She's crazy."

When Sun motioned for Anita to let her back, Levi changed his mind. "Fine, I did it. I killed him."

"What?"

"I killed him. Kubrick. That was all me."

"Why? Did he abduct me? Were you partners?"

"Partners? In the abduction and rape of a seventeen-year-old girl?"

"I'm just trying to understand."

"You're going to think what you're going to think. Nothing I say will change that."

"Bullshit."

"You've made up your mind, Vicram. And even if you haven't, the fact that you need a test to prove I'm an honorable person pretty much leaves us out in the cold."

"I did it!" Hailey said as she ran back to them.

"Hailey, what the hell?" he asked, his tone like a razor blade.

"Shut up. I killed Uncle Kubrick."

Levi crossed his arms over the expanse of chest he carried around. "Okay, how did he die?"

"What?"

"How did you kill him?"

"With . . . I—I shot him. With a gun."

He smirked at Sun, then asked Hailey, "What kind of gun?"

"I don't know. I don't remember. It was a rifle."

Levi deadpanned her. "Will you arrest me already?"

"Why?" she asked him, wondering if he knew. "How'd he die?"

He stepped closer and bent down until their mouths almost met. "I stabbed him through his cold, cruel heart."

Sun felt like he'd just stabbed her through the heart as well. She nodded to Quincy, who took him to processing.

"Wait," Hailey said, trying to grab ahold of Levi's arm as Quincy handcuffed him. "What just happened?"

Quincy escorted him to processing.

"You and your brother were playing a game. He won."

"Please, Sunshine, let me confess. I was . . . he did it for me."

"Don't listen to her!" Levi shouted as Quincy escorted him away.

Sun waited for him to get out of earshot, then asked Hailey, "What do you mean?"

"I—I can't explain."

She sat at her desk. "I need more than that."

Hailey took a seat across from her and closed her eyes.

Sun recognized the shame immediately. She knew it all too well from her time at Santa Fe PD.

"He—Uncle Brick hit Jimmy."

Sun stood and took the seat next to her. By the look on her face, he'd done it more than once. "Hailey, I'm so sorry."

"He'd been verbally abusive to him for years. I did everything I could to keep them apart. But I didn't know he was hitting him. We just thought . . . he falls a lot, you know?"

Sun nodded and gave her time.

"Then Levi found out, and—" She filled her lungs, the breath shuddering through her. "A judge will look kindlier on someone like me killing him rather than my brother. The family needs him. If Levi goes to jail and Uncle Clay takes the reins of the business, Jimmy will have nothing when I'm gone. Clay will run it into the ground. Or just turn it over to his connections in the South."

"Hailey, I can't just—"

"Brick was a piece of shit, Sun." A sob retched from her throat, and Sun took her hand. "In more ways than one."

"I'm sure he was, but—"

"He broke his arm." Another sob escaped her. She covered her face for a solid minute, struggling for control of her emotions. She swallowed hard, then continued, "That day. The day Levi went after him. Uncle Brick yanked Jimmy off the tractor so hard he broke his arm." She covered her face again, overcome by guilt. From behind her hands, she said, "He was three."

Sun's vision blurred with a wetness that was stinging the backs of her eyes. Disabled kids were so vulnerable to bullying and abuse. She knew the statistics. The heartbreaking, mind-boggling statistics.

But what now? On the one hand, none of this had anything to do with Sun's abduction. On the other, Levi had killed a man. For all the right reasons, sure, but unless it was self-defense . . .

"We'll figure something out, okay? I promise."

Maybe she didn't lose her sixth sense in the move, after all. Levi was good. She knew it. She could feel it to the marrow of her bones. But that wouldn't be for her to judge. She would have to leave that to the DA, but she'd damn well make sure they knew the particulars of the case.

After Hailey left, Sun buckled down. No more distractions. They had to find out who'd abducted Sybil before he tried it again.

24

Being an adult is like folding a fitted sheet.
Don't worry. We can help.

—SIGN AT DEL SOL MENTAL HEALTH RESOURCES

Sun had Principal Jacobs get Auri personally. He brought her to the front where Sun waited, the look on her face one of concern until she saw her mom.

"What's going on?" she asked.

"I need to talk to Sybil, but I'd like a friendly face there. You up for it?"

Auri almost jumped into her arms. "Totally. Thanks, Mom."

They drove to the urgent care center and met up with Marianna and Forest St. Aubin.

"I hear we have you to thank for finding her," Forest said to Auri.

She shook her head. Quite vigorously. "It was a group effort."

They pulled Auri into a group hug. She let them.

"Do you think she's up for some questions?" Sun asked them. "Our guy is still out there. She could have seen something or heard something without even knowing it."

They glanced at each other, then Mr. St. Aubin nodded. "Just not too long?"

"I promise. You ready?"

Auri nodded and seemed to mentally brace herself as they went inside her room.

"Sybil?" Auri said softly. The blinds had been pulled and the lights turned low.

A tiny figure in the bed shifted. "Auri?" she said, her voice hoarse.

Auri rushed forward. "Sybil, I'm so glad you're okay."

"Auri!" Sybil latched on to her, and they hugged for a solid ten minutes. They both cried, and Sun sent up a quick thanks for having a kid like the one he'd given her.

Their reunion gave Sun a chance to check out the room. If their suspect could get Sybil out of a home with state-of-the-art security and through a window in the laundry room with no one the wiser, he could possibly get her out of the hospital window. The facility was only a one-story. Otherwise, she would have her moved to the second floor or higher. The windows didn't open, but could they be opened with a tool of some kind?

She was trying to think of any possible way the suspect could get into the room.

The quickest and surest way would be to wait until the guard went to the restroom. If there wasn't another guard around, they would put a nurse in charge of keeping people out, but nurses were busy people. And emergencies that could call a nurse away from his or her post happened.

The truth was, Sybil was far from safe. They needed to move her as quickly as possible.

"How do you feel?" Auri asked her, breaking their hold. "Do you feel like it's over?"

Sybil released a sad sigh. "I don't know. I don't think I'll believe it's really over until my birthday passes and I'm still alive and breathing, which could happen thanks to you." Tears sprang to her eyes again.

"Thanks to my mom," she said, gesturing toward her. "Do you remember her? You met last night?"

A line formed between Sybil's delicate brows. "I think so."

"It's okay, sweetheart." Sun stood beside her daughter. "You had other things on your mind."

She smiled shyly.

"So, I got your letter, and I've studied your diary. I hope that's okay."

Auri helped Sybil to sit up and got her more comfortable. "It's okay. Is that how you found me?"

"We found your note," Auri said. "The drawing you taped under your desk at school before winter break."

"You found it?"

Auri nodded. "You knew I was coming."

She shrugged, like it was no big deal. "Everyone knew you were coming. Your mom won the election."

"But you knew I was coming and you left the drawing for me. The note to me in your letter led me to it."

"Clever girls," Sun said.

They brightened.

"Would you mind if I asked you a couple of questions?" she said, treading carefully.

"Sure. I'm okay."

Sun took in every aspect of her demeanor as they spoke. Every gesture. Every word. Every tone in her voice and direction in her gaze. Not because she didn't believe the girl. Far from it. But sometimes people don't tell the whole truth because they are embarrassed or they don't think it's important.

She lifted a plastic bag. "Sybil, do you recognize this button?"

She took the evidence bag that contained the button they found at her house. "Yes," she said, thinking back. "That's from a backpack I used to have when we lived in Chicago."

"Like this?" She showed her the picture Anita had found.

"That's it."

"But you lost it? Any chance that button had fallen off and was still in your things?"

"I don't think so. The backpack was pretty new, and that button held one of the pockets closed. I think I would've noticed if it came off."

Sun took a quick note, but Sybil added, "Oh, and I didn't lose it. It was stolen. Right out from under me."

Sun stopped writing. "Stolen? From where?"

"I was at the park with some friends, and we were all sitting on this bench. We all had our backpacks either under the bench or beside our feet. I was sitting on the end, and the backpack was right beside me one minute and gone the next. Nobody was around or anything. Just the usual joggers and stuff, but nobody stopped to talk to us. And none of the other kids saw anything, either. We all kind of freaked out."

"I bet you did."

That was what Sun needed to know. The last time she'd seen the backpack and the chances the button ended up in her possession. That meant her abductor had been stalking her for a very long time.

If he was brazen enough to steal her backpack in broad daylight with a group of kids looking on, what else was he brazen enough to do? Was he a chameleon? Could he blend? Become invisible?

This guy was right under their noses. She could feel it.

"Did you see or hear anything else?" she asked her.

"Yeah," Auri said, "you'd be surprised at how the smallest detail will lead to something big."

The two girls were holding hands like they'd been best friends for years. It warmed Sun's heart but also broke it. She wasn't planning on staying in Del Sol long enough for them to get to know each other much better. She was close to solving her abduction. She could feel it.

"I know this is going to be hard to believe, but everything I put in my letter is what I saw and heard. I really don't have much else. He hardly talked, but when he did, his voice wasn't really deep. It was just normal."

"What about an accent? A speech impediment of any kind?"

She shook her head. "I'm sorry. I didn't notice anything like that."

Marianna came in then, carrying a new pitcher of water. "How's it going?"

"Good," Sybil said. "Have you met Auri?"

"Well, your dad and I just about smothered her, if that's what you mean."

The girls giggled. Marianna poured Sybil a fresh glass of water, then went around to the other side of her bed. "Are you cold? Do you need another blanket?"

"I'm fine, Mom."

Mari tucked a strand of hair behind Sybil's ear and encouraged her to lie down.

"Can Auri stay? Just for a little while?"

Auri offered them both pleading looks as well, and Sun had to admit something awful. She didn't want to put Auri in the line of fire. If the suspect did come back, if he somehow managed to get to Sybil, what would he do with Auri if she got in his way?

"I don't see why not," Mari said. "But just for a little while. You need to rest."

"Please, Mom," Auri begged.

"I guess you can miss a couple of more classes today. I have to go back to the office for about an hour. I'll swing by to pick you up when I'm finished there. How's that?"

The girls looked at each other and giggled in excitement. Sun had never seen her daughter get so excited about being friends with anyone before, and she wondered if she'd missed that part of her life as an insanely busy parent, or if Auri had missed that part of her life as the daughter of a law enforcement officer.

Sun watched the two for a minute, marveling at a little dimple Sybil had where her ear met her temple. An adorable attribute for an adorable girl, and Sun remembered reading a story about them in college. In some folklores, the rare dents were considered very lucky, and it was said that the bearers would gain great wealth throughout their lives.

She hoped so. Sybil could use a little luck after the life of fear she'd led.

"Sybil, if I send one of my deputies over later, do you think you can try to remember everything the suspect said to you? No matter how small?"

"Sure." She said the word, but the last thing Sybil wanted to talk about was her abduction or the man who perpetrated it, and it shone through in the tone of her voice. Sun understood all too well.

"Thank you, sweetheart. I'll be back," she said, doing her best Arnold Schwarzenegger impersonation.

Auri rolled her eyes, and they giggled.

Auri and Sybil had a lot of catching up to do. Auri told her new friend everything that had happed to her since she'd started school, including the broadcast news bit, and Sybil told Auri about her own run-ins with the infamous group Lynelle and the Lackeys, Sybil's euphemism. Auri liked it. It had finesse. Spunk. And alliteration. Cruz would be proud.

"One more time."

Auri exhaled loudly and flung herself back on the bed. Sybil had insisted she crawl on the bed with her so they could watch a rerun of *The Vampire Diaries*, but they ended up talking the whole time instead. "Dude, I've already told you seven times."

Sybil counted on her hands. "Nope. You've only told me six times."

After a soft laugh, Auri told her friend once more about the first time she saw Cruz reading in class and how captivated she'd become listening to his poetry.

"I was captivated by him, too, only it had nothing to do with his poetry."

"Right?" They giggled again and were still giggling when a nurse named Jessie, if his nametag was to be believed, came in with sodas and sandwiches.

He offered them a smile. "A little bird told me that you both like Orange Crush."

They looked at each other.

"You like it, too?" Auri asked, surprised.

"It's my favorite." She popped the top on her can and looked at Auri. "It's like we were meant to be."

"I agree."

"These are ham and cheese, but I can get something else if you'd like."

"No," Sybil said, "these are great. Thank you."

"Enjoy."

When he left, they naturally had to talk about how cute he was.

"Nursing is an excellent profession to go into," Sybil said. She took a bite, then added, "He should go back and become a physician's assistant. They make even more money."

Auri took a huge swig of the orange stuff. "I thought about going into medicine."

"You changed your mind?"

"Yeah. I think I'm too much like my mom. I think I need to go into law enforcement."

"Really?" Sybil said, shifting to face her better. "That's fascinating. I don't think I could do something like that."

"Why? You're good with puzzles. That's half the battle."

"Yeah, but I'm not good with people."

"You're good with me."

Sybil beamed at her. "I am, aren't I?" She took another bite, then said, "Okay, really, one more time."

Auri gave in and, after a moment, had her friend sighing in puppy love bliss. Then she sobered. "I'm so sorry about everything that happened to you."

Sybil shrugged and ducked, trying to play it off as no big deal when it was anything but. It had haunted the poor thing her entire life, and now it was almost over. This deep fear she'd been waiting for. Auri couldn't imagine how she felt, and she didn't pretend to.

"Do you feel better about it now? Will the dreams stop?"

"I don't know. It's not my birthday until tomorrow. I think I'll feel better the day after."

Auri nodded in understanding and smiled sleepily when Sybil's lids started drifting closed.

"I'm so glad you're here, Auri."

"Me, too, Sybil."

"Oh, I just remembered something," she said, her voice getting farther and farther away. "He told me he did everything for my mom. The man who took me. He said she needed to know what it felt like."

"What?" Alarm rushed through Auri. She had to tell her mother immediately. And she would have, too, if she could just . . . wake . . . up.

Sun checked in on the team processing the well house before grabbing Quincy from the station for a coffee and a sandwich at Caffeine-Wah. She'd decided to send Deputy Salazar to watch over Sybil and, if possible, talk to her about what happened. Salazar was a natural; she just didn't know it yet. She had a way of putting people at ease.

Unfortunately, there was a flip side to that. Because of her sweet disposition, people often underestimated the young deputy. Hopefully that would change over time.

Zee met them at the coffee shop, and Richard and Ricky instantly fell in love with the stunning beauty. But that was okay. Zee instantly fell in love with their eyeliner, and Sun realized she might have a way to get the lowdown on the secret sanctum sanctorum of the baristas' makeup routine sitting right under her nose. Or at her left elbow.

"How is he?" Sun asked Quincy when they sat down with their food.

He stopped chewing and spoke through a mouthful of Monte Cristo. "Hell. No."

She gaped at him. Her best friend. Her most trusted confidante. "Why 'hell no'? I'm the sheriff checking up on a detainee in my care."

He swallowed. "Nope. You'll have to go talk to him. I refuse to be a go-between."

"But he won't talk to me. Possibly ever again. And he did actually confess to a murder."

"Yeah, to keep his sister out of jail," Zee said.

"Please, she had nothing to do with it." Sun took a bite, then said, "We're missing something, guys."

"Mayo. I forgot to ask." He grabbed a packet of mayo and sat back down.

"No. Something much more vital. I feel like our suspect is so close I could touch him."

"Like in a carnal way?"

Fine. When Quincy joked about something so serious, it usually meant he was so frustrated he didn't know what else to do. She was right there with him.

Marshal Deleon walked into the shop in all his slick glory. "I knew I'd find you guys here. What's good?"

A soft gasp came from behind the counter at the insolence of the implication that there was something on the menu that *wasn't* good.

Sun fought a grin. "Everything here is good."

"Fantastic." He went up to order while Quincy and Zee wiggled their eyebrows at her.

"Stop it," she whispered, pretending to be appalled. "You look ridiculous. And he's probably married."

"He's not," Quincy said. "I checked." When both gazes landed on him in surprise, he said, "For Sun. I could tell he liked her."

"Mm-hmm," Zee said, adding a healthy dose of skepticism to her voice.

"May I?" Deleon asked, and three heads nodded in unison. "Thanks. Great job on the St. Aubin girl. What a coup."

"I guess. How is your search going?"

"Don't get me started." He took a sip of coffee, then looked back at the proprietors, clearly impressed with their concoction. "We thought we had a solid lead. Turned out to be nothing, so we wasted a whole day."

"Sorry about that." She considered telling him the truth, but she needed to talk to Darlene first. If anyone would know where Deleon's fugitive, Ramses Rojas, was headed, it would be Darlene. Sun could pass on the information without ever involving her mom's best friend. "How long are you staying in the area?"

The grin he offered her would have melted the knees of a lesser, and less-in-love-with-Levi, girl. Unfortunately, every breath she took seemed to confirm her affliction to a greater degree.

Still, dude was hot.

"Trying to get rid of me already?"

"Not at all. I'm just trying to figure out if that offer for a drink still stands."

He was about to take a bite of his smoked salmon croissant. He stopped, his sandwich hovering mere centimeters from his mouth. "Yes, it is."

"Great. I'd love a mocha latte with extra whipped cream."

His grin turned evil. "Would you?"

"And chocolate sauce. In the shape of the Mona Lisa."

He put down his sandwich to give her a suspicious once-over. "You're plying me with your feminine wiles?"

"Not at all. I left my feminine wiles in my other pants. And I very rarely ply in public."

"Want to tell me what you *are* doing, then?"

"Nothing dastardly. I just thought you might give me the low-down on the inmate you're looking for."

"Fugitive. The second he escaped, he became a fugitive."

"Ah, right. I watched the video of the escape. The footage from the transport van?"

"Let me guess." He sat back in his chair. "He didn't actually participate in the escape. And he didn't hurt anyone."

"It just seemed like a very well-thought-out effort. A coordinated attack. Like it had been planned for weeks. But I noticed in a field report, Ramses wasn't supposed to be on that transport."

"You're right. He didn't participate in the hijacking. And he didn't hurt anyone. But he also didn't stop them from hurting two of our finest. And he did escape with the others."

"Four."

He took another sip, wiped his lovely mouth, then asked, "Four?"

"There were four hardened criminals against one man."

"Ouch," Quincy said, ever the wordsmith.

"I saw the looks they gave him, Marshal. It wouldn't have ended well had he tried to intervene."

"Are you saying he's an upstanding citizen and we should just let him go because he's a good guy?"

"No. I'm saying, when you do find him, try to give him a chance to turn himself in." After all, Darlene Tapia wouldn't help anyone she knew was a danger to society. Sun would bet her last shiny nickel on that.

"What do you think is going to happen? Do you think I'm going to gun him down in the street?"

She grinned, letting the appreciation she felt for him show. "No, I do not, Marshal Deleon. That's not your style."

He grinned back. "I'm glad you noticed."

"So," Quincy said, shifting in his chair, "the sib and I are going to interview Mrs. Usury. She owns the land the well house is on."

Sun blinked at him, his words—or more importantly *word*—sinking in. Sometimes, when a piece of the puzzle fell into place, a jolt of electricity rocketed through her body. Not always, but that rush of adrenaline, that high, was quite addictive.

Her gaze darted between them, then she asked, "What did you just say?"

Quincy shrugged. "We're going to interview Mrs. Usury."

Sun closed her eyes. Maybe she was wrong. Maybe . . . she didn't know, maybe it was just a word. Just a nickname. Maybe *Syb* meant nothing.

"What's going on?" Zee asked.

It was so thin, so far-fetched, she didn't want to say it out loud for fear it would disintegrate and drift away. But the dimples, for lack of a better term, on Sybil's temples matched another set she'd seen recently for the first time in her life. And she didn't believe in coincidences.

She grabbed her jacket and said to them, "Meet me at the urgent care center."

"Was it something I said?" Quincy asked, scrambling after her.

She skidded to a halt at the door. Quincy and Zee, who'd been hurrying to keep up, almost plowed into her.

She turned to them, her mind racing with all the fragments she'd missed, all the clues that were right there in front of her. She'd just never put them together.

But even now . . . she had to know for certain before she started pointing fingers and making accusations. Then again, what if something bizarre happened and she died in an accident on the way to the urgent care center or she had an aneurysm or the zombie apocalypse was nigher than anyone had imagined.

She took out her notepad, wrote two words onto a slip of paper, and stuffed it into Quincy's front pocket. "Do not look at this unless I die unexpectedly."

"Really?" he said, unimpressed. "This again?"

He had a point. She used to pull the very same antics in school, whenever she suspected someone of wrongdoing but didn't want to call them out in case she was wrong. But back then, it was more of an insurance thing. That way, if she were wrong, no one would be the wiser. But when she was proven right, she could gloat that she'd figured it out first. Win-win.

Maybe she had been destined for a career in law enforcement, after all.

Holding up a finger over her lips, she said, "Complete radio silence."

They nodded, and she sprinted to her cruiser.

"Marianna," Sun said, running up to Sybil's mom as she swiped her card at a vending machine.

Before she found Mari, she'd ordered Quincy and Zee to join the guard and Deputy Salazar at Sybil's room, telling them to allow no one, absolutely no one, entrance until she got there. Then she went in search of Marianna St. Aubin.

The woman's face showed signs of severe stress, and when Sun ran up to her like a shopping addict during a fire sale, she thought the poor thing would faint.

"I'm sorry," Sun said, holding up her hands in surrender. "Everything's okay. I just have a couple of questions."

Mari put a hand over her heart while Sun scanned the small snack area that had been decorated to look like a piazza in Italy. Absolutely charming.

"How is Sybil doing?" she asked in the name of social niceties.

"I just checked in on her. She's asleep."

"Good. Good." She led Mari to a small table and had her sit. "I have what could be considered a very delicate question to ask you."

She laced her fingers around the soda can she'd been drinking from. "All right."

"Does your husband have any children from another marriage?"

"Forest? No. Well, none that we know of."

"We? Or you?"

"What are you getting at?"

Sun took a deep breath, hoping she was not starting something she couldn't back up. "I could be wrong. I don't want you to worry he's been lying to you, and I would be talking to him about this, but my deputy said your husband had to make a quick trip into Santa Fe."

Mari's lips thinned. "His daughter was almost murdered, but God forbid he miss an opportunity to get his wine into another national chain."

"I'm sorry."

She smoothed her frown. "No, I am. He's been working so hard. I do understand. And this meeting was set up weeks ago. If he missed it, he may never get a second chance, but some things are just more important, you know?"

"I do," Sun said, though she saw his side, too. In Mr. St. Aubin's eyes, his daughter was safe and sound. He could resume his normal activities without worry.

If only that were the case.

"But I have to say," she continued, "he's never told me he had a child with anyone else."

Sun pulled her lower lip between her teeth. "And . . . you?"

The flash of emotion on Mari's face told her everything. She dropped her gaze to the bank card she'd put on the table. After a long moment of contemplation, she swallowed and said, "He doesn't know."

"Your husband?"

She nodded. "He doesn't know that I had a child. It was . . ." She cleared her throat and began again. "It was a mistake."

"Mari, we all make mistakes. It's nothing to be ashamed of."

"I didn't tell my parents for months, until I could no longer hide the evidence."

"How did they take it?"

She shook her head as though embarrassed. "Anger. Disappointment. Humiliation."

"So, not well."

"Nope. Not my parents. See, everyone else makes mistakes. My parents are perfection incarnate."

"Oh, I think I met them at the fairy ball in Fantasy Land."

She chuckled, but the memory was a bitter one. "Two hours after I told them, we were at an adoption agency, filling out papers."

"I'm sorry."

"No," she said, shaking her head. "I am. They made me feel so ashamed." She locked a determined gaze onto Sun's. "I will never let anyone make me feel that way again."

"Good for you. Did you know the father well?"

"Not really. We'd met at a party. Both of us drunk. He owns a plumbing supply company in Chicago now. Married with three kids."

"Did you ever tell him about the baby?"

She shook her head. "I know what you're thinking. He had a right to know, but my parents threatened to kick me out. I was only sixteen, and they did not want *that boy* in our lives. Like it was all his fault."

And once again, Sun offered up a silent thank-you to the powers that be for giving her Cyrus and Elaine Freyr.

"I left home soon after that. They never looked at me the same again. I was lost for so long, and then Forest happened." Her face brightened as a happy memory bubbled to the surface.

"I was a waitress working the night shift when Forest St. Aubin walked in. Or, well, stumbled in. He was so drunk." She laughed at the memory. "I let him sleep it off in a corner booth, then got him a cab when my shift ended. He came back the next night to apologize, and the rest is history." She looked at Sun then, as though pleading for her to understand. "They didn't even let me look at him before they took him. The baby." She dabbed at the wetness on her cheeks.

"I know what you're going through, Mari. If you ever need someone to talk to."

"Oh, honey, you can't possibly."

She took Mari's hand. "I can, actually."

When her meaning sank in, Mari cupped both her hands around Sun's. "Did you—? What happened?"

Sun felt the corners of her mouth tilt up, and she whispered, "Auri."

Mari's hands flew to her mouth. "Oh, my god. She's amazing. She's . . . Should I have kept him? Should I have tried?" A fresh round of tears slid down her face.

"No, Marianna. You can't compare your situation with mine or anyone else's. You did what you had to do."

"Wait." The truth was sinking in at last. "Is he . . . Did—did he do this?"

Already knowing what the answer would be, Sun brought out her phone and pulled up a picture of one of her very own, Deputy Lonnie Price. Or the man posing as Lonnie Price.

She angled the phone for Mari to see, and the blood drained from Mari's face a microsecond before she dove for a trash can by the door. She emptied her stomach as both the heaving and a round of sobs shook her shoulders.

"Yes," she said through the sobs. "That's— He came to my door."

"What? When?"

She wiped her mouth on a napkin, then sat back down. "Sybil was tiny. Maybe four? And this kid rang our bell. His parents were sitting out in a car, and I recognized them from the adoption agency. I knew instantly who he was."

"You'd met the adoptive parents?"

She nodded. "Only once, but they seemed nice. He told me who he was and asked if he could live with me." Her hands pressed into her mouth, and she sobbed. "What was I supposed to say? Forest didn't know. I was so afraid he would look at me like my parents did because I'd lied to him."

"Mari, this is not your fault."

"No, it is. I grieved for him every day and yet, I—I turned him away." She broke down again. "Is that why he's doing this? Oh, my god. He doesn't know what that did to me."

"He's doing this because he's hurt by his past, Mari. This is not your fault. But right now, I have to find my deputy."

She had no choice. She had to leave Mari in agony as she texted Quincy. "On my way. Read the note."

Hurrying toward the recovery rooms, Sun turned the corner and saw a stunned expression on Quincy's face. Zee's jaw dropped when she read the note, but Sun pushed past them and into the room.

A tuft of red hair poked out from the blankets on the bed where Sybil slept. Sun scanned the room. Rushed into the restroom. Turned a full circle, then looked at the state officer who'd been assigned to guard the room.

"Where's Auri? Where's my daughter?"

He stepped in and checked the area. Deputy Salazar followed, panic draining the color from her face. "She was just right here."

Sun ripped back the covers and almost cried out. Auri lay sleeping in Sybil's bed. She hugged her. But then, "Where's Sybil?"

Marianna stumbled into the room.

"Who's been in here?" Sun asked the officer.

"No one. Just a couple of nurses."

The charge nurse stepped just inside the room, her face the picture of shock.

"Which nurses?" Sun growled.

"Her," he said, pointing at the charge nurse, "and a male nurse."

The nurse shook her head. "We don't have any male nurses on duty today."

"Son of a bitch," Quincy said. "Lock it down!"

He ran to get security to lock down the facility as her other two deputies and the state officer checked the immediate ward.

"I need surveillance yesterday!" Sun shouted, then gestured for the nurse. "She's not waking up."

The nurse sprang into action, pressing the emergency button to call for assistance and rushing to Auri's side. The area flooded with medical personnel as the nurse checked her vitals.

"She's okay," she said. "Her passageways are clear. Her pulse is strong. She's just asleep."

"He drugged them. How did he get Sybil out?"

"Where's my daughter?" Mari asked, and Sun was worried she would pass out.

"He was pushing a cart," the state cop said when he came back. "I didn't think anything of it at the time."

Of course he didn't. This wasn't his fault, but Sun wanted to rip him apart, anyway. Price could have killed her daughter, and he could still kill Marianna's.

"Sunshine," Mari said, terrified. "Please."

Sun ran to her and gave her a hug before calling in every city, county, and state employee in the area, from the highway patrol to the water department.

Price would know they'd discovered Sybil missing, but not that they were onto him. With any luck, he would keep up the game and report to the urgent care center to help in the search.

"Auri, honey?" The nurse put a cool compress on her forehead and was patting her cheek. "Wake up, love. Can you hear me?"

Auri groaned, and Sun almost fell trying to get to her side.

"Auri? Sweetheart?"

"Mom?" she said about half a second before she lurched toward the side of the bed and heaved over the side of it. Orange liquid spilled onto the floor.

Sun held her hair, smoothing it back and fighting hot, angry tears.

"Mom?"

She laid her back as the nurse cleaned her up and swabbed her brow and the back of her neck. "Auri, are you okay?"

"He's still here." Her voice was a thin shell of its former self. "He won't leave."

"Who won't leave, sweetheart?"

"The suspect. He wants Mrs. St. Aubin to see. I don't know why."

"I do." Sun motioned for Quincy to come in. "Did Sybil tell you this?"

Auri nodded. "I tried to tell you, but I was just so tired."

Sun hugged her to her. "It's okay, bug. We'll find her."

Her lids drifted closed just as she said, "What would Lisbeth do?"

"Let's get her to an exam room," the nurse said. "Get some fluids into her to flush out the drugs."

Sun let them take her, then called in her parents, instructing them not to leave Auri's side.

25

Caller reported his wife missing for eighteen months.
Is starting to get worried.

—DEL SOL POLICE BLOTTER

Price didn't fall for it. They'd locked down urgent care for four hours as officers searched the place from top to bottom. Nothing. Not a trace of Sybil or Price. So they expanded their search, bringing in the helicopter and cadaver dogs to comb the area directly behind the urgent care center.

Once they'd lifted the lockdown, Sun's parents took Auri home, and Sun did something she'd never imagined she would. She got the number for Chris De los Santos from Deputy Salazar and texted him, asking if Cruz could go stay with them. Mostly to sit by Auri's side, to comfort her, but the kid knew how to handle himself. If anything should happen, she had no doubt he would do everything in his power to keep them all safe. It was a lot to put on a teenage boy, but desperate times . . .

She explained the situation to Mr. De los Santos, told him there was a slight chance of danger. He texted back that it sounded exactly like something Cruz would jump into the middle of with or without an invitation.

She really liked that kid.

The surveillance video clearly showed Price—they continued

to call him Price because they still didn't have an ID on the guy—going into the room pushing a cart and leaving a few minutes later, so whatever he'd given the girls was fast-acting.

They hadn't blocked the roads quickly enough. He could be well on his way to Colorado by that point. Or Arizona or Texas or even Mexico.

But she also agreed with Auri. Price wanted Marianna to suffer. He wanted her to pay for giving him up for adoption. That could be his only motivation.

"Wait," Sun said. They were still in the urgent care center, and Zee was reviewing the footage in the security room when something caught Sun's eye. "Go back."

Zee rewound the video. "This is where he goes into the room."

"Yeah, but look at that cart. That's not big enough to fit a person. Even a tiny one."

"You're right," Zee said. No way he got her in there. Does that mean—?"

"She's been here the whole time?"

Zee, Quincy, and Sun exchanged glances before taking off toward the outpatient recovery room they'd had Sybil in. They practically burst through the door, but all the officers were out of the building, searching other areas and canvassing the town.

They tore open every door and drawer in search of a tiny redhead to no avail. But they did find a set of metal springs and levers.

"What the hell?" Zee asked, but Sun and Quincy immediately looked at the recliner by the window. It was a hospital chair that folded out to a bed should someone need to stay with a patient all night.

They stepped closer and noticed a tiny pool of blood by the back foot. Quincy knelt down and lifted the chair gently to peek under. Then he pushed it over.

"Motherfucker, she's gone." He grabbed his hair and doubled over in frustration.

But Zee was looking at what was left of the inner workings

of the chair. A long lock of hair had gotten tangled in the mecha-
nisms, and Price had apparently pulled it out when he took her out
of the chair. "She was here the whole time. He took her while we
were looking at other footage."

"This is not happening," Sun said, very aware that it was. And
Sybil was going to pay for their mistakes.

"Thank you, Lieutenant." Sun disconnected the call she'd made on
the way back to the station, very curious as to why Price had come
with such a stellar recommendation.

Of course, she hadn't hired him, but she'd read his file. And
the reason he'd received such stellar accolades was because he'd
assumed the identity of an actual officer in Detroit. An officer who
was very surprised when Del Sol did an inquiry on him when he
hadn't applied there.

Sun wanted to know how the former sheriff didn't catch that.
Then again, maybe he did. According to her investigation into
Redding, the guy was certifiable.

Agent Fields put out feelers in Detroit to try to find out who'd
adopted Marianna's baby so they could at least get an ID and possible history. But that wasn't going to help them now.

Since the game was clearly up, they plastered his face all over
the news and social media, begging for any sightings. Any tips on
his location.

And that was where they were when Sun walked into the
station. Salazar gestured toward the holding cell in the deputy's
room. The one in which one Levi Ravinder currently resided.

"He's really upset," she said, looking much like a deer in head-
lights.

And then Sun understood why. A thunderous crash echoed
throughout the area, shaking the walls and knocking dust off the
ceiling.

"What the hell?" She marched over to the holding cell and
opened the solid outer door.

Levi stood in all his angry glory behind a set of bars, his expression flat except for the fact that his warm caramel irises had caught fire. Metaphorically.

She did not need this right now. "What the hell, Ravinder?"

"Open the door, *Vicram*."

"Um, no?"

"Where is she? Did you find her? Is she okay?"

Sun's shoulder sagged. "We're still looking."

Before she even finished the sentence, he kicked the bars so hard she was afraid he'd broken them. The crash made everyone in the room jump, and she realized his hands were cuffed behind his back.

When he spoke, his voice was quiet. His tone lethal. "Open. The fucking. Door."

"Why?" she asked, frustrated. "Do you know something we don't?"

"I can help look for her."

"Right."

"I've done it before. It's what I do."

"I know, Levi. I know you do. You found Jimmy, and we wouldn't have found Sybil the first time without you, but this time is different. We don't even know what area to focus on."

"The first time?" he asked as though confused. "Sybil is missing? Again?"

"Yes. Who did you think we were talking about?"

He stepped back and sat on the cot. "I thought it was Auri. Holy fuck."

"Why would you think that?"

He leaned his head back against the wall. "I saw the picture your deputies were handing out. It looked like Auri from a distance."

Why did she feel so ingratiated to him? Why did the fact that he cared that much for her daughter give her such an incredible sense of pride and gratitude?

He stabbed her with a determined glare. "I can still help. You know I can."

"We need to narrow down the search area first."

He sighed, leaned his head back again, and closed his eyes.

"If I open this, are you going to behave?"

"Probably not."

At least he was honest. "I'm coming in. And I'm going to uncuff you, but you have to be nice and stop trying to tear down my station."

He looked at her. "Aren't you supposed to do that through the cage?"

She opened the barred door. "Yes."

He stood when she walked in, but he didn't turn around. Not allowed to have anything in the cell beyond his clothing, he wore only a T-shirt that molded to his sculpted biceps like spray paint, a pair of jeans that fit comfortably loose, and socks.

And he was looking at her as though he were famished and she was made of strawberries and whipped cream.

"You'll have to turn around if you want those off."

"Let me help."

"If I need you, I'll come back."

With deliberate slowness, he turned and let her unlock the cuffs. They'd dug into his skin, leaving grooves in his wrists, and she tamped down the surge of anger that jolted through her.

Her team showed up after she locked her prisoner back in his cell, and they studied a map, scouring the area for ideas while Levi stood at the bars and watched.

"There are dozens of empty cabins this time of year," she said. "We can't possibly check them all before tomorrow."

"Who says he'll wait until the sun comes up?" Quincy asked. "Legally, she turns fifteen at midnight."

He was right. It would be callous of them to assume he would wait a second longer than his warped brain told him he needed to.

"Wait," Salazar said. "What about Mrs. Usury's place? She's all alone out there since her husband died, and Price did take Sybil to their well house. Maybe he knows her or knows she's vulnerable."

"Get someone out there," Sun said. "Recon only."

Quincy snapped, pointed at his twin, and headed for the door. "We're on it!"

Zee followed him, and Sun looked up at Tricia Salazar, the young deputy with wide-set eyes and chipmunk cheeks. That caring disposition, that deep concern for the well-being of others, was why the girl was on her team. Every agency in the world needed someone with a sense of empathy, a gentler view of the world. Someone who saw things through a softer shade of rose-colored glasses.

"It won't take them long to get to Mrs. Usury's house," she said. "In the meantime, what else do we know about this guy? You've spent the last six months getting to know him."

Salazar's expression became strained. "He was that guy, Sheriff. The one who's impossible to get to know. He never really talked about his life. He never went out for drinks after a shift. We didn't even know where he was living for the longest."

"And after a while," Anita said, walking up and handing Sun a cup of coffee, "we quit asking."

Salazar looked like she carried the weight of the galaxy, her guilt so evident.

"Deputy," Sun said, "no one saw this coming. This is not your fault."

"It kind of is," she said, twisting her hands. When Sun raised a questioning brow, she explained. "I vetted him."

"Yeah, well, I vetted him, too. I vetted all of you. He slipped through all our fingers."

The girl nodded, then steeled herself to face the challenge ahead. "We checked his house again a few minutes ago. No sign of him."

"And you never saw him with anyone? No friends or known associates?"

Both women shook their heads. He was probably too busy stalking the St. Aubins. Sun was a little surprised no one in the household had noticed him. But that was the thing about Price. He was so very ordinary. So easily dismissed.

Sun's phone rang. It was Zee. She put her on speakerphone.

"Hey, boss." Her voice sounded sad, and adrenaline shot through Sun's body. "I didn't want this over the radio."

"No," she whispered.

"I'm sorry. He's definitely been here. Mrs. Usury is dead."

"Mrs. Usury?" For some reason, she turned to Levi, and he stiffened.

"It looks like he's been staying here for a few days. He must've wanted to keep an eye on Sybil while he had her in the well house."

She studied Levi's beautiful frame. His solid jaw. His full mouth. His presence was comforting. "If he was staying at her residence, why go to the well house from the opposite direction?"

"To throw us off," both Levi and Zee answered simultaneously.

"Just in case," Levi added.

"Well, it certainly worked. He's not there now?"

"No," Quincy said. "But his patrol unit is, and it's still warm. There are some tracks beside the house, but hell if I know how old they are. Either way, looks like we just missed him."

"And it's getting dark," Zee said. "We need to get on this. We need the tracker."

Levi grabbed a rifle from the back of Sun's cruiser. He started to take off, but he turned, grabbed the lapel of her parka, and pulled her close. With his mouth barely inches from hers, he said, "Keep your head down, and try to keep up."

He didn't wait. He took off at a dead run, following the tracks left in the snow, as the rest of the team did indeed try to keep up. Sun, Quincy, and Zee ran through the snow and brush as darkness crept in around them, and while Sun lost any sight of tracks a half mile back, Levi kept going at a breakneck speed.

Then, without warning, he slowed his pace so they could catch up. Their breaths fogged in the air, the altitude making breathing even harder. He knelt and held up a fist, signaling for them to stop.

They gathered around him and took a knee. "We're closing the distance. We need to strategize."

"What?" Sun gasped for air. "We need to catch up to them. That's a good strategy."

"No, we need to take the high ground." He looked at Zee and then at her rifle, a rifle she carried like a newborn in her arms. "How good are you with that?"

"Very."

"See this?" He pointed to a disturbance in the snow. "He was dragging her before. Now he's carrying her, so I don't know if she passed out or if he's caught on to the fact that we're behind him and has picked up the pace. He's going for Joey Bachicha's hunting cabin. He must've been scoping out this area for months to know it's there. We can't let him get to it."

"Why?" Quincy asked. "Besides the obvious."

"The obvious being the fact that any cover is good for him and bad for us. That cabin has no windows at all. He'll force a stalemate and kill her before we can even get close."

Sun nodded in understanding. "We need to get to that cabin before he does."

One corner of his mouth lifted, just barely, as he studied her. "Remember that state track record you broke in high school?"

"Levi," she said, still panting, "that was a long time ago."

When he only stared at her, apparently giving her a minute to come to the same conclusion he had, she caved.

"Fine. We'll go around this ridge and get to the cabin while you two"—she looked at Zee and Quincy—"come in from behind." She leveled a hard look on Zee. "If you get the shot, you take it. He went to a lot of trouble to get to Sybil. He will not hesitate to kill her. His sole purpose at this moment is to make his biological mother pay." She pointed to Zee. "Sniper." Then to Quincy. "Spotter." Then she took hold of Zee's shoulder and gazed directly into her eyes. "If you have to shoot him in the fucking back, you take the shot."

Zee nodded just as Levi grabbed Sun's arm, lifted her to her feet, and took off. And she thought he'd taken off at a dead run before. He flew through the trees, and it took everything in her power to keep up with him.

The snow and altitude made the last mile feel like a hundred. She'd lost feeling in her legs a while back, but it didn't make them any lighter.

Still, they were so close, her adrenaline kicked in. Then he stopped and pointed two fingers down the mountain. A cabin, barely visible in the moonlight, sat to the side of a small clearing.

Thanking God for the full moon, she fought to fill her burning lungs and slow her pulse. She looked at Levi as he studied the terrain. His magnificent profile against the snow-covered backdrop made her ache more than the run did.

"Don't," he said, his voice hoarse.

She frowned and followed his gaze to the clearing. "Don't what?"

He reached out, grabbed the front of her jacket, and pulled her close. She stumbled against him and put her palms on his chest for balance.

The fog of their breaths mingled as he looked down at her. As he ran a gloved thumb over her mouth. As he bent closer, his gaze locked onto hers like a predator. "We have to get down this mountain, and we have to do it fast."

"Okay."

"And if you keep looking at me like I'm some kind of hero, you're going to be very disappointed in the long run."

"I don't think so."

He held her chin to study her face, then asked, "Ready?"

She nodded, but Quincy's voice invaded the moment. "Are you guys making out?"

They were using a short-range in-ear comm set. She gritted her teeth. "What part of radio silence—"

"We have eyes," he said.

They both turned and looked at the clearing. Price was just emerging from a tree line, heading for the cabin.

"Fuck," Levi said, and he pulled Sun down the mountain.

They half ran and half fell. Sliding through huge drifts of snow, they landed on the side opposite of Price and Sybil. She could only pray he didn't see them.

"She can't get a shot," he said, peering around the side of a stack of firewood.

She looked around him. He was right. There was no way Zee could take the shot. He had Sybil draped over him. "Son of a bitch," she said. "Ideas?"

"You're the idea person," he said. "I'm more of a 'let's get in front of him and blow him away' kind of guy."

"We have to get her away from him."

"Agreed."

She drew in a deep breath, her stomach raw from all the acid pumping into it. "I have an idea. Zee, stay sharp."

"Always," she said, her voice as calm as the breeze on a summer's day. She was already in the zone, centering the crosshairs on her mark, slowing her pulse.

She explained her plan, then said, "He's got to be exhausted. I'll get her away from him. You just make sure he doesn't make it into the cabin with her should I fail."

"Don't fail," Levi said.

She looked at his profile again, studied it, a mere shadow in the dark.

"Don't," he whispered as Price got closer.

The man was groaning, straining against the weight of the fourteen-year-old over his shoulders and the resistance of the snow at his feet.

They realized she was awake. Her whimpers drifted over the snow.

"Levi," she whispered.

He reached back and took her gloved hand into his.

"If I do fail," she started, her voice as quiet as the snow, but he turned to glare at her before she could finish. She shook her head, determined. "If I do fail, will you take care of her?"

They both knew she wasn't talking about Sybil.

It took him a long moment to answer. When he finally did, he echoed Zee's sentiment when he said, "Always."

She nodded and ducked behind the woodpile as Levi slid onto the porch of the cabin from the back and slunk around to the front to head Price off.

Price started to take the first step when she realized he was carrying a hunting knife in one hand, and she almost lost her nerve. He could do so much damage to Sybil in such a short amount of time with that knife, but she had no choice.

She eased from behind the woodpile just as his foot landed on the first rung of the steps. That was Levi's cue, and he played his part beautifully.

"Can I ask what you're doing here?"

The plan was to make Price think Levi owned the cabin and was in residence.

Not expecting company, Price stumbled back in surprise. It was the opening she needed. She rushed him from the side, grabbed hold of Sybil, and pulled with every ounce of strength she had.

At the same time, Levi shot off the porch and, while Sun did succeed in getting Sybil away from him, she also succeeded in allowing Price to get a firm hold of her instead.

Before Levi could get to them, in a move startlingly quick, Price had his arms around her and the knife at her throat. A knife that was longer than her forearm.

"Back!" He gave Levi a warning glare as he dragged her backward.

Levi slid to a stop a few feet from them and raised his hands.

"I will slice her fucking throat so fast she won't even know it until she sees her blood spraying onto your face."

"Price," she said, her voice calm.

He was beginning to unravel. All his plans spoiled.

"This would have worked if that idiot Redding had won the fucking election," he said. He laughed helplessly. "Oh, my god, that man was so stupid."

"Can I ask your real name?"

"Why, Sheriff? You gonna be my friend?"

"If you'll let me."

"Yeah, well, you can cut that psychobabble shit right now. How did you know?" He kept moving with her, turning her as he scanned the distance as though he knew Zee was out there trying to get a shot. "How'd you figure it out?"

"The divot," she said. "The one where your ear meets your temple."

When Sun had originally seen the slit in Price's temple, she'd thought it was part of the injury he'd sustained chasing dogs in the middle of the night. Part of the scrapes and bruises when, as he put it, the bushes attacked him. She was wrong.

"Sybil has one, too," she said, her breath fogging on the air. "It took me a while to make the connection, but once I realized you were somehow related, it all fell into place. That kind of dimple is hereditary. And it's pretty rare."

He pulled her around again. "No shit?"

"Sybil doesn't deserve this."

"Where is she?" he asked, spinning her around as he scanned the trees again.

"Who?"

"Zee!" he yelled into the quiet night. "I know you're out there, gorgeous. Let me see you or she dies."

"Zee's not here. We didn't have time to wait for her."

He hugged Sun to him, his mouth at her ear. "You know, Auri and I have a lot in common."

"Yeah?"

"I was a surprise to my mother as well."

"Really?"

"Only my mother threw me away. Of course, the minute my adoptive mother got little ole me, that bitch got pregnant and suddenly I didn't matter anymore. They had their dream kid. I was an inconvenience. Do you know what they did to me?"

"Why don't you tell me?"

"They took me to meet her when I was fifteen." He laughed, the sound bitter in the quiet night air. "I stood on the doorstep to this . . . mansion and rang the doorbell while my parents sat in the car. And Marianna St. Aubin answered the door, her redheaded daughter nipping at her heels. I told her who I was." He squeezed her tighter as the memories washed over him. "I begged her to take me in, but she said I had the wrong house. Told me to never come back and closed the door on my face while my parents laughed."

Sun felt the sting of the blade a second before she felt a warm drop of blood slide down her neck. He was getting angrier by the second. She needed to change the subject. "The deputies at the station said you've been a great cop."

He scoffed. "You giving me my job back?"

"I think you have a lot to offer the world."

"Where are you, Zee?" he shouted, completely ignoring her.

She heard Zee's voice in her ear. "Can you drop?"

Levi gave the barest shake of his head, but she nodded. If she could get a hand underneath the blade, she could drop to the ground and give Zee the shot.

Levi glared at her, but she ignored him. Closing her eyes, she offered up a prayer and counted off with her fingers out of range of his vision. But before she could drop to her knees, Price fell to his and took her with him, hugging her to his chest, his chin on her shoulder, his mouth at her ear.

"No, no, no, no, no, no, no, Sunshine on My Shoulders. No cheating." His breaths came in shallow gasps as adrenaline coursed through him. "No cheating."

"I'm not going anywhere."

He pulled her even closer, his grip like a vise around her ribs. "How about we both go, huh? I take you out, and then Zee takes me out, and everything is right with the world."

"As long as Sybil is okay."

He burst out laughing. "Oh, she's dead, beautiful. Or she will be soon."

Sun stiffened and glanced at the unconscious girl in the snow. "What do you mean?"

"OD. She kept fighting me. I got pissed off. I've been told I have anger issues."

"What did you give her?"

"The usual, GHB. Still, I did want to gut her. Leave her in little pieces on Marianna's porch, just like she left me."

"You don't know how hard that was for her."

He was rocking her now, making peace with whatever demons possessed him, preparing to die. Question was, would he take her with him?

Zee came back on. "One inch to your left, in three . . ."

"I'm sorry it's come to this, Price."

". . . two . . ."

He looked at her from over her shoulder, tears shimmering in his eyes, and whispered his real name. "Cory."

". . . one."

She turned to him, tilted her head to the left, and put the tips of her gloved fingers on his jaw. "Cory."

Blood exploded across her face, the execution of the order happening so fast she almost lost consciousness. His head shattered before she even heard the shot.

Levi dove for the knife before Cory's muscles could tighten in reflex and cut her throat. Something she hadn't even thought of. He held on to the blade until Cory's muscles realized his brain was no longer in control.

It was barely a second. Maybe two. But it seemed like an eternity until he went limp and fell to the side. Sun scrambled to get to Sybil. Zee and Quincy ran toward them as Sun and Levi checked her.

She was still warm. Her breaths were shallow, but she was still warm.

The medics arrived in a helicopter and stabilized her enough to fly her out.

The cabin, which was normally accessible by road, had been cut off due to the snow. If not for small miracles, Price . . . Cory could have just driven Sybil there and killed her before they could get to them.

Clearly, someone was watching out for Sybil. She wondered if it was the same entity that had given her the premonition in the first place.

After the helicopter took off, another one landed, blowing ice-cold bursts of snow around them. They would secure the scene and take Cory's body to the OMI.

About twenty minutes later, the cavalry arrived. The engines of several emergency ATVs echoed in the clearing, and time was running out. Sun had been busy organizing the emergency personnel, but now she had to decide what to do with Levi.

She looked over at him as he leaned against the porch rails. He'd saved a life tonight. Possibly two. But he'd also confessed to killing his uncle.

His gaze didn't waver as he watched her. Then, as though he were taking a stroll on a beach, he put a hand in his jacket pocket, tipped an invisible hat, and disappeared into the darkness surrounding him like he belonged to it.

She let him go.

For now.

26

Church parking only.
Violators will be baptized.

—SIGN AT DEL SOL CHURCH ON THE ROCKS

Auri woke up in the middle of the night, partially on her grand-parents' sofa, the buttery one she'd helped her grandmother pick out, and partially on the chest of a boy.

Cruz lay asleep underneath her, his long frame stretched across the length of the sofa. Only it didn't fit, so his feet, still clad in an old pair of running shoes, hung off the edge and rested on a side table along with a hideous ashtray Auri had made her grandparents—who'd never smoked a day in their lives—at summer day camp.

She blinked in the low light, her head still spinning from be-ing drugged, and looked across the room at a man sitting in the matching recliner. The one with a rifle in his lap.

Auri rocketed from a sleepy haze to a startlingly lucid aware-ness. She jumped and tried to fling herself off Cruz in a flurry of arms and legs and blankets. Her extremities were twisted and trapped, and she lost her balance. The floor rushed to get up close and personal with her face when two arms wrapped around her torso and scooped her up.

She landed right back where she'd started. On top of none other than Cruz De los Santos.

"You're okay," he said, his voice soft and calming. "You're okay."

She melted into the rich warmth of his dark irises. Then she remembered her grandfather.

"Grandpa!" She twisted around to look at him. "This isn't what it looks like!"

But when she spotted him, he'd put the rifle aside so he could double over in laughter. Another round of laughs emanating from the love seat caught her attention, and she turned to see her grandmother prone on the chair, giggling it up.

"My falling is that funny?"

"No," she said, trying to sober. "The fact that you thought your grandfather was here to chaperone."

They doubled over again, and Auri almost cracked a smile. Cruz tucked a strand of hair behind her ear, fighting a grin himself, and Auri gave up. She laughed softly, feeling more than a little sheepish. Then a realization dawned.

"Hey," she said, glowering at her grandparents. "What makes you think I don't need a chaperone? This could be exactly what it looks like. You never know. We could be in the throes of passion right now."

Cruz choked on air as Auri's grandparents exchanged humorous glances and burst into laughter again.

"I'm sorry, hon," Elaine said, wiping her eyes. "It's just, your arms and legs flying about? You looked like a spasmodic starfish."

Heat spread across her cheeks. "Thanks."

Cruz offered her a sympathetic grin, but not too sympathetic. He brushed the backs of his fingers over her cheek, and she giggled and ducked.

Then everything hit her at once. Cruz. Her grandparents. Sybil. Her mom.

She shoved off her potential boyfriend, fought a dizzy spell, then sat up and refocused on her grandparents. They took her cue and sobered instantly, a knowing smile on their faces.

"Mom?"

Cyrus nodded. "She's okay."

Cruz sat up and took her hand.

She swallowed and asked, "Sybil?"

Elaine expression softened, and something akin to sympathy flashed in her eyes. "She's going to be fine. They got to her just in time."

The emotion Auri had been holding in for days threatened to erupt out of her. A happy sob escaped her, and she pressed her hands over her mouth as the news sank in. Then she sprang forward and hugged her grandparents.

"Your boyfriends left."

Sun gave Quincy the barest hint of her attention as she strolled past his desk. None of them had gotten much sleep, but her inquisitive daughter made her tell her everything the minute she'd gotten home. She'd skipped the plasma facial, but she did tell her that Zee had delivered a fatal shot. She wanted Auri to have that closure.

But the story put Auri into a mild state of shock. Either that or she was figuring out how she could put it into a novel and get rich. Sun knew she'd see her daughter's memoirs on a store shelf someday.

"I don't have a boyfriend." Clearly.

"Not boyfriend. Boyfriends."

She stopped and lowered her sunglasses so she could give him just enough of a glare to spur him to finish his story.

"Agent Fields got called back to the Albuquerque office. And the marshals' work here was done."

"Done?"

"The fugitive was apprehended last night in Santa Fe after robbing a convenience store and falling asleep in the getaway car.

While it was still in the parking lot!" He snorted, then pointed to his eye but gesturing to hers. "That's pretty."

Somehow, she'd managed to get a black eye. She didn't even remember how, and then Zee suggested it was from the concussion of the shot. Sun didn't think it worked that way, but who was she to argue?

Zee was on mandatory leave pending an investigation into the shooting, but she'd shown up to file her report. Quincy gestured a greeting, his smile a tad awestruck.

Sun understood. Any woman who could take out a target at night, in a highly stressful situation, at fifty yards, and avoid killing her boss deserved a fair amount of respect.

"Get me that file, will you?"

He put his booted feet on his desk and crossed them at the ankles. "Well, now, that's not really my job, is it?"

She ignored him and walked to her office.

He put his feet down and jumped up. "Okay! I'm on it, boss!" After a moment, he added, "Which file would that be?"

"The one on the fugitive, Ramses Rojas."

Anita walked to her office door, her curly blond hair pulled into a messy bun that made her look younger than her thirty-plus years. "There's a Mrs. Sorenson here to see you."

Sun groaned. "This again?"

"She has a chicken."

"Oh." Sun hopped up to look into the lobby. "She does indeed."

Quincy handed her the file she'd asked for. "Why does she get to call it a chicken?"

"Did you know that Anita is a fifth-degree black belt in a secret form of martial arts that's so deadly it's banned in every country in the world and she can kill you with cheese spread?"

He studied the tiny lady for a solid minute, then walked away.

Anita giggled. "Should I let her back?"

"Yeah, put her in the interview room."

"Oh, and there's a Mr. Madrid, too."

"Wonderful. Put him in the other interview room."

"We only have the one."

"Okay, the supply closet, then."

"You got it."

But much to Sun's surprise, they insisted on seeing her together.

Mrs. Sorenson, a sixtysomething with neon-red hair, held on to Puff Daddy like she'd been reunited with the love of her life. Which she very well could have been.

"He was just lost," she said, laughing nervously.

Mr. Madrid chimed in. "Yeah, and Ida . . ." He glanced past the giant rooster in her arms. "May I call you Ida?"

She almost blushed. "Of course."

Sun fought the muscles in her eyes, whose knee-jerk reaction was to roll like a heroin addict mid-high.

"Ida thought I took him, but I would never."

Honestly, she could hardly look at the man. He was covered in more cuts and bruises than an MMA fighter. It took everything in her not to crack up.

Quincy was not suffering from the same malady. Even though he was in the observation room, she could hear him laughing through the two-way.

She turned around to glare at him, then turned back to what could be a potential problem for a long time to come. They lived across the street from one another and were always arguing. That was not a problem. It was when they filed formal complaints and pressed charges and then suddenly dropped the whole thing a few days, or weeks, later.

And it was getting ridiculous.

"I'm sorry, Mrs. Sorenson, but once the complaint is filed, it has to be taken to court."

They both gaped at her.

"It's never worked that way before," she said.

"I know. It's a new law. If a complaint is filed, the suspect must be arrested, and it must go to trial. You'll, of course, be called in to testify, and you can tell them it was all a mistake when you do. But by then, wow, I can't imagine the legal bills you're going to rack up, Mr. Madrid. I wish there was some way—"

"Well, there has to be," Ida said. "I don't want Ike—may I call you Ike?"

He nodded and ducked with a grin.

Seriously? They'd been squabbling all these years and they were just now getting to know each other on a first-name basis?

"I don't want Ike to have to go through that."

Sun took out her handcuffs and stood. "Can you please stand and put your hands behind your back, Mr. Madrid?"

"What?" Ida jumped to her feet, upsetting Puff Daddy. His massive wings flapped several times, and feathers of all shapes and sizes went airborne.

That was when Sun could hear both Quincy's and Zee's laughter through the two-way. And that was when she gave in to her eye muscles and let them roll.

"I'll refuse to testify against him!" Ida said.

"Well, there's only one way you can do that, but—"

Their gazes shot to her face in unison. "How?"

Sun shook her head and sat back down. "It's impossible."

"No, it's not." She calmed the rooster with several aggressive strokes.

"Okay, I'll tell you, but you aren't going to like it."

"Sure we will," Ike said. He had such a kind face, she hated to do this to him, but someone had to give them that little shove.

"The only way the ADA can't force you to testify is . . . is if you're married."

Both members of the upcoming wedding party stood motionless, neither willing to address the situation first.

"And even then, it's only if you're married before I have to get this paperwork to the courthouse. Today. At 4:00 p.m.," she prodded. "And I just can't see that happ—"

"No, it can happen." Ida looked at Ike and nodded.

He nodded back at her. "Today by four."

Sun shrugged. "Okay, then. I guess, without an eyewitness, I'll have no choice but to drop the case. If I get a copy of your marriage certificate by the end of the day."

"You'll have it."

They started for the door, but Ike turned back and whispered to her, "Can you thank that nice deputy for me? If not for him, I don't know what would've happened."

"Which one?"

"That Price fellow. Puff escaped, and he spent half the night helping me find him. I mean, I only had him because I saw him out by Route 63 and I was going to give him back, but then he got out and that nice deputy—"

"Cory," she said, her heart sinking for what had to be done. "His name was Cory."

"Well, thank him for me, will you?"

"I will. Congratulations." Sun blew out a deep breath, trying to come to terms with how things can go so horribly wrong one minute and so wonderfully right the next.

Quincy walked up to her. "You realize she's going to do a lot worse to him than what the chicken did."

"Funny thing about that," Sun said. "I have a feeling he's going to enjoy it."

He made a face. "Ew."

He started to walk off when she said one word to him. "Bo."

Turning toward her, he put his fingers on his chin in thought. "Who?"

She stepped closer. "I don't like being in the dark, Quincy."

"Who does? That shit's scary."

"I'm afraid of ghosts," Zee said, not helping.

"Lieutenant Bo Britton," Sun continued. "The only deputy on the payroll who gets paid to do absolutely nothing."

Quincy grinned. "Well, he's been a little preoccupied."

"Where is he?" He started to talk, but she interrupted. "And if you say 'who,' I will throw darts at your spleen. While it's still in your body."

"Ouch. Aggressive much? I was going to ask what day it is."

Sunshine tried to pry her teeth apart, but he held up his hands in surrender.

"No, really. I have to know what day it is before I can tell you."

"Fine. It's the ninth."

"Oh, right. Sybil's birthday. Well, we can go see him now."

"Who?"

"Really?" he asked, his expression flatlining.

They drove to the Del Sol Mortuary and, after a heated discussion with the mortician, Quincy led Sun back to the embalming room.

"Quincy, what's going on?"

"A wife and two kids," he said as the mortician opened a cold chamber and pulled out a tray with a handsome older gentleman.

"Sunshine Vicram, meet Lieutenant Bobby Britton."

"Quincy," she said, having had enough death for the time being.

"Bo passed this morning."

"He's frozen solid," she said.

"Yeah. He . . . froze to death."

"Quincy, damn it."

He lowered his head. "Bo passed away two weeks ago while hunting. He had a heart attack, but he was two weeks away from retiring with full benefits instead of that bullshit they offer you if you retire early. Two weeks, Sun."

She said nothing, so he continued, "He married late. Has two small kids. A wife who loved him more than air. They're devastated." He moved closer to her, begging her to hear. "They deserve this."

The mortician stood back, clearly nervous about the whole thing now that the sheriff had arrived.

"Did Redding know about this?" She would have been very surprised if the former sheriff had agreed to it. He cared about no one but himself.

"Hell no. Just a handful of us lackeys."

After offering Bo a silent prayer, she turned to the mortician. "He died in the line of duty last night during a manhunt."

"Yes, ma'am. Sheriff. I'm sorry for your loss."

If ever there were a town that could pull this off, it was Del Sol. After all, they'd pulled off a fake husband for her.

"We'll be taking care of all the funeral expenses, if you could arrange that."

"Of course."

"Quincy," she said, walking him out, "you have a lot of paperwork to illegally alter and hope it doesn't come back to bite us on the ass."

"I hate paperwork, but for once, I'm not complaining." He stopped and faced her. "Thank you, Sunny. And if you really need to be bitten on the ass . . ."

She slammed a hand over his mouth to stop him. "I'm good."

He chuckled from behind her hand and asked, "Where are you off to?"

"I need to ask Darlene Tapia why she was harboring a fugitive."

As she walked off, he called after her, "You already know, don't you?"

"I have my suspicions."

Sun stepped outside with a tray of fruity drinks in her hand. No one needed to know it was just 7 Up with food coloring and orange slices.

"I love Sundays," Auri said, angling her face toward the round ball of fire in the sky. "They're so relaxing."

"Don't get too relaxed," Sun said.

Auri opened her eyes and took a drink off the tray. "Can you believe two days ago we were in our winter coats and today we're tanning?"

"That's New Mexico for you." The temp had risen to a downright balmy seventy-five degrees, but there was still snow on the mountains. The sun sparkled off the white peaks, reminding the sheriff it was still midwinter in the Land of Enchantment.

Auri, Cruz, and Jimmy Ravinder were sitting on lounge chairs in her front yard. Which was basically her parents' backyard.

"How can it be so sunny and warm today, when it was all drizzly and cold yesterday? This state is weird."

"Your face is weird," Sun said, reverting to her favorite joke.

"Did you talk to Sybil's mom?" Cruz asked.

"I did. Sybil is fantastic and, well, glad to be alive. She's coming home today."

Auri bolted upright. "Can we go see her? Please? We've been texting, but it's just not the same, and she's been in the hospital forever."

"She's been in there two days."

"And?"

Sun felt the corners of her eyes crinkle. "If it's okay with Marianna. But first, I have a favor to ask." She looked at Cruz. "Both of you."

"And me?" Jimmy asked, his dark blond hair ruffling in the light breeze.

"And you, but I'll need you to hang back with me. Help me with operations."

"I can do that." The excitement in his eyes was contagious, and her daughter leaned over and hugged him.

Sun loved that he was like a brother to Auri. Had been since that day on the cliff over seven years ago. If Sun had known, things would have been a lot different the last few years.

Water under the bridge now, but she'd missed so much. She'd just have to make up for it.

"Ask away," Cruz said. He wore his army jacket and goggles for the tanning session. No clue why.

"Okay," she said, but Auri interrupted her before she could get two words in.

"I know that look."

"Not this one. I just bought it."

"Nope." She pointed at her suspiciously. "You've had that one in the back of your closet, waiting for the opportunity to wear it again. It's that 'I'm about to do something dangerous' look."

"Okay, you caught me. But before I tell you the plan, I have to know, do either of you have any experience buying drugs?"

One hour later, with the help of one Darlene Tapia, Sun sat a few yards away from an orange Chevy long bed, faded with large patches of rust on the roof, that should have been retired from duty in the '80s. Her daughter and her daughter's potential boyfriend strolled up to the window of said orange Chevy long bed.

If her hunch was correct, the man sitting in the driver's seat was a pretty great guy. This would be the ultimate test to prove her theory either right or wrong.

"Zee? Quincy? You got eyes?"

"Twenty-twenty," Quincy said.

Zee came on the headset, her voice, her tone, smooth and re-laxed, reflecting that razor-sharp focus the makers of Adderall would kill to bottle. "I got 'im."

"Great, well, don't shoot him yet."

She chuckled softly. "Copy that."

"Jimmy?" she said to the kid looking through the binoculars beside her. "You good?"

He gave her a thumbs-up.

Cruz's dad let her use his son without question, and she realized they had an incredible bond, much like she and Auri had. That trust shone through. Hailey was a little harder to convince. Sun had had to swear to her that Jimmy would be nowhere near the action.

If Sun had this guy figured out, and she liked to think she did, there wouldn't be any action.

The guy in the truck, a tattooed Latino with a buzz cut and an attitude a mile long, sat facing the icy water at the lake, his mind a million miles away if the fact that the kids walked up to his window and he still hadn't noticed them was any indication.

"You okay, baby?"

"I'm okay," Auri said into her mic. "I have the best backup team ever."

"Damn straight you do," Quincy said.

"Damn straight you do," Jimmy echoed.

Auri knocked on the window, and Sun realized the guy had been aware of the two kids stalking him, after all. He rolled the glass down without turning his head, but he'd been watching them in his side mirror.

He finally gave them a once-over then asked, "Yeah?"

"Um, we were told you had illegal drugs for sale."

Sun almost lost it. Holy cow, her daughter would never make it as an undercover cop. Not necessarily a bad thing.

Cruz stepped up to the plate. "We want to try mescaline. The good shit, not the knockoff. You got any?"

Suddenly, Auri's choice in potential boyfriends was being brought into question. He was good. A little too good.

The guy laughed. "Man, you have come to the wrong place. Who told you some shit like that, holmes?"

"My friend Lucky," he said.

"Well, your friend Lucky is a liar." He leaned closer to them. "Haven't you heard? Drugs are bad."

"Come on," Cruz said, pushing it. "Do we look like cops? We just want to try it."

"You know what you can try?"

"What?" Auri asked.

"You can try to get the fuck outta my world, because if I see your skinny asses trying to buy drugs again, I am going to rip you apart. Both of you."

Cruz laughed it off and took on the persona of a gangster. "Fuck you, man. What are you gonna do?"

In a move that happened so fast even Sun was stunned, the guy opened his door and had Cruz by the collar and thrown against the truck.

While Auri's hands shot to cover her mouth, Cruz signaled that he was okay, waving his hand by his side in negation, letting them know not to come in just yet.

The guy leaned in close.

Cruz stared him down, refusing to break eye contact. The kid was good.

"You know what they do to pretty boys like you in prison?"

"Stop!" Auri yelled, and Sun's adrenaline skyrocketed.

"That's it," Sun said. "This is over."

Auri literally turned around to her—or to her position, as it was doubtful the girl could see her mother past the shrubs—and scowled at her, lifting her hands and shrugging, every ounce of her demeanor screaming, "What the hell?"

She was acting? Seriously? Maybe she did have the chops for undercover police work. Not that she would wish that on her worst enemy.

Sun canceled her orders and said, "Sorry, bug. Carry on."

She shrugged again and shook her head, then went back to her promising career as a soap star. Or a hardened criminal. Either way.

"Stop it! Let him go!" She ran up to the man and tried to pull him off her potential boyfriend—her descriptor—and Sun cringed.

All he'd have to do was swing his elbow back and she'd have a broken jaw.

Instead, he confirmed Sun's suspicions. He let go of Cruz and wrapped an arm around Auri to restrain her, to try to calm her down.

"Stop, sweetheart. I'm sorry. I won't hurt him, I promise."

"That's what I needed," Sun said. "Let's go."

Quincy turned on his siren and lights and stormed the beach, so to speak, as Zee, Sun, and Jimmy emerged from their hiding places.

The guy threw his hands up in anger and hit his palm against the truck. Not hard enough to do any damage, however. Then he saw the rifle that had been aimed at his head and paled.

Zee opened the bed of his truck, rested her secured rifle there, then rushed forward to handcuff him.

He didn't fight her, but he wasn't happy. "Man, this is some bullshit. I didn't even do anything."

"You assaulted a teen," Sun said. "For starters."

He laid his head back as Zee got the cuffs around his wrists. "This is such bullshit."

"Yeah, you said that."

Jimmy's face was one solid smile. "Yeah, you said that, scumbag."

"That's it," she said to him. "No more *Miami Vice* reruns for you."

27

Caller reported 50 lbs. of green chile stolen from his freezer.
A national manhunt is under way.

—DEL SOL POLICE BLOTTER

Back at the station, Sun sent the kids to Caffeine-Wah for mocha lattes, instructing Richard and Ricky to use decaf in Auri's.

"Can we come back?" Auri asked her. "You know, for the thing?"

Sun nodded, then went in search of a wanted fugitive.

She stepped into the interview room and sat across from a very perturbed Latino. Opening the file she'd been studying, she said, "You have quite the record, Rojas."

He played with the chain that held him cuffed to the table, metal scraping against metal.

"You did well while you were inside. You got a bachelor's in criminal justice in under three years. I'm impressed."

Nothing. He refused to even look at her.

"Just one thing—you did it all using your name and inmate number. But to go to school, you have to use your social. And that social doesn't match your name or your inmate number."

When he finally met her gaze, his was cold and full of distrust. "Not every Latino sells drugs, you know."

"Really?" She called out the open door to her half-Latino BFF. "Cooper, do you sell drugs?"

"Every chance I get."

"What about you, Salazar?"

Tricia giggled, then said, "Only on weekends. I don't want it interfering with my law enforcement gig."

"Good girl. Escobar?" she asked her feisty admin.

"My name is Escobar. Duh."

Rojas nodded. "You're funny."

"Really? Like funny hmm or funny ha-ha? 'Cause I've been contemplating stand-up."

A knock sounded on the doorframe, and Auri peeked inside the interrogation room while Cruz parked himself against it, cradling a cup of coffee.

"Can I come in?" she asked.

"Of course."

She walked in with two cups and sat one on the table. "We brought you a hot chocolate. I didn't know what you liked, but most people like hot chocolate, right?"

He spared her a quick glance, seemingly surprised she was talking to him, then returned to sulking.

It didn't faze her. "I like your name. I'm going to name my firstborn after you. Is that okay?"

"That's so sweet," Sun said before coming to her senses. "Wait a minute. You've already named your firstborn? When did this happen? Why didn't you tell me?"

The minx flashed her a grin of pure mischief.

"Well, what if you have a girl? Ramses is a little gender-specific."

Auri giggled, pushed the cup closer to the interviewee, and left the room.

"Wait, this isn't going to happen anytime soon, right?" When she still didn't get an answer, she yelled, "I know where you live, Cruz!"

Her prisoner ignored the drink and kept his razor-sharp gaze averted, but she had a feeling he didn't miss much.

"You gonna try your hot chocolate?"

He finally offered her his attention, but not in a good way. If looks could kill and all.

The grin she felt spread across her face surely rivaled anything Jack Nicholson could have conjured. She leaned forward and whispered, "Try the hot chocolate."

He scalded her with a heated glare, but couldn't help himself. He looked at the cup. Auri had written his name on it in thick black marker.

His name.

Not his brother's.

Poetry Rojas looked back at Sunshine, his poker face in shambles.

He'd have to work on that.

"What is this?"

"I know who you are."

He sneered at her. "You have no idea who I am."

"Maybe, but I know who you're not, and you are not Ramses Rojas."

He held on to his sneer for dear life, but she could see it starting to give.

"Because he was picked up a couple of days ago when he fell asleep in his getaway car after robbing a Loaf 'N Jug just outside of Santa Fe."

His sneer faltered.

"And I'm fairly certain he did it on purpose."

His gaze dropped to the picture she slid across the table.

"The latest mug shot."

An involuntary parting of the lips told Sun that his brother being arrested was about the last thing he'd expected to hear that day.

"It's nice to meet you, Poetry."

When she'd first read his name, Poetry Romaine Rojas, she'd wondered if it were a typo and they'd entered his street name. As luck would have it, that was his actual name, straight off his birth certificate. His mother was apparently very into literature. And salads. And it would explain his only known alias: Lettuce.

If Sun's plan succeeded, she was so calling him that.

From what she could uncover between her research—which she stayed up half the night doing—and Royce Womack's investigation, Darlene Tapia used to watch them when he and his twin brother were growing up in Albuquerque. She'd lived next door. And she was about the only family they had after their parents died, but because she wasn't actually related and she didn't meet the criteria to become a foster parent, they went into the system and she never saw them again.

Until a few weeks ago.

Poetry leaned on his elbows and pressed the palms of his hands to his eyes.

She leaned over and unlocked the cuffs.

He removed them and then covered his eyes again.

"I'm sorry about your brother."

Overcome with emotion, he only shook his head.

"I just have one question for you. How the hell did you do it?"

He cleared his throat and said, "Sorry for the act."

"The tough-guy act? I'm sure it came in handy in prison."

He raised a brow. "You could say that."

"But really, how the hell did you pull this off? Your fingerprints wouldn't match your brother's, and yet you went to prison for him? For three years? Why? Did he have something on you?"

His laugh held more sadness than humor. "You said you just had one question."

"I'm sorry." Sun had to admit, this was the most fascinating thing she'd ever seen during her entire career in law enforcement.

He showed her his hands. More to the point, his fingerprints. They were covered in scars. "I chew them. You know, to hide my prints. The COs used to laugh at me. They'd remind me I was already in prison. I was already convicted. No use in trying to hide my identity now."

"I'm stunned you pulled this off. I'm beyond stunned."

"They don't care, you know? It's not like they compare your fingerprints once they have you. You could be the pope, as long as they have someone in that bed come lights-out."

"But how did you even end up in your brother's place?"

"He was out on bail. He skipped. I was mistaken for him and hauled in right before the trial."

"So, you just went with it? You let them believe you were your brother? That you'd committed armed robbery?"

"I owed him."

"You spent three years in prison for something you didn't do. You did time for your brother."

"What was I going to do? Rat him out? I got busted. They thought I was him. I just let them."

"I am astoundingly impressed."

"Don't be."

"I hope he knows how lucky he is."

"He's not that lucky. We all have penance to pay."

"That we do, Poetry."

"How did you know?" he asked her, seeming impressed himself.

"The footage from the transport van and the mug shot."

"What about them?"

She slid some screenshots to him. "You guys did a good job keeping your tats identical, but you must've gotten a new one in prison." She pointed behind her ear, indicating the cross he had that ran from behind his down the side of this neck.

"You caught that? Damn."

"Well, that and you've clearly eaten better than he has. He's gaunt compared to you."

He looked at the mug shot again. "He doesn't look well."

"Maybe prison will do him good? Get him clean?"

"Prison doesn't do anyone any good." He took a drink of the hot chocolate. "Your kid's pretty great."

"Yes, she is."

"So, is that why you dragged me in here? To gloat?"

"No, I can gloat anytime. Would you like to see your brother? I can arrange it. On one condition."

He'd gone from intrigued to wary in the time it took to snap. "Oh yeah? What's that?"

"I have an opening. I need a deputy."

He stilled again, only this time, his expression would suggest he was questioning her sanity. Why were people always doing that?

"You have the instincts. You clearly have the guts. You're level-headed AF. You have a bachelor's in criminal justice. You're like the poster child for entry-level law enforcement."

"Right, only you forgot a couple of things. I'm a convicted felon. And I just spent three years in prison."

"No. Your brother is a convicted felon. You haven't spent a single day inside. You've never even been arrested. I checked."

He took another swig and shook his head. "Look, I appreciate the vote of confidence, but I'm not your guy."

"You saved that little girl's life."

His surprise shone through in glowing Technicolor. "That wasn't—I didn't mean—that wasn't what it looked like."

"You didn't jump off a cliff onto a frozen lake to save a little girl's life?"

"Yeah, but it's not like I gave it a lot of thought. It just happened."

She held out her hand. "Welcome to the force, Deputy Rojas. I'm your sheriff, Sunshine Vicram."

A set of dimples emerged when he offered her the barest hint of an astonished smile. He took her hand. "I can't believe this."

"I know. Aren't they soft? I use extra moisturizing lotion. A girl can't be too moisturized these days."

He breathed out a laugh as though unable to wrap his head around the events of the day.

Quincy appeared at the door. "I know what you're thinking," he said to him. "That you're the only identical twin on the force. Nope. Me and Zee. It'll be hard to tell us apart at first, but you'll get used to it." He flashed Rojas a thumbs-up, then left.

"Hey, isn't Zee the one with the rifle?"

"Yes."

"So, they're not really—"

"No."

He nodded and looked around the place, sizing it up. "Do I have to wear a uniform?"

"Yes."

Despite the fact that the Del Sol County Sheriff's Station brimmed with people of all shapes and sizes, many dressed in black, the atmosphere was subdued and somber. A woman in her late thirties held on to two small children with one hand and a tissue with the other, while others in the room stood with hands folded as they waited.

Sun nodded to her dispatch.

Anita pressed the button on the mic. "Dispatch to two-seven-two."

The room went completely silent. Moments passed as people waited with a solemn respect.

Anita tried again. "Dispatch to unit two-seven-two."

The woman in black buried her face in Quincy's lapel and sobbed. He picked up her youngest child, then hugged her to him, fighting back tears himself.

Anita's fingers curled around the mic, her knuckles white. "Final call for unit two-seven-two, Lieutenant Bobby Beauregard Britton." She didn't wait as long this time. Her emotions barely contained, her voice cracked when she came on one last time. "Two-seven-two is ten-seven. Badge number fourteen-twelve is at end of watch. Rest in peace, Lieutenant. You will be missed."

The deputies gathered around Mrs. Britton to offer their

condolences. Sun took Auri's hand, her daughter's eyes shimmering with unspent tears. Cruz scooted closer to her to offer his support as well.

Zee walked up just as Auri and Cruz stole away to a corner, ostensibly to check their phones.

"Mrs. Moore brought muffins," Zee said, gesturing toward the lobby.

Sun looked over at the giant basket of the cursed pastries, wondering what could possibly be next.

"According to the muffin count, the world is going to end sometime in the next week."

"Great," Sun said.

Zee gave her a quick hug before heading toward the widow.

A woman spoke beside her. "This was quite beautiful."

Sun turned to see Mayor Lomas standing next to her, holding a paper cup of something red. "Mayor. Thanks for coming."

She nodded, the tips of her bob brushing the tops of her shoulders. "Of course. Have you thought any more about my offer?"

"Offer?" she asked, confused. "Oh, you mean ultimatum? Find out who the mythical Dangerous Daughters are or else you'll expose my sordid past?" She leaned closer to the pretty blonde. "I think some high school kids beat you to the punch."

A sly smile stole across her face. "Oh, I bet there's more. Something you don't want getting out. Am I right?"

What on earth could she know?

"I just hope you find them. You know, for Auri's sake."

A wildfire erupted in Sun's core. "Did you just threaten my daughter?"

"Why would I do that?" she asked, then turned to walk away.

She went to stop the woman when a shadow slid over her. She looked up and into the startlingly handsome face of Levi Ravinder.

Drawing in a deep, calming breath, she said, "Pretty brave, Ravinder. You showing up here since we never finished processing your arrest."

"He was a friend." Clean-shaven, possibly for the first time in years, he wore a charcoal jacket and a black button-down that set off the darkness in his hair and contrasted with the warmth of his amber eyes.

"I'm sorry for your loss," she said. "You left in a hurry the other night."

"I had places to be. Are you going to charge me or not?"

"With a felony count of having places to be?"

"With murder."

"Ah. We're still investigating."

"Well, let me know."

"You'll be the first." Her focus kept wandering to the hand wrapped around a coffee cup from Caffeine-Wah, his long fingers dark against the white paper. When it looked like he was going to leave, she said, "I didn't get a chance to thank you. For the other night. You went above and beyond, and I'm not sure how to repay you."

He turned her jaw to get a better look at the thin red line across her neck. His touch sent a shock wave of electricity shooting through her.

His amber eyes glistened as he studied the wound. "I was almost too late."

"Almost is okay. I'm good with almost. I saw your truck parked at Barbie's this morning." Barbie was an amazing mechanic. "I hope everything is okay."

"Routine."

"I would offer you a ride home, but I don't think you'd want your family seeing me drop you off."

The look he planted on her, glittering and dark, sent a warmth spiraling through her entire body until it pooled deep in her abdomen. He leaned closer and asked, "What have I ever done that would make you believe I give a single, solitary fuck what my family thinks?"

Auri's voice wafted toward them, breaking the spell he'd temporarily placed her under. "Hi, Levi."

He tore his gaze away and offered her daughter his complete attention. "Hey, Red."

"You clean up well," she said, and Sun almost snorted.

He flashed her a blinding smile and pulled her into a hug. "Back atcha."

She beamed at him, and Sun saw something there. Something pure and unconditional. Her daughter loved him. Possibly as much as Sun did, though in a very different way.

Zee walked up then and gestured a greeting to Auri with a nod before giving Sun her attention. "Sheriff, can we talk in your office?"

Quincy stood behind her. Auri left Levi's embrace long enough to give Quincy a hug, then she returned to Levi and summoned Cruz with a wave. "This is Cruz," she said to him.

Levi gave the kid a once-over, then, as though Cruz had met his approval, offered his hand.

"Mr. Ravinder," Cruz said. "I like your moonshine." When Levi lifted a brow, he rushed to add, "Not the taste. I've never tried it. I don't drink." He cast a nervous glance at Sun. "I mean, the fact that you sell moonshine. Legitimately. Without that whole crossing-state-lines and revenue-men-knocking-down-your-door thing."

"Yes," Levi said, his eyes shimmering with humor. "That does help."

Before she burst out laughing, Sun turned to Auri. "I'll be back in a jiff."

Her daughter let out a loud sigh. "The demands of being a sheriff. We're going to run over to Caffeine-Wah and pry the truth out of Richard and Ricky if it's the last thing we do."

"The truth?" Levi asked.

"They have a supersecret eyeliner trick we've been trying to steal for years."

"Ah."

Sun laughed softly and leaned in for a hug. "Give 'em hell, and remember—"

Auri raised a hand to stop her. "I know what you're going to say. If they refuse to spill this time, replace their cans of tuna with cat food and threaten to turn them in to the health department."

"Attagirl."

Levi grinned at Auri, the affection in his eyes genuine, and Sun could hardly believe he'd been a part of her life for years. A positive part of her life.

She offered him a quick nod, then led Zee and Quincy into her office. After closing the door behind them, she sat at her desk.

Zee didn't sit down. She handed Sun a report. "It seems a kid was injured a few years ago. He went into the urgent care center and was treated for stab wounds."

"Okay," she said, scanning the document.

"The guy had AB negative. Same as the blood on Kubrick Ravinder's clothes."

Sun's gaze shot to her face, then back to the report. "Who was it?"

"That's just it. They don't know." She pointed to the chart that showed where the stab wounds were. Three lacerations clustered just underneath his left rib cage. "The kid gave them a false name. They had no choice but to take him into surgery immediately. Then the minute he woke up, he bolted."

"Security footage?" Sun asked.

Zee shook her head. "Not back then."

Small towns. And Del Sol was smaller than most. "How did you get this chart?"

"Well, see, this is where things get a little sticky."

Quincy sat across from Sun and whistled. "Uh-oh, sibling o' mine. Whatever did you do?"

She cleared her throat and said softly, "I may know a guy."

"Like, carnally?" he asked.

"Quincy," Sun said, her tone exasperated, "I am going to rip out your thyroid."

"Right. My bad."

The woman was clearly having a difficult time coming to terms with what she'd done. Quincy was not helping. "Go ahead, Zee."

"So, yeah, I kind of asked him to look up people in the area with AB negative blood. Without a warrant."

"Thinking outside the box. And?"

"There are only three, barring Auri, and two of them could never have fought with a man the size of Kubrick Ravinder and lived to see another day."

"Why's that?"

"He couldn't give me their names, of course, but I told him the circumstances and he said one was a ninety-year-old female who'd had two hip replacements and the other would have been no more than six at the time of Kubrick Ravinder's death."

"Oh yeah. That does narrow it down a bit. So, we're left with this kid?"

"Yes. Look at the date," Zee said softly.

She scanned the admittance date. The same day, over fifteen years ago, that an unidentified male dropped Sun off at an emergency room in Santa Fe.

Quincy rounded the desk and stood reading over her shoulder. "The question we need to be asking ourselves is, was this kid a part of the kidnapping scheme or not?"

"Exactly," Zee agreed. "Did he endanger your life, Sheriff, or save it?"

That night, Sunshine Vicram made sure the redhead was fast asleep before going to the closet in her master bedroom. She pushed her clothes aside to reveal the corkboard she'd been using for the last couple of years. Ever since she'd decided to find the man who'd assaulted her and prosecute him to the fullest extent of the law, she'd used the board more as motivation than anything else.

Her suspects were displayed in a random order, because she couldn't connect any one of them to the crime. Yet each of them either had motive or opportunity, and until now, that was all she'd had to go on.

Pinned to the top of the board was a generic silhouette representing the unknown assailant. The one who'd abducted her. The one who'd assaulted her. The one she would hunt down if it was the last thing she did on this earth.

With fingers trembling, she took down the silhouette and pinned a picture of her number-one suspect. Only one question remained: Was Levi Arun Ravinder her assailant, her savior, or a little of both?